dixi
books

Necdet ÖZKAYA was born in Antakya in 1959. After graduating from Ege University Faculty of Medicine in 1983, he worked at all levels in public and private health institutions and organizations in Van-Erciş, Antalya and Istanbul, respectively.

He has two poetry books (*Solmasın Yüzün*-2000/3 editions, *Su Damlası*-2004) and thirteen novels that have been previously published; *Ellerinden Kaydı Hayat* (Okuyan Us Publishing House-2013), *Luke Is My Name* (Bilge Karınca Publishing House-2014 / 1st Edition), *Ansızın Değişir Hayat, Uzun Bir Gece* (Destek Publications-2015), *Kıyılarına Vur Adamın, Kimliği Meçhul, Kişiliği Belirsiz, Kimsesiz, Kaybedilmiş, Roman Hayattır, Edebiyat Başka Türlü Anlatmaktır, Mimoza Koyu'nda Bir Kış, Koru Kendini, Bir Daha Hiçbir Ana Doğuramaz Seni, Dillere Destandır Dilim* (Yeni İnsan, Publications).

The author also has a story book published by GOA Publications in 2016; Queen of the East (Orientis Apicem Pulcrum)

www.necdetozkaya.com.tr

ozkaya.necd@hotmail.com

Necdet ÖZKAYA

LUKE IS MY NAME

dixi
books

Dixi Books

Luke is My Name
Necdet Özkaya
Translator: Lara Vural
Editor: Cherry Carlson
Proofreading: Andrea Bailey
Designer: Pablo Ulyanov
1st Edition in English: September 2023

ISBN: 978 -1- 913680- 80 -0

1. Fiction 2. Historical Fiction 3. Antioch

© Dixi Books Publishing
293 Green Lanes, Palmers Green, London, England, N13 4XS
info@dixibooks.com
www.dixibooks.com

Necdet ÖZKAYA

LUKE IS MY NAME

dixi books

The Voice of the New Age

For Semiramis Özkaya Kış and Kemal Kırar...

CHAPTERS

FOREWORD

BETWEEN ANTAKYA AND TARSUS

The world of Biblist Luke, examined in-depth by Necdet Özkaya, is also the world Özkaya himself lives in. Just as Evangelist Luke, Necdet Özkaya is a physician with a passion for literature. With his second novel, My Name Is Luke, Özkaya gifts Luke's noble character to the lands he lived in, to modern Turkey.

Those lands, formerly known as Antioch, is now Hatay, where Özkaya also spent a part of his life. These vital traits reminding one of Luke are de nitely not futile, but rather correspond to each other perfectly. The characters in the story and the re- read of history bears in the reader the desire to look at these lands from the eyes of the Antioch region and the early Christian period. The novel creates an emotional enthusiasm - that would please the majority of readers - transitioning from the past and the future. This type of literature may be applied to various periods in history.

What's surprising and is also a "first" with certainty is the perspective of a modern Turk, who does not deny his identity, diving deep into the Christian-Anatolian world. According to Marc Bloch, history cannot actually be written without bridging the gap between the past and the now. This novel brilliantly stands out among its peers within the vast literary scene in today's Turkey.

The serious comparison made with Evangelist Luke is extremely important. As the physician of Antioch, Luke is a human prism in which all existence and history can be seen; through him, one can gain a brand new perspective.

Necdet Özkaya knows that Luke was a true friend of Paul of Tarsos, who was one of the most imporant apostles of Jesus. Luke could completely absorb the message of the apostle of delle GENTI, thanks to his closeness with Paul. Luke was a student of Paul and it is enough for Özkaya to introduce him as a Jew: The expression "Luke Is My Name, I am a Jew from Antioch" occurs frequently in the text. According to the overall knowledge of Christianity, however, Luke was born and raised in a pagan environment in accordance with the faith of the Romans residing in this land. Nevertheless, this is not the ambiguity that is pointed out; the literary interpretation is extremely fitting to Luke's character.

Luke was raised with pagan traditions he was familiar with; later approached towards the Jewish world Christianized by Paul and this world has become his. We see a man who inherited the spiritual purpose of Saint Paul and this is what constitutes the basis of Necdet Özkaya's novel.

It takes true skill to peek into the lives of the characters; to observe situations, incidents and ancient documents with spiritual depth and to reveal a new archaeology with these observations. Yes, it is archaeology itself that allows one to relive events of the past and creates an even stronger atmosphere than watching a movie, when true passion is present.

With this novel, the Turkish reader will nd the opportunity to rediscover the - mostly true - names of the milestones constituting the past of his/her country and meet a new archaeology of the land. Meanwhile, this is an invitation to a journey set out through the archaeological excavations in the region where Luke, the precious student of Paul the Apostle, was born in.

We wish that the name Luke is the name of many readers as well.

Alberto Fabio Ambrosio O. P

Former Priest at Church of Saint Peter and Paul in Galata, Istanbul

CHAPTER ONE

EDITOR'S NOTE

I knew my friend Yiğit Kaya for long years. He was a well-educated, intelligent, spunky, sporty man who knew much about archaeology and history. Besides a few languages he spoke, he also read and wrote ancient Greek very well and was lately forcing himself to learn Latin.

One day, at my office in the publishing house as I was going through the final drafts of the books before printing, I saw his name on the screen the moment I looked at my ringing phone, answering the phone eagerly.

He was the starring person in the incidents the newspapers have been writing on and the TVs were broadcasting for days; incidents which were both mysterious and bitter. I didn't have the chance to meet him for months. I did not know what he was up to, besides the mysterious incidents I was following on the media, and I was very curious about how his life was.

He spoke about an old text and explained to me that he was writing about some incidents he experienced in these past months, which were hard to believe. As an editor with a sensitive nose, I understood what he meant immediately and exclaimed with excitement that we would be pleased to publish it.

He was just starting to tell me that we could publish his work in case we accept the only condition he had, when I interrupted him and said that I accept all his conditions without objection. I recall my statement with the same excitement I had in the moment.

What he called "condition" was nothing difficult or impossible - he wanted his writings to be published as they are and wanted absolutely no intervention from us on his chapter ordering.

I understood, from the way he spoke and his voice, that he will not make concessions on this matter. Besides, I was not a person who had the ordinary professional concerns to prevent a book, written by one of the people seen most frequently in the media, from being published by the of1ce I was working and managing; not to mention I had immense confidence in Yiğit Kaya.

You will find the rest of the story on the next page; we haven't touched a single punctuation mark in the text, just as we promised him. There is not one word more, or one less from the original text he's written.

Wishing you a pleasant reading.

1.

1. WE LISTENED TO HIM IN THE CAVE WE GATHERED

We believed in everything he said. We were listening to Him, whatever he says, however he describes what, with our mouths wide open.

We were gathering in a thirteen feet deep cave. We climbed up the foothills of the mountain. We were walking without drawing any attention, as if we were out there collecting herbs to heal our wounds.

Women were bending over to the ground, carrying their children. They sat, collected herbs they were familiar with, smelled them and put them in sacks bound to the sides of their skirts.

We were passing by them without a word, entering through the mouth of the cave and taking deep breaths as soon as we were in; the cool air rejuvenated our numb souls.

We were walking towards the man we wanted to reach, who was filled with the Holy Spirit, with slow steps - calmly and quietly without hurry. His inside was full with the Holy Spirit and he was telling us about that. The teller was coming from where He is, telling us about Him, his pain, his experiences.

We were drinking the water that leaked from the cave walls and puddled in the deep hollow. We were putting the water on our faces, understanding that we were resurging.

We were looking at his face, in his eyes, on his body as if we saw Him in every corner of the teller; feeling the pain he went through in our hearts and weeping together.

We were gathering with a quiet, calm and slow walk; without making ourselves seen by the residents of the neighborhood next to the cave. The women sitting on the ground, collecting herbs, were entering the cave last with their little children and were washing their and then their childrens' faces with the leaking water that puddled in the hollow.

The water increased as we drank and used it, it wasn't decreasing or ooding. It was like a refreshing, cool potion.

We were sitting on the ground of the ten feet wide cave and listening to the teller;

never wanting for the tremor of our souls through the things told to end, cease or vanish. For the teller was coming from where He was.

His face glimmered, his eyes and hair shimmered and he was speaking with his soft voice, caressing our souls.

We all listened to him, including little children and babies, without a sound; for he was coming from where He is, with his inside full of the Holy Spirit.

We weren't asking questions. He understood the questions we were to ask and continued to answer and explain with his voice as calm as always, that caressed our souls.

2. HELLO, I AM YİĞİT KAYA

In a walk I attempted to continue as my steps inclined backwards, I dreamed that I proceeded forwards - the opposite direction to my steps. As my dream faded, I opened my eyes to see the woman sitting on my left. "Solmaz," I mumbled. She didn't look at me, instead continued gazing towards the road, "You slept," she said, "You slept well."

I had reclined the right front seat of the fast car I was sitting in and said to Solmaz, "I'm going to rest my eyes for a little bit." We set out from Istanbul at exactly six in the morning. After giving a short breakfast break, we continued towards Bolu and gave another break when we were close to Ankara.

Ten years ago, as I was walking in the wide halls under the high ceiling of the faculty in Ankara, I couldn't help but notice the movement of the body in front of me, the body of a tall young woman that was wrapped inside her tight jeans under her slim waist.

My steps became quicker and I found myself walking in front of her in the hall, then turned back immediately as if I just came up with an idea. I was mesmerized with the young woman looking at me. I looked at her short, blonde hair, dark blue eyes and her porcelain skin as if I've known her for hundreds of years and I smiled. Smiling back looking into my eyes, she extended her hand and spoke to me.

"Hello, I'm Solmaz Başaran, do you know where the student office is?"

She looked right into my eyes, shaking the hand I extended with a tremble, as if wanting to make her existence felt.

"Hi, I'm Yiğit Kaya." She told me her name together with her surname, so I went along and said my name together with mine.

The day I went to the Faculty of Archaeology, where I studied for the last two years, and which now griped my soul, the beautiful girl was there to experience the same nightmares I went through - it was the first day of registration.

I didn't leave her side for the entire registration process, I could also not take my eyes off of her face, her tight jeans, her slim waist and her dark blue eyes.

As Solmaz went through her registration, I simultaneously went through the process to leave the department of Archaeology after studying there for two years. When I showed her my examination results allowing me to transfer to the Department of History, she looked at my face with eyes not able to believe what she has seen. Nevertheless, she didn't ask why or question my reasons. The moment we nished our work at the student of ce, we went to the faculty's cafeteria and dove into a deep conversation, as if we knew each other for hundreds of years.

There were two oors between Solmaz's department and mine - we were studying on different oors of the same building. After that day, we continued to meet at every opportunity, during each class break, with the same hundred-year acquaintance that we felt the first day.

In the little apartment I lived alone in, where I took Solmaz to give her all the books, magazines and notes related to the Archaeology department after my two-year study, her deep blue eyes and my black eyes came together in the closest distance possible. I was the first man of Solmaz Başaran.

As we continued driving from Ankara, I told Solmaz that I was tired; so she sat in the driver's seat without a second word from me. She drove with pleasure and with expertise. I sat in the right front seat, reclined it and closed my eyes.

When I woke up from the dream I had, the rst thing I saw was her blonde, straight and shimmering strands of hair that were cut short, hanging downwards from the top of her head. "I had the same dream," I told Solmaz. "And we are going there for the same dream of yours," she said.

We were living together for ten years and Solmaz was now twenty-eight years old. In the rst days we met, we tried out the white scale of the old man who measured heights and weights on the street - just so that he is happy and that he earns a little money. When the white-haired old man told Solmaz, "One meter and seventy-one centimeters" and told me, "One meter and eighty centimeters," I hugged the woman I loved, joked to her, "What's up, kiddo!" and kissed her cheek. She looked at my face with her ever-pleasing, sincere smile and dark blue eyes, then pulled my hair. I grabbed her waist, so slim that I could almost encircle with one hand, and moved it down her wide hips, as if by accident.

This is what upset her the most; she perceived my move towards her hips as if I was making an emphasis on the part of her body she disliked the most out of nding it "too wide." She always got upset about her hips and I always wanted to upset her about it.

Every time I woke up, with every fading dream for the past ten years I saw the same beautiful face and dark blue eyes; silently wishing that I will continue seeing the same face for the next few decades as well.

"Did I sleep long?" I asked her. "Yes you did, for exactly ve minutes!" Solmaz said. She smiled with the face I wished would never fade, and eventually looked at my face with her deep blue eyes, even if for a short second.

I turned my head towards the road and read the sign that said, "Adana - 60 km". Looking at her, I asked, "You liar, I slept so long, why haven't you told me?" "You needed rest..." she answered and looked at my face with her beautiful, loving and happy eyes. "Whatever it is you're looking for, we will nd it - don't worry, we're going. We will search for it and we will definitely find it. And - did you call Dimitri?"

I told her I did, that we are going to have dinner together. I slowly straightened my seat and gave a wet kiss from the side of that beautiful woman's face, on her lips, as she drove the fast car. She looked at my face and smiled at me with the most beautiful smile, winking at me.

3. CHARON WITHOUT A FACE

We were looking at the slopes of the Stauris Mountain and Charon was looking at us with his missing face. The "Hell Boatman" was rowing non-stop in the underground rivers and we knew, we believed that he would one day take us on a boat. He had a head, a cloth over his head, but no face, Charon's face was of stone. He had been looking at the city from above, for two centuries.

We were sitting on the ground and picking herbs, as always, from the foothills of Stauris Mountain. We were collecting the yellow, white and red flowers that bloom when the cold ends and the weather gets warmer; we were smelling them and filling our bags with them. The healing magical power of Stauris Mountain was mixed with all the herbs, plants and flowers of the mountain.

We were boiling these herbs and flowers; we were drinking their water no matter what the illness we were targeting, and made our children drink the juice. We never got ill, whoever was ill was getting better. It seemed that Stauris Mountain was a physician who healed without speaking.

We used to go to the foothills of the mountain every week, sometimes even every three days. We entered the cave of Stauris without getting crowded, accumulated or attracting attention. We were washing our faces, the hands and feet of our children with the same holy water. The water was as much as we used, it never overflowed or increased.

We were drinking the same holy water and sitting on the stone and rock floor of the cave without making a sound. We were removing the darkness of the cool cave, which we entered in groups of three, by igniting the torches we brought with us and starting to listen to the holy man who was clean, pure and whose every word we believed in.

He first used to look at everyone's face in the cave, smiled and closed his eyes, reading a short prayer, wishing health and a long life for all of us. Then he opened his eyes and started his speech, which we couldn't get enough of listening and never wanted to end. He was telling what he said softly, with a voice that caressed our soul. All of us, even our babies, were listening to that holy man in belief, without blinking. He was a holy man, because he was coming from where He is.

4. DIMITRI ÇAĞLAYAN

We took a short break in Iskenderun, where the highway outside the city center took us and is now turned into an industrial city, without stopping by in central Adana. We cleaned the windows of our car after filling its tank and I told Solmaz, who I was tired now, that I could drive the car. I sat on the left front seat, without listening to her telling me how she wasn't tired and that she could drive the car until the end of the journey.

It was the beginning of July and Iskenderun was quite hot. I closed the windows of the car and turned on the air conditioner. Solmaz started to to caress my hair with her left hand and asked once again, whether I called Dimitri. I told her I called twice.

Dimitri Çağlayan was my classmate at the university first. Later on, my hardworking (!) friend lost two years and studied in the same class with Solmaz. I took pictures when they threw their caps in the air at their graduation ceremony with Solmaz. We were the same age with Dimitri. Our medium-sized, overweight friend with a big belly started to lose his hair from the top of his forehead and then his head already when he was a university student. He was born in Antakya and worked in the city's world-famous museum.

Curious about eating and cooking, Dimitri started growing his majestic belly starting from the first day I knew him. The main topics of our conversations were the dishes Dimitri described with enthusiasm and their preparation and presentation techniques. He used to lose himself talking about these. He exploded with enthusiasm and calmed down in the last minutes when he explained the presentation techniques, which he attached great importance to, then began to describe the technique of preparing a new dish this time without a break. We used to joke and say, "Dimitri Çağlayan is flooding like water…"*

*Çağlayan (Turkish): Waterfall.

He was only "Dimitri" whenever we spoke about professional subjects, life, love, relationships, separation, pain - in short, everything except food preparation and presentation techniques. He was "Çağlayan," though, whenever we talked about all matters of food with appetite and great enthusiasm.

Dimitri was able to show his achievements only after university, which he could only finish in six years. He suddenly bloomed and became the favourite of all high-level museum officials with his diligence, honesty and the new important archaeological artifacts and ruins he managed to discover.

In our last phone call, he said that he would wait for us at Antakya Museum. While telling about the location of the museum, when I asked him to book a good hotel he knew, he got stuck with his usual sincere and friendly attitude when he explained that he would definitely not be able to accept such a thing and would be uncomfortable if he could not host us in his house. So I joked as usual, "Dimitri Çağlayan is flooding like water!"

My phone rang while looking at the smiling face of Solmaz, as I was telling her about these. "You are late, brother, the museum has already closed, there's the building of the former Hatay State National Assembly, now a pudding palace, almost across the museum very close to it, I'll wait for you there." As soon as he finished speaking, Dimitri gave one of his classic loud laughter.

The old National Assembly building was right next to the Asi River, which divides Antakya from the middle. The cut stone was quite alive and had an appearance that gives one confidence when viewed from a distance. We parked the car somewhere near the Asi River and started walking with Solmaz, arm in arm, on the road next to the river.

"The Orontes River, now known as Asi River, which brings abundance and happiness to everywhere it touches, is now far from being rebellious, as you can see. It tries not to flow but almost to leak. The journey of Lebanon, which starts from the Bekaa Valley and lasts for nearly four hundred kilometers, continues without interruption by dividing Antakya from the middle into two, ending at the Mediterranean shores of Samandağ district. The Mediterranean Sea and the Asi River blend together there, like two lovers who have been separated for many years, they hug each other tightly - not to be separated again. "

Solmaz listened to what I said, carefully looking at my face. From the road next to the Asi River, the waters in the river bed we looked from above were almost completely withdrawn. Sewage water that continued to flow to the river bed were trying to infiltrate through the gaps they found, find ways to flow and continue their journey. It was July, hot and the magnificent Orontes River of the past was emanating very unpleasant odors in the hot weather. It looked like a very wealthy man who had lost everything, or an ancient city full of ruins, destroyed by earthquakes. There was no trace of its rebelliousness* anymore; instead, it had a sad, unhappy, depressed image of the poor river that could not flow. Listening to these, Solmaz looked at my face, smiling as she squeezed my waist between her fingers as she hugged me with her right hand. "Our authority on history, Yiğit Kaya, is getting at it again," she said. I put a small kiss on the cheek of the woman I love.

*Asi (Turkish): Rebellious.

The National Assembly building of the Old Hatay State was now transformed into a pudding palace. We started to climb the stone stair steps of the building, together with Solmaz. Dimitri, who was sitting at a corner table in the terrace of the old building, which was surrounded by glass, jumped up as soon as he saw us. We hugged, kissed, laughed loudly and disturbed those sitting at the side tables, and we sat down on comfortable chairs. Dimitri had gained a little more weight, lost more hair and his forehead was wide open.

"Let's have a tea here and get up, go home, rest a little, take a shower if you want - my home is big. I absolutely do not allow you to stay in a hotel, I am alone in the big house, my brother will come a few days later, you can meet him too, when you see my house, you will understand what I mean and the why there is no need to stay in a hotel anyway. Even eating pudding here is forbidden now, get really hungry, I will take you to a good restaurant in the evening, you will meet the best dishes and kebabs, appetizers you have never seen before, and you will be very happy while enjoying these meetings. "

It was Solmaz this time, who said what needed to be said: "Flooding again, Dimitri Çağlayan!"

We got up laughing from the "Pudding Palace". We went to the car. Solmaz was driving, Dimitri sat next to her and I on the back seat. We drove towards a neighborhood with the navigation of Dimitri, laughing, having fun with small jokes. Te neighborhood was a very old settlement with its historical houses, narrow streets, stone-paved places, and the waters running along the grooves. We could perceive the age of this place from its smell, air, and from every point we looked at, through the walls, doors, rain gutters of the homes. The old neighborhood smelled of history with its narrow streets.

We parked the car in the area near the entrance door of Dimitri's house. This parking place, where the two house walls intersected, was an empty area where the parked car will not block the traffic of the street in any way. We took our backpacks and suitcases from the trunk and looked at the width of the large courtyard that Dimitri entered: the large number of room doors, each opening to the courtyard. This was a house that could be a nice, sweet, charming and very comfortable boutique hotel. Looking at our face and showing the room doors with his hand, our lovely friend asked: "Do you understand the unnecessity of the hotel now, love doves!"

5. WE USED TO ESCAPE FROM THE TUNNEL IN THE CAVE IN ORDER TO HIDE

As he started to speak, he would first look at the high ceiling of the cave; close his eyes as if he saw the face of someone looking at him, read a short prayer and make his first words heard in a low tone. He would open up as he spoke, his voice would get louder, and he'd continue at a faster pace. He was excited and we all listened, without making any noise, forgetting to even breathe, without taking our eyes off his sacred face. We would write all that he said in our hearts. As he approached the end of his speech, he would slow down again, lower his voice, and read a new prayer in a tone we could hear this time.

We wouldn't forget a word of what he was telling, we couldn't forget it. It was as if a divine hand would put it in our minds, and none of us would want it to end; we would want him to speak for hours and days. It was as if the narrator spoke in His voice.

We were afraid of the neighborhood next to Stauris Mountain, of those living in the neighborhood. When we listened to the holy man, we would leave two people outside the cave. One would wait at the foot of the mountain, close to the neighborhood; the other would be right in front of the entrance to the cave. When the brother, who was waiting at the foot of the mountain, would see people coming from afar, that could be dangerous; he would stand up immediately, unwind the rope he tied to his waist, take the bag filled with grass and flowers, and turn it over into the ground. Then he would crouch down to the ground again and pretend that he was choosing what's useful to him from what he had poured and begin to put them back into his bag. This was a signal given to our other brother waiting at the entrance of the cave. Our brother, who received the signal, would slowly stand up from his seat, enter the cave, go to the holy man without worry and said a few words that only He could hear. The narrator would then begin to slowly walk towards the tunnel on the back wall of the cave, stand right in its mouth, wait for all of us to enter, entering the tunnel himself last. We would walk with torches in our hands; without stopping, speaking and making noises.

The tunnel was too long to end even if we walked for hours. After a while we would stop, sit in the space and start waiting. Our brother, who was waiting outside of the cave, would come and tell us that the danger had passed, sometimes after a short and sometimes a long time. We would then return to the cave of Stauris Mountain.

6. YOU ARE VERY STYLISH, LADY SOLMAZ

The rooms were next to the large courtyard after the entrance door of the house, around an inverted letter "U", and the space of the letter was a large courtyard. With a fifteen-step staircase stretching up from the high street wall of the house, the windows of a large room that seemed to be built later were visible from below.

"I will give you this room, love doves, I just got it built, there is a bathroom and a toilet inside the room, let's get up there, I think you will like it."

The room was really nicely furnished. It had a large bed, bedside tables, wardrobe, mirrored wardrobe, two armchairs and a large bathroom that passed through the room. There was even a bathtub in the bathroom and the toilet was inside the bathroom. Dimitri had a balcony built in front of the room; an embroidered table and four iron chairs with the same patterns were waiting for our chat hours there.

"Let me leave you two alone, get some rest, when you're ready, you'll go downstairs. I had reserved our place from the restaurant, you do not need to hurry, even if we go at night, the guys there would leave our table empty, but still, do not wait for until ten o'clock. Let's go and ask how all the appetizers, dishes and kebabs waiting for us are doing! "

It was obvious that Dimitri was hungry. He is in fact usually hungry, but today it was evident that he had a different enthusiasm because he knew that we would meet the rich cuisine he had told us for years.

We locked the door of the room and pulled the thick curtains of the big window. Solmaz started to undress in front of the mirror and I started to look at her beautiful body, which I watched with a fascinating admiration that never faded a bit for ten years, with the same admiration, interest and hunger. When she took off her thin shirt and bra, I couldn't stand it when I looked at the view that I saw from the mirror and then her narrow waist, which appeared under the tight jeans that she had started to take off, so I hugged the woman I loved.

"No, Yiğit, behave… Now we will take a nice warm shower together, get dressed and go downstairs without keeping Dimitri wait too long. We're going to eat, I'm so hungry, aren't you hungry?"

I couldn't tell Solmaz that I had hunger for other things. So I undressed as well and we took a shower together. The cruel woman repelled all the attacks I attempted during the shower!

When we went downstairs from our room, Dimitri had turned on the lights of the courtyard. He was sitting next to the small fountain in the middle of the courtyard, which he lit with dim lights. From the sprinkler of the pool, the waters rising upwards were mingling again, making pleasant and uniform noises. Our friend created a real meditation environment. He looked at us with a smile.

"Mrs. Solmaz, you are very stylish and beautiful as always and I think you will never change, you will never get old."

My dark blue-eyed lover looked really beautiful with her dark blue slim dress hanging down by the two thin straps that left her shoulders exposed. I looked at Dimitri and this time I told him the sentence that needed to be said: "Flooding again, Dimitri Çağlayan!" He stood up and I hugged my friend - we really missed each other. We started walking with Dimitri, who said that we do not need to go by car and that the restaurant with drinks is close, is in the ancient, narrow and historical ancient streets. Solmaz was walking between us.

The weather was very cool compared to the first hours we arrived. The humid and sweltering climate in İskenderun was replaced by cool, dry and rapidly blowing cool winds. We were walking under the comforting effect of this.

Dimitri was greeting everyone, men, young, old people, sitting on narrow streets, in front of their houses, on the rugs they opened to the ground. He didn't miss a single person. He spoke Turkish with some, and Arabic with others, and Solmaz and I knew that our friend was loved.

We reached *Antakya Food Restaurant* ten minutes after we left the house. The restaurant had a very warm and pleasant entrance on a narrow street with large glass windows on its wooden doors and ivy roses stretching from the sides towards the door. The man, who stood at the door, greeted Dimitri immediately with a large smile on his face, as soon as he saw him. They spoke Arabic initially, I couldn't understand. Then our friend introduced us with the same warmth, this time the man spoke Turkish, asked us how we were doing. Anyone who watched us from outside could have thought that we had known the man at the door for years, that we had not met for a long time, and that we were fulfilling our longing now.

We entered the restaurant and met another "Forty-year-friend" in his fifties, with a belly, white beard and a smiling face. They spoke Arabic and hugged each other with Dimitri.

"Let me introduce you, Semir Yağmur, the owner of *Antakya Food Restaurant*... He is the real master of the appetizers, dishes and kebabs I have been telling you for years. Although he has succeeded in reaching the boss position from cooking, even dishwashing, he's always in the restaurant's kitchen and prepares most of the appetizers and kebabs with his own hands; he owe this majestic belly to the dishes he prepared, sir!"

In describing these, Dimitri was trying to grab the majestic belly of the owner of the restaurant with his left hand, hugging him from the waist with his right hand. He introduced Solmaz and then me to the friendly boss. We walked to the garden of the restaurant all together. In the middle of the large garden, there was a fountain with a square shape and a jet of water in the middle of it; the tables on the sides of this fountain were the most desired and reserved for respectable people. Semir Yağmur took us to one of these; almost all tables were already full except this one.

Solmaz and I sat opposite the chairs closest to the fountain, Dimitri sat on the chair next to Solmaz. With a behavior that I thought was an important rule of hosting as, boss Semir Yağmur sat in the chair next to me for a short time. He spoke so closely and sincerely that anyone who watched us could think we had met for many years. When I recalled that we saw the same behavior from the attendant at the door, I thought with a smile that this warm-bloodedness was a local structural feature and behavior. People we encounter every day in Istanbul, in big, giant buildings, elevators, corridors, streets, streets, car parks and walking paths refrain from even saying a "Hello!" with their foreign, repulsive, cold attitude and remembering that, I suddenly shuddered.

The boss called one of the waiters dressed in uniform with black pants, white shirt and black thin tie. He was a tall, thin young man, who was around twenty-five years old.

"Adorn the table with our appetizers without asking what they want... Let there be nothing missing, tell the kitchen, prepare them in small plates and fresh, let's not feed our guests with appetizers... You drink rakı*, right?"

*Rakı (Turkish): An alcohol-drink made of twice-distilled grapes and aniseed.

Semir Yağmur asked this in such a natural and ordinary manner that those who heard the tone of his voice would think that there was no other alcoholic beverage. He got up from our desk, saying he was glad that he knew us and shaking each of our hands, one by one.

Shortly afterwards, the tall thin and young waiter came to our table with the big tray he carried. He carefully placed the tray in his hand on the smaller and lower rectangular table next to the table. He started to transfer small, white and round porcelain plates on the table. Dimitri counted the name of the appetizer on every plate put on our table; swallowing, with his mouth watering, with great pleasure!

"Look at this hummus, topped with pepper and pine nuts roasted in butter... This is a bean paste, this is a green olive salad, this is walnut-stuffed pepper and this is tomato-pepper paste... Now you can see the roasted eggplant, with yoghurt, öcce, wrap filling, tahini tarator, and the king of the tables, the salad made with zahter gathered from the Antakya mountains, that is, the miraculous plant you know as thyme... Locally-produced olive oil is added to all those dishes except hummus."

While Solmaz and I were content with looking at the beauty of the appetizers in the confusion of the first moments, Dimitri had already cut off the tip of the steaming sesame pita and made his first move towards the buttered nuts of the hummus.

In the first tray, we were content to watch the skillful and experienced fine movements of the young waiter, who added half a glass of rakı, cold water and two pieces of ice without asking us, from the large bottle of rakı wth ice-cold steam all over, to the thin tall glasses on the table. Cups steamed from cold in a short time under the influence of hot air. Dimitri looked at the white and cold composition in the rakı glass he received with appetite, brought it towards his nose, sniffed it and raised his glass first to Solmaz next to him, and then to me.

"I missed you so much, welcome, I was really happy because I can see you again, it's a short life, here we are today and we will not be here tomorrow. We lose ourselves while we work, we do not call those who are closest to us, we do not visit and postpone everything all the time, to the future; we ruthlessly forget the possibility that tomorrows may not happen... Come on, to our health and friendship... "

Solmaz acted faster than I did, laughing and said the sentence to be said to our lovely, sincere and old friend: "Flooding like a waterfall, Dimitri Çağlayan!"

Laughing together, we started to consume appetizing appetizers at our table with pleasure. Dimitri was constantly talking... He was talking about the excavations they made, the floor mosaics they found, sculptures, old coins, manuscripts. This successful archaeologist explained that every point in the region has an ancient artifact, that they find hundreds of thousands of years of sculptures, mosaics, money and similar historical artifacts, whereas *Antakya Archeology Museum* can no longer find a place to exhibit these finds, therefore many important ancient finds are kept in warehouses, that the *museum* is one of the most important museums of the World and that he is so proud of working there and being able to contribute.

He lifted his glass again and this time, tapping it on our table, took it to his mouth and consumed the first glass of rakı. I strang along with my friend, finishing my glass in a sip. I was trying to forget my anxieties, fears, nightmares. I looked at his face and forced myself to speak in a low and calm tone: "I have been having the same dream for a long time, Dimitri. I had no discomfort the first day I saw it; it was even very interesting… I told Solmaz about it, we thought of it as an ordinary dream. Then I started having the same dream once a month, once a week and recently almost every day, I see myself in the same place; there are the same people around me and we try to fight the same struggle… I started to wake up with fear now, I wake up in sweat and I can't sleep again, I struggle until the morning."

Dimitri, who could not understand anything, looked at me with a facial expression saying that he could not understand, and turned his anxious face into Solmaz as he waited for her to help.

7. WE WROTE WHATEVER HE SAID

We were writing on the same day. We wrote whatever he said and did not forget. Even if we forgot a word, we thought we would have made a big crime, an irreparable mistake.

*"Let your mysterious inner being be your ornament with the beauty of a calm, quiet and soft soul." **

He was giving lessons like this and similar to us, and we were all writing what he said to reach those who came after us; we did not forget and did everything to not forget.

We placed these things in earthen jugs so that what we wrote wouldn't be found by our enemies; we hid them in caves on steep cliffs, in cavities of cracked rocks or buried them in the ground.

I was also writing our own story. If these writings reached centuries later; even later, I wanted everyone who read to learn what we were experiencing.

If it reached centuries without being lost, disappeared, and erased, I wanted for those who read it after a long time to learn about the difficulties we experienced and the pain we suffered. If you are reading this now, and if you can understand what I wrote, it means I have reached my goal and I can now peacefully maintain my eternal sleep in eternity.

*"Avoid bodily passions that fight against life. Avoid them, because you are a foreigner in this world, temporary, only a guest."**

He was telling us that our bodies and souls in the world are temporary, and he taught us that we should live this temporary time without fighting, away from bodily passions and without taking lives.

He was a holy teacher and he was teaching sacred lessons. We were learning and getting enlightened. With the enlightenment, we were reaching peace.

At the end of each speech, he would get quiet for a short time and turn his face to the ceiling of the damp cave; closing his eyes and sitting still, quiet, calmly and quietly, like a rock.

In those moments, we would literally feel deep in our hearts, in the hidden corners of out souls, that he blessed us all with the prayers he reads.

He would remain like a quiet, silent holy rock, and we all saw Him as our father; because this "Sacred Rock" came from where He was.

From St. Peter.

8. ARCHAEOLOGIST DIMITRI ÇAĞLAYAN, A MONUMENT OF APPETITE

Solmaz first looked at my face, then looked back at Dimitri; she reached for her rakı glass, hesitant to tell or not, to finish the white drink in her glass.

"You should tell Yiğit, that would be more accurate, you should start from the very beginning. You should start from the first year, when we first met you, and with your reasons for leaving the archeology department. I found it strange that you would leave a department you'd have studied for two whole years, discarding those years, I believe Dimitri might have found it strange as well. I tried on my own to analyze your reasons of not loving the archeology department and wanting to change it, and reacted with understanding; but now I understand that not loving it was not your only reason. The nightmares you are having recently make me unhappy as well, and the person who can help us the most is fortunately our best friend; It's you, Dimitri."

Dimitri did not understand anything. Solmaz completed her speech and was not staring at me, he was looking at Solmaz, with a gesture that exhibited that he did not understand anything.

The young waiter, who filled our empty cups, came to my aid, taking the remaining pieces of the bread mostly consumed by Dimitri, and brought a hot sesame pita that just came out of the oven. I didn't want to talk yet, I wasn't ready for it. Yes, I could tell the woman I had lived with and loved for years, Solmaz, all my feelings, fears, anxieties and worries and I did not feel any discomfort; I was talking to Solmaz as if I was before a mirror and telling everything to my reflection in the mirror. But now, I did not think and feel ready to talk about my dreams and discuss my nightmares as comfortably with someone other than Solmaz, even with one of my closest and oldest friends.

Actually, Dimitri was the person who could help me most after Solmaz with his job, the city he lived in, his personal characteristics and sincerity. However, I did not want to ruin this beautiful night, when we were having a good meal in a good restaurant with nice meals, and I did not want to make my old friend sad. Dimitri didn't push, he didn't ask or question. He knew well that I was going to tell him when the time came and that I would ask for his help. He called the waiter and told him to collect the appetizer plates that mostly he ate and to start the "hor d'oeuvres" with a loving, mischievous and impatient tone. "We would like boiled and fried kibbeh, bring one piece of kaytaz pastry each, give a piece of bread, don't forget that bread with peppers!" he said.

Continuing to count, Solmaz interjected, "What are you doing, appetite monument, what will be of the kebabs you have been praising for years, won't we be full eating what you just said?"

The "appetite monument" had resolved the issues Solmaz had brought up with the recommendation of eating only a little bite from the ends of each "hor d'oeuvres" dish. Solmaz desperately looked at my face, pursed her lips and fell into an accepted silence. My blonde lover had stated to get cold later in the cool hours of night under the dim lights of the restaurant; when I asked the waiter for a shawl, Solmaz sent me a small kiss only I could see. It was a gift of my understanding.

"The year I finished high school and entered the university exams, all I wanted was to be a good archaeologist, I listed all the archeology departments of the country in my preference list. When the exam results were announced, I had one of the happiest days of my life. I couldn't believe it, I won the archeology faculty in Ankara. I was so impatient and happy, I had completed everything required on the first registration day. And I met you on that first registration day, Dimitri. "

It seemed strange to my old friend that I started to explain at once, unexpectedly, without anyone asking or pushing. Solmaz was looking at me with confirming eyes. This time I hit the base of the rakı glass on the table myself, I raised my glass, holding it high for a short time and tossed it down. They both reciprocated my action.

"While I was studying in archeology, I started to compare myself to a young doctor candidate who studies in the medical school and finds a few symptoms of every illness he reads, thinking he is sick and turns into a hypochondriac. I was very unhappy with what I was told, what I read, and what I learned. This unhappiness was increasing day by day, I started to drift away from the department I was studying in and I thought I had to solve this problem. I re-entered the university exams and this time, on the days when I learned that I have entered the history department of the same faculty, which I wrote only that on my preference list, I met the woman of my life."

As soon as I completed my last sentence with my eyes on Solmaz, we raised our glasses to the health of the woman I love. The woman I love knew that I was trying to save time and taking various ways to get away from the subject, she was getting upset and angry at that; however, she also couldn't put the happiness she felt from the words of love I said, the praiseworthy flattery I made as well. What woman wouldn't like being praised anyway?

"I don't want to annoy Dimitri from the first day by explaining more on this beautiful night, we are here for a few more days anyway, now order our mixed kebabs, let's eat and leave. Tell me yourself tonight if you want, Dimitri, what are you doing, how is your brother? "

The kebab specialist old friend was looking at my face lovingly and listening to what I was saying, his eyes flashed and even filled with tears. I knew he got emotional. We knew that his parents died a few years ago, in a painful and strange traffic accident, in their car, and that he had only one brother. We found out about the accident very late and we could only share his pain by calling him on the phone. We couldn't attend the funerals, both of them were lying in the Christian Cemetery of Antakya. He had his tombs built and visited them regularly.

He was telling us, with eyes filled with tears, that they had rough days. The house we stayed in, a few lands and some cash was left for Dimitri and his brother. He sol done of the lands, renovated the old house and decided to continue the rest of his life in this house, to give his last breath here.

The "hor d'oeuvres" lined up in the large serving plate brought by the young waiter had an appetizing appearance and was smoking hot steam. The moment I lifted my head from the large round porcelain plate as beautiful as a painting, which I thought Dimitri would begin to explain and introduce right away, the expected speech started: "Look, this is called 'Kaytaz pastry,' ground beef is used in this, you take it life this, bite it and swallow it after having the taste of it on your palate." He continued to explain even while chewing and swallowing. For a moment I thought that Dimitri could be a good advertiser, for he was talking without stopping: "This is a dumpling prepared with serious labor, which we call 'Sembusek'. Look at it and bite, you will realize that the dough was rolled in thin layers like baklava. Well, how about this, this is called 'Additive Bread'. If you see the things added to it, you wouldn't believe your eyes and here is the king of our table, 'Pepper bread'. Attention, it burns and scorches! It makes you leap into the air, you get thinner as you eat, your metabolism speeds up..."

I made a decision that I would do whatever Dimitri did, as he would take a piece of that variety in his hand, look at it, bit it with appetite, started to chew it and then sent it to his stomach. I was determined to implement this decision. I did the same thing he last did as well. I extended my fork towards the Bean Paste that came on a separate plate and at that very moment I resembled myself with the quiet, silent, poor and addicted state of an alcoholic, who couldn't take his hands off the bottle even though he filled at least an evening's full capacity. She warned me as always: "Enough Yiğit, don't eat more, you won't be able to sleep and turn in bed until morning, you will have nightmares."

Not losing any opportunity, Dimitri said, "He's already having the nightmares, Solmaz, let him eat as much as he wants so that the nightmares he has don't go waste!"

I was looking at the bean paste as I was listening to this conversation. Anyone who'd watch me or Dimitri, any other guest would have thought that we were out of famile, that we hadn't eaten in days and that we probably thought if we couldn't consume all the food on the table, we would be kidnapped from the table right away.

"He's right, Solmaz… The nightmares I've been having, let them do their work; you should also take the risk of losing sleep fort he sake of these dishes, you should try all kinds, believe me you will not regret it. Look, you can never find the taste of this hot pepper in this pepper bread, the thyme and extra virgin olive oil anywhere else! Could you ever think that an ordinary bean dish could be prepared in such a delicious way?"

Solmaz looked at me and Dimitri with a dismissive facial expression. I will not be able to explain how our grilled meat, greased and peppered breads and onions with sumac, parsley, and our attitudes, movements, breathing style and attacks towards them; I do not want to even mention the efforts of Solmaz to prevent me and Dimitri; because it couldn't go beyond being an effort, neither Solmaz's attempts nor any other force anyway!

9. DID HE BLESS ORONTES, OR DID ORONTES BLESS HIM?

We would walk towards the shores of the Orontes River and when we arrived, we would wait for Him to sit on the shores first. He was getting close to the river bank, kneeling and washing his face, arms, shoulders with the water he took in his palms.

We couldn't understand whether He blessed Orontes or Orontes Him.

In the direction of the flow of the river, besides Him, we would line up to the shore and we were washing our hands with the waters used by Him, at that moment we would understand that the blessed Orontes blessed us with its cool water as well.

We would find a gap between trees, bushes and reeds that grew up on the banks of the river and sit right across him. He would remain silent, quiet, calm, like a holy rock, for a short time, and begin to speak as if he had grasped the hearts of all of us; at that moment, when he'd start talking, the moment we heard his voice and understood what he was saying, we would change, took on different structures and put our souls in the arms of peace.

"Share the feelings of people other than yourself, share their pain, joy and love each other, be humble, be compassionate, be merciful." *

We would understand, memorize what he said, and write everything he said after the first moments we left beside him.

He was coming from where the Holy Son was. He saw all the suffering he had experienced with his eyes and could not help. He was experiencing the trouble of not being able to do anything, and was trying to fulfill his duties without making us feel the pain of the spirit he had ruined.

He was the "Rock" of the Holy Son, the most trusted, and the closest.

The Orontes River flowed non-stop; The sounds of the branches, leaves, bushes on the shore and the reeds extending into the water, accompanied His voice, and He was telling us about the Holy Son.

We knew that what he was saying and telling us was what he was told and said to him; it was all important, and it had to be passed on to the people who came after us, to our children, our grandchildren, and from them to their children and grandchildren.

That is why we wrote all that he said, filled the earthen jugs and hid them in the caves of the Stauris Mountain, and sometimes buried them in the ground.

From St.Peter.

10. I FELT LIKE I LIVED AROUND HERE, TWO THOUSAND YEARS AGO

The boss and waiters went out of the old restaurant and saw us off. We could understand the need for a good walk after such a rich and dense meal from the weight that collapsed on us and the discomfort in our bellies. Our bodies, full stomachs and satisfied brains were saying to us, "Walk, walk non-stop."

We were walking slowly, swinging from one side to another, with Dimitri, and Solmaz was walking upright and laughing at us. She was making fun of both of us. "If you hadn't eaten those last desserts, at least, and you even put an ice cream on it." Dimitri replied instantly: "Come on Solmaz, they'd beat you up if you come to Antakya and sit at a rich table and not eat künefe after drinking plenty of rakı. But you are right, the ice cream on the künefe was unnecessary and it was too much!"

I was trying to understand the rationale of telling the unnecessity of a small ball of ice cream on top of the dessert, after having eaten and drunk so much; but instead, I was surrendering to the captivity of my drunk mind and throwing strange glances at my friend, who was indeed a monument of appetite.

We entered the narrow streets again. On a windy and cool night, Dimitri greeted all the people of the neighborhood, sitting on the rugs and carpets they laid in front of their old houses, resting their backs on thick and hard pillows. He spoke Turkish with some, Arabic with others, swore at some, and they laughed loudly all together. Warmness was the common feature of the people of this region. They were giving sincere greetings to me and Solmaz, whom they never knew and saw for the first time. All the men of the neighborhood were giving admiring glances to Solmaz, they could not take their eyes off her.

With her blond hair and dark blue eyes, they thought my beloved had come from a foreign country; and she continued her charming walk with her stylish dress in my arm, not minding any glances towards her. If I could look at this beautiful woman that I have been together with for ten years with this endless admiration for a long time that never faded, it was quite natural for those who saw her for the first time to look at her with glances that could be included in all sorts of definitions; and these glances could also contain negative meanings as well as hunger, admiration and longing.

When we got home, Dimitri lit the dim yellow lamps of the wide courtyard, and he turned on the fountain in the middle of the court-yard; we looked at the drops that rose up from the puddle under the yellow lights and fell back into the puddle with graceful curls, listening to the song of the waters.

We sat on the chairs next to the pool, and Dimitri gave Solmaz a black cardigan fors he started to feel cold in her dress with her shoulders exposed.

"Here I sit every night, listening to the sound of water drops; I perceive that my mortal life is actually an integral part of an endless movement, in those lonely moments. The water coming at the end of the sprinkler pipe rise up and every drop is swung in different directions, pouring into the pool where they come back and making the sound we are hearing now. After a very short time, the same drops swirl again to the heights and mix again into the same pud-dle they came from. Life is that simple, uncomplicated and clear. There's no need for complex philosophical analysis, searching for hidden meanings, and asking unanswered questions, I think and I hold tightly to the values I have. "

Was he really thinking that way, or was he giving secret advice to his depressed friend, me? In fact, he was telling me about the meaninglessness of bad dreams and troubled days that I had had for years; you are born, you grow up, rise up in the sky and mix again into the puddle you came from like a drop of water. You min-gle in the ground and when the time comes, rise to the sky again only to return where you came from. My old friend told me this in a clear, simple way in its most understandable form. I looked at his eyes with a facial expression that said that I understood and accepted what he was telling, and I started talking slowly with a very low volume.

"It seems to me that I lived here two thousand years ago. Starting from the first minute I arrived, I had a feeling that I came back to where I was born, I didn't even feel for a moment that I was a foreigner here. I feel myself as part of the wind blowing for two thousand years, the waters of the flowing river, the old streets, the houses, and the warmth and I cannot believe myself; I see in my dreams that I am the survivor of the fights, debates, the resident of those painful and troubled days two thousand years ago.

I research, read, and whenever I see that I have a place in an old event, fight, struggle, discussion, I get scared because I can't resolve it, I wake up sweating as if I am just out of a fight, I look at my hands and I only notice the marks of dried blood that only I can see. I wipe my face with my hands and feel the smell, warmth, stickiness and taste of the warm and fresh blood smeared on my hands. I am trying to understand what belief, belief principles, mentality and morality, behavior, and methods of movement affect hundreds of millions of people with all their existence for two thousand years. Starting from the day I learned that Antioch is the second most important city where this belief is spread, developed and its principles are written, I started to think that you are a very lucky person."

Dimitri looked at my face, smiled and turned his gaze into the drops of water splashing from the fountain of the pool, expressing that he had a lot to tell. The water was rising into the sky, falling into drops, and every drop of water mixed again into the puddle it came from.

"Come on, let's sleep now," Solmaz said. "We'll talk longer tomorrow, we'll be here for a few more days anyway."

When she stood up, I understood that I surrendered once again to the poetic beauty of the woman in front of me under the dim yellow lights, accompanied by the sound of water drops rising from the pool, and I did not regret this voluntary surrender. I stood up and followed her with my unbalanced walk. We headed upstairs from the courtyard and entered our room, I brushed my teeth, undressed until I was completely naked and threw myself under the thin blanket of the wide bed. I wanted to sleep, I was tired and I just wanted to sleep; I didn't want to have any more of those nightmares dividing my sleep and I wanted to start the next day refreshed, rested and carefree from the first moments I woke up.

I was lying on my back on a piece of warm soil covered with wide and white daisies, looking at the sky, I was sweating despite the cool winds blowing, I was soaked in sweat, two mysterious arms were hugging my body burning in flames, caressing my hair, thin long fingers, warm breaths were blowing in me from my lips. A warm, wet and writhing tongue that entered and exited my ears was writing yesterday, today, and tomorrow on my soul, with a thin pencil that had a trace but did not hurt, I was beginning to carry a heavier load on my body. I was wiggling, wriggling and surrendering with fear, intimacy and incredible harmony that were the opposite of the delusions that I thought I did not know; this voluntary surrender and captivity, which is another meaning of surrender, did not cause any discomfort to me and I wish this captivity would last a lifetime.

I opened my eyes and met the eyes of the beautiful woman on me. She was sweating and her breathing was accelerated, her heart was beating rapidly; I responded at the same speed… We stopped, stagnated and hugged each other, tightly.

"I wouldn't be able to waste the aphrodisiac effects of the Antakya appetiers, dishes and desserts, sir; you asked for it by entering in bed naked." She was still on top of me, her heartrate had slowed down. I hugged the woman I love tightly and slowed down my breath and heartrate, kissing Solmaz on her cheeks.

11. CAVE CHURCH ON STAURIS MOUNTAIN

He would stand in front of us with his thin long body, white beard and well-shaped face, looking at our face. We would then understand that we were very lucky to be able to see His face, hold his hands, and be blessed by Him.

When we listened to the speeches that asked us to throw ourselves in the arms of a life that has melted and destroyed all ambitions, away from all fights and war; and asked us to surrender ourselves, we understood that a fight-free life could be lived.

Every speech, every sentence, every word he was telling us spoke of these; like a teacher who loves us all, he was carving what he said to the depths in our soul, that would leave marks. His stories would erase, destroy and vanish every bad thought from inside of us.

Traders from Mesopotamia, Arabia and India were meeting with Egyptians, Greeks, and selling or exchanging valuable goods they brought in the markets built alongside the Orontes River.

As the weather got dark, we would visit these merchants sitting in front of the tents they set up next to the river and at the tables on the ground. One night, we shared the table of someone who came from Arabia, another night the table of someone from India.

After a few sentences they heard, a few stories he told them, every community, every trader, every visitor of the city could understand His greatness, His difference from other people and His, the first moment they knew him.

Returning to their country, Mesopotamian, Greek, and Egyptians were telling about this man they knew wherever they went, his upright stance like a rock, and the words, experiences and suffering of the Holy Son he was near.

"Ekklesia" the Greeks we knew and trusted named our meetings on the Stauris Muontain, and they sometimes attended our meetings as well.

We would go to Stauris's cave together write every word He said first in our soulds, hearts and minds, later on the papyrus and deerskin that we will keep in earthen jugs. We would listen, knowing whose words they actually were.

12. HISTORIA MAGISTRA VITAE*

The rocks of the mountain, which was different, strange and un-like any other, were cracking; the writings that had been hidden for centuries were swept to the ground. I was reaching with my hand, touching the old leather and gently stroking their surface as if I could hurt them, that they would scatter as soon as I touched them. The rocks of the mountain that collapsed and cracked were rolling from my right and left, and not even a single pebblestone touched me. I was slowly taking the old and worn leather roll, which I touched, from the ground, standing up and walking towards the mountain being demolished without haste. I was standing in the mouth of the old cave of the mountain for a short time, looking at the old city from above and entering into the cave; I was taking ten steps and entered its narrow, dark, long tunnel, starting to walk without knowing where I was going. As I walked, I felt that I was rising, chilling in the cool air of the tunnel and feeling cold. I was carrying the old and hardened, leather-covered leather roll like a fine glass-ware that would be dispersed and turned into dust at any time. I was walking through the narrow, dark and cold tunnel, and it was as if the closed eyelids of the faces hidden in the walls of the tunnel had been opening and looking right into my eyes. I was shivering, scared. The lights reflected from the brightness of the eyes under the opened eyelids were illuminating the dark tunnel, I was afraid of the brightness of these dead eyes and was trying to accelerate, run through the tunnel; However, the narrow and flat tunnel did not allow me to. I was throwing myself out of a window of the tunnel without

History is the teacher of life.

harming the written leather I had in my hands. The light of the shining sun of the day did not allow me to see anything at first; I closed my eyes tightly, waiting for a short time and slowly opening. The first thing I saw was the well-shaped rock that was carved into the rocks of the mountain, overlooking the city for two thousand and two hundred years without a face. Suddenly, the rock had a face and introduced himself to me with a smile.

"Charon is my name, I'm a boatman..." he said.

His loud voice shook the mountain and larger rocks began to roll off and towards the skirts of the mountain, and despite all my fear, I couldn't squeeze the old leather in my hand – it felt like they could be shaken, destoyed into pieces at any moment. I was looking right into the eyes of Charon and the boatman's new face was disappearing in an instant. The faceless rock continued to wait with a stance, which would not reveal where he was looking with the veil on his head, and continued his two-thousand-and-two-hundred-year watch.

* * *

I opened my eyes and looked at the ceiling. The light of the new day was leaking from the window. Despite the thin blanket on me, I was in sweat. I've had the bad dream I've had for years; The rocks falling down, shaking and cracking, the cave that I entered, the narrow tunnel I walked, the old leather scroll with writings on it, and the narrative I couldn't read, but tried to understand by hovering my fingers on it – old days, fights, quarrels, blood, torture and tears... I was shivering as I remembered.

Years ago, I told Solmaz about the dream that I didn't mind on the first day I had it but later started to have the same dream every day in sweat, making me jump awake from my sleep. She had listened to me and whispered a few words of love to help me calm down. After that night, when the number of nights I woke up with the same dream of the same boatman increased, even though she could not clearly say it, she mentioned that we could go to a psychiatrist. I pretended I didn't understand it and started not to tell her about my nightmares.

I looked at Solmaz, she was sleeping face-down. I stroked her blonde hair, she muttered and opened one eye halfway, smiled at me as if she was dreaming, closed her eye again, turned her head to the other side, pulled a knee towards her belly; I stripped the thin blanket on her and watched her naked body admiringly for a while, then covered it again. I realized that I could not sleep any longer and went into the bathroom, took a long, warm, relaxing shower. I dressed quietly and went down to the courtyard of the house, sat on one of the chairs next to the fountain. The birds were singing wildly, having morning conversations. I listened to their morning concerts, I tried to understand the words of the songs that cut the silence of the morning, I could not understand, I thought I could understand if I made a serious effort for it; I did not spend that effort…

* * *

After studying for two years in the archeology department, I entered the history department of the same faculty and completed my education in the normal period of time. As soon as school was over, I started to work as a "History Consultant" in a tourism company. I was working at the headquarters of a large international company in Istanbul. My good knowledge of French, English, old and new Greek helped me a lot. In addition to the history consultancy, the managers of the company wanted me to participate in cultural tours of private groups as well and started to pay me a lot of money apart from the salary I received.

We were picking up groups of ten, fifteen, and twenty people, all of whom were from abroad and very wealthy, from hotels where they were staying in Istanbul with private and well-equipped buses, taking them to places they wanted, wondered about, read, researched and wanted to see, together with other guides. These were generally three-day cultural tours. All of the participants were well-educated, cultured and wealthy. We were visiting all the historical buildings, ruins, museums, mountains and caves of the places we went and I was making our tours more enjoyable with scientific narratives, interesting stories, incredible connections, ongoing discussions for thousands of years and gossip. We were climbing the mountains, setting up small tents and going overnight, sometimes on deserted slopes. We were singing songs, lighting small fires and cooking beautiful local dishes with the joint efforts of the group's guests.

Sometimes we were diving in the sea, took photos and tried to fish in deep, cool waters. After each tour I attended, the participants of the tour would send messages of thanks to our company headquarters and their phones expressing their satisfaction, the lines of happiness and constant praising me strengthened my place in the company day by day with the result of a very high raise in my salary. While I was doing my job as a historical consultant, which I knew well, I learned about the subtleties of this work almost as much as a professional guide. Praising letters, messages, e-mails of especially women, mostly female tourists, about me attracted the attention of the boss of the company, and he would joke every time we met:

"Mr. Yiğit, eight of the fifteen people who participated in the last Cappadocia tour you went were women, and we received thank you messages from each of these eight ladies. I just say for your information. Some of them liked your way of speaking, fluent expression methods, and some praised that you are multicultural and knowledgeable. Others talk about your broad shoulders, narrow hips and athletic body, agility. They want to come again next year and be sure that you are with them in their tours, we respond positively to all of them, just so you know. If you want, leave your position as the History Consultant and become a professional guide, what would you say? "

It was the boss, who was joking with a michievous smile and not making it obvious, and of course I wasn't letting his jokes unanswered:

"Historia magistra vitae."

He looked at my face and understood what I said in Latin, which he knew well, but continued to joke:

"But the ladies who convey their messages of thanks are more about your approach to life and your athletic body than your history teaching!"

The boss was having fun with me, and I knew that as these jokes have increased, this was a sure signal that a raise on my salary was on its way soon, as well as a good additional payment. I was never mistaken.

This work started to hinder my job as a history consultant and I started to do this job only, working almost like a full-time guide; however, the boss, who wanted me to be on these tours, which earned him quite well, could not object to this hindering. I mentioned Solmaz Başaran one day at a meeting to the boss, he was interested and immediately called her, who became a new archaeologist, to meet her the next day. I ignored the touchy and frustrated attitudes of the "Human Resources Director" who normally arranged recruitment meetings. As the boss said he will hold this meeting himself; I was trying to escape my glances from the chubby red-cheeked human resources manager.

Thanks to the country's well-planning (!),archeology graduates who are well above the needed number were often unable to find jobs or had to work in different jobs outside their profession that were not related to their education. They felt lucky even if they found any job positions such as experts in insurance companies, marketing staff in phone dealers, cashiers in markets, drivers in minibuses, unskilled workers in brick factories, salespersons in air-conditioning shops, marketing of make-up materials and so on.

On the day she graduated from the archeology department, I took photos of Solmaz with her cap and black gown, which she threw in the air; she was really happy; she did not yet know the realities of life and the cruel face of unemployment. She was not yet aware of the difficulties of entering a job she could work in her own field. On the same day, I photographed Dimitri, who graduated together with Solmaz, with his cap and gown, he looked confident and quite happy. However he managed, Dimitri was accepted to work in the famous and large museum of the city where he was born, just three months after finishing school.

Solmaz was unhappy, depressed and sad, after having nowhere left that she applied to work as an archaeologist and every door was closed to her face. Months later when I told her about my boss' request to meet her, she happily hugged my neck. I had taken the opportunity and slid my palms from the thin waist, which I hugged with both hands, towards her raised hips; this was a behavior of mine that upset her every time, scolding me: "Don't be spoiled!"

However, I liked everywhere on her body. For years, I have been a fan of uniquely beautiful navy eyes, healthy, fresh blonde hair, skin, lips and a thin waist shaped almost by a master painter and proportional areas underneath. Every time I told her about them, she would happily look at my face and smile; bu whenever I started to describe the regions underneath her waist, she would scowl and silence me. I would not be silent, however, and I would continue to describe them taking a few steps backwards, with an attitude that is ready to escape at any moment. In the beginning, she would get seriously upset at this, but over time, the cruel beautiful woman started not to mind them!

We were living together in a small apartment in Kartal district of Istanbul. We were on the fourteenth floor of a gated building complex on *Yalnız Selvi Street*. Princes' Islands (Buyukada, Heybeliada, Burgazada and Kınalıada) were right across us. When the weather was nice, we would put little candles on the turn off all the lights and watch the flashing, blinking lights of the islands together.

We went to my workplace together the next day and Solmaz was seeing the place for the fist time. I introduced her to my colleagues. The boss arrived at the office around 10.00 in the morning and had a one-on-one meeting with Solmaz in his room, eventually deciding to hire her with a not-so-bad salary for start in order to help me and cover my missing work in my position as the history consultant.

I understood the boss; he was trying to make sure that everything works in a timely manner at the company while at the same time, calculating how he could send me to culture tours more frequently and for longer periods of time, knowing that Solmaz couldn't object too much as she's new. Our boss was a smart, intelligent and a good tradesman, making the sensitive calculations of how he could make these culture tour organizations work, which was paying the company well, as well as how he could increase my dependence to the company.

I moved away from my thoughts with the stimulating notes of the birds' morning symphonies, which are now voiced by higher-volumed chirps. The rising sun started to illuminate a corner of the courtyard with its bright light.

The door of one of the rooms opposite the fountain area I was sitting at opened and Dimitri appeared in his clothes, which was a mix of sweatpants and pajamas. More precisely, first his imposing belly appeared and then Dimitri himself. He was yawning, rubbing his eyes and smiling, voicing his first complaints: "The ice cream on the kebab we had at the end of the meal was heavy, we shouldn't have eaten that ice cream, I turned in bed until morning, how are you?" I answered my cheerful friend, thinking about the abundance of kebabs and appetizers that each of us eat almost in three-person-sized dishes.

"You're right, Dimitri, we ate each dish appropriately and we would be as light as a bird if only we haven't eaten that ice cream on top of the dessert!" He came up to me, scratching his head and laughing, and sat on one of the chairs in front of me. "Could you sleep comfortably, did you like the room?" I told Dimitri that we liked it and had a comfortable night except the nightmares we had because of our overly full stomachs.

I told him that it was a habit of mine to wake up early, that I was trying to understand the lyrics of the song that the little birds sang on the trees of the garden, and that I could solve this language by spending a little more effort and listening to them for a few more mornings. He naively looked at my face and smiled again. "You can solve it; if I don't remember wrong, you were interested in Latin after English and French, how's it going?"

I looked at the branches of trees, which remained empty after the birds got frightened and left due to Dimitri's loud noise with his walk, talk and laugh. I tried to perceive the silence that collapsed in the courtyard.

"Silentium post clamores."*

He did not understand what I said, and I did not tell him the meaning. He knew the meaning of the words "Silentium" and "Post". He asked me what "Clamores" was, I told him so my friend resolved the meaning. "So, now, with the opposite practice, let's break the silence of the morning, prepare a nice breakfast with you, make noise and wake up Solmaz, we haven't eaten anything since yesterday, aren't you hungry?" I looked at Dimitri's face with painful eyes and told him that I was hungry in a tone I did not believe.

Silence comes after noise.

The door of the kitchen was opening to the wide courtyard. I walked after Dimitri, we went into the kitchen and he started to place glass storage containers with white plastic lids that he took out of the refrigerator on the table in the kitchen.

"I will visit the museum shortly after breakfast, then I will go to Stauris Mountain, as you know, Saint Pierre Church, the first church in the world, is on this mountain. We had to close visits to it a while ago.

Large cracks have occurred in many parts of the mountain in the sections above the cave, large pieces of rock are tumbling and rolling, and they can be very dangerous so we closed it to visits, thinking that the church could be damaged as well. One night, when no one was around, a few rocks fell down and fortunately no one was where the rocks fell. We have created a security zone and closed the historical church, we are working on strengthening the dangerous parts of the mountain, if you want to come, you're welcome. "

I listened to Dimitri silently and with a chill, I stopped, paused, and suddenly felt that my mouth was dry.

The destroyed, cracking mountain, pouring rocks and the church cave beneath them; I thought of my fearful dreams, my forehead and armpits began to sweat. Looking at my face, Dimitri tried to understand the reason of my silence and my pale color, but he could not.

"Did something happen, your face turned pale, are you alright?"

13. WE WERE FISHING IN
THE ORONTES RIVER

He taught us how to fish. We were riding on big boats together. He was riding the front rowboat with the three people he took with him, and we were rowing in the waters of Orontes.

He was telling us where to stand, how and where to throw our nets in the river that is twisting, accelerating, slowing down, stagnant; as if he was talking to the fish in the waters of the river.

When we pulled the nets where he stood at a place, with his eyes staring at the water of the river, after having thrown the nets all at once and waited, we had a hard time holding the contents of the nets, the fish overflew from our boats. He was gathering us on the shore and starting to tell us the story.

"I was a fisherman, a simple, self-contained, ordinary, small man with no purpose, earning his living by fishing on the lake. He saw me and 'Now forget fishing and come with me, I will teach you to hunr people, to reach the souls of people who are unbelievers, who do not know where they are and why they are. You will reach these unbelieving souls and put faith in them,' he said to me.

"I was a fisherman, I leaned on a small, ordinary life and was doing the only job I knew, I was fishing. First He hunted my soul, then he taught me to hunt a soul. "

We took the fish that we kept in the deep waters of the Orontes River to the city and distributed them to everyone.

The smell of smoke and fish rising from the fires we burned on the bank of the river covered the sky.

We were singing songs, playing games, our neighborhoods were ringing with the cries of joy.

No *fisherman of the city, young or old, old or new, anyone who has been doing the job for a long time or has just learned it, no fisherman was as skillful and lucky as His.*

It was as if the fish knew that he was in the boat floating in the waters of the Orontes River, never leaving around His boat until they came out of the river.

"I was a fisherman... I was not a fisherman ever since he said to me, 'Come with me, we will hunt people now.'"

We were looking into his eyes, we knew and understood exactly who kept Him from fishing.

14. LEARNED BEHAVIOR

I sat on one of the chairs next to the kitchen table; My heart was beating fast. Dimitri put what he took out of the fridge on the table and looked at my face. I took a deep breath and said that my blood pressure may have fallen. He filled a glass of cold water and gave it to me, his cheer had vanished.

I couldn't tell Dimitri that the dream I've had for months is similar to what he's just told me, he wouldn't take me seriously even if I said it, or would think I am insane; he's ask me to do what Solmaz suggested, to tell a psychiatrist about my problem. I said nothing, and I told him that I would rest a little in the room, that he should come home after he is finished at the museum and that I would go to the Stauris Mountain with him. He accepted what I said without a word.

I climbed up the stairs with difficulty, resting, stopping and trying to calm my palpitations, I entered the room without making any noise. Solmaz was still sleeping with light mutters. I laid down next to her, put my hand on her bare back; she jumped up awake, my hand was cold, she looked at my face and told me I didn't look well. For a while I did not speak, could not speak. Then I said with a low volume that I woke up with the same dream in the morning, and I told Solmaz, who was listening to me with worry, what Dimitri had said. She thought this was one of my usual jokes first, but when she realized that I was serious, she threw the blanket away and sat cross-legged on the bed. She was naked.

"We came here for this anyway, we've been researching for months and together we realized that this is the only place we should come. Now calm down, and believe that you will get the answers to all your questions here, I'll be there for you as always.

I reached forth and kissed the lips of this beautiful woman. I knew that she was upset and was worried about me, and I was getting angry at myself because I was upsetting her. An emotional, sensitive and delicate woman she was, like a flower that could fade at any moment. When I told her about these or mentioned them, she would scold me with a harsh attitude.

"Are you crazy, of course I will be with you, we will share bad days as well as good days; Everything may not always go well, we will have hard times and we will overcome all the difficulties together; you may have mental problems, all of us may, will you leave me alone if I experience a crisis tomorrow? "

Solmaz was determined to see the problems and troubles I had, the fearful dreams I had, as a simple and ordinary mental crisis. But I knew that these were not a spiritual crisis; I wanted to follow the traces of my problems, troubles hidden deep in my nightmares, which I couldn't understand.

A small caterpillar that comes out of the egg and curls over the green leaves displays a very appetizing image to hungry and gluttonous birds flying in the air. However, that little caterpillar has to grow, develop and survive; it bites the leafstalk of the tree, which is the leaf's only connection with the branch, bites, gnaws on it and cuts all of the feeding paths of the leaf. So the leaf gets dry, curls as it dries and takes on a round, cylindrical shape. The little caterpillar lies right in the middle of this cylinder, it thinks that it can no longer attract the appetites of hungry and gluttonous birds looking from above; however, it is mistaken. The hungry and gluttonous bird dives towards that one leaf among the lush green leaves, the only leaf that is dry, yellow and curled! Swallows the delicious caterpiller in an instant.

In the second step, another caterpillar behaves more carefully; it gnaws on three leafstalks this time, leaves the three leaves to dry side by side and lies in the middle of one of them, hides and becomes invisible. The hungry and gluttonous bird looks from above, dives in for one of three dry and rolled leaves among the lush green leaves; understanding there is no caterpillar, it shakes to get rid of the remains of dry leaves between its beak and moves away quickly from the other two rolls of dry leaves.

The caterpillar took the precautions of not being found and not being caught; it has bitten the stems of three leaves, dried three leaves standing next to each other and devoted itself to completing its development, safely spending the time required in one of them. It reduced the chances of being caught by hungry and gluttonous birds to one third, and reduced the chances of these birds attacking dry leaf rolls they saw.

Now, is this the mind, can we call it intelligence? As we try to talk about them and resolve the mysteries of this mysterious behavior, the familiar caterpillar, which has completed its development in the dry leaf roll and turned into a blue, yellow, green or white butterfly, has already started its free flight from one flower to another.

"Learned Behavior..." Learned behavior; passwords inside the cells, attitudes that were memorized for hundreds, thousands or even millions of years, habitual behavior could produce more consistent, logical, and accurate behavior, actions and results than many other highly intelligent behavior.

This was my problem. I thought that the reason for my repeating dreadful dreams that Solmaz sees as a mental crisis, an important problem, was the same as the problems experienced by the caterpillar; I knew that I was at least as smart as that little caterpillar and I felt like I had to find solutions; I wanted to complete my development, turn into a butterfly and fly freely; I wanted to fly on unique flowers and smell them.

I stretched my arms and hugged Solmaz's naked body, sniffed her hair, but she jumped out of bed, saying that she was going to take a shower. I looked at her bare back and hips from behind, I said I could soap her back in the shower, she thanked me and said with a smile that she knew very well what could come after soaping and that she had tried it for years and memorized it as "Learned Behavior". I helplessly accepted the situation, with my back on the pillow, I started to watch the movements of Solmaz's shadow, visible from the shower cabin.

My cell phone on the nightstand began to ring, Dimitri was calling. "I prepared the breakfast, on the table in the kitchen, I also brewed the tea, just so you know, the stove is on, I'm leaving, I will come back after completing my work at the museum, be ready in two hours." I hung up, saying I will be ready. Solmaz came out of the bathroom with her white bathrobe. She asked with curiosity, who the call came from at the eartly hours in the morning, I told her what Dimitri said, and she said she wanted to come with us. I confirmed her request by bending my head forward; she had to come and see with her own eyes that something similar to dream that I had seen for years actually existed.

I watched Solmaz get dressed. I watched her pulling her tight jeans, which she usually wore, towards her waist. She constantly complained, saying that if we continued to eat like we did the day before, we would go back to Istanbul gaining a few kilograms.

"After a certain age, people should pay attention to what they eat and drink. When we were young, we were able to metabolize everything we eat quickly, our bodies burned all of them, it is not like that anymore, it is easy to gain weight as you get older and it is very difficult to lose. "

I reminded her that she was only twenty-eight years old, and I told Solmaz that I would voluntarily accompany her and support her in all physical activities that would prevent her from gaining weight. She looked at my face; a sly, cunning smile appeared suddenly on the edge of her beautiful lips.

We went down to the courtyard together, the flock of small birds that saw Dimitri out of the house had returned and perched on the branches of the trees, singing their morning songs in a different tone this time. When we entered the kitchen, we paused for a moment when we saw the abundance of the rich table and its varieties Dimitri described as breakfast, and we swallowed, looking at the appetizing view. Steam that smelled of brewed tea were spreading from the teapot to the ceiling of the kitchen.

"Remember, Yiğit, you may need to work for months to lose the weight you have gained in an instant, be careful!" I looked desperately in the face of my tough teacher.

I said, "It takes a lifetime to love, a minute to make love." She looked at my face, roughly. However, I was only trying to explain to her that I confirmed what she said, but she could not understand, so

I had to explain. "You should understand the words "to love" from the lyrics of this old song as "To lose weight"; and the word "making love" as "eating"… We know that women are trying to lose weight for a lifetime; even now I see a vivid example of this in front of me. In this sense, we can perceive the "Love-Lose Weight" duo as a synonym. For those like me, you should perceive the actions of "making love-eating" as a synonym. I have an orgasmic pleasure from eating. In other words, we can sing the lyrics of the song as follows: Losing weight takes a lifetime, eating takes a minute... Are we on the same page now?"

"Alright then," said Solmaz. "After that, go to bed with good food, I will sleep on the sofa in the living room, so this is how you can meet your need for orgasm!"

While I explained that the food plates I will enter into the bed should be oval and dark blue in the shape of eyes and that it is an indispensable choice for all pies to have a fresh, fluffy, appetizing appearance, I slowly extended my hand and caressed her tight hips. As always, she scolded me: "Don't be spoiled!"

I filled our teas in the white porcelain cups prepared by Dimitri. We sat opposite each other and I took a small piece of feta cheese, two slices of tomatoes and cucumber on the plate in front of me, I started to eat by cutting small pieces from the ends. She looked at my face and scolded me again, my harsh teacher: "Don't overdo it!"

However, I had watched her and took the same amount of everything she took on my plate, I was doing the same as whatever she did on my own plate, with similar movements; From the tip of the cheese, I cut a small piece with a knife, stuck the fork and gently pushed it into my mouth.

"I have to call Gizem," said Solmaz. "We haven't talked for two days, she didn't call as well, I wonder how she's doing."

Gizem was Solmaz's only sister. The year I met Solmaz, she was an eight-year-old, a cute, active, naughty little girl. She grew up in the past decade, became taller and became a young girl at least as beautiful as her older sister. A few centimeters shorter, a little fuller than Solmaz; she was a very cute, blue-eyed, lively young girl with auburn wavy long hair who liked to joke. She graduated from high school a year ago, was interested in English literature and succeeded in winning the "Department of English Language and Literature" in the first university entrance exam she entered. It is unlikely that we will ever forget the happiness she experienced the day she learned the results; she screamed, ran from one room to another in the house, hugged us on our neck, sang songs. We took her to Ankara together with Solmaz, we first completed her registration process at the faculty, and then we completed her entrance procedures for a good, clean, high-quality girls' dormitory.

Solmaz's mother and father were intellectual, well-cultured, understanding and loving people. Both were retired teachers. Starting from our student years, they did not react against me living in the same apartment with Solmaz, they would tell me that they trust and love me; and I was always respectful towards them. When we finished the faculty, they wanted us to come to Istanbul and they never opposed us living together. In particular, aside from asking the question, "When will you get married?" We never heard a sentence that might even evoke the question. They were really good, honest and well-cultured people.

Solmaz told Gizem that we were in Antioch, told her about Dimitri, told us that he was hosting us at his home and that we were on vacation for three more days. When she said that she could come where we are and stay with us, for our friend's house was quite big, even I heard the crazy Gizem's cry on the phone in Solmaz's ear.

When Solmaz went back to the room to take her sunglasses, I attacked the storage containers with the open lids on the table and started to swallow them without wasting time, without chewing too much; sediments, crushed green olives, pepper with walnuts, salty yoghurt with thyme, honey, jams, butter... We attacked each other like longed friends, we hugged and wrapped each other, we became one body! When Solmaz came back in the kitchen, I corrected the surfaces of the breakfast dishes in the storage boxes, closed the lids and started to put them in the refrigerator.

"When you get up from the table without eating too much, you feel yourself more comfortable, Solmaz, I will always do what you do from now on." She looked at my face, first she looked at the boxes I started to put in the fridge, she nodded, shripped her lips and said nothing, she couldn't say anything.

Dimitri came towards 10:30, I told him that Solmaz would come to Stauris Mountain as well. We turned off the heat under the tea and left the house together.

15. WE WERE LISTENING TO CEPHAS IN THE CAVE

They called our meetings "Ekklesia" in Greek. We were eagerly waiting for the time when we would come together and listen to Cephas. We missed his voice, his stance and the things he was telling us.*

We started to call the cave of Stauris Mountain a "Church". Wen ever spoke about the location of the cave, where it was, we never even spoke about it being a cave. When we said "Church," we all would understand what was being said and continued with our meetings.

Cephas lived in Jerusalem, he was the closest to Him and he remembered every every speech, every word of him, conveying all of them to us. We knew what he was telling transmitting to us and everything he said came from Him.

In fact, we were not doing anything to be afraid of, nor were we doing things that would disturb anyone. What Cephas told us were a prase for life, humanity, kindness and benevolence.

However, we were afraid, we knew that increasing the number of our people and accepting our beliefs more and more would disturb the rulers of the city, and Cephas did not want to experience the suffering he had experienced before.

We continued to dig and advance the tunnel in the cave, namely the "Church", into the Stauris Mountain; because the number of people coming to listen to Cephas continued to increase rapidly day by day.

Rock.

We have started to become a bigger crowd. We all knew each other, we knew we have the same belief, but we all followed the privacy rules that Cephas constantly reminded and warned us about.

We questioned and asked everything that came to our mind, what was told us:

"What is the name of our faith, what is the name of our community?"

Cephas looked at our face, paused, thought for a while and spoke in a slow, calm manner that could be heard by the entire community in the cave church of Stauris, telling us the name of our community for the first time.

The name of our community and belief was not used even in the city where He lived, and after Jerusalem, it was mentioned for the first time in this first church in the World in Antioch, where our faith spread most and was accepted rapidly for the first time in the World. It was the first time this name was used and voiced and it was Cephas who was saying this; now he blessed us all with this name.

16. AT THE WORLD'S FIRST CHURCH

It was as hot as the day before. We got in the car, closed the windows and started the air conditioner. We proceeded in the old and narrow streets of Antakya. Dimitri was navigating the path we would take from the front seat. The streets we passed smelled of history; old doors of the old houses, windows, plastered walls, children playing in the narrow streets, and even old people who were asleep in front of the walls had not changed for thousands of years. We traveled on the narrow street to the south of the city.

"Did you spend the night comfortably, Solmaz?" asked Dimitri to his classmate sitting in the back seat. "No," said Solmaz. "I will never comply with you and Yiğit again, no matter how much you insist, I will eat at my own measure. You have great food and if I lose control, I will have to go hungry for months to lose the weight I will gain here in a few days. I will not comply with you and I will sleep comfortably at night." Dimitri laughed warmly, hopping his belly; he said that what he saw the day before was just the beginning and that there are many special dishes to offer. Solmaz listened to him, grimacing her beautiful face.

Dimitri warned me to turn right from the street going south of the city, and when I turned, he showed the mountain right in front of him. "This is the 'Cross Mountain', formerly 'Stauris Mountain'. Look at the left side of the mountain, do you see the sculpture there?"

We looked at the relief on the mountain, that was well-carved but didn't have a face, so it looked like an incomplete painting. "That's Charon in mythology, the 'Hell Boatman...'" The sculpture on the mountain is exactly two thousand and two hundred years old. A great plague epidemic started in the city during the rule of Antiochus Epiphanes IV, known as the second founder of Antioch, they couldn't prevent it so many people have died in a very short time. They tried everything to stop it; however, the plague epidemic did not stop. In order to plead with the Gods, they started sculpting the face of 'Hell Boatman Charon' there on the mountain. The plague epidemic stopped before its completion, the sculptors gave up in those days and did not finish their work. If you pay attention, the Hell Boatman doesn't have a face. History writes it like this: "The plague epidemic has stopped and they gave up sculpting." I do not think so, I think it's as if the sculptors thought of a face for a 'Hell Boatman', how they should sculpt it, they could not figüre it out and decide, and they left it in this state when the epidemic stopped... Don't you think it's possible?"

I couldn't understand if Dimitri believed what he was saying it or joking. He was talking about something he was competent and we were listening to him with interest. "Charon would take money from the dead to take them in his boat, so when they buried the dead, they put money in their palms. Charon is someone who takes bribe in mythology. You know, those who take bribes are cheeky; they want a separate fee to do the things they already have to do, they do not do it if they don't take it, they delay the work and make things difficult... Charon is the first one to get bribery in world history. I think the sculptors did not carve a face to the Hell Boatman because of this; it has been like this, faceless, on the mountain for two thousand and two hundred years!"

I stopped the car in the large parking lot at the end of the road, a few boys came running to the car, they opened our doors and in their local accent, they said, "Welcome!" to us. The moment they saw Dimitri, they ran away from us. "They tell the history of this place to the tourists who come here, they have nothing to tell me!" said Dimitri.

We walked to the far side of the parking area and looked up at the historical building at the foot of the mountain. I trembled and felt that sweat droplets began to appear on my forehead at that moment. I dried my forehead and face with a paper tissue from my pocket and tried to calm down with deep breaths. It was as if I knew this place that I had come to for the first time, I was born here and I felt as if I lived here, had never left here for years and that I have died here. I was filled with the excitement, bitterness and happiness of a sad person who longed for the city, the neighborhood and streets he spent his childhood and youth in, and never forgot these places.

"Are you alright?" I was startled by the question of Solmaz. "Your face is red, you're sweating," she said to me. I said I was fine, I forced myself to smile, I held her hand, squeezed it, and said I was very good. I also explained to her that I felt as if I had returned to the place at the foot of the mountain where I lived years ago and that this feeling did not bother me at all. She was the one who could understand me the best. She looked at my face, smiled with an worried expression, and squeezed my hand back... I was able to return to the day when Dimitri started talking. "The first church in the world is what you see across us. St. Peter's Church or Saint Pierre Church as the French call it."

Dimitri spoke not like out frend but authoritatively, confidently and clearly like a serious bureaucrat, an important official of one of the most important museums in the world, the Antakya Archaeology Museum – and he was.

"After Jerusalem, Antakya is the most important city where Christianity developed. The word 'Ekklesia' means community or meeting in Greek, the word 'Church*' is derived from this Greek word and survived to the present day. In fact, Peter or Simon was a fisherman, while they were throwing nets with his brother Andreas in the Sea of Galilee, they met Jesus Christ on the shore of the lake. He told Petrus, whose name was Simon at the time, and Andreas, "Stop hunting fish and come with me, you will hunt men from now on," then named Simon "Cephas," meaning rock. This person was going to form the solid foundation of the church that was going to be built, and was as strong and durable as a rock floor. Peter is always remembered as a very important saint in the history of Christianity, the first of his twelve disciples. After the crucifixion of Jesus Christ, he came to Antakya and founded the first church in the world, he stayed here for seven years. "

*Kilise (Turkish): Church

Dimitri was proud to tell, I understood that he was honored because he was born in one of the cities that was of great importance in the development and spread of the religion he believed in.

"In the Bible, the holy book of Christianity, in the 'Acts of the Apostles' section, while mentioning a community that is not yet mentioned by a name, it is written that the name 'Christian' given to the previously unnamed community was given in Antakya, did you know? Antakya is such an important city. I think it is very important that the community of the most widespread religion in the world (which is believed to be 30 percent of believers in the world according to reliable sources) found a name here in this city. This situation and the important history here are not known enough. However, these and other historical facts can be explained more skillfully and the city can be turned into a center of attraction. Antakya, whose economy is strengthening, can return to its glorious days. *The Queen of the East* was the old name of Antakya.

Dimitri turned around and pointed the distant mountain with his hand.

"Look, Stauris Mountain, which you see before you, was sacred before Christianity as well. In many parts of the mountain, you can find very old sculptures, carvings, caves, tunnels, corridors. I will tell you about the people gathered in this first church of Christianity, their historical significance, the meetings of the founders of the world's most common religion in the cave church of Antakya.

First of all, St. Peter, the first apostle of Jesus Christ. Jesus calls him "Cephas", meaning "Rock". Cephas, Kiphas, Petrus, Simon, Simeon, The Rock are the names of the first apostle. Approximately ten or twelve years after the 33rd year when Jesus Christ was crucified, he came to Antakya, and for seven years he stayed here and founded the first church in the world.

"It's not over, I just started. Paul and Barnabas, one of the most important names of Christianity, also come to Antakya and hold their meetings with St. Peter in this cave-church. I can tell you the importance of Paul as follows: One of the most important personalities that shape the foundations of Christianity, the foundations of belief. There are four canonicals, that is, four Bibles accepted by the authorities: Bibles of Matthew, Markos, Luke and John. The author of the Bible of Luke is a very close friend and physician of Paul. Luke is also from Antioch. It is accepted that the Antioch physician Luke wrote the 'Acts of the Apostles' section, which is one of the most important parts of the Bible. It is known that he wrote this section according to Paul's narratives, being his close friend. "

Dimitri spoke and we were keeping our silence. We didn't want to interrupt his excitement.

"We can talk about the importance of Antakya on the most wide-spread religion in the world for days. If you want, we can talk about these topics in our next chats; for now, let me show you the first church in the world. Let me show you the first church in the cave of the Holy Stauris Mountain, where St. Petrus, Paul, Barnabas and Luke held meetings... Let's close our eyes and try to hear the divine speeches made two thousand years ago. "

We climbed the steps from the car park area to the cave at the foot of Stauris Mountain and reached the locked iron gate of St. Peter's Church. I looked at the wide empty space visible through the openings at the top of the iron door and the solid-looking iron cage that stretched over the cave, my heart began to race. I felt that my forehead, hands, and armpits began to sweat, my mouth suddenly dried, I staggered, and grabbed the iron on the door in front of me. "What happened, are you okay?" asked Solmaz. I was shaking with the same emotions, I felt as if I had run, sat, talked, discussed, frightened and constantly found peace in the vast area that I could see through the gaps of the iron door, centuries ago. I was in the similar dreams I've been having for months; I was awake and living the dreams I had seen. "That's enough for today," I said to Dimitri. "I'm not feeling well, let's go home, we'll come again tomorrow.

I sat on one of the steps and took my head between my hands, I deeply inhaled through my lungs. I closed my eyes and thought of the similarities between the place in my dreams and the place behind the locked iron door. I tried to perceive the acrid, frustrated, sad and pale emotional states of people who returned to where they were born, raised and lived centuries ago, I forced myself to feel as if I was experiencing what they experienced. I felt like I was in a vacuum; I could not perceive anything, I could not understand, and I could not experience. As soon as my palpitations stagnated, I slowly stood up. Dimitri and Solmaz entered my arms, we walked towards the car, sat on the back seat and looked through the closed window of the car, to Stauris, the holy mountain of thousands of years.

17. STUDENTS NAMED CHRISTIANS IN ANTAKYA FOR THE FIRST TIME**

We were listening to Him in the cave where we gathered on the Stauris Mountain, his face was radiating holy lights. He was telling us about the great suffering he experienced and the good, beautiful and happy news that he received while experiencing these suffering.

He was telling the gospel of the Son who rose to the sky. He explained how they received the news that they were going to be baptized with the Holy Spirit, and a few days after receiving the news, a strong wind from the sky filled the house they were living in, there were loud sounds, things like fire-tongues had spread around and fell on them, all of them were filled with the Holy Spirit.

We were listening quietly, almost without breath, to Cephas, who was filled with the Holy Spirit. As soon as we saw the drops flowing from his eyes, we were all starting to cry.

Cephas was constantly telling us about the moment when the Holy Spirit appeared, heard and that they were filled with it. He almost seemed to blow the breaths of the Holy Spirit, which filled him; we were cleaned, purified and hugged each other with great living power.

Cephas was telling us that one of those who were in the same house when the Holy Spirit rained on them was Barnaba and that they sent this good person to Antakya, next to us. We knew those days and knew Barnaba, who was full of the Holy Spirit as well.

Christiyanos (Greek): Followers of Christ, Christians.

From the New Testament: Acts of the Apostles.

Barnaba held meetings in the cave of Stauris Mountain, and tied us to his belief with the things he told us in his sincere and heartfelt speeches. Our number was increasing day by day.

With the peace and happiness he felt from our increasing number, Barnaba had gone to Tarsus. He brought Saul to us, whom he had found after having searched for him for days, unable to find and was about to lose hope.

They remained in Antakya for a year; Barnaba and Saul had spoken, told, discussed, taught, and tried to learn from even the little ones, in their humblest ways. Our number was increasing day by day.

They looked at us through a high rock, thirteen steps deep and ten steps wide, where we gathered in the cave and had now difficulty in fitting.

When they put their hands up, we were all silent, even the little children and babies among us were silent. Our community, which has been increasing day by day, had no name yet, and they first called here with our new name in the cave of Stauris, on Stauris Mountain of Antakya:

"Christianos... This is the name of our community now." they said.

We got this name in Antakya and it was mentioned for the first time in that cave...

We carried hearts in our bodies filled with the Holy Spirit, that would spread, announce, tell and teach our name and belief with this name to Jerusalem, Damascus, Cyprus, Psidia, Pamphylia, Perge, Konya, Listre, Derbe, Macedonia, Thessaloniki, Veriya, Athens, Corinth, Ephesus, Rome and all around the world.

Peter, Cephas as the Son named him, was looking at the seven-foot-high ceiling of the cave where he spoke and we listened to him, as well as at the rock floor on the ground, and was trying to understand why Christ named him "Cephas" in our first temple in the World, that we now called "Church." As soon as he understood it, he was beginning to tell us.

"You are the solid Rock on the floor of the church!" Barnaba said to Peter.

"The church will rise above this solid Rock floor!" Paul added.

At the end of the ritual, we were going out in groups of three or five people, quietly walking away from the cave and collecting daffodils that opened on the foothills of Stauris Mountain. We were collecting and gifting them to our women.

I was one of the first to leave and without losing time, I was heading to my house in the Jewish neighborhood to reach my patients, who were waiting for me.

18. AMIK LAKE, NOW AMIK PLAIN

As I moved away from St. Peter's Church, Stauris Mountain, which I looked again, looked quite ordinary with its grass, shrubs, trees, rocks, slopes and skirts. However, I knew that it was not an ordinary mountain. Stauris was a mountain where the people who lived in this city for thousands of years came in all their desperate and hopeless moments, climbed to it, shaped its rocks, dig tunnels, hid, celebrated their rituals, collected flowers, plants, insects and considered its water holy, blessed themselves with its water and were attached to it for thousands of years.

I looked at Solmaz driving the car from the back seat where I sat, I stretched my hand and caressed her hair. She looked at me in the rearview mirror, our eyes met, I smiled and whispered to her that I was feeling better. She read my moving lips and smiled; her beautiful dark blue eyes smiled with her. I knew she was worried, that she was uncomfortable and that she wished that I would be away from these nightmares as soon as possible. I told her what my dreams were and she also knew as far as I explained, where, in the skirts of what kind of mountain, that these dreams took place. Was she able to understand the reasons for the moments when I was shaken, my breath became faster, and sweating cold from recognizing the incredible similarities between the mountain we saw and the mountain in my dreams? I do not know and did not want to talk about this matter in front of Dimitri; I fell silent and closed my eyes again.

I woke up from my short sleep with a phone ringing insistently and the cry of joy from Solmaz. "Gizem, crazy girl, where are you?" I found this question strange, they had just spoken a few hours ago. Being an old sister isn't easy, I thought. Especially when the younger sister is ten years younger than you, you probably feel she is like your own daughter. With her left hand on the steering wheel, her right hand on the phone in her right ear, Solmaz enthusiastically shouted the words of love.

"Gizem bought a plane ticket for tonight at eight, she's coming to Antakya, apparently she is very curious about these places, missed us as well and wants to meet Dimitri... We can go to the airport at nine o'clock, right?" Solmaz asked. I was also revived at that moment, I felt better. "We have many rooms," Dimitri said. "I was always very curious about Gizem, we can meet her at the airport together, and if Yiğit feels good, we can go out to dinner."

"Let's not have dinner, let's stay home tonight and chat next to the fountain," I said to Dimitri. He turned back and looked at me; when he saw my alive, no-longer-faded face, he was enthusiastic and said, "Alright, friend, tonight I shall show you my great expertise - I will teach you how to burn the barbecue, how to make a real grill in coal fire, I will show you that." I stretched my hand and shook Dimitri's hand that was reaching towards me.

We passed through the narrow streets of Antakya slowly. I looked at the sad walls of the obsolete houses of the old neighborhood, sincerely smiling faces of the little boys running around our cars with love, and the wrinkled faces and hands of the old women, men sitting on the cushions placed next to the century-old door.

When we arrived in front of the house, Dimitri got out of the car first, opened my door and looked at me with an expression saying that he wanted to help me get off. I smiled and said that I was good and quickly got out of the car. My loving friend of the house opened the outer door to the courtyard with the key he took out of his pocket. "You two rest well, there is enough food in the fridge that can feed you for days, but it's all cold! I am going to the museum, if you are determined to stay home in the evening, I have to shop, we can't casually grill with ordinary meat." As he was speaking, I and Solmaz, we were looking at the plump face of our friend, an appetite monument, with loving smiles.

We entered the wide courtyard of the house with Solmaz and sat opposite the armchairs next to the small fountain. "I am fine," I said, looking at the face of the woman I loved, who was looking at me with worry and trying to understand what was happening.

"Don't worry, it's good we arrived. If I hadn't told you about my dreams in advance, if I hadn't described the places I saw in detail, you would have thought that I was dreaming; whereas you saw it too. I see Stauris Mountain! When I saw that I could not believe it, that is the reason why I got pale, sweated through my whole body, felt bad was because I recognized the incredible similarity. In addition to this incredible resemblance, when I saw that mountain and the cave of the mountain, the vast area in front of the cave, I felt as if I had returned to my home, where I had previously lived, grew up, walked, run, talked. I was shaken by these feelings, Solmaz. I know this place, I know it to the finest detail and these similarities scare me, it shakes me, my own self. Can a person continuously dream of a place they have never come, seen or lived in? "

She was looking at my face with a worried, anxious and irritable facial expression, she could not understand me or perhaps I could not explain myself. However, she was the only person I could tell about the mysterious and restless situation I experienced, she was my friend who knew me best; my weaknesses, confusion, fears and anxieties in all detail.

"I'm trying to understand you," she said, and continued in a calm, low tone.

"I try to perceive what you experience and feel. While you are having trouble understanding your situation, you should give credit to the difficulties I am experiencing while trying to understand you. If I had not known your dreams, if you had not told me about the nightmares you had seen for years, if you only described the place in your dreams after our visit to Stauris, I would have definitely taken you to a psychiatrist without listening to any objection. I don't want to scare you more by telling you about the fear I experienced when I saw the mountain, the iron door opening to the cave in the mountainand the solid iron gate that laid on the cracked rock about to collapse. When I saw the excavation area where some of the walls of the old houses in the lower parts of the cave's parking lot were exposed, I remembered that you told me about the old houses in this area as well."

The things the woman I love told me did not contain any accusatory statements, she understood me, most importantly, she did not see me as an ill owner of mentally disturbed moods. All of my night-mares were like those many people sometimes experience, as if the conversations, debates, quarrels, actions, sensations that already happened, were happening again. You meet any of your acquaintances, sit down and talk, that acquaintance prepares to tell you an event and you guess what he will tell, without telling that person and you say inside yourself, "I have experienced these things before, I knew this moment…" This was the only definition of all the anxiety and fears I experienced, with its clearest, simplest and uncomplicated expression.

July's burning and scorching sun was high up in the sky and we started to sweat in the open area next to the small fountain. The moment she said, "Come on, let's get to our room; take a warm shower, sleep a little, you can be sure that it will be good for you," I told her I can accept this suggestion only if we take the shower together. She knew very well that starting my juiciness again meant I was feeling good, so she tried to explain that she could think about it by puckering her lips, pretending to make an angry facial expression.

We stood up and started to climb the narrow and steep stairs built against the front wall of the courtyard towards our room, Solmaz walking in front of me. I touched the appetizing, provocative area, which looked incredibly dull in her very tight jeans, with both of my hands extended, I knew she would be angry; I wasn't mistaken and she said with a smile that if I act like that, we cannot take a shower together. As I tried to explain that the criminal was the aphrodisiac food we ate the night before, the cruel woman turned back and shook the index finger of her right hand against my face.

She wanted me to calm down, get rid of all my anxiety and she was the only one who could accomplish this. She calmed me and relieved me of all my concerns in the shower we took together. We laid in the wide bed in our room together, I looked in her navy eyes and hugged her. I sat my eyes on the ceiling and waited for my fluttering heart to rest.

* * *

We were on our way to the airport, twenty kilometers from Antakya. Both sides of the wide street leading to İskenderun were filled with factories, hotels, hostels, student dormitories, car galleries, clothing stores, furnishers and large buildings of the university. The vast void, once the "Amik Lake", has now turned into "Amik Plain". The political power wanted to create new agricultural fields years ago and dried the waters of the lake, changed the flow direction of all the streams feeding the lake, and constructed irrigation channels by draining the accumulated water in many ways and thus obtained a gigantic plain. Hatay Airport was established somewhere in the middle of this fertile plain.

People have been arguing all the time: Environmentalists who argue that the drying of a natural lake is murder, the villagers who advocate the correctness of the process, since they were able to plant their own fields with the lands given to them, opposing people, claiming that an airport can not be built here, looking at the puddles that transformed the runway of the airport, which was formerly a lake bed, into a lake with heavy rainfall. They were discussing all together and without listening to each other... Dimitri, who explained these, supported the side that defended the construction of the airport. He told us that this airport, which was built between Antakya and İskenderun, would help the region catch class and that Antakya, which has an important place in the history of Christianity, would develop rapidly thanks to visitors from all over the world.

He explained that about thirty percent of people believing in God around the world were Christians, that the name of this religion was used for the first time in this city, and that the scriptures were written very clearly, unambiguously and without controversy in the *Acts of the Apostles* section, after the first four chapters of the Bible. He told us that it is known all over the world that historical events, talks, gatherings, rites, meetings that have been told, written, read for many thousand years have occurred in this city; however, acts with the good intentions in our country are not appreciated enough. Some malicious people would try and prevent such acts with questions like, "Are you making Christian propaganda, are you missionary?" His voice was timid, anxious, and it revealed that he wasn't willing to accept this situation.

As someone who earns his living from history, dealing with a profession that is of a mix of tourism and history, even I did not know very well what Dimitri told us on our way to the airport. He said that he would continue to tell us more in our later conversations. At that moment, I decided to thoroughly research and learn about the history of this city.

Approximately twenty kilometers after leaving Antakya, we left the İskenderun road and took the direction towards the airport. If there was no delay, the plane had to land at 21:00. We left our car at the parking lot and walked towards the *Arrivals* gate. Solmaz was very excited and enthusiastic. "My baby is coming, my sister is coming," she said non-stop. She was telling us about her longing, her sincere love and devotion to her brother, she told us about her nice, cute, beautiful pranks and was explaining about her playful personality. We were listening to her, smiling.

At 21.20, Gizem came out with her suitcase, which she dragged from the *Arrivals* gate with her hand. She looked pretty stylish with her light blue short-sleeved shirt as tight as the black pants she was wearing with thin heels. The moment she stepped outside the gate, Solmaz waved enthusiastically to her sister.

With her brown long hair, blue eyes and deep dimples appearing on both cheeks, she started walking towards us, showing her white teeth, and hugged her sister as soon as she arrived. She first told her sister words of longing, love, and devotion and then turned to me, the crazy girl. She repeated the same words of love to me, with the same sincerity. I started telling her about Dimitri; that her older sister was his classmate and that he had eaten with great devotion in order to form his magnificent belly that I showed by pointing with my hand. Dimitri looked at my face, stroked his imposing belly with both hands and said that if I stayed only for a month in Antakya, I could have a belly of the same size and that I should not be jealous. Then he turned to Solmaz and whispered that her sister was more beautiful than her. "Of course my sister is beautiful," Solmaz said and hugged Gizem again.

We walked towards our car with the enthusiasm, happiness and loud laughter created by Gizem. The wind was blowing in a refreshing, stimulating coolness. Even though it was July, the large, flat and wide Amik Plain was cooled by the relieving air much like huge ventilators directed from the mountains to the large area.

Solmaz and Gizem sat in the back seat, talking about school, their parents; they laughed constantly and hugged each other. I listened to them with a smile and thought I loved and missed Gizem as well. Dimitri turned around and said that there is a barbecue party in the evening and that he would introduce a small portion of Antakya cuisine. So our crazy girl threw one of her sincere screams. We passed slowly through the narrow streets of Dimitri's neighborhood. In the streets illuminated with yellow pale lights, the old, the young, women, men, children, babies and residents of the neighborhood, sitting on the cushions laid in front of the doors of their houses and leaning on the pillows, watched us pass them by, slowly and calmly.

We took Gizem's suitcase and entered the wide courtyard of the house. Dimitri lit the yellow lamps that created a warm atmosphere, touched a button and turned on the fountain, so we listened with interest to the sound of water, which provided peae and comfort. Gizem thanked the host, who said he could stay in the room directly opposite the fountain and headed to her room with her older sister. She was totally crazy, and sympathetic! While ahe was walking towards her room with her older sister, she spoke, laughed and did not hesitate from throwing tokes at us.

We put the meat flavored by Dimitri with various spices, fats, yoghurt and some ingredients that I did not know, from the refrigerator, and put them on the table in the kitchen; there were appetizers, thin breads, greens, a large bottle of rakı, glasses, knives, forks and everything to make this barbecue party complete...

"As I burn the barbecue, you keep carrying those on the table to the pool, Yiğit. If you want to be a barbecue master, you must be a good apprentice first," Dimitri said to me. I told him that I did not want to be a barbecue master, I wanted to be a "master of eating grilled meat ". He said he would not give me anything to eat and I would be hungry if I do not work and carry the kitchen materials to the pool, with a threatening attitude… So I quickly carried everything from the kitchen table…

19. WE UNDERSTOOD OUR TEMPORARINESS, THAT CEPHAS TOLD US

We were no longer afraid of falling rains, lightning flashes, blowing storms and deafening thunders.

Scorpions, snakes, spiders and predators no longer appeared before us anywhere. A snake on our way was quickly hiding among the bushes, any scorpion with a lethal poison that passed by our toes was quickly disappearing among the stones and rocks. The poisonous spiders were running away, leaving flies and insects falling on their nets. Predators withdrew completely to the peaks of the mountains.

Gazelles, beautiful-eyed gazelles; they were looking at us with curiosity from the green hills where they ran and the plain of the mountains where they ate fresh grass. They were approaching us like the sheep, goats and cows that we fed at home, and they were saying, "Take us." "Take and write His words on our skins."

We were taking them, loving them, and we were embellishing what He was telling us, on their bodies and skins. Letters, words, sentences, stories and mysterious moments that can resist centuries could only reach generations of our grandchildren and the grandchildren of their descendants through the skins of those beautiful gazelles.

All these things I'm telling, correspond to the days He came to the city. They reach the days when He came and told us about the moments when the Holy Spirit fell upon them, shaking our souls and captivating our hearts.

We listened to everything He told us by looking into His eyes. We were writing everything He said, every word that came out of His mouth, all His sentences into our brains, minds, and souls, and then in the first moments when we left him, we were writing them on the skins of the beautiful-eyed gazelles who surrendered themselves to us.

We had the option not to write, we had the option to not do anything to convey to our grandchildren what Cephas said about his experiences and his sufferings; but it was coming from inside of us, "Write them!" a voice was saying, "You must write!". In the middle of the night, this voice was taking us out of our beds and we were writing every sentence that He said, told us, things we understood and could not understand.

An ordinary, simple and pure fisherman, reviving, elevating and glorifying the touch of a hand touching his head; however, we were trying to resolve the secrets we could not understand, and we could not.

While sitting in a room, we were trying to understand the meaning and sanctity of the light that flows into the room, quiet and still, the unresolvable movement that fills the soul of everyone. We understood and engraved them on our soul in indelible letters.

We were looking at the face of Cephas. We were watching his lines as hard, clear, sharp and clean as a rock. We waited for him to stand up, put the water from the deep hole of the cave in his palms, put it on our heads and face and bless us all. As soon as he finished what he was saying, he would stand up and look right in the middle of our eyes with the power of the Holy Spirit, which fills His entire body.

We felt ourselves superior, privileged, valuable and strong enough to account for all of our life experiences on the last day we will live.

He was with us; he was telling us every moment we lived in the past, that we are living today and that we will live tomorrow. We were trying to convey what we understood to the other days of the next thousands of years.

We now knew that our bodies, blessed by the pure and clean water leaking from the rock walls of the sacred cave of Stauris Mountain, were not very meaningful and we could understand our transience as described by Cephas.

Cephas was like a real rock. He was mature, hard, unchanging and unchangeable, and He never changed.

For many years during His stay in our city, we wrote every word that He spoke in the cave, at home, in the small rooms of the houses, in the courtyards, in the shadows of the trees in the courtyards, without a missing word or exaggeration. We explained every sentence to those who did not listen, and made them understand.

While explaining to us our importance, our value and who we are, He continuously made us understand our transience. We were all temporary in this world, only what we did was permanent.

20. GRILL PARTY

It was a cool, light windswept, quiet and joyful July night. The barking of dogs, frog sounds, and the timbre of the rising and falling songs of the crickets were accompanied by the preparations for a beautiful dinner. Dim yellow lights hitting the branches, leaves, flowers of the wide courtyard and the sounds of the drops rising from the fountain and pouring into the puddle heralded a beautiful, pleasant, happy and sincere barbecue party. I felt myself ready to melt in the joyful and loving arms of a stillness that I could not experience for months. I wanted to get away from the unhappy effects of bad dreams and nightmares I had had and to bring my depressed spirit to healthy harbors.

The orange light of the fire that hit the wide face and forehead of Dimitri, who ignited the coal he placed inside a high-legged enameled grill in a corner far from the fountain and the table beside the fountain, displayed a pleasant color combination with the yellow lights of the garden lamps.

I slowly carried all the plates, forks, knives, glasses, steamed rakı bottle, seasoned meats, appetizers and breads he placed on the table in the kitchen.

I was placing what I carried my carries on the table, paying attention to the order and symmetry so that four people can sit opposite to one another. The two would sit on one side of the table, and the other two on the other. The intonation of the joyful and happy voice of Dimitri, who tried to create an air flow over the barbecue with the folded newspaper in his hand and tell me by crying out loud about the tricks of burning a barbecue, was disturbing the quiet and calm atmosphere of the cool night. He was constantly joking with me: "Well done Yiğit, you are working well, you really deserve these beautiful meals, I will definitely not starve you tonight ..." and just at that moment, he was laughing with his his splendid belly jumping.

Solmaz and her sister walked out of the door of the room where Gizem will stay. Gizem changed her outfit and was now wearing a one-piece thin sleeveless blue dress with yellow, white and green florals on it. She looked extraordinarily beautiful in her dress that stretched below her knees. The tone of the blue of the dress on her was the same as the tone of the blue of her eyes. As if it was planned, we released a long whistle together with Dimitri at the same time, and told her that she looks very pretty and that her dress suits her very much. The crazy girl jumped into the air happily, came next to me, kissed my cheeks and ran to Dimitri with the same speed, kissing him on the cheeks as well.

I could not understand whether the reddening of Dimitri's face, smiling with a crimson face, was caused by the flames in the gril lor by the kisses of Gizem. He was trying to make Solmaz angry again by telling her that her sister looks prettier than her; but Solmaz didn't mind him, hugging Gizem and caressing her hair. "I want to wear something comfortable as well, I might have a hard time taking these tight jeans off after dinner," Solmaz said and headed towards the stairs that go up to our room. I told her in my silliest mood that she shouldn't tire herself, that I would most gladly volunteer to take off her pants. As I was talking, Dimitri shook his index finger as if he was scolding me, accompanied by Gizem's festive laughter.

Gizem looked carefully at the symmetry in the arrangement of the plates, knives and forks I placed on the table. Making a thumbs up with her left hand, she silently approved of the arrangement then helped me carry the other food from the kitchen table.

I looked at the inexhaustible beauty of Solmaz, who was coming dowstairs to the courtyard, accompanied by the rhythmic sounds of crickets and dogs barking from afar, under the dim yellow lights illuminating the stairs. The words we used to praise Gizem, as well as the whistle we blew for her, came out of our lips again – this time for Solmaz. She looked at out face and smiled shyly, the woman I love.

Dimitri was putting the onions, tomatoes, green and red hot peppers, which were grilled on the barbecue's hot coal, on separate plates. As the Head Grillmaster was looking at the rakı that I prepared in thin tall glasses like thirsty little boy, I went to him and gave him one glass. He lifted the steamed glass in his left hand into the air to say cheers and took a big sip of the white liquid, with wishes of health and happiness. We all raised our glasses as well for cheers, making the same wishes with a smile. I carried the plates on the counter next to the barbecue to the table; smoke was still coming from the onions, tomatoes and peppers. The fumes of steaks and meatballs, which started to cook between the steel grill on the hot coal, rose to the sky from the courtyard, which was lit up with dim lights, and swelled all our appetites.

Gizem and Solmaz sat on the chairs opposite to each other next to the fountain. I was standing and finishing off the drink in my hand enthusiastically, with new wishes. The Head Grillmaster cooked half of the meat he prepared and brought it to the table, and I was getting ready to fill our glasses for the second time when he sat down next to Gizem.

The night was cool, quiet and full of joy with continuous winds. We felt more enthusiastic and happy with the effect of the alcohol we consumed. We attacked the steaming meat and appetizing starters as if we were just out of famine. Solmaz and Gizem, who watched our fast and impatient movements with smiles, took one meatball each with their most polite attitude and stuck their forks into the small pieces they cut with the tip of their knives with the same politeness; they were like teachers who taught me and Dimitri the rules of etiquette. Unfortunately, we were the most lazy students of this "etiquette lesson". We continued our attacks on the plates, inflating our cheeks.

"There was an important meeting in the museum today. They came from the Ministry of Culture, we talked about the restoration of St. Peter's Church, we explained them what we have done so far. They want the restoration to be completed and the church to be opened to visitors as soon as possible," the Head Grillmaster spoke, as he stood up and walked to the side of the barbecue. He carefully placed the remaining meat on the grill with the blackened tongs he held.

I suddenly got stagnant. Reaching towards my glass with her first glass of drink, Solmaz said, "Let's drink!" She didn't want me to be so stagnant and lose my enthusiasm. I looked at her and smiled, I reached towards her cheek and put a light kiss on it, looking at her again with an expression that said, "Don't worry, I will get rid of all my troubles, I will overcome my depression." Solmaz understood me, she smiled again and this time, she was the one to reach towards my cheek and give me a kiss.

Carrying the cooked meat to the table, Dimitri continued to explain as he sat next to Gizem: "St. Peter's Church is considered the first church in the world, I can take you too tomorrow if you want to see it as well. It is also known as the Cross Mountain at the skirts of the Stauris Mountain, and it was sacred even before the years when Christianity was born and spread. You must see it, I think you will like it and be touched. Antakya is the most important center of Christianity after Jerusalem; the most important city where the religion spread, developed and is discussed. The most important people and apostles of religion came to this city, gathered in the cave on Mount Stauris. If you are interested, I can tell you the rest after seeing the cave church tomorrow. "

Gizem looked with great interest and curiosity in the face of Dimitri next to her. I also looked; and tried to understand the cause of his downward, emotionalized face and slowing movements. He raised the glass of rakı he held in his right hand and a few incomprehensible words spilled from his lips. He looked to the right of the chair he was holding and then looked at our face again, tried to speak slowly, could not speak, apologized and stood up and walked to the side of the barbecue.

I stood up and hurried towards Dimitri, held his hand. He and I were under the ecstatic effect of the alcohol we consumed. I knew that calm and quiet personalities could change under the influence of alcohol. I knew that the most stagnant personality structures could suddenly change, become aggressive; and those with happy and calm behavior, the most respected people, could suddenly become unhappy, depressed, crying ceaselessly. We were just at the beginning of the night and I didn't want this beautiful night to be ruined at all.

"Our name is 'Minority', we are the minority, we have internalized a secret snoring, being humiliated, or even often being ignored. We are always treated like stepchildren. We feel the belittling eyes of some of our most civilized, even well-educated friends, as soon as we turn our backs. It is a form of behavior that comes from the past, you cannot change it, you cannot delete it, and you learn to pretend that there is no such disdain over time. However, these people named as "Minority" love this country at least as much as you; they do military service, produce jobs, pay taxes, and carry the concerns that every citizen carries."

Now I could better understand the reason why he suddenly stagnated and seemed sad; but I also knew that unhappy, sad, anxious and constantly irritated structures could also lie beneath many seemingly happy, cheerful, carefree and comfortable structures. I waited for him to continue what he said without asking anything; I would try to listen to him, make him vent and relax without interrupting him. His eyes seemed to be over-blooded in the redness reflecting on his face from the grill. He was silent for a moment without talking, and as if it was not himself, who was just walking around the peaks of emotionality, saddened, eyes filled with tears, with his voice trembling; he said, "Let's change the subject, Yiğit, let's not spoil the beauty of the night."

At that moment, he smiled with a thought that suddenly came to his mind, looked at my face, and suddenly he dived into new topics, apart from what he had just talked about: "I forgot to say, my brother comes tomorrow morning. He called me in the evening, he was in Adana. He said he would catch breakfast in the morning, which is a good coincidence, he could also meet Gizem. His name is Nikola…" I understood from his uninterrupted speech and his attitude, which showed that he did not want me to interrupt him, that he really wanted to change the subject and tried to make me forget about his previous extreme emotionality. I complied and started to behave like he wanted me to, asking questions about Nikola without returning to the previous topics. Solmaz and Gizem were listening to us quietly next to the fountain.

I took the plate on the table with the chilled meats in it and placed it back on the grill with the burning coal. Gizem started to ask Dimitri questions about her brother. The curious girl found out with a few questions that Nikola is twenty years old, he is a fourth-year student at the medical school in Ankara, he is handsome and poet-loving, he wrote poetry, he admired Che Guevara and looked like him, he knew the history of Antakya as good as a historian, he was constantly doing research about it and was keen on the food of the city he was born in.

Towards midnight, we carried the table altogether to the kitchen, poured water over the ashes in the grill, cleaned everywhere and retreated to our rooms. It was a long and tiring day. I and Solmaz hugged each other in the big and wide bed in our room and tried to sleep without talking.

We were not aware of the disasters, unhappy and secretive events that will happen in the coming days. We didn't know any-thing and thought we were living in the arms of a happy life yet.

21. LUKE IS MY NAME

Luke is my name. I am a Jewish person from Antakya. I live in my house, in the Jewish neighborhood of the city where I was born, raised and recognized life. My physician, my patients and their relatives say that I am a good physician. I heal my patients with medicines made from herbs, flowers, leaves and bark, from the mountains, plains, valleys. The yellow, white, red flowers that I collect and their leaves in every shade of green become a remedy for a different disease, and I can look at the face of every healing patient with the happy face of a person who has reached peace, succeeded, and did well.

I also use the water that leaks from the walls of the cave on the Stauris Mountain, which accumulates in the cavity of a rock. First I collect bark, grass, shrubs, thorns, flowers, leaves, branches. I wait and let them dry. I crush some of them alone with others, dust them together and mix them with the leachate of Stauris's cave; no water creates a healing effect as strong as the leaking water of the cave in the medicine that I prepare.

Luke is my name. I am a Jewish and a physician born in Antioch. I write about the events I have experienced and seen, the stories of the holy people I know and believe, on the skins of gazelles that I have prepared. I try to make them reach thousands of years later and ensure that they are not forgotten.

If you can read these things I've written, it means that they reached to you. I don't know who the reader, you are, and I don't know how long later you are reading these; but now you know who I am: Luke is my name, I am a physicial from Antioch and a Jewish.

The good person Barnaba came to Antioch and later brought Paul from Tarsus here. Our friendship with Paul started the moment I met him and never ended during the days-nights I listened to him without blinking. I am also the physician of Paul, I am the believer and his close friend, who wrote what he told me on the skins of the gazelles.

We gathered around Peter, who came from Jerusalem and stayed in Antioch for seven years, listening to what he told for hours in the cave. Barnaba, Paul and I were in the front row.

Peter brought the grail used by Christ at the Last Supper, from Jerusalem. We'd pour the water leaking from the walls of the Stauris cave in the grail, passing it from hand to hand and taking small sips from the now differentiating water inside the grail, being blessed. The grail was in Antioch now and it was going to stay in this city forever. I brought all my patients, who I couldn't heal, to this cave, to the meetings in the cave and let them drink a little sip of water from the grail that Peter handed to us. I saw that my patients who could not recover for a long time had recovered in a very short time, and that I saw that my belief was growing and I was telling Paul about this, enthusiastically.

Luke is my name. I am a physician and a Jewish from Antioch. I wrote these writings on the skins of the gazelles with the same hands I held the grail of Christ, drinking the leaking water of the sacred cave of Stauris Mountain.

22. DANTE'S HELL AND CHARON

Despite all my tiredness, I could not sleep. Solmaz was lying on her chest in the bed. I looked at her face on the soft pillowi listened to her calm and regular breathing; then I got out of the bed with little movements, trying not to wake her up. I turned around and looked at her face once again, she pulled her left knee towards her stomach and turned her face to the other side. I got dressed and went out of the room, it was around three in the morning. I wore my sneakers and went downstairs, pulled the slider of the front gate and opened it. I thanked Dimitri inside for not having locked the front door with a key, besides the slider.

I got in my car and drove towards where I should, through the quiet streets. A few dogs napping at the edge of narrow roads, in front of the doors of the houses, looked at the car's rotating tires and never barked, lifting their heads without disturbing their posture. I went up to the main street about a hundred meters from the house; There was an old mosque right across the street and the intersection of the street, and a church right behind it. It felt strange to me at first to see the bell of the church in a very close range with the minaret of the mosque, and then I perceived it as a clear and simple expression of the city's tolerance for centuries. There must have been a Jewish temple closeby, as this place I was at was a very old Jewish neighborhood and the desription, "Ecumenical Triangle" would best suit here.

I made my way to the southeast of the city. I continued my journey until I saw the sign that read "St. Pierre Church", which pointed to the mountain. I drove up the steep slope that I learned during the dat and parked the car in the wide lot at the lower parts of the church. I got off the car and quietly closed its door. I wished that there is no nightguard or a security guard, and even if there is one, that he doesn't see me. Without stopping by the front door of the church, I headed towards the pathway that stretched to the left and upwards, started to walk fast towards the sculpted face od the Hell Boatman on the rocks of the mountain, which I only saw during the day from afar. I reached Charon in a short time, stood across him and thought of Dante; Dante Alighieri.

I remembered the lines in the Divine Comedy's *Inferno* section, which talked about Charon. I looked at his missing face and without raising my voice, I started to recite the lines of Dante's Divine Comedy, as if there was someone in front of me.

"Thereat, with shame-suffused and downcast eyes, and fearing lest my talking might annoy him, up to the river I abstained from speech. Behold then, coming toward us in a boat, an aged man, all white with ancient hair, who shouted: "Woe to you, ye souls depraved!"*

**Aged man: Kharon/Charon.*

I looked at the cover over his head, he was pretty well carved, and Hell Boatman had been standing on the rocks of Stauris Mountain for exactly two thousand and two hundred years; in other words, he started to look at Antioch from the slopes of this mountain already one thousand and five hundred years before the year Dante wrote the Divine Comedy and talked about Charon. I continued reciting Dante's *Inferno*.

"Give up all hope of ever seeing Heaven! I come to take you to the other shore, into eternal darkness, heat and cold.

And thou that yonder art, a living soul, withdraw thee from those fellows that are dead." But when he saw that I did not withdraw, he said:

"By other roads and other ferries shalt thou attain a shore to pass across, not here; a lighter boat must carry thee."

To him my Leader: "Charon, be not vexed; thus is it yonder willed, where there is power to do whate'er is willed; so ask no more!"

Thereat were quieted the woolly cheeks of that old boatman of the murky swamp, who round about his eyes had wheels of flame."

Charon quietly listened to what I recited to him, and when he saw that I wasn't leaving as well, he understood my determination;

he knew that there is no use in him trying to prevent me from leaving and that I would never steer away from the road that I was on. He started looking at the city he had been looking at for two thousand and two hundred years.

I continued to climb up from the sculpture of the Hell Boatman, towards the cave church. I wanted to reach small hollowed out areas in the upper parts of St. Peter's Church, carved by human hand. Who was pushing me, why did I want to do this, and what was I looking for? I didn't know many things and I was trying to analyse the reasons for what I was doing. However, I had to reach Stauris's secret compartments, no matter what.

I was no stranger to climbing mountains, wandering on deserted mountains. I continued my walk through the iron cage that stretched to the upper parts of the church, and when I reached that level, I began to carefully descend into the cavities on the iron structure. I put my fingers on a ledge, clinging to the stem or branches of a solid bush, trying to safely descend to the church, trying not to slip and roll down. Suddenly I saw the sound of a guard whistle and a beam of light stretching from the door of the church to the parking lot; I held my breath and stopped. That should not have happened, the night guard of the church should not have woken up!

Once again, the guard blew his whistle and the dogs of the squatter neighborhood across from here started to bark in a strong choir. I looked from above; I could see that a shadow was walking nearby, scanning his surroundings with a flashlight. He was walking towards my car.

I had done something I should not have done and parked my car late at night in the parking lot where no other cars were left. I qucikly started to climb in the direction I came from. I shouldn't have been seen where I was. I approached the parking lot in the lower parts of the church, walking through the path I came from, passing the Hell Boatman. I paused for a short time and waited for my breath to become regular, wiped the dust off my outfit, wiped the sweat on my forehead and walked towards the middle-aged security guard, walking around my car, whistling, looking at its plate and illuminating it with a flashlight.

He didn't see me until I got very close to him. He was staring into the car with his head against the left side of the windshield. I was only a few steps awat from him, suddenly he startled with the breaking sound of a dry branch under my foot, a few low and meaningless words came out of his mouth and he reached for his pistol with his idle hand. He looked frightened and very scared. I put my hand in the air and said that the car was mine. Without taking his hand off the pistol in its case, he pointed the flashlight to my face and asked who I was, what I was looking for here at this time of night; with the anxious tone of a strict but a scared, frightened person. I smiled, trying to look comfortable; I told him that I was a tourist guide, that I would bring a group that would come in the morning to these mountains and the church cave in the afternoon, and that I wanted to see this place, which I knew beforehand, before I brought the tourist group. He listened to me carefully, without blinking, then shook his head. I told him that now I want to go back to my hotel and said that I wanted to rest, showing him the left front door with the key in my hand. He understood me and stepped aside the car.

I parked the car in the space in front of Dimitri's house, and I slowly opened the door and looked at the empty courtyard, wishing that nobody had woken up. I walked in and pushed the doorslide back again. I climbed up the steps of the stairs, when I entered the room, Solmaz was still sleeping. The blanket on her was opened and her nightgown was stripped towards her thin waist. I quietly undressed and lied next to the gorgeous woman. It was approaching six o'clock and the sun was rising. I closed my eyes and thought about the mad, crazy journey I had done in the last few hours. I thought of the mountain that I climbed with great thuds that I couldn't resist, even though I shouldn't have, then I left myself in the arms of sleep that surrounded me.

*"A good soul never goes across from hence; if Charon, therefore, findeth fault with thee, well canst thou now know what his words imply."**

I fell asleep, remembering a few lines from Dante's *Inferno*…

* * *

At eight o'clock, Solmaz, Gizem, Dimitri and I were setting up the breakfast table and listening to the songs of the birds choir in the courtyard, chirping with the cool winds of the morning. We were just filling up our second tea glasses that we heard the sound of three blows hitting the front door. Smiling, Dimitri stood up, swinging to the front door and almost flying away, opened the slider and hugged the young man who entered. They hugged each other enthusiastically and sincerely. When they separated, he said, without taking his left hand from his brother's waist, "This handsome man is Nikola. My brother and the only thing I have in life," Dimitri was telling us about the young man he pointed at with his right hand.

The young man with a tall beard and a thin, muscular body walked next to us. We greeted him, standing up. We didn't miss out on Gizem and him, looking at each other. They shook hands and couldn't take their eyes away from each other as they introduced themselves. Dimitri introduced me and Solmaz to him; he quickly summarized who we were, how we became friends and how close we are.

As Nikola was explaining that he was a fourth-year student at the medical school in Ankara, he was constantly looking at Gizem's face and saying how unfortunate it was that he did not come to know such a beautiful girl until now, even though they were studying in the same city. None of us could understand when our crazy girl's face blushed from this sudden and unexpected intimacy. We all could understand that Gizem liked the young doctor candidate as well, from the way she looked and how her eyes shined.

* Dante: Divine Comedy – Inferno III (The Gate and Vestibule of Hell)

[Dante Alighieri, The Divine Comedy of Dante Alighieri. The Italian Text with a Translation in English Blank Verse and a Commentary by Courtney Langdon, Vol. 1 (Inferno) (Cambridge: Harvard University Press, 1918). English version.]

I was looking at Nikola's face and feeling like I had seen him before, his face was no stranger to me. Probably Solmaz felt the same way, fors he asked Nikola whether they had met before. The young man hardly took his eyes away from Gizem and looked first at me, then to Solmaz, smiling. He said that he was sure he never met any of us anywhere, and that if he did, it would be impossible for him to forget these two women, Solmaz and Gizem, who had such extraordinary beauty.

This young man was incredibly practical, intelligent and flirtatious. We laughed together, we all liked this friendly young man. "That is how my brother is, he jokes around with the people around him, he took it as principle to continue life laughing, not making a big deal out of problems, after all those painful things we've been through." Nikola looked at his brother, and began to speak slowly, with a smile that fits his face. *Stand up straight and smile. Let them wonder why you are smiling."* As he spoke to his emotional, sad brother with a smile, we shouted simultaneously with Solmaz, "Che Guevara!" as if we agreed to do it together.

As he continued his smile, he said, "Yes, my close friends call me 'Che'," he said, and then he extended his hand first to Solmaz, then to me. However, we were only saying who the famous sentence belonged to; we were also then able to analyze, where that feeling of having met before and that feeling, "We know this face," came from. Nikola was almost an exact copy of Che Guevara, with his face, hair, beard, mustache and skin color.

We took another chair next to the table and bspent our happy moments of breakfast together, playing around with jokes and laughs flying in the air.

If I could, if there was a way, if I could know the method; just at that moment I would stop time, and I wouldn't let another minute pass.

Quote by Ernesto Che Guevara.

Nikola moved his chair closer to Gizem. As he was complimenting her, saying, "For so many years in Ankara, in the same city, what a bad luck that I have never seen this beautiful girl," Gizem was now relieved and now gave quick replies to the young man, without blushing. "You are not considered to have lost anything, you have seen me now, it is not easy to make up the lost times; but it is very important to start from somewhere."

As she pulled his chair away from the young man, who approached Gizem beyond normal standards, she said, "Don't get too close, please, you just have to look. I very much like a saying from our ancestors: 'Too much closeness brings early separation'… Please don't forget this saying." Gizem wasn't quiet against the smart jokes of Nikola, she quickly replied back to him, with smart comebacks.

Starting from the first minutes we just met, we had established a sincere intimacy as if we had known each other for years, and this seemed very natural to us all. There was laughs in the air; we were having happy, trouble-free, carefree and friendly hours, thinking that these white, clean days would never end.

However, I couldn't know that those happy hours in the early morning would be the beginning of mysterious and painful days to come.

23. ACTS OF THE APOSTLES

*"In the church at Antioch there were prophets and teachers: Barnabas, Simeon called Niger, Lucius of Cyrene, Manaen (a childhood companion of Heod the tetrarch) and Saul. While they were worshipping the Lord and fasting, the Holy Spirit said, "Set apart for me Barnabas and Saul for the work to which I have called them." And after they had fasted and prayed, they laid their hands on them and sent them off."**

Luke is my name, I'm a physician from Antioch. I take care of my patients in a room of the house where I live in the Jewish neighborhood and try to cure them. Paul is my close friend. I wrote what I just talked about, in the second book I wrote earlier. I explained the acts of the apostles, the places they went, the difficulties and the pain they experienced, and what they did.

The Holy Spirit appeared in the church on Stauris Mountain in Antioch and I was there too. First, flames rained inside the cave, that did not burn, then the rocks, stones and the soil on the ground lit up, filled us, we closed our eyes and reached peace, comfort, maturity and faith.

* New Testament: Acts of the Apostles – Acts 13 (1-3)

"Set apart for me Barnabas and Saul for the work to which I have called them," said the Holy Spirit. We listened, heard and obeyed the commandments.

Barnabas and Saul (Paul) set out at the command of the Holy Spirit and headed towards Seleucia, Cyprus, Pisidian Antioch, Lystra, Derbe.

*"After passing through Pisidia, they came to Pamphylia. And when they had spoken the word in Perga, they went down to Attalia. From Attalia they sailed to Antioch, where they had been commended to the grace of God for the work they had just completed."**

*"When they arrived, they gathered the church together and reported all that God had done through them, and how He had opened the door of faith to the Gentiles. And they spent a long time there with the disciples."**

They stayed for a long time in Antioch. They told us where they went, what they saw and where they lived.

Luke is my name. I write all that I have seen and experienecd on the skins of the gazelles living in the mountains of Antioch so that they are known, remembered and not lost... If you can read these now, it means I have reached my goal.*

* New Testament: Acts of the Apostles – Acts 14 (24-26)

** New Testament: Acts of the Apostles – Acts 14 (27-28)

24. CUR, QUOMODO, QUANDO?*

Nikola slowly brought his chair closer to Gizem, and reached towards the blue hairclip holding her hair. Expecting an upset expression from Gizem and for her to say something like, "You've gone too far now, it hasn't even been ten minutes since we met!" suddenly I saw a smile on her face much like Che's. First I was stressed, then I was relieved. We understood that our crazy girl also liked the young doctor candidate. We didn't say anything, and we joined the same game. In the afternoon, we talked about all the places that Dimitri will take us, which all smell of history.

Nikola said, "Gizem I must take you, you must hear the history of this place from me," and suddenly we saw that he took the blue hairclip holding Gizem's shiny, wavy hair and jumped up like a mischievous boy who accomplished his mission. "You will no longer see this blue hairclip capturing such beautiful hair, I am seizing it now; I take revenge of it capturing the strands of this beautiful hair!" Then, Nikola placed the blue shiny hairclip in the right front pocket of his jeans. We watched his comfort, sincerity, his carefree attitude and smile with interest. He really looked like Che…

He mentioned the Silpius Mountain first. He spoke of the Antakya Walls that stretched from this mountain to the Stauris Mountain next to it. He told us that they were the longest walls that survived after the walls of Istanbul, how these walls that stretched out for twelve thousand meters have protected the city, that one of the first dams of the worls, the "Iron Gate," was still standing; he talked about the closeness of the cave to the church, that the other name of the Silpius Mountain was Habib Al-Najjar and that the first mosque in Anatolia was called by this name. He talked about the carpenter, who gave its name to the first mosque in Anatolia, was one of the people who believed and accepted the faith of Christianity in the city when he was a Jewish; speaking continuously without break, with breathless excitement.

* Why, how, when?

We stopped, paused and listened to the young doctor candidate with our mouths open. We all listened with interest, including the elder brother, who is an expert of the city's history as well as of and all the findings as an official of the city museum, I, the historical expert, and Solmaz, a successful archaeologist.

I was tired due to the little runaway trip I've after midnight, the mountain I climbed and the tension I experienced. I couldn't get enough sleep. I told them I want to rest, sleep and think all day. I told Solmaz that she may join the two crazy people in their mountain trips and when I said that, she looked at me with a harsh expression. I understood that the woman I love couldn't leave me alone in this state. As Dimitri was talking about the intensity of his work, I thought that he was actually preparing the ground for his brother to travel with Gizem alone. He reached his goal, afterall…

Towards noon, we withdrew to our room with Solmaz. The two crazy, energetic young people, who were sincerely fond of each other, were leaving the house with their black backpacks through the door opening to the narrow street.

All I wanted was to sleep. I wanted to relieve the tremors of the merry-filled dinner we had in the night before, the night I couldn't sleep, the huge rocks that fell rolled down in the cave church under the mysterious Stauris Mountain I have been to, the cracks on the skirts of the mountain, the cavities created hundreds of years ago by human hand and the armed security guard who walked towards my car; the tremors created by all of them in my soul.

I went up to the room without waiting for Solmaz, undressed and laid in bed. I slept without interruption; no dreams, no nightmares, just calm sleep.

And I woke up with the warm touches of two white and soft arms wrapped around my neck. I didn't know how long I slept and I had a throbbing headache. "How are you?" said Solmaz. I couldn't understand what she said. "Did you sleep well?" she asked. "Are you going to wake up now?" She looked angry and nervous. "They still haven't arrived!" she said. "Who?" I asked. "Get up and wash your face, it's evening, it's seven o'clock and they're still not back!" As my darling spoke, I really couldn't understand who she was talking about.

I sat up in the bed. I tried to keep my head, which weighed down a few tons, up, looked at her face and said, "Who is still not back?" forcing myself.

She pulled his arms away from my neck and reached for her phone on the nightstand, without saying anything. She spoke very briefly and looked at me with her most anxious, fearful face, "Dimitri doesn't know where they are!" she said. I told her to call Gizem or Nikola, in a silly way. She said that she had called Gizem and that her phone wouldn'tbe reached even though it rang for a long time. She also told me, fearfully, that she didn't know Nikola's phone number. I took my phone from the other nightstand and called Dimitri, hastily. He also told me that he called Nikola after Solmaz called him and that his phone wouldn't answer.

The world had suddenly changed as soon as I woke up. I tried to get rid of all the bad and negative thoughts in my head. I looked at Solmaz's sad and worried face. I mumbled a few words in a low voice, to comfort her; however, even I didn't believe what I said. I called Dimitri again, asked for Nikola's phone number and quickly called him. The phone rang, rang and unfortunately there was no answer. I unconsciously called Gizem, but she didn't pick up either.

We looked at each other's faces without knowing what to do and what we should do. "Please, do something, find my sister," Solmaz said to me with a pleading, tired and helpless expression. With an attitude that I didn't also know what I was doing, I picked up the phone again, calling Gizem first, then Nikola. The phones rang for a long time but there was no answer. Solmaz and I were in the arms of increasing fear, worry and hopelessness.

There must have been more we could do; we weren't going to beat the fear and discomfort inside us by staying next to the phone, hoping for a positive response to our calls and by waiting for them to call us. I called Dimitri quickly and immediately, and I told him in a worried tone that he should come home and that we should evaluate the situation together without losing time. While my friend told me that he has called his brother many times and that he has not received any response, he tried not to make me feel the fear he is experiencing, but he was failing at it.

We gathered around the table in the courtyard together with Dimitri, who came home shortly after. Solmaz was thinking with her elbows on the table, her head in her hands, never speaking. It was already after seven o'clock, the sun had set, and it was getting dark. We were looking at each other's faces, meaninglessly and desperately. We wouldn't be so nervous if their phones were switched off or never rang. At least we would have thought that their phones were not receiving signals from the places they visited, we would not be alarmed and afraid. However, the phones that ringed and not opened despite our calls repeatedly frightened all of us and caused hundreds of negativities to attack our minds.

"Let's go to the police," Solmaz said. "Let's go now, let's not waste time. Something bad might have happened to them, they may need help. Let's not be late, please!" Dimitri, who said that it would be appropriate for us to wait for a while, was trying to speak with a contrived comfort he did not believe himself either.

"How long will we wait, it got dark and they are still not back. They left the house at noon, shouldn't they have been back by this time, at least to call us and tell us that they would be late?" I caressed her hands on the table. "You're right," I said. "I do not think that they can be so irresponsible, but I do not find it appropriate to go to the police immediately and make the situation more complicated. Let's wait a short while and continue to call; If we cannot reach them or they are still not back, we will go to the police anyway." She looked at my face, as if she was trying to understand whether I was talking like that because I believed so, or to relieve her.

Solmaz stood up with hope, walked to the room where Gizem was staying, opened the door and stood in front of the door, taking her phone to her ear. I understood that she was calling her brother. There was a possibility that Gizem had forgotten her phone in her room and that's why she could not answer. She waited and soon closed the door with a desperate facial expression. Dimitri did the same thing in front of Nikola's room, and he desperately returned to us.

We couldn't believe this situation. Just this morning, the day had started happily, peacefully and joyfully; and now we had reached an unhappy night, full of fear, anxiety, that what we couldn't figure out what was happening. We also knew that these young people, who are smart, consistent and university students both, and that we knew they wouldn't be so irresponsible to cause us such anxious hours like now.

Solmaz was looking at her watch for a while and then to the screen of her phone, exhibiting quite uneasy behaviour. She wasn't asking anything or speaking. Dimitri broke the silence: "Did they tell you where they went? You were together until noon after I left fort he museum. Did they tell you what they were going to do?"

I told Dimitri what I heard. I said that I heard that Nikola was talking about the Silpius Mountain, the walls on this mountain, a place called the "Iron Gate" between Silpius and Stauris mountains, a mosque called Habib Al-Najjar and that he would take Gizem to these places.

Dimitri paused first, turned his eyes towards the sky and thought for a while. Then he suddenly stood up from his chair. "We cannot go to all the places you said at this time, but Habib Al-Najjar Mosque is very close, we can go on foot. Let's first look over there, maybe they're there, or at least we'll ask the people there if they've ever been there.

We locked the street door of the house from the outside and quickly walked to the main street through narrow streets. The main street, where we walked to the southeast of the city, looked as tired, worn, dusty and old as the houses standing on its two sides. The fearful moments we experienced were reflected in our souls and continued to increase our anxieties. The despair that I never thought of when I was passing this street the day before was throwing our souls into dark corridors with what we experienced tonight. Side-walks of the old street, the asphalted road, old houses with their rusty doors, rusty windows, dusty windows, painted and non-plastered walls; they were all coming towards us, making us feel cornered.

We walked for ten or fifteen minutes. Where we wanted to go was at the corner of intersection between the Street that descended towards the Asi River and the street we were walking on. Habib Al-Najjar Mosque, the first mosque in Anatolia, was built on a Roman pagan temple, used as a church, then converted into a mosque in the early years of Islam, then was used as a church again during the Crusades when the city was occupied, after a while it was converted into a mosque again. The temple was built in an old Jewish neighborhood; where Paganism, Judaism, Christianity and Islam were at the same place, under the same walls, blessed with the same purposes, on the same piece of land; what would it tell believers, what would those who understood and believed could understand from it?

Even though the carpenter, who gave the mosque the name of Habib Al-Najjar, was the first person to accept Christianity in Antioch, all believers who knew that this mosque was called with this name thought that this "dear Carpenter" was a Muslim!

We entered the courtyard of the mosque and looked at the rooms lined up around it from the outside. We looked at the seated groups of all men. They turned their gaze quietly towards us, especially towards Solmaz, the only woman in the courtyard. They were trying to understand what we were doing and why we came at this late hour of the night. Dimitri went to someone he knew and explained the how Gizem and Nikola looked, to the man; he asked if he had ever seen them today. He was a man in his sixties, fat, bearded, and hunched. He thought for a moment, and without saying anything, signaled us to follow him with his right hand. He walked to the northeastern corner of the mosque and next to a mausoleum asked the tired man who pulled his knees on his stomach, leaning against the wall, sitting on the ground, thoroughly old, weak and almost waiting for his death. The old man replied in Arabic, slowly speaking in a low voice that hardly came out, and closed his eyes. He muttered words which I thought were prayers, moving his thin and dry lips. I suddenly shuddered when I realized that "John and Paul" were written on the tomb beside him, where he was leaning against.

Translating to us what the old man told him in Arabic, Dimitri was a little relieved with what he heard. He saw the two youngsters in the afternoon towards one o'clock, they looked very happy and enthusiastic, they stayed for about an hour in the mosque's court-yard and gave him some money as well. They were constantly joking with each other and talking; the young woman was listening to the long-haired, bearded man with interest; they took photos of the tombs, the mosque and him, and left the mosque with the same cheerful attitude after an hour.

When we walked back home, it was almost midnight. The information we received about Gizem and Nikola, the walk we took and the cool air revived us all. We turned on the lights of the court-yard and sat again in the dim lighting, next to the fountain. Without talking and dividing the work; Solmaz called Gizem and Dimitri called Nikola at the same time and they hung up their phones with unhappy, anxious, sad and sullen facial expressions that we were now used to. Unfortunately, there was no answer.

I thought of what Nikola told us before he left the house at noon and he gave them their names. One of them was the Habib Al-Najjar Mosque, which we just visited. They went there and stayed for about an hour. I tried to remember the other places he had mentioned. The young doctor candidate's eyes were shining as he spoke of Silpius Mountain and the walls on this mountain. I also remembered that he was excitedly telling about a place called "Iron Gate"; between the Silpius and Stauris Mountains. He spoke enthusiastically about the huge and incredible structure and the importance of its survival for centuries. I was trying to capture small clues from these details that I remember, and I was trying to understand what these two young people were trying to do, as we had not heard from them for almost twelve hours. They did not respond to any of our phones, although being sane, consistent people who just met each other.

I also told what I thought about, to the woman I love and my old friend, who were sitting at the table, unhappy, anxious and afraid. I said with excitement that they went to the mosque, which Nikola first mentioned, so they must have visited the other places he mentioned as well and that it is very important that we check these places as soon as possible; even, if we are able to go, we should go right away. Dimitri looked at my face with the anxious expression that settled in his face that day and never went away, and said that we could not go at this late hour of the night, we would not be able to do anything even if we went there, we could not get help from anyone, we could not find anyone to ask questions to, and again he stared back at the screen of his phone on the table.

My friend was right. What could we do in the dark of the night? We were talking about steep cliffs, caves, walls stretching thousands of meters, deep pits, corridors and tunnels and two mountains stretching for kilometers. Aside from the blind darkness of the night, we knew nothing about the mountains that stretched out to the eye, even if we went in daylight, we might have have to look for them days on end. As we don't know exactly where they went, we didn't have the slightest clue.

Solmaz said that as soon as the sun rises in the morning, we should start searching in the mountains and that we shouldn't call neither Gizem, nor Nikola by phone any more. She said that if they see and hear we are calling them, they would definitely respond, and even if they cannot answer at that moment, they were mature and responsible enough to know what to do in the first moment they are available. She added that if they can't answer the phone, there is a high possibility that something negative might have happened to them, so we shouldn't be draining their phone batteries by continuously calling them. She explained these with an expression of fear, together with her increasing worries. She said that we can most definitely find out where they are from their phone signals when we apply at the corresponding authorities. We whispered to her, as if we promised her that we will comply with everything she said.

We weren't tired. We wouldn't be able to sleep even if we went to bed, but a hard and long day awaited us in the morning. We had to be rested and strong, with both our minds and bodies. We turned off the lights of the courtyard, which witnessed happy and joyful laughs the night before. The happy courtyard had turned into a sad and gloomy emptiness. We went to our rooms and struggled to sleep until the early hours of the morning, trying to sleep without speaking.

* * *

What have we done? What mistakes have we made to deserve these unhappy and fearful moments, to stay under these ruins and those walls falling on us? What were we paying for as a small, joyful little ensemble of the day before?

What could be the reason for me experiencing the dangers moving under the shaken land, while trying to embrace the inner serenity that I was trying to reach in this blessed city of the centuries?

I could not sleep; whereas I knew that I had to sleep and rest for we had to cross mountains, slopes and cliffs early in the morning. I was also sure that I would go out right away, right now, without wairing, if I knew that the woman I loved wouldn't prevent me. Neither the blind darkness of the night, nor steep slopes, sharp rocks, thorns in my flesh could prevent me! What have I done, what mistakes have I made that could cause me to experience these unhappy and fearful moments!

I turned slowly to the side and I saw the drops coming down from the eyes of the woman I loved, on her cheeks. She was crying quietly and tightly holding on the thin piece of fabric we couldn't cover ourselves with. She was crying silently and was trying not to put me in unresolvable situations. I pretended not to see her crying, I closed my eyes tightly. In fact, I wanted to rebel and shout, I was desperate; I couldn't, I couldn't do anything. I should not have. I was silent, I did not speak, I could not speak, and I could not say anything that could comfort her. I stretched my hand and touched her thin arm; I caressed, hugged her and opened my eyes with difficulty. She looked into my eyes and tried to understand what I wanted to tell; I thought she understood, I forced myself to explain, but I understood that I could not explain anything to her.

* * *

Silpius Mountain. The mysterious mountain overlooking Antakya, the tired city of centuries, the magnificent mountain neighbor of Stauris, the holy mountain of thousands of years; what did it hold for us, what days was it going to give us, what was it going to take from us, hide from us, give it back to us when the day comes? Was it going to ever give it back to us? We know nothing, and we couldn't understand.

We left the house at the earliest minutes of the morning, when the darkness of the night began to dissipate, we started the car and passed slowly through the narrow streets. We never talked to each other. We parked the car to the left side of the road from the beginning of the mountain where St. Peter's Church was located, to a place near the place where the mountain ended. We started to climb, following Dimitri, from the narrow street a little ahead of where the new museum was built, towards the hills of the mountain rising before us.

We were trying to walk, climb, search and catch a hint, albeit small. Dimitri knew where Nikola could go from his previous accounts, trips and climbs in this area. We started to climb without waiting, advancing from the solid and printable parts of the sharp rocks, passing the paths and protecting our legs from hard thorny bushes. We never lowered our speed, after about forty-five minutes we reached the slope of the mountain, which was not very high.

After walking for a while on the hill, we proceeded about thirty minutes further on the asphalt road that we encountered towards the west, towards Altınözü district, and continued our walk towards the valley between the two mountains. The path before us was a narrow road that had been walked on for at least two thousand years.

The river flowing between Silpius Mountain and Stauris Mountain was a river called the "Parmenius River" or "Onnopnicles River" in ancient times. This river, which flows insanely during the rainy periods, feeds, fills, carries and flows by dragging everything that comes in front of it; these days turned into calm, almost never flowing puddles formed in certain places. In some places we were walking on the dried river bed, in some places from the path of the centuries that passed the left of this bed.

When we went through a passage rising from the rocks opened like a narrow corridor from the shore of the Parmenius River, we looked at the incredibly large structure that appeared suddenly before us with Solmaz, with the eyes of people who saw an unexpected formation in a place they never expected. Between Silpius and Stauris mountains, the structure built of solid and cut stones stretched up from the flat rocky ground of the river bed at the base of the valley.

"The Iron Gate," said Dimitri. "One of the first dams of the world, the Arabs call it "Bab Al-Hadid", built by Justinian, which reigned in the five hundreds AD. The raging waters of the Parmenius River have been built so that they do not flood the city and cause danger, and as you can see, it has been standing for exactly one thousand five hundred years. Nikola used to visit this place very often, come, let's walk on it and examine it thoroughly."

We walked on the stone building, following Dimitri, who said that it was the largest of the four gates opening to Old Antioch and that it was called the "Iron Gate" because there was an iron gate next to this dam at that time. We stood right in the middle and looked down; the white rocks, which are flattened and polished by the waters hitting from twenty to twenty-five meters deep, and the height of it made us dizzy. We quickly pulled ourselves back.

It was so easy to fall down and be split into pieces at once with a simple, small and minor mistake or an unnecessary step. We carefully studied every place we passed; the surrounding hills, trees, bushes and tried to find a familiar item; but we couldn't find anything.

"Where are you, where did you go, why are you hiding, did something happen to you?" These and similar questions were constantly crying in my numb brain. "Are you hiding because of a sudden love, an unintentional act, embarrassing feelings, an unexplained behavior, to allow time afterwards?" I was asking and repeating the same questions non-stop. These could be the most innocent reason for such loss or hiding, and I wished it would be so.

We left the Iron Gate and continued walking along the historical path. Soon we looked at the depth of the valley from a high point of the mountain we arrived; the roofs of slums, small gardens bordered by wooden fences, and caves at the foot of the mountain and rock recesses used as animal shelters were constantly breaking our hopes. The stench of straw, fertilizer and urine rising from animal shelters reached the height we were at. We went down quickly and walked towards Stauris Mountain from the small bridge over the Parmenius River, which is now called "Hacıkürüş". The moment I lifted my head, I saw the cut stone sidewall of St. Peter's Church and the big rocks, which rolled off the mountain to the steps of the stairs next to this wall.

I stopped and stood at the steps of the staircase where big rocks fell down, at the garden where the steps descended, at the flattened sheet iron trash barrel under a large rock, the sad view of a tree that was shattered from the bottom, and the security guard who stood by the side of the scattered, sad landscape. I looked at his bored, sullen and ugly face.

I felt the same flaming hellish image of my meaningless nightmares as this image in ruins, scattered, cracked, and fire did not affect me as much as the first day I saw it. I felt secretly happy about it, being embarrassed of my happiness. We were looking for our missing relatives, we couldn't find them, couldn't even find the smallest trace and I was still thinking about the similarities of the places in my meaningless nightmares, with the place we were at. I was embarrassed, I was really embarrassed of myself.

"Passing is forbidden!" the bored, sullen and ugly-faced security guard said, pointing two meters ahead of the red-white plastic security strip. Dimitri took out the task card from his pocket and held it near the tip of his nose, showing it. The official immediately apologized for not being able to recognize the museum official, jumping up from the rocks he was sitting on. We asked about our relatives to the guard of the rocks falling from the mountain. He said that he was on duty the day before as well and that he had never seen anyone similar to the people we described; as we left, he shouted from behind us that we should ask the other officer waiting in the north of the safe area.

Passing by the rolling rocks, we quickly walked towards the guard at the other end of the forbidden area. The moment we arrived, I was trying to understand this even more bored, sullen and ugly-faced officer, who was trying to greet the high-level bureaucrat of the museum to which St. Peter's Church was officially affiliated, and his friends.

The moment Dimitri started describing the people he was asking for, the man interrupted him and he said that the previous day, he was on duty at the same place, telling us that two people, one a young woman and the other a long-bearded, long-haired man, came to him and asked him to enter the forbidden zone around two or three in the afternoon. He said that he told them that he can't allow that and asked them to leave this area for their own safety. He was out of breath, explaining these. We all could understand that he exaggerated the last part and that he was trying to show us how careful he was in his profession.

Suddenly we found ourselves in a wave of warm hope. I thought the security guard smiled and his exhaustion had passed as well. With a new wave of speech, he explained that the two people thanked him after his warnings and that they walked towards the mountain through the pathway that lead to the Hell Boatman, and that he never saw them again afterwards.

They did not know that I came here two nights before, after midnight, stood in front of Charon and the other nonsense I've done. I waited for Dimitri to walk ahead, and followed my friend, fearfully, as if I was walking this path for the first time and that I didn't know anything about it.

We came in front of the relief on the mountain and looked at the missing face of Hell Boatman. We looked at the pebbles under the hewn, the tunnel window very close to it, the crumbling vents, the round goat excrement scattered around the environment, the yellowing grasses, the drying shrubs and the hills of Stauris, the holy mountain of thousands of years, where we found no clues.

There was no good news that could give data, information, findings and hope other than what the security guard told us about their encounter the day before.

It was past eight in the morning and the sun was rising from the east of the city. We left Charon's statue quickly and started to walk towards the narrow Street where we parked our car, next to the construction of the new museum building. We were next to the car in thirty minutes.

I painfully looked at the clenched hands and the helpless face of Solmaz, who said that we should now apply to all relevant places and report that our relatives have disappeared. We never called them after the night to avoid draining their phone batteries. I told her to call. She looked at my face as if something good and new had come to her mind and quickly dialed the phone in her hand; took it to her ear, waited a short time, and looked at me in fear, as if she saw a brutal predator. "Gizem's phone is off."

It was news that I never wanted to hear, I was shaken, I felt my heart beating faster. I looked at Dimitri's face without saying anything, and he did what he had to do quickly, called Nikola quickly, he held his phone in his ear for a short moment, and whispered that his brother's phone was off, in a hopeless, desperate, fearful tone. Solmaz started to cry, shaking, sobbing. I held her left hand softly, tightened it and tried to say that she should not lose hope; a few words spilled from my lips that I had trouble believing even myself.

The anxious brother said that we would report a loss to the police officer in front of the Police Headquarters we had reached, and started walking towards the entrance door of the building. We followed him and entered an environment with on-and-off sounds of police radios.

We told the young official of the Office, who was dealing with missing cases, about everything, the problem we had, our calls, all the information we could ever give, phone numbers, that their phones were on at night but off this morning, no longer being reached. When one of us was done speaking, another one of us immediately explained all the information that was missing, which must be said and given, without breathing.

The young police officer on duty, who wrote down all the things we said, sometimes interrupted us, asked small questions and noted down all the answers he received. He recognized our desperation, our fears and the pain we felt, and he continued his work in a non-hectic manner that would allow us to calm down.

He explained to us that according to his experiences, especially young people, who disappeared and could not be heard from, came back after a day or two, they generally did not encounter negative results and they would sometimes leave for emotional, sometimes economic reasons, that they sometimes want to be alone in places where no one is, that they want nobody to reach them, try to give their relatives lessons with little anger. He told us that those people usually returned to their homes on their own, without giving any explanation. Was it really the experience he had, or was the young police officer trying to comfort us? I couldn't understand.

In particular, we asked for the records of the last twenty-four hours of the phone operator of the numbers we gave, whether a signal could be reached or not, that they should quickly get summaries of the narrowest localisation, that they shouldn't lose time about it and kindly asked to be informed of those records as well. The young officer said that he isn't authorized to decide in such matters, but that he will speak to his commanders and let us know as well, with a sincere attitude that pitied our desperation. He stood up, stating that he should start working as soon as possible, shook our hands and walked us out of the room. Before he left us in front of the door, he repeated twice that the phones we gave numbers of must always be on, so that they can reach us.

We got in the car and came home desperately. The sun was hitting the yard from above, and it was very hot. We went to the living room. Daylight leaking from small windows on thick stone walls could not illuminate the room enough. We sat on the sofa that laid along the windowless walls. Hand-woven thick rugs covered the sofas. Thick and firm pillows leaning against the wall had the same patterns as the rugs.

We didn't talk for a while; we looked at the ceiling, looked at the carpet on the floor, the rug on the cedar, the patterns of the rug, the thick stone walls, the dusty windows of the small windows, the tree-carved shelves, and we just thought. We were trying to understand the causes of the disasters and destructions that may have happened, and the bad luck of the happy and carefree community of the day before, not being able to reach any conclusions. I was the first to break the silence of the gloomy room, I started to speak without raising my voice, often pausing and in a calm style.

"We are all unhappy, and scared of what happened. We can't think very well and therefore can't achieve healthy results. We also know that we all sincerely wish that nothing bad had happened to Gizem and Nikola. Now, if you want, let each of us explain the reasons that come to our mind. Everything we think of and say can be absurd, meaningless, irrational, or against the usual course of life. It doesn't matter, let's say what we think is here now to each other. You see, maybe we can reach a really important conclusion from the most meaningless thought, and catch a clue. "

They looked at my face and then gazed around the room, as if they were looking for something. They paused, not saying anything, and looked at me as if they were waiting for me to speak and to express my thoughts first.

"I think nothing bad has happened to them, at least I wish it is so. They are both young and beautiful people, you have seen how they looked at each other with interest and how they got close at once. We let them go alone and of course we should have, in what age do we live! I don't know how to say this, but, perhaps in the mountains they went, in the deserted places where they were alone, I wonder if they have gotten closer than appropriate and some things have happened between them that they could not explain to us... So maybe they are waiting for some time to pass to explain to us, I think of stuff like this. I prefer that what I think is true, instead of something bad having happened to them. "

None of them responded, they listened to me and started to scan the room again with their eyes.

"Since you have not commented on my words, this means that you did not find what I think is illogical or unreasonable. So I continue: What would you do if you had experienced something similar to what I told you and you were about eighteen or twenty? Wouldn't you want to get away and wait for your thoughts to become clear, wouldn't you try to gain some time to tell your relatives? I would have done so. Where did these young people come from? From Ankara, so Ankara is the place where they are most likely to go… I think they both went there together and we can find them in Ankara, they are trying to save time to explain or digest somethings," I said and went quiet. Now I started to wait for them to start talking, to make a good or bad comment.

"So, why did they not answer their phones, how can they even turn off their phones - when will they call us?" Solmaz asked one after another.

I suddenly said that they might be waiting for their thoughts to become clearer. I talked about the possibility of a serious crisis and waiting to get rid of their depressed emotions again. I couldn't answer Solmaz, who asked "why" they didn't answer their phones, "how could they" turn off their phone, and "when" they will call us. I asked with a voice that only I could hear: "Cur, quomodo, quondo?"

25. BELOVED CARPENTER: HABIB AL-NAJJAR

The carpenter lived in a cave on the side of the path of Silpius Mountain, which was full of high, steep and pointed rocks, close to the Parmenius River, with rocks, bushes and elongated grass covering the gate of it. He carved wooden idols for the pagans of Antioch and the wooden idols he carved were always met with the admiration of the idol worshipers. Habib Al-Najjar made his livelihood by carving the tree stumps and thick branches he cut from Silpius Mountain and made them with these wooden sculptures. His son was affected with leprosy. That is why he lived in a cave on Silpius Mountain. He was desperate to be able to do nothing for his son, whose illness worsened day by day, his skin became thicker, creating wounds that did not heal.*

One day, he sees two men walking from the pathway next to the Parmenius River to Antakya, he goes to them and invites them to the cave where he lives with his son, asking them to take a breath and rest. (The tense had changed, from the past to the present.) As they sat in the shade in front of the cave, the Beloved Carpenter asks them who they are and what they do. One says "John is my name", the other says "Paul". They say that they went to the city to explain the teaching of the Holy Son and that they could heal patients who did not recover.

*   Beloved Carpenter.

The carpenter shows them his son with leprosy, the cause of a deep pain and despair in him, asking them to heal him. Immediately at this moment, John and Paul perform a miracle without waiting and quickly, the child with leprosy heals.

The Beloved Carpenter, who was filled with happiness by looking at the face, arms and legs of his healed son with a miracle John and Paul performed without expecting anything in return, becomes the first believer in the religion that the apostles of Christ were trying to spread in Antioch, telling everyone in the city about his experiences.

However, the pagans throw John and Paul into the dungeon, for they were against Paganism and were trying to explain the new religion. Then another apostle comes from Jerusalem, this rock-hard man was called Peter. He also tries to explain this religion to the people, try to get them believe in it, try to hunt them.

The Beloved Carpenter runs towards the people to prevent them from hurting, imprisoning, or even killing the apostles, who were speaking and performing miracles at the skirts of the Silpius Mountain. He asks for the people to believe in them, that he has seen the miracle that healed his son with his own eyes. The pagans kill the Beloved Carpenter with stones and bury him where he dies.

Luke is my name. I am a Jewish and physician from Antioch. I wrote the story of the Beloved Carpenter, the good man, one of the first believers in Antioch, on gazelle skins and if you can read them now, you will carry this story on to thousands of years later.

26. AT NIKOLA'S APARTMENT IN ANKARA

We got in the car at six in the evening. We told Dimitri that we can reach Ankara only after midnight and he was sending us off with a sad and anxious facial expression.

We were going to Ankara. In the talks we had on the sofas in the living room of Dimitri's house, which were covered with embroidered rugs, we thought that it was not right for all of us to stay in Antakya to receive news, and that the young people were likely to go to Ankara, the city where they studied and lived in. We could not stand anyway, we were standing up, uneasy, wandering aimlessly in the room, thinking, sitting for a while, standing up again, wandering in the courtyard again and throwing desperate and fearful glances at each other's face.

Dimitri said that Nikola lived alone in a small house in Ankara, gave us the key he found in his brother's room as well as the address of the house.

We were going to the city where we studied the university, we got to know each other and fell in love with Solmaz, and we often had happy memories. Our visit to the city, which would usually be happy and joyful trips, was not with the same happiness and calm ths time; we left our most important values, our relatives behind and felt as if we would not see them again. A small light, a hope, a possibility forced us and allowed us to move quickly on the wide asphalt road.

When we left this city for the holidays of the university, we always looked forward to coming back, to our little flat with Solmaz, living happily with jokes, pranks, laughs, cooking and making love. I looked at the wide highway road and thought how much I would have liked this trip to be like that. We lived in this city for many years, happy, carefree, without a problem. After the last two days, which we experienced great fear, this city has turned into a city of unknowns, where we went to search of our missing relatives, in my depressed soul.

The breakfast we prepared for the table next to the small fountain in the large courtyard in Dimitri's house, our conversation accompanied by cheerful laughters, the knocks on the front foor, the young doctor candidate much like Che Guevara who entered in the house, the beautiful Gizem being quickly affected by the handsome young man, the closeness between them, perhaps "love at first sight", them leaving home at noon and not being able to hear from them since that time, their disappearance, sudden disappearance... It was painful, what was happening, really painful. They were moments of unhappiness, that were hard to remove, and those that I wanted to have never experienced. How could I endure these real life difficulties and sufferings, when I had difficulty in even enduring the nightmares, fearful dreams that I had experienced for years?

How could I tell Solmaz, who knew about my depression and had problems with this situation as well, that I was also responsible for what happened to her sister? If we hadn't made this trip because of my fearful dreams, nightmares, if we haven't been to that city, if Gizem didn't come to visit us and never met the young doctor candidate, if they never went up in the mountains together, if we never let them alone, if nothing had happened between them... Now, we wouldn't be experiencing these hopeless moments, these scary seconds, nightmarish hours and this worried journey.

We headed towards Ankara with the hope that we'd find them side by side, facing each other; what if we couldn't! I didn't even want to think about it, I quickly removed all negative thoughts from my brain. I gave all my attention to the road before me, which seemed endless, wishing positive, good possibilities. I wanted this road and for these bitter days to end, as soon as possible.

We reached Ankara two hours after midnight. Despite all my insistence, Solmaz couldn't even blink an eye. She adjusted her seat backwards but was still unable to sleep. She never spoke. She either didn't listen, hear the questions I asked and the things I told her to distract her; or gave them meaningless, uninterested answers. It was as if she wasn't with me.

We moved quietly through the deserted and still streets of Ankara. We reached Kavaklıdere and passed by the Kuğulu Park, and at the beginning of the road turning left from Tunalı Hilmi Street, I understood that it was the place we were looking for when I saw the name of the street written on the blue-white sign attached to the wall of a building. I entered Bestekar Street without hesitation. The street was lively even in this late hour of the night, life was ongoing with full speed and the lights were flickering with the vibrant chaos of many colours.

Neon signs on the entrance doors of the bars, white vapors rising from the pans of tripe soups illuminated with bright lamps, scents of vinegar and garlic scattering everywhere, the rhythmic sounds made by the kokoreç maker who cut the lamb intestines cooked in front of the grill car on the sidewalk with his sharp blade; young and beautiful girls trying to cover their opened legs while trying to get in comfortable cars in front of the bars, their attentive but insincere attitude, drunk people leaning onto trees with their unbalanced walks; they all felt like we entered a new and a different world.

I parked the car on the sidewalk in front of the building with a pharmacy on the ground floor, illuminated with dim lights. We looked at the old and three-story, yellow-coloured, faded, tired, worn-out building for a while, without getting out of the car. The ground floor, where the pharmacy was, contrasted the other two floors above it. It displayed a young, new and extremely dynamic image with its clean and wide windows, dim but clear lights, medicine boxes placed on the shelves, natural hemorrhoid syrups attached to the front windows, shampoos for hair growth, tablets that enlarge the penis and increase sexual power.

The two floors above were not the continuation of the ground floor, where the pharmacy was. These floors contained a separate world and different lives were lived there, they looked like an old man who was tired, worn and waiting for his death, with its dusty windows, faded paint and spilled plaster from the walls. No light leaked from any window; with their curtains drawn in different colors, they abstracted themselves from the bustling world on the street, and surrounded the dark rooms where quiet, calm and different lives were lived. I looked at the sad upper two floors again and opened the car door.

We passed a road that looked like a narrow corridor between the side windows of the pharmacy and the plastered, unpainted garden wall of the neighboring building and arrived in front of the entrance gate of the building. The old iron door with chipped paint was closed and locked, and I suddenly shuddered. I recalled that the keychain Dimitri gave us had a single key, I immediately took out the key ring from my left pocket; two keys were swinging at his tip, so I was relieved at that moment, we weren't going to have to ring anyone's bell at this time of the night. We entered the building with the first key I tried and I touched the electric switch at the beginning of the stairs that went up, now all the stairs were lit. We started to climb upstairs with Solmaz following me.

I thought that the combined stinks of mold, onion, urine, burnt oil, toast and moist laundry that completely encircled the interior of the old building could not be removed even if the building was ventilated for years. I forced myself to breathe in from my mouth and to breathe out from my nose and not to smell whatever it was, that could not be found in any environment other than the similar buildings of that world.

There were three apartments on the top floor of the building, we came in front of the apartment overlooking the small garden at the back. We were breathing heavy after the steps that we rushed and the intense excitement we had, our hearts were beating rapidly. I touched the faded, yellowed button of the bell. We waited, no sound came from the house. I touched it again, and this time I rang the bell for a long while. There was nothing - no voice, no sound, no motion, no noise. I inserted the key in the lock, twisted it twice and opened the wooden door, painted in oil. We entered the house with Solmaz, lit the lamp of the hallway at the entrance and closed the door after us. There was a kitchenette right next to the entrance door and a bathroom right next to it, the doors were open. There was another corridor crossing the hallway at the entrance and two doors were opening here, both of the doors were closed. We opened the double-winged door first, it was the living room of the house, we opened the other door, and we saw that it was a large bedroom. Suddenly I felt that my hopes were exhausted and my legs were shaking.

Nobody was at home. The youngsters, who were going to bring us in carefree arms of life and to end the fears we had for two days, that we were looking for and unfortunately could not find, were not at Nikola's apartment either, where we hoped to find them. I hugged Solmaz, who started crying, took her to the living room and helped her to slowly sit in a chair. She was shaking and sobbing.

I looked at the walls of the hall and read the text on one of the hanging pictures, which startled me. There were at least three pictures, posters or texts hanging on each wall of the hall, and I first saw this writing: *"If you want to find it, you must search for it."* It was a large poster of Stauris Mountain before me, the photo was taken from afar in colour and I recognized it at the first glance. No word, no sentence, no writing could shake and scare me as much as it did at that moment.

I looked at the side wall and a large, black and white poster of Che Guevara was hanging; I looked at his face and was once again surprised by his similarities with Nikola. *"The warrior may lose, the non-warrior has already lost".* I knew that this sentence written under the poster belonged to Che Guevara, who looked at us from inside the picture and whose main profession was medicine.

There was a similar couch in the living room to the one Solmaz was sitting on. There was a rectangular table with four wooden chairs around it, a handmade rug on the floor and a bookcase full of books. *If you want to find it, you must search for it…* I got up and walked around the other room, kitchen, bathroom. It was a typical student flat; however, everywhere around the apartment was remarkably clean, all parts of the house were carefully wiped, dusted, floors swept. I entered the bedroom, turned on the light, and looked at the large poster in the middle of the wall on which the head of the bed rested, and the inscription below. It was also a picture of a familiar place: the Iron Gate, which stood upright between the Silpius and Stauris mountains, and of the historical dam, built of thick and solid cut stones, which are one thousand and five hundred years old. Nikola wrote two sentences with a black and thick pencil:

"They brought it here and hid it / If you want to find it, you must search for it."

I read and tried to understand the sentence I saw in the first picture and the new sentence written on it, several times; I forced myself but I could not understand anything. Only Nikola could make a connection between the posters, pictures, photographs, words and sentences on the walls of his house, which he furnished and decorated in line with his own interests, thoughts and perspective.

As I left the bedroom, I looked at another quote by Che that was hanging next to the left side of the door: "If you don't have enemies, it means you never succeeded in life." I ached with my unsuccessfulness in life, based on the logic of that saying. I had none, really had no enemies, and I did not want to spend a single second on enemies or hostilities in any period of my short, small, simple life, even on a single day.

The kitchen and bathroom were clean like the other parts of the house. I opened the refrigerator in the kitchen, it was not very full, I took a can of beer, broke off the lid and tossed it down my throat; I drank, sipped it and I didn't take it away from my mouth until my throat burned. I went to Solmaz, I asked whether she would like to eat something and she looked at me with a painful expression, as she told me she didn't want to. She said that my theory, about which I was very hopeful, has collapsed and that we couldn't find them here either. I didn't say anything, didn't argue with her.

I tried to raise hopes with my words that said that we would stay here until morning and that it wouldn't be right to make any interpretations until the next day. I didn't believe my words either but I tried to keep our hopes alive. I put forward many reasons like they might be having fun somewhere outside, and that there is a possibility that they may be back by the morning, and others alike. She didn't listen to me, she stood up, grazed the curtain she held until the end and opened one of the windows; she tried to breathe in the clean air that suddenly filled the room; with her face, nose in the darkness.

I went to the kitchen and bought another can of beer. I took a little sip this time and examined the colourful magnet collection on the door of the refrigerator, big and small. I tried to analyze the complex table created by the different lengths, shapes and patterns created by the names, addresses and phone numbers of kebab restaurants, dry cleaners, pharmacies, raw meatballs, pizzerias, cleaners, restaurants, bars, night clubs written on the magnets; I couldn't analyze it and tossed the beer down my throat again.

I started to line up the magnets to the top right of the refrigerator, separating places on Bestekar Street, where this building was located. I looked at the lined-up, colourful magnets of one pizzeria, two pita restaurants, one kebab restaurant, one pharmacy, two bars and a nightclub. I eliminated those except bars and nightclubs from the eight magnets I separated, thinking that they were probably not open at this time of the night. Two bars and a nightclub remained. I did not know the difference between them, but I was trying to group them by following the definitions on the magnets.

I finished my beer, took the three magnets as well as the Che poster in the bedroom, put them all in my pocket. I tried to tell Solmaz that I would go out and do a little research. "At this time of night?" She looked at my face as if she wanted to say that. "Yes," I said. "There are places that can be visited especially at this time of the night, places that are closed during the daytime, places to be opened at the latest in the night... I will have a little visit to these places, my phone is on, the places I will go are on the street of this building. I will not go far, I'd be there in a minute, the moment you call me." She nodded, approving. I said that I would take the key of the house with me, as I was leaving the living room.

I entered the world of neon lights - bright, lively, fake, shallow and empty. I started walking past full, stinking garbage cans. There were cats and innocent-faed dogs inside the garbage cans; they looked at me for a short moment and continued with their search by bending their heads back forward into the can.

I took out the magnets in my pocket and ordered them according to their street numbers. I smiled when I realized the ironic similarity of the "Güftekâr* Bar", which was the first Bar that I encountered in the direction I was walking. I entered the bar, saluting the attendants at the door.

- *Bestekar: Composer, *Güftekar: Song lyrics writer.

It wasn't very crowded inside. I sat down on one of the high stools in front of the tall bar counter, without listening to the waiter who insisted that I'd sit at one of the tables – not even looking at his face. A middle-aged woman with her dyed blonde hair and excessive make-up smiled at me from behind the bar counter and asked me what I'd like to drink. Then she handed me the beer I wanted, with its bottle. I looked at her, smiling, and took out the Che poster from my pocket after taking a sip from my beer. "Nikola!" she shrieked. "All the girls here know him, he comes here frequently, he doesn't drink much but when he does, it's almost impossible to stop him… Why are you looking for Nikola?" she asked, curiously. I said I was a relative of his, that we couldn't see each other for a long time and that I lost his phone number.

The barmaid with the excessive make-up looked at my face and called some of the girls sitting at various tables. One of the girls sat on the stool on my right and two of them on my left. One of the girls sitting on my left, probably around 20 years old with her hip pointed way back on the stool, asked the woman behind the bar counter with a sincere innocence, "Will the gentlemen take all three of us?" "No honey," said the barmaid, smiling, "This gentleman wants me as well, he'll take all four of us." I joined in the laughs of the other girls, who understood the joke.

I told them I was looking for Nikola Çağlayan. They first looked at each others faces and then winked at the barmaid with their witty smiles. They told me they knew the young doctor candidate, that they sometimes go to his place, that this man has a very interesting character who always talked about searching for something, not being able to find it and that he was going to, one day; at mountains, walls and thousand-year-old pathways on the mountains. They said he was very polite, he treated them well, cooked good food and that they always had a good time with him.

The phone number they gave me was the same one as I had, but I saved it on my phone as if I didn't have it. A woman with bright yellow hair told me that he used the expression, "If you want to find it, you must search for it," like a slogan. I asked them when they saw him last. They told me altogether that they haven't seen him almost for a month and that they were starting to get worried.

I was searching whether someone has seen him in the last days. They knew him in the other bars and nightclubs I went into as well; they knew his name too, but they all kindly told me that they haven't seen him for a month. I left the bars full of lights, noisy music, alcohol, young female bodies, smells of smoke and mold with a brain, feelings and thoughts numbed by the beer I drank, with my increasing hopelessness.

None of the midnight people who knew Nikola has seen him in the last month. Almost all girls, waitesses know him in the last two places I visited as well; they knew his name an deven remembered the expressions he used like a slogan, with careless attitudes: *"If you want to find it, you must search for it."*

I went back home, opened the door slowly and quietly walked towards the living room. Solmaz was lying on the couch in the living room, with her eyes closed. I wished that she would be sleeping and could get some rest, and I sat down in one of the armchairs, stretched my legs on the chair I pulled in front of the armchair and closed my eyes with the numbing effect of the beer. I fell asleep.

I woke up with birdsongs filling the room from the window Solmaz opened at night, my head was throbbing. My legs on the chair were numb, my entire body was söre. I looked at Solmaz and she was just as I have left her at night. I stood up with difficulty and went into the bathroom; washed my hands and face, hair; I even put my head under the cold water from the tap and didn't pull back until I was very cold. As I dried my face, hair and the back of my neck with the towel, I didn't like what I saw in the mirror at all; there wre bags under my eyes and my beard was overgrown. I combed my hair with the brush I found in front of the mirror and left home again. It was close to eight in the morning.

I saluted a 20-year-old youngster, who was opening the pharmacy and wiping its winsows. I got in the car that I parked on the pavement in front of the entrance of the pharmacy last night, took it down the pavement. The youngster came up to me and thanked me for opening up space in front of the pharmacy. Without saying anything else, I immediately asked him whether he knew Nikola and whether he did, when was the last time he saw him. He answered to me withs surprise. He told me that he hasn't seen him for a week, that he knew him well, that sometimes he'd help them when the pharmacy was too crowded and even the pharmacist ladt liked Nikola very much. I left, thanking him.

When I got back home, I found Solmaz awake; she was washing her face. I stood at the bathroom door and asked how she was. She looked at me as if she wanted to say, "How do you expect me to be, I'm naturally not well," then she turned her face back towards the mirror on top of the sink, without saying anything. I started to tell her about the places I've been and the people I've talked to. Solmaz was wiping her face, I continued to tell her as she walked past me towards the living room and I followed her in the living room. She told me that it made her sad that no one has seen Nikola especially in the past week and that if she heard someone has seen him in the last two days, that she would have hope again. I also told her about the conversation I had with the youngster at the pharmacy.

There was nothing left to do at Nikola's place. We closed the window, put the empty cans of beer and other garbage in a bag and left the home, leaving everything as we found them.

We were headed to the female dormitory Gizem was staying at. I looked at the sullen crowd of Ankara, in the morning traffic on their way to work... The city was almost like a big government office, with the majority going to work every day at exactly 9 am, leaving work at exactly 6 pm and trying to get back home as soon as they can.

When we went to the dormitory, we directly went to the room of the dormitory manager, whom we met before. The manager woman greeted us with enthusiasm. She turned on her computer and told us immediately that Gizem left the dormitory exactly three days ago at 17:15, that she didn't take her stuff with her and informed them that she would come back three days later, take her stuff and go to Istanbul, next to her parents. She also added, gazing at the ceiling, that if she didn't calculate it wrong, Gizem must be returning today to take her stuff from her room.

Yes, she was indeed going to come in three days, take her belongings and go to Istanbul. If everything went normal, she would come back to Ankara after her vacation in Antakya, which was a small break she took, take her belongings and gto to Istanbul to spend her two-month summer break there.

I wished it would be so; as we sat in the office of the dormitory manager, I thought about how much I wanted Gizem to come to us with her usual enthusiastic and crazy attitude, jump the moment she saw us, hug us and say, "Wait for me, I'll be right back with my stuff."

We left our phone numbers to the manager women, writing them on a small piece of paper. We told her to call us immediately if Gizem comes here or calls her, especially indicating that this is very important.

"I have to call my parents," Solmaz said. "What will I tell them, how can I even explain what happened; they'd both have simultaneous heart attacks!" I listened to her quietly, started the car's engine and told her that I can send her to Istanbul with the first plane. "G oto them, see how they are, and tell them what happened slowly in a suitable moment…" I said. She thought for a while without looking at my face and said, "Yes, you're right. It would be better if I was there and supported them dealing with what I'll tell them. I don't want to experience the pain of losing my parents after everything we've been through now."

Without repliyng to her, I drove the car towards Esenboğa Airport. I didn't leave the airport until the plane, which took off at 12:30, disappeared from sight.

I called Dimitri, he answered the phone immediately and his voice was full of worry and curiosity. I told him what we've been to. I explained to him that we couldn't find any clue, no new information, no hopeful development, that no one has seen Nikola in the last week, and that Gizem left the dormitory in the evening she came to Antakya. There was a moment of silence on the phone – I thought he hung up. Just as I was about to take the phone away from my ear as well, I heard Dimitri's exhausted, sad and hopeless voice, once again. He told me that he called the police officer that we talked to, early in the morning; and that he just went to see him. He said that there are no developments yet but that he'd call me immediately if he finds out anything new. There was another silence and he asked about Solmaz. I told him I sent her to Istanbul. I explained to my sad, hopeless friend about Solmaz's exhausted, destroyed, fearful state and that I wasn't so different as well.

I left the airport and drove towards Kızılay, fastly through the streets. I wanted to g oto Nikola's place fort he last time – examine the pictures, posters on the walls of his apartment; look at his writings – there should have been nothing left that I missed.

I couldn't find a place to park my car in front of the apartment. So I waited for the female driver who tried to get out of the parking spot about fifty meters away from the building, and quickly parked my car there.

The pharmacy on the ground floor was crowded. I opened the locked front gate and went upstairs without hurry. I quietly opened the door of the apartment, entered inside and shut the door with the same quietness. There was a sound coming from the kitchen, I thought whether I could be mistaken… Was I dreaming?

I walked fast towards the open kitchen door, thinking how right I was in coming back again to Nikola's place, that the lost youngsters have finally come back home and how they could account for all the pain and confict they've put us through… But my hopes fell, once again.

There was an old, weak woman wearing a scarf, washing something in the sink with her back turned to the door. The moment she heard the sound I made, she quickly turned towards me and looked at me with fear. I tried to calm down the old woman; I told her I was a friend of Nikola's, that I stayed in this apartment last night, I left early in the morning and that I returned to get my remaining stuff. She smiled, turned off the water she left on; wiped her hands and sat down onto one of the chairs next to the small table in the kitchen. She pointed with her hand to the other chair, telling me to sit down. I quietly sat down where she showed.

The old woman told me that she's been cleaning this apartment for two years. She explained that she'd come once a week, clean the apartment and takes the small cash Nikola leaves every month on the kitchen counter; that she has never seen the doctor candidate for months and that she enters the apartment with the key he gave her; that she goes back home after locking the apartment when she is finished. That's when I understood how clean Nikola's apartment was, despite it being a student's flat.

I asked her what Nikola is like. She looked at my face as if she wanted to say to me, "Aren't you a close friend, why are you asking me?" and she started speaking, as she thought what reply I could give her. She was speaking calmly with lots of pauses, thoughts… "He's a nice young man, I haven't seen anything bad from him, he always treats me good, always pays me timely. I am retired, and my retirement salary is barely enough for my rent; so I survive off the money he gives me. What can I do, I'm alone, my children aren't calling me either…"

She paused at that moment in her speech; wiped the tears falling from her eyes towards her cheek; she gulped and started speaking to me again: "He always told me that he was looking for something, and that he will surely find it one day; but he never told me what he was looking for and when, where he would find it…"

She thought for a while and started speaking fastly, as if she remembered something: "He spoke about mountains, he told me, in the days we'd meet, that the true, eternal, never-ending life can only be seized through these mountains. I would listen to him without understanding what he was talking about… I'd always ask him, whenever I saw him, whether he could find what he was looking for, and that I was praying for him so he could find it. He'd get happy and always tell me, 'If you want to find it, you have to search for it.' Now I've memorised these things he always said."

I gave the old woman some money; she didn't want to take it. I insisted that she should take the money and I slowly slipped it into her old purse on the table. I said goodbye to her, thanking her, and closed the door from behind her.

I folded the pictures, posters, notes on the walls and newspaper articles in the drawers carefully. I collected some books from the bookshelves and placed them all inside a bag. I called Dimitri and told him that I came back to Nikola's place, that I saw an old clenaing lady and that I am now heading towards Antakya.

I understood where I must search for them: Mountains, walls, jungles, fortresses... It was just like Nikola had said: *"If you want to find it, you must search for it."*

27. I AM A JEWISH PHYSICIAN FROM ANTIOCH

*"Then the apostles and elders, with the whole church, decided to select men from among them to send to Antioch with Paul and Barnabas. They chose Judas called Barsabbas and Silas, two leaders among the brothers."**

*Apostles who came to Antioch brought us a letter. We waited for them in the passage between Silpius Mountain and Stauris Mountain, and when they came, we went to Stauris's cave with them all together. They read the letter written to us at the meeting in Jerusalem. Important advice was given and the writings encouraged us all: "You must abstain from food sacrifices to idols, from blood, from the meat of strangled animals, and from sexual immorality. You will do well to avoid these things. Farewell."** This is how the letter ended.*

"You should avoid the meat of the victims offered to idols, blood, meat of slaughtered animals and prostitution. Stay well." the letter ended.

*"Judas and Silas, who themselves were prophets, said much to encourage and strengthen the brothers. After spending some time there, they were sent off by the brothers in peace to return to those who had sent them. But Paul and Barnabas remained at Antioch, along with many others, teaching and preaching the word of the Lord."****

Barnabas and Paul remained at Antioch for a while and then Barnabas went to Cyprus along with John, and Paul went to Syria and Cilicia with Silas.

**New Testament: Acts of the Apostles – Act 15-22*

***New Testament: Acts of the Apostles – Act 15-29*

****New Testament: Acts of the Apostles - Acts15-32, 15-33, 15-35*

Luke is my name. I am a physician from Antioch, I am a Jew. All that I have told are "Acts of the Apostles", I have told them separately, I wrote them and entrusted them to believers so they will be read even hundreds of years later. What you read now is my story, what I have been through, what I saw and what I listened from those who are filled with the Holy Spirit.

When the rock-solid Peter came and stayed for many years at Antioch, he told us about his last dinner with Jesus Christ as well, when we gathered in Stauris's cave. As he said that Christ gave him the chalice he had used in this last meal, that he brought it with him and wanted it to stay at Antioch forever, he looked around at the believers gathered in the cave and looked at me. He said, "Dear physician, take this sacred chalice and fill it with water, make all your brothers and sisters drink from that water so they would be blessed forever." I stood up, went to Saint Peter and took the chalice from him with trembling hands. I filled the chalice with the water leaking from the walls of the cave, waited impatiently for all believers to pass along and drink the water inside, and handed it back to Kifas.

Much later, Peter gave me that chalice as he was leaving Antioch. He told me to protect it well and that he wishes for it to remain forever in this city, at Antioch. I took the chalice with my trembling hands and the great excitement I had, with my heart's unresting beat and lack of breath, I thought for days what I must do fort he chalice to remain in this city forever.

Luke is my name, I am a physician from Antioch and I am the protector of that holy trust.

28. LIFE CHANGES IN A MOMENT

Starting from the first minutes of my departure from Ankara, I thought of everything we've been through and I couldn't believe. I was watching with surprise how everything can turn around when we thought everything was going well and we were leading a good, happy, content life; all good could go bad and that moments filled with fear and disaster can happen at any moment. I was trying to analyse reasons for it, forcing myself but couldn't reach any positive conclusion.

I really didn't see any of the details of the long road I was driving fast on, which seemed like it never ended – the traffic lights, trees on the side of the road, mountains, hills I crossed – I saw none of them. I was doing what I was supposed to, like a mechanical doll; trying not to take my eyes off the road, stopping where I must stop, slowing down where I must slow down, speed up where I have to speed up, continue my journey towards the city I must go to and I wanted to complete this journey as soon as possible.

I didn't even know where the two young people were after they disappeared without a reason and we couldn't hear from them again; I didn't know what they were up to, whether anything negative had happened to them and this situation was consuming the hopes I was trying to keep alive, with each passing day.

I was trying to remember the speeches and sentences of the young doctor candidate, whom we only saw for a few hours, so I could catch a hint. Without taking my eyes off the road I was driving fast on, I was forcing myself to see whether there were any details that I missed or skipped.

I knew that I couldn't and shouldn't make any judgement about the personality type, thoughts, ideals and extremities of a young man in his twenties; whom I only saw for a few hours.

Immediately after the old cleaning lady had left the apartment, I also left there, taking all the pictures and posters on the wall, the notes I thought he'd written, sloganised sentences and anything alike. I took a few books that drew my attention, a few note papers I found between the pages of the other books, cut out newspaper articles, columns and placed them next to the pictures in the plastic bag.

I wanted to Show Dimitri all of them and wanted to speak about many details like his brother's personality, mental state, emotional fluctuations, extremities, beliefs, political views, goals and many others. Diitri could best know his brother. A detail that seemed little, unimportant and unnecessary to me or to someone else could be very important for Dimitri and I could catch indispensable hints as much as I could understand the value of it.

It was midnight when I reached Adana. I was quite tired and hungry. My eyes were closing and I was trying to resist the intense sleep hovering on me. I opened the window of the fast car and tried to remain awake with the chilling effect of the crisp air. After driving like this for a while, I thought that I can't stand this, that I could fall asleep and have a bad accident. So I parked the car at the first gas station that I found; I flattened my seat and closed my eyes. I forced myself not to think about anything and I fell into a deep sleep, immediately. I just slept – away from nightmares, disappearances, worries, fears – I threw myself on the peaceful shores of a different world.

I must have slept for about half an hour. I got out of the car, went in the restaurant next to the gas station and washed my face with cold water. I had a light meal there and started driving again. Even that short break, that small, short sleep helped me to be more awake and supported me to continue my long journey without endangering my life, driving with a more careful technique.

I reached Antakya around 4 am. I called Dimitri as I approached his house and he answered the phone immediately. With a tired and worried voice, he told me that if I didn't call him, he'd call me himself. I parked the car in the empty slot in front of his house. I found my friend in front of his house, waiting for me. We hugged and looked at each other's face with sadness.

I entered the courtyard of the house with the plastic bag I took from Nikola's apartment. I left it at the table next to the small fountain and threw myself on a chair. I was tired, exhausted. Dimitri also looked tired, he said that he barely slept until my arrival; I felt my tiredness went away when I looked at his unhappy face filled with sadness.

I saw that he looked at the plastic bag I left at the table. I told him that I took it from Nikola's place and started taking everything out of the bag. There was a book on the 1098 Crusades, a large poster of the walls of Antioch, a photograph of the Iron Gate with a large writing of "Bab Al-Hadid," a photograph of Che Guevara, a poster of the movie *Raiders of the Lost Ark* starring Harrison Ford, a watercolour painting of Saint Peter, a representative sketch with lights shining from it, with the writing, "*Holy Ark,*" White paper with writings of scripture on the *Ark*, a large photograph of the Saint Peter's Church, another middle-size photograph of the church's inside that was taken with a wide angle, the black-and-white photograph that depicted the entrance of the tunnel inside the cave church with the writing: "*If you want to find it, you must search for it,*" newspaper articles, yellowed columns, a representative Picture of the Holy Grail… I took whatever was in that bag, put it on the table and waited for Dimitri to speak – he was looking at my face without a word and trying to understand how these objects could help us.

He really looked tired, his beard was overgrown, he had bags under his eyes and he was far from his usual joyful and happy state. He started speaking, slowly…

"I knew that my brother had a special interest and admiration for Che Guevara, because he physically looked like him and because he was also studying medicine. He knew almost every sloganised word of his by memory, and repeated them at every chance… You know that Saint Peter is the first Pope; so I can only connect his interest in Saint Peter's Church and the Holy Grail to his religion, his sect. We are Catholic. And Nikola passionately believed, like many others do, that this lost grail or chalice was brought to Antioch, was hidden here, couldn't be found and is still hidden to this day, to be found somewhere, one day.

I believe his interest on the Walls of Antioch could be about the Crusades in 1098 and the occupation of the city. The Holy Ark remains to be an important and unbelievable secret for more than two thousand and five hundred years. Nikola believed that this Ark was brought to Antiock and was hidden here, and is still hidden somewhere around here. When he found out that this was also written in important religious scripture not only of Christianity but of your religion as well, he started to research and investigate it even more passionately and with determination, asking me hundreds of questions about it. The Iron Gate, "Bab Al-Hadid" in Arabic, is the continuation of the walls between Silpius Mountain and Stauris Mountain and Nikola had special admiration fort his structure. Whenever he came to Antakya, he would take that long way, climb the mountains, go to that Iron Gate and would sit on the one thousand and five hundred year old stone structure for hours."

When he said that it's getting very late, it was almost morning, the birds were chirping in the trees. He suggested, with a tired voice, that we would sleep for a few hours and greet the coming day with at least a bit of rest. I put everything on the table – pictures, posters, books, columns – back in the plastic bag and went up to my room.

I laid in the bed, the sheets and the pillow smelled of Solmaz. I wondered what she was doing; how she told her parents about the difficult days we've had, how she told them about their disappearance, what kind of reaction she faced. I understoof that I can no longer question my thoughts or judge what happened. I was very tired and there were many things I had to do, many places I had to go, and many things I had to search for in places I was going to go after waking up; I wanted to find those things and I was going to search fort hem with passion – I had to.

I slept for about two hours. I woke up, rested my back against the head of the bed, took out the columns cut out from newspapers from the plastic bag on the nightstand and randomly chose one. It was an article cut from the black-and-white printed page of a local newspaper in Antakya. The name and the photo of the columnist was on top of the column. I started reading Mehmet Ali Öztaş.

"Dear readers, we promised you in our column last week that we would tell you about the Walls of Antioch; we hold our promise and start telling.

The walls in our city were constructed during the Greek, Rome and Byzantine regions. In the ancient writings of famous travellers, it is said that the length of the wallswere fourty-four thousand feet. They are the longest walls after the walls of Rome and Istanbul. Even though eighteen great earthquakes, wars, occupations and fires have destroyed a majority of them, the part of the wall that is neighboring Habib Al-Najjar Mountain, formerly known as Silpius Mountain, as well as to the Cross Mountain, known as the Stauris Mountain is standing erect to this day. The giant structure stands on Hacıkürüş, formerly known as the Parmenius River and is known as the "Iron Gate." This structure was constructed by Justinian in the 6th century and as it has great importance in the controlling of flood water, it also acted as a bridge.

We advise you to read carefully the next information we will give to you. Ten thousand carpenters, seven thousand masons, nine thousand donkeys and nine thousand porters worked int he construction of these walls, that could stand erect for centuries. Five thousand people carried rocks from the Asi River, ten thousand people worked on the block stones, a thousand people cut trees, two thousand and five hundred people worked in brick kilns, a thousand blacksmiths and five thousand carpenters did the other work. A total of eighty thousand people put their hard work in the construction of these walls.

We now look at the still standing walls that we can see from afar. We look at them and think; what makes them stand to this day despite great pain and disasters like eighteen great earthquakes, fires, wars, great occupations must be a big and unbeatable force. These walls could keep the greatest armies outside of the city for months and prevent occupations, and they must definitely have a secret. We will continue our research and share all the secrets we find out, everything interesting and unknown, with you.

We will talk about the Holy Ark of the Covenant, the Holy Grail and the Crusades in 1097 in the next weeks."

After reading the column, I placed it back inside the plastic bag, together with the other things I put there. I actually wanted to go downstairs after reading the other columns as well. I looked at the clock, took out the columns I placed in the plastic bag once again and started looking at the one on top of the others.

The local newspaper columnist Mehmet Ali Öztaş had an interesting, different writing style. What he wrote captivated the reader immediately and one couldn't leave the writing without finishing it, after reading the first sentence only. It made the reader finish the writing with curiosity until the last word. At least, I noticed that was the effect of it on me. I looked at the column on top of what I had in my hand, and started reading it with the different effect of the writer on me, with curiosity:

"Have you ever thought that the Holy Ark of the Covenant and what is being told about the Holy Ark in the Islamic resources, on an ark made out of locust bark that was lost since 587 B.C. are actually not different arks but the same ark?

Have you ever heard that this Holy Ark contained the first written versions of the Ten Commandments in the Torah, together with the rods of Prophet Musa and Harun and was initially hidden at the Suleiman Temple in Jerusalem?

Did you know that when Prophet Christ was crucified, an apostle filled a chalice with his blood and put that chalice inside the Holy Ark, hiding the ark to bring to another city?

Have you ever read that Qor'an's 248th verse of Bakara Section speaks about the Holy Ark as a "Casket" and informs that the casket has "Sekine" – meaning calmness, quietness, contentment – as well as remnants of Prophets Musa and Harun?

Have you ever heard of the Hadith Scripture by Jalaluddin Al-Suyuti in Al-Hawi lil-Fatawi, which said, "The reason why He is called His Holiness Mahdi is because he shows a way for it which is hidden. He will reveak the Casket (The Holy Ark) from somewhere called Antioch."

Have you ever read Kitab Al-Fitan written by Naim bin-Hammad, which says, "The Mahdi sends an army to fight the Greek. His knowledge of fiqh (Islamic law) is equal to the knowledge of ten men. He will reveal the Holy Casket of Sekine (The Holy Ark) from the cave at Antioch."

Yes, dear readers, religious authorities, whose words can not be argued, inform us that the Holy Ark is in Antakya. In this case, what is left for us is to believe what is said and to wait fort he Mahdi, who will find that Ark. We will wait with patience and faith."

I put all writings of Mehmet Ali Öztaş back in the plastic bag, for I knew if I only looked at one sentence in a column, I couldn't stop myself from reading the entire article. I took a shower, got dressed and quickly went downstairs to the courtyard, where Dimitri waited for me. It was almost half past nine.

I told Dimitri about what I've found at Nikola's place, what I've read in the columns I brought with me. I told him that I was weirdly captivated by the writings, not knowing whether it's because of the writing style or the mystery of what's being told. Dimitri, one of the important experts of Antakya's rich history, told me that he knew Mehmet Ali Öztaş well and that he is a careful researcher.

As we were speaking, he took his phone in his hand and dialled a number. From his first words, I understood that he was coling the police officer we spoke to, when we made the application of missing people. I listened to their conversation quietly. I found out that there was nothing new, surrendering with increasing worry and fear. I waited fo a while and called Solmaz, but her phone was off. I didn't insist, I didn't call again and thought that there were no good, new and important news I could give her anyway.

We split the work with Dimitri. He was going to go to the Security Directorate and make face-to-face meetings; especially invesigating where the last phone signals of Gizem and Nikola came from, where they had their last phone call; and whether this information arrived from the phone operators or not. I, on the other hand, was going to climb the mountains once again and try to find the smallest hint, a sign, a clue.

Immediately after this decision, I drove the car on the road I now knew very well and parked it away from Saint Peter's Church near the new Antakya museum building construction, where I previously parked it. Without hesitation, I started climbing the mountain. Forcing myself not to see the rocks, thornd, escaping lizards, flies, insects of the mountain and found myself on the asphalt road that lead to Altınözü district. I quickly walked on the hundreds-of-year-old pathway between the two mountains and looked at the magestic view of the Iron Gate, its impressive architecture and how contemporary, strong and magnificent it looked even though it was constructed one thousand and five hundred years ago.

The Iron Gate, "Bab Al-Hadid," as the name stated on the picture I brought with me from the walls of Nikola's apartment, pulled me to itself with a weird feeling of curiosity that came from inside me, whose reason I could not understand. I was looking at the structure with interest, curiosity and fear I couldn't quite understand, approaching the magnificent structure, which seemed different with each step I took. I knew that this magnificent structure, which took an important place in the life of Nikola, could be a significnat tool for us to reach these young people we were searching for – and I was unreasonably afraid of it.

"If you want to find it, you must search for it."

29. O THEOPHILUS

O Theophilus,

By looking at, thinking and understanding the Father, the Son, who bless this city that I was born in, raised; and the Holy Spirit that has fallen upon us; we set aside all sides in us that we see privileged, significant or superior; just like He taught us.

O Theophilus,

I work as a physician in order to sustain my life and I work non-stop by adding my night to the day so that many patients can achieve health. I am happily watching the healing of a baby with a fever, a woman with a headache or an elderly with chest pain, after the treatments and recommendations I give; and the moment I see their happy faces, I understand how I love this profession even more, I see myself important as someone privileged. Here I can remove this profession that I love very much as well as all the privileges it provides to me, and that is an important feature that each of us have sincerely learned, just like He taught us.

O Theophilus,

We know that we are rid of all evil thoughts, become more fair, will never steer away from the truth until the ends of our lives with each knowledge we listened to, believed and engraved in out hearts from Peter, Barnabas, John and Paul in Antioch; and despite this unbreakable power we reached, all of us also know that we could be destroyed with the smallest blow of Him, we try not to live wrongly and try not to harm, not even unintentionally, anyone - no plants, insects, birds or even ants; just like He taught us.

O Theophilus,

The precious believer and beloved of God; I quickly wrote what you have learned on the life of Christ from the first book I wrote for you, and then on the Acts of the Apostles I wrote later; starting the the first day it was being told me, without waiting. It didn't matter whether it was night or day; I learned lessons from each incident I saw, listened to, and experienced myself; I wrote them for you, and wished that what I have written would be transferred forever, from one generation to another; just as He wanted.

O Theophilus,

We, all believers, have seen the grail used by the Son, that Peter brought to Antioch; drunk the strong, healing water inside that was more effective than all medicines that could be developed for centuries. I keep that Holy Grail and I will keep it as long as I live; it will remain forever in this city, in Antioch and when it's found, it will continue to bless the Stauris Mountain, its cave, Silpius Mountain, Parmenius River and everyone who lives here even if centuries have passed; just as He wanted.

O Theophilus,

You also know that an Ark is being talked about, that is lost for centuries, and that it was brought to Antioch, the city we live in. I feel and believe that the Lost Ark is somewhere around here. One day, when the day comes, when the time is up, we believe that a believer will most definitely find that Ark in this city; perhaps in a cave in this city, perhaps on mountain peaks, perhaps near a riverbed; just like He made us believe.

O Theophilus,

I'm the man you know, and know very well even. Luke is my name, I'm a physician from Antioch; I am Paul's friend and companion; I am a constant companion of his journeys. I am the author of what I see, what I listen to, and all that Peter and Paul speak of; just as they teach, tell, and believe.

30. IF YOU WANT TO FIND IT, YOU MUST SEARCH FOR IT…

I looked at the shiny rocks of the pathway that were flattened due to being walked on for centuries, at narrow passageways between the rocks and at the walls that could survive centuries, standing from the very peaks of Silpius Mountain to the plain. I thought of all living creatures that walked on this pathway for thousands of years; traders, clergymen, caravans, Crusaders, camels and horses carrying loads. I was so close to the Iron Gate, which stood right across me and has been standing there for one thousand and five hundred years. The structure, built with the joint efforts of thousands of people with the aim to control the crazy waters of the Parmenius River and to be a bridge between the Silpius and Stauris Mountains, looked magnificent.

This place was the largest of the four Gates opening to ancient Antioch, and I knew that there was an iron gate there that doesn't exist today, that one could enter the city through this gate and that armed guards stood watch all day in this passage called the Iron Gate, *Bab Al-Hadid* in Arabic. I also knew that the people, camels, horses, donkeys, sheep and goats passing this gate were counted and the prepared reports were sent to the architect of the Iron Gate, Justinian – even that a tax was received from these entrances and exits.

This city protected its mystery, magnificence and significance against great fires, floods, raids, occupations, pandemics and eighteen great earthquakes. I thought that the city was similar to a strong queen, who insisted on living and not falling, not dying against continuous damage, betrayals, strangling and torture: "Orientis apicem pulcrum…" As it was called on the magnificent ancient days: "The Queen of the East…"

I continued to walk, trying to get away from worrisome thoughts, and approached the massive dam/bridge through the narrow pathway next to the Iron Gate. When I looked down from the structure I climbed on top of, I felt my head spnning and my feet numbing; it was very, very high and I thought with chills that if someone fell from that height, he/she would have no chance of living, that all bones on his/her body would be broken to pieces. A small, wrong step taken towards the gap in front of that one-meter wide place I was standing on, a short fall on the flat white rocks of the Parmenius River right below the high structure, the body hitting the rocks, bones shattering to pieces, the last breath, and the inevitable end... I had chills. I felt cold drops of sweat flowing from my back.

I walked towards the Stauris Mountain over the Iron Gate. Walking on the pathway reaching downwards from the mountain, I reached the very bottom of the giant dam. The Parmenius River, which was filled with the water flowing from the mountains, was dry as desert; there was no water in the riverbed except small puddles.

As I approached the very bottom of the Iron Gate, I retreated and moved away from the giant structure in order to escape an intensely disturbing stench, which increased gradually and made breathing very difficult. I stood at a distance the stench decreased and there, I could see a dark and deep space in the middle section of the one-thousand-and-five-hundred-year-old structure, where it met the riverbed. The bricks and rocks making up the wall of the lower sections of the place, where the structure intersected with the riverbed, fell and a dark cave was formed that was about three meters wide. I couldn't calculate the depth of the pit.

I took a deep breath and filled my lungs with air; then hurried with a fast run towards the dark hollow under the Iron Gate. When I was right in front of it, I paused for a moment and I entered the dark cave. I held my breath and understood that this dark hollow was the place where the stench was emerging from. I waited a bit so my eyes could get used to the darkness. I took two steps forward and right then, I was about to fall on a smooth, heavy object - I saved myself the last minute.

I took out the lighter from the pocket of my pants, leaned towards the object that almost tripped me and I screamed wildly with the incredible fear and terror I felt from what I saw; I walked back with difficulty, got out of the cave under the giant structure, turned my back and started running unconsciously on the dried river bed. I was screaming and crying frivolous words. Soon after, I was able to perceive the situation I was in and stopped, kneeled, put my forehead on the dry riverbed and burst into tears. It was the body of Gizem that started to stink, which I found in the cave at the bottom of the Iron Gate. It was unfortunately the source of the stench that consumed all my hopes.

Although I was sure that the corpse in the dark place belonged to Gizem, with the pale face and matted eyes I could see for a very short time, I decided to re-enter the dark pit with the slightest hope I had left. I stood up, wiped my tears with my hand and started walking into the dark pit with my shaky legs. My soul was shattered, I felt a pang of grief; I was destroyed, crushed.

I was no longer disturbed by the odor, which increased in severity as I approached the cave-like cavity; I crouched as I entered the pit, grabbed the body from the armpits, dragged it out, and left it on the white rocks in the riverbed, which were flattened by the waters flowing from high above. I looked at her face, at her hair, her clothes I recognised, her shoes. It was Gizem, unfortunately the body that began to rot and stink belonged to Gizem. I started crying again; I could not believe it, I could not believe anything in any way and the sad point we were at.

As soon as I saw the corner of the white paper, that came out of the front pocket of her jeans, I pulled it out and put it in my left pocket. I took out my phone and dialed the number without hesitation; but there was no answer. I called over and over again... I insisted on calling and the moment there was an answer, I told Dimitri everything without a pause... I told him everything – everything I was through and the point we were at. With my destroyed and crushed soul, I tried to explain to him where I was. With my incredible hopelessness, I asked him not to call Solmaz or not tell her anything if they speak. Then I sat on the ledge of a rock that stretched towards the riverbed, a few meters away from Gizem; staring at the dead body lying across me.

I turned my gaze upwards from the bed of the Parmenius River, looking at the asymmetrical posture of Gizem's body, the image that revealed all her bones broken even under her clothes, with her bruised hands, arms and face. I looked at the giant Iron Gate, almost twenty meters high, and the path lying on the cut stones and bricks that stretched between the two mountains. I could understand that all the bones of anyone falling from this height would be shattered, and every time I looked at Gizem's body, I could perceive it with the asymmetrical posture of her arms and legs.

It was possible to fall from such a height as a result of a simple mistake, for example, a step taken incorrectly, or a small dizziness, foot slip, darkening of the eyes.

* * *

About an hour after I found the body of Gizem and called Dimitri, I saw the crowd convoy approaching us and I couldn't get up. I sat on the rock without moving as the police, gendarmerie and a few others dressed in civil outfits – one woman and three others I thought were museum officers - descended carefully towards the riverbed.

I saw the officers looking at the dead body of Gizem, whose bones were shattered, with pity in their eyes. They searched the areas I showed, where I found the body, at the dark pit, everywhere around the Iron Gate, on the paths we walked, around the stones, under the rocks, in the bushes, in the areas hidden by the grass – unfortunately, they couldn't find anything.

They placed the dead of Gizem in a corpse bag, pulled the zipper and started walking along the path they came from, holding the bag on each end. Four people were carrying the corpse bag, walking with sadness along the ancient path.

I wasn't aware of anything – neither the Forensic Medicine Institute we waited in front of during the autopsy, the Public Prosecutor's Office we went to testify, the asphalt street we drove back home through, nor the pavements and anyone else on the streets. I couldn't gather my thoughts. I felt weak, insufficient and lonely as someone poor who lost his emotions and can't know what or who he was. We threw ourselves on the chairs next to the fountain in the courtyard, as soon as we got back home.

I thought of what I should do. How could I tell Solmaz about this situation! How could I tell her that her sister was dead, that she had fallen over an old high structure on a riverbed that had dried up, maybe she had been even been thrown off, that I found her corpse with all bones of her body crushed and the things that happened afterwards!

It was one of my desperate and weak moments that I wished that never happened, that even when I was aware that it was indeed happening, I wished that I was having a bad nightmare and escape it by waking up. I wanted to wake up, get away from the nightmare I was having and get rid of that torment.

After the autopsy, they did not give us back her clothes, phone, money, identity card and any other similar belongings. They told us that they will examine them for a while and I quietly listened to the person, who told us that they could give us back all her belongings after the pathology, toxicology and other work I couldn't understand. I looked at their faces, dazzled, without understanding what they were telling me, as they told us that they will hand us all her belongings in case nothing suspicious comes out from the autopsy report.

I asked Dimitri what we should do. He was also destroyed; he looked at me with a crushed, sad and fearful expression. I could understand that he was trying to hide his fear that his brother might have experienced the same end.

I saw a small cloud of hope passing over Dimitri's face when the officers, who searched seriously and meticulously all over the void where I found the body of Gizem, the Iron Gate, in the surrounding caves, hollows, under the trees and bushes, could not find anything related to Nikola.

He told me that he did not know what to do and he moved his eyes in the dark corners of the courtyard, where he hadn't lit a lamp despite the darkening weather. I reluctantly extended my hand to my phone and pressed the screen with fear; and I quickly pressed the off button the moment I heard the uniform-toned voice, telling me that the person I was trying to reach was unreachable or her phone was off. If I called again, I knew it was possible to reach; whereas I did not call, I called once and fulfilled my duty. If Solmaz was to answer the phone, what could I tell her? How could I explain to her what happened?

It was almost half past ten, I stood up to get to my room and asked Dimitri to not answer in case Solmaz called him and to let me know right away. As I climbed the steps of the ladder rising towards the room, I took out my phone from my pocket and turned it off; I was not feeling like I had the emotional and spiritual maturity to explain or speak about what happened with the woman I loved.

I entered the room, put my hand in my pocket and I was startled. My hand had touched the folded white paper that I took from Gizem's pocket, and I completely had forgotten it. I sat on the edge of the bed, opened the folded paper and looked at it for a while... I just looked at it; I did not read, I could not read. I did not know what to expect if I did read it, and I did not want to be shaken once again with a new kind of pain.

I waited a short while, and then I opened the folded paper, thinking "let it happen." I knew Gizem's unique and beautiful handwriting, but what I read didn't belong to her.

You will find it in the holes,

Of the cracked walls,

Of the destroyed temple;

If you want to find it, you must search for it.

I knew the last sentence from the writings he hung on the walls of his apartment; it was Nikola's handwriting, I continued reading:

You will surely find it,

In the great void

Of the cave in the middle

Right above the temple,

I read it a few more times. It was a poetic narrative, and I felt that it contained a password, hid what it wanted to tell in between words, and that there could be separate meanings in sentences. I thought but could not reach a meaningful conclusion.

I put all the pictures, posters and writings that I had taken from the apartment of the owner of the handwriting in Ankara; I compared the handwriting, I read everything several more times; I tried to make a connection between them and the last poetic narrative I've found. I closed my eyes and thought about all the sentences written by Nikola in handwriting, and forced myself to understand, to make new meanings, and to solve the secret codes that I thought existed. I stopped at a moment when I focused on the meaning of the writings and the connections between them, I opened my eyes and I solved the mystery of the narrative right then.

I now knew what to do and where to go. I gathered all the writings on the bed, put them in a bag and laid on my bed to get rid of the fatigue collapsing on me and the exhaustion of my soul. I tried to sleep, I turned around but could not sleep for a long time. It was hot, very hot…

* * *

I woke up from my uncomfortable sleep, I was sweaty, my entire body, my hair, and even the pillow I put on my head were wet. I looked at my watch, it was approaching three. "It's time," I said to myself, "You have to go, and complete the job you have left incomplete."

I quickly got out of bed, entered the bathroom, washed my hand and face, tried to get rid of the sluggish effects of the nightmares I saw. I looked in the mirror above the sink and I was even more disturbed by the shabby look of my face reflected from the mirror. I turned off the light in the room, and as I did a few days ago, I quietly went down the steps. I went out of the house, started the car and drove without any hurry towards the place I have to go, reach, search and find, no matter what, through the history-smelling streets of the city, that was thousands of years old.

I did not feel well, I constantly thought of Solmaz and I was almost drunk with the lack of sleep. I couldn't think straight and I had ridiculous thoughts.

I wanted to remain under the dust of the road on the street I was driving, walking on, remaining there forever. I wanted to disappear inside my clothes, not be remembered and be erased as much as possible. I just wanted to remember the moments I couldn't erase Solmaz from my heart. I wanted to disappear in the hours of the days, that were like Solmaz. I didn't want to live the moments, when she erased me from her heart, and I wanted to increase the time I could walk with her.

Could it be? Could I protect the woman I love from the spears of misfortune when she wasn't there, as I missed her like crazy, in her white clothes, that fit her perfectly?

Could you heal our losses, my love, our pain, any day, the love that looked like you, our memories, the moments when you said you will never erase my name, our souls you were going to heal, our selves, our wounds?

Love, my love, you must throw everything aside – the moments you put me out like a candle, the minutes I waited, the pouring rain, everything – and you must return to me in the moments I miss you... I miss you...

What could I tell you? How could I answer any of your questions? How could you understand what I tell you?

I was talking to myself and talking nonsense, it was really nonsense, and I was doing it intentionally. I forced myself to push away, throw aside and destroy all ridiculous and meaningless thoughts.

At the intersection of the street with another street, I approached to the right side of the road and stopped. I looked at the minaret of the mosque I saw on the left, opened the car door, got off the car, locked it and walked towards the temple of the centuries, "Dear carpenter, Habib al-Najjar, are you comfortable where you're lying?" I asked in a whisper.

I entered through the stone gate of the once pagan temple, the old men sitting in the courtyard looked at my face, and I looked back at their faces; I walked without waiting, I walked towards the tombs in the rooms that smelled musty. A cool wind blew suddenly in the warm courtyard, I reached the graves, "Are you here?" I asked. "We're here," said John, Paul, and Peter, whom I could not believe. Leaving the illusion, nonsense and hallucinations I experienced, I escaped to the courtyard again.

I passed through the carved stones and steep walls of the centuries-old pagan temple, then church and now mosque. Without looking at the old men sitting under the small windows, I went back on the street and headed home.

I opened the door of the house, walked quietly and entered Nikola's room. For a moment I felt that my head was spinning and my stomach was nauseous. Trying not to fall, I sat on the floor and tried to breathe deeply, I could not stand the feeling so I fully stretched myself on the floor. I couldn't understand what was happening to me, I wasn't well at all. Soon I got upright and looked at Nikola's backpack at the corner of the room. I took the bag and poured everything inside it on the hand-woven rug on the floor. What I was going through was a complete revolt, similar to the feelings that would be experienced in a big riot. It was a deep rebellion that I felt against me finding the dead body of the beautiful and crazy Gizem, whom I loved so, not being able to do anything about it.

I looked around Nikola's room once more, went out with his backpack and entered the room right next to his, in the room where Gizem stayed. The room smelled of Gizem - of jasmine, daffodils and cloves; of youth and madness. The scent of the room was far from the stench of the corpse I found during the day, the rotten human scent and the inexorable, heavy and hard-to-breathe scents of hell. I thought about the smiling face of Gizem and said, "Charon," inside. "Don't take her, don't bother, you will not be able to get her, your ways are not the same." The Hell Boatman did not respond to me, at that moment I thought he continued rowing in the underground rivers.

I wanted to forget what I experienced didn't want to experience, everything negative I could not understand or perceive; I was at the apex of emotionality and I didn't care about any kind of reality. I looked around the room where Gizem stayed, the bed where she slept, the clothes that were left there as she put them - I looked at them and cried. I wiped my flowing tears with my hand. I always remembered the first time I saw her dead body and the weight was becoming increasingly difficult to carry. I meaninglessly thought how much I wished I never found Gizem's dead body, I knew that I couldn't think healthy. I wasn't well at all – I cried without stopping, sobbing, forcing myself not to make a lot of sound.

I meaninglessly looked at the walls and had to quickly sit on the sofa next to me, I took a deep breath and forced myself to stand up. I wanted to stand up, walk, run, search, find, shout and scream but I couldn't – I couldn't do anything…

It was a night that was dark and cool, which made me feel my loneliness even deeper. I was going to go to the carved face of Charon on the mountain, look at his non-face, and climb the cold rocks of Stauris Mountain.

I must not have been caught in the mess of the dark and the pitch-black rocks; I must not have get caught in the pitch-black treachery of dark nightmares and burrows.

Neither the streets of the ancient city, nor the structure of the old pagan temple next to the street, converted into a church and then into a mosque - none of them could tell me anything.

In the moments when I longed for my days that I could breathe comfortably and smoothly, I stretched my hands and tried to atch a life that was calm, content, happy and full of beauty. I couldn't grab it, hold it – I couldn't hold onto life.

Without caring about anything, I went back out of Dimitri's house and drove through the streets of the city, which smelled of history, mold and moisture; slowly, trying not to make too much noise. I parked the car far from the cave church, I got out of the car and walked fast towards the harsh cliffs of Stauris Mountain.

What I experienced was a ritual; I wanted to believe them, not to deny them, not be silly and be rid of all negativity.

Everything that happened were like a ritual; the paths I walked on, the caves, walls, giant structures, dark recesses, regular cavities – they were like important rooms of the temple, where the ritual was organized.

I threw my brain aside, full of confused, blurred and pointless thoughts; I forced myself to forget all the pain I've been through and threw away my being and memory, to places far from me, like a dry leaf.

It was right in front of me, Stauris; We glanced at each other, smiled at each other and I quickly started to climb it… I softly caressed the rocks, stones, trees of the mountain. I looked at the deep hole I saw in a hidden place of the mountain where I climbed and started walking and tried to illuminate the dark space with the lantern in my hand; The fig, plum, oak and juniper trees that suddenly enlightened looked quite magnificent; I tried to perceive the life struggles and power of development of trees that can reach such a size in such a cave-pit,

I stood on the Stauris Mountain, looked at Silpius Mountain right across it and its walls extending into the deep valley. I thought about the important functions that the walls protecting the city have undertaken for centuries; I tried to imagine the days when the city resisted the Crusader Army for two hundred days under its siege and finally failed as a result of betrayal.

Standing on the cliffs right above the church cave, I looked at the city for the last time, without worrying about the bushes and thorns stinging my legs. I let myself flow with the Orontes flowing right in the middle, as I flew a river bed; without aring about the rocks, bushes and trees of the flat mountain.

Rocks rolling from a collapsed, cracked mountain were looking at my face. I looked at all of them; I did not care about rocks that broke, shattered and rolled into the gaps below. My thoughts were blurred, now I wanted to get rid of all my crises and chaos.

* * *

I sat at the top of the Stauris Mountain, at the far end of the steep cliffs that extended to the cave-church below. Taking deep breaths, I forced myself to calm down and think more correctly, more healthily. I looked down from where I was sitting, to the steps of the stairs of the church, to the garden, to the parking lot, and to the massive rock masses scattered all over the place. I knew very well that I could roll down with a piece of rock that could break off at any moment from where I was sitting and that I wouldn't even have the slightest chance to survive if that happened. I thought and shuddered. Without losing time, I must have gone down from the steep cliffs into the gap in front of the cave, which I could see below, enter the cave-church and continue my search.

I knew that this would not be like the mountain climbs on touristic trips I have been to before. I stood up from where I was sitting and started to descend slowly from the steep cliffs. I was paying attention to everywhere I stepped and grabbed, trying to descend without haste towards the wide gap I could see below. This time I was determined, I was going to complete the work I could not complete in my previous trial and I would enter the church no matter what happened; I wanted to enter and find what I was looking for.

I quickly completed the last few meters and reached the space in front of the cave, taking a deep breath. The security guard of the church wasn't around. I hoped he was deep asleep. I walked towards the entrance of the St. Peter's Church without losing time. I held the small flashlight that I attached to my belt and scanned all over the place; I illuminated the ceiling, the floor, the sculpture of Peter, the stone throne, everywhere inside the church with the flashlight in my hand.

I took a few steps, walked to the middle of the cave and stopped suddenly with a startle; it stinked terrible, I shivered, felt sore, stayed where I was and tried not to move. The smell was terrible and heavy, much like the stench at the place I found Gizem. I tried to get rid of all negative thoughts that came to my mind.

I knew the inside of the cave-churh from the pictures I saw at Nikol's house. There must have been a tunnel here. I took another step or two towards the heavy, rotten smell and tried to find the entrance of the tunnel by illuminating the walls with the flashlight. I found it and walked in fear, stood right at the entrance; I was afraid of entering the tunnel, the increasing heaviness of the rotten stench was making my stomach sick and I was trying hard not to vomit. I knew I would not be able to stand for a second and run without looking back if I was not determined.

I forced myself into the tunnel and two meters from the entrance of the corridor, I encountered the bruised corpse of a young man with long hair and beard, sitting on the ground and resting his back on the wall of the tunnel. It started to rot and stink. I scared myself with my own scream and quickly got out of the tunnel.

It was heavy. This last incident was really heavy now. What I was going through were much worse and scarier than the nightmares I've had for years. "My God," I said to myself. "You shouldn't have let me go through these, what wrong have I done that you punish me like this?" After a short moment of hesitation, I entered the dark tunnel again with determination.

Nikola's body was weird – without the heavy, rotten stench, one could think he was resting, sitting on the ground of the tunnel with his back on the wall. He was holding an empty box of antidepressants. I quickly went through his pockets. The stench was becoming more and more unbearable. I found a blue hairclip in the left pocket of his jeans – it was Gizem's. I found a folded white paper on his right pocket, I took it with me and I threw myself outside the tunnel of the centuries, to the cavity of the cave-church, after forcing myself not to faint. I walked towards the garden outside the cave and the moment I reached there, I filled my lungs with the fresh, cool air.

I sat right in front of the temple of thousands of years, I looked at the blue hairclip that I held in my left hand, I thought of Gizem. I remembered the moment when Gizem looked and smiled angrily as soon as Nikola mischievously smiled and took the blue hairclip off her hair. I thought about the point we were at, a few days after those hours, when we were all happy. Unhappiness aside; I thought of our pitiful state, we had collapsed, scattered and were inside inexorable disasters. Could life suddenly slip like this from our hands?

I put the blue hairclip in my pocket and looked at the folded white paper I held in my hand. I opened it slowly, not knowing what I was doing, seeing Nikola's handwriting I now recognized. It was written in two separate sections, one four and the other six lines. I tried to read it. All the letters looked blurry,

I wiped the tears in my eyes, tried to calm myself, tried to perceive the situation I was in and tried again to read and understand what was written on the paper.

You will find it in the holes,
Of the cracked walls,
Of the destroyed temple;
If you want to find it, you must search for it.

I knew I had read them before. I started reading the other lines quickly. I was hoping to find new sentences.

You will surely find it,
In the great void
Of the cave in the middle
Right above the temple,
Where it waited for two thousand years,
If you want to find it, you must search for it.

It was the same. What was written on this paper were the same sentences I read on the paper I found in Gizem's pocket. Now I could better understand the meaning of the lines I memorized and I knew very well what I had to do.

In all the paintings he hung around his apartment, Nikola tried to give secret messages to those who could understand. He had hung pictures of the Iron Gate, St. Peter's Church, the interior of the church and the tunnel inside, everywhere around his apartment – and the moments when I found the corpses that began to rot in the places depicted in these pictures were unfortunately the moments when the worst disasters of our lives have begun.

I now knew that Nikola, who gave mysterious messages with pictures, posters and writings he hung on all the walls of his apartment; insisted on trying to explain something, a place, repeating it twice with the ten-verse writings I found in his and Gizem's pockets. I thought about it. "If you want to find it, you must search for it." Yes, now I wanted to search for it and find it, so I had to.

I looked at the paper in my hand and read the first three verses once again: "You will find it in the holes / Of the cracked walls / Of the destroyed temple."

I raised my head and looked at the upright, cracked and destroyed body of Stauris Mountain that stretched into the dark sky. I looked at the cavities, gaps, pits and monk burrows seen in the upper parts of the sacred cave of the mountain. Nikola was writing about here, I no longer had any doubts. I would find it in the holes of the cracked walls of the destroyed temple... "The destroyed temple" was the St. Peter's Church itself.

I re-read the first five verses of the second part of six strings with great curiosity in my heart. "You will surely find it / In the great void / Of the cave in the middle / Right above the temple / Where it waited for two thousand years."

I finally understood; I was now able to perceive the secret information the verses were trying to explain, which I couldn't make any sense of when I first read them. I stood up without waiting and forced myself to climb up, move, reach and find by grabbing the steep cliffs, cavities, pits, plants and trees of the mountain I descended to. I climbed quickly and non-stop. I proceeded to the caves described in the ten-verse poem. I didn't even care about the jagged rocks hitting my knees, thorns stinging my arms, shrubs, bushes, vines and stones scraping the skin of my hand.

I reached the caves above the church and threw myself into the deep hole that I expected to be right in the middle and then made sure it was there. I sat on the plain at the entrance of the cave. I needed to rest. My heart was beating like crazy; I needed rest and to calm down, with my heart and my whole self.

It was a monk cave where I was waiting; It was one of the places where you could perceive the moment you experienced; you could understand what that moment was, how and where you were – with the moments that were slow and rid of all haste. It carried the evil moments of nightmares I didn't even want to see in the last moments of my life, which could stop my heard with crises; I didn't even want to breathe in the winds of this place.

"God," I said, speaking loudly and listening to the echo of my voice in the cavity of the cave. "God, what are these? The destroyed mountain, rolling rocks, cracked walls, what are these? Isn't it enough that I haven't been sleeping well for years, with the nightmares you showed me? My sleep, which turned into a brutal torture, the suffering you put me through – isn't it enough? What do you want from me? I stopped, rested, and waited for my heart palpitations to rest.

I was in the cave Nikola described; I wanted to find it, so I was going to search for it. I took out the flashlight in my pocket and turned my back to the city where thousands of lamps burned, touched its button and looked at the light reflected on the walls of the monk cave. I crawled forward, looked at the invisible cracks of the sacred mountain cave. I reached forth with my shaking hand, towards the brown scroll, that the flashlight in my hand illuminated. I touched it, caressed its texture, which was hard and soft at the same time. I grabbed it and pulled it slowly towards me. It felt as if it was going to fall apart and turn into dust if I forced it.

Without releasing the part I was holding, I put my other hand down the enlarged hole of the monk cave and the moment I understood that I reached the very bottom, I pressed it upwards and I took out the entire scrolls, which were bound in the shape of a cross. I sat down and took the previous treasure that I removed from the crack in the mountain. My hands were shaking, I could not touch it. I just looked at it; it seemed as if the parchments were covered with a thin layer of wax, it was clear that they had been treated recently.

I looked at it fearfully, I could not touch it; it felt like everything would suddenly dissolve, turn into dust and fly around the holes of the cave if I tried to touch it and untie the leather strings binding the scroll.

I couldn't touch it; I grabbed the flashlight and looked at the two Greek words, which were visible at the very top of the scroll, which I could barely illuminate. I tried to read it, understand it and perceive it. There were two words, written in capital letters.

I read: "*O Theophilus!*"

31. DEAR MR THEOPHILUS

O Theophilus,

My dear brother who "loves God", all the events and experiences I have described in the two previous books I have written to you are correct from start to finish. You must believe all of the things this physician from Antioch - who is living a simple, self-contained, small and simple life - says.

"Mr Theophilus,

*Many people attempted to write the history of what happened between us. Indeed, the witnesses of these events and servants of the word of God from the beginning conveyed them to us. As someone who has carefully studied all these events from the beginning, I found it appropriate to write them to you in order. So that you know the accuracy of the information given to you."**

The first two books I wrote to you will reach out to you as soon as possible. Read it, understand it and tell everyone you know and do not know about it.

The third book, which I continue to write, addressed to you, will never reach out to you, and you will not be able to read it. I am now dedicating all my remaining time from my hours as a physician to this book.

This third and last book that I write will be very different from my first book, in which I spoke about the experiences, miracles, suffering and advice of the Holy Son; as well as the second book, in which I wrote about the Acts of the Apostles filled with the Holy Spirit.

My writings will be embroidered on the skin of the beautiful gazelles living in the mountains of Antioch. I hope for these gazelles to live thousands of years more, continue their species and never disappear.

**Luke's Bible, 1*

O Theophilus,

When I complete this book, which I am currently writing - before I wrap it, I will also place that valuable relic among the scrolls. I will also place the mug, brought by Peter from Jerusalem in the previous evening of the day Christ was crucified, used by Christ with his last disciples and first students, touched his lips, and which was entrusted to me by Cephas to protect it. I will place it inside, wrap it up and hide it in a hidden place in one of the caves in the upper parts of the church on Stauris Mountain, perhaps in a crack formed on the mountain.

O Theophilus,

I am a physician from Antioch and a lonely man. I will put the item that was entrusted to me to protect and preserve in an iron box and thus follow Peter's request, who wants it to stay in Antioch for centuries, and perhaps make it found by good people, who will possess the power to take every precaution to avoid it being taken away from this city thousands of years later when it is found.

O Theophilus,

My dear brother who loves God. People may experience pain, suffering, earthquakes, fires, sieges, invasions and wars. We must not give up against any difficulty that we may experience and should not leave the right path that we believe in.

You know as well as I do, that the more the bow stretches, the further the arrow can go; that the blind darkness of the night is always greeted by the bright day, and that good can come out of the bad. You live, believing in it.

32. YOU MAY FIND IT IF YOU SEARCH FOR IT

My heart was pounding, I was breathless. I was trying to perceive the importance and value of the scrolls I found. I untied the buttons of my shirt and placed the scrolls on my chest. I could not climb the steep rocks of the mountain with the scrolls in my hand.

I started climbing without trying to hold on the wrong place and without hurrying upward from the monk caves of Stauris Mountain. It could lead to huge turmoil and unresolvable mysteries if the security guard saw me or if my dead body was found with a historical treasure on my chest in case my life ended on the jagged rocks with one foot slip, on top of the dead body of Nikola that will be found in the tunnel inside St. Peter's Church.

I was sweating, but I continued climbing with more careful, slower movements. I skillfully stepped on the ridges of the rocks; I paid attention that the plant stems I was holding were strong with deep roots. I placed my fingers inside the rock gaps with the right technique and I was finally done climbing. I took out the scroll that I placed on my chest, took it in my hand and started walking on the hills of Stauris Mountain. I descended towards the construction of the Antakya Museum, whose lights I saw from the top of the mountain. I finally could go over the car through a road that could be a good hiking route, with its hills and pathways. I did it; I was able to complete everything I had to do without getting caught, being seen or suffering an accident.

I carefully placed the scrolls in the backpack in the trunk and drove the car along the dark and deserted street, carefully leaving them on the seat next to me.

I entered the house with the backpack I had in my hand. Dimitri wasn't awake yet. I took a deep breath in the courtyard with no one there; whereas this instant relief was meaningless… Because I had to talk to him as soon as possible. But how could I tell him all I had done, and that I found his brother's dead body inside the cave church tunnel! How could I say that! How could I explain to Dimitri, even if not him, to the police, to the gendarmerie, to the prosecutor - the complicated connections of the man who found the dead body of Gizem in a pit at the bottom of the Iron Gate the day before?

I climbed up the stairs, entered my room and locked the door. I left my backpack on the bed with care and I went into the bathroom, undressed, washed myself, and washed, and washed… I wanted to purify myself, my brain, my soul and clean them, remove the pain I had recently experienced.

I got out of the shower, put the backpack I left on the bed in the corner of one of the shelves of the wardrobe; I closed the wardrobe door and threw my tired body on the bed. I was feeling exhausted, destroyed and helpless. If I could, I would sleep for hours. I closed my eyes, forced myself to calm my collapsed and broken soul; I tried not to think about the recent events and to expel all difficulties from my brain. I fell asleep…

I could hear the sound of a regular ticking of metal on the windows. I forced myself to open my eyes. Trying to understand how long I slept, I listened to the sound of the tap on the room window; I quickly got out of bed, opened the curtain and saw the sad face of Dimitri behind the window. He said, with a tired tone, that it was late and he was worried about me because I still didn't wake up. I said I was about to come down.

How could I explain… How could I tell him that I found Nikola's body and how could I complete this difficult, complex and painful task… I was thinking, forcing myself, but I couldn't find a suitable and easy way. I quickly got dressed, took the backpack in the closet and went down to the courtyard. I sat on the chair opposite my silent and sad friend sitting next to the small fountain. He looked at my face and never spoke. I knew that he was waiting for me to start speaking. I started talking without waiting, thinking, without even needing an introduction…

I said, "Nikola is in St. Peter's Church, Dimitri." He did not understand, could not understand; he initially could not perceive what the sentence meant, the sentence I said as if it was anything ordinary. His face took an expression that he didn't believe it, then he looked at me... Without waiting for him to ask any questions, I told him about everything I did and everywhere I went – except the scrolls I found - during the night, as he was sleeping.

I painfully listened to the screams of Dimitri for his only relative in life, his brother Nikola, which lasted for minutes. Only when he calmed down and became able to talk and understand what I was saying, I stood up, went to the car, left the backpack I took with me in the trunk and quickly went to the police station where we previously reported Nikola missing.

It took about one and a half hours for all nevessary notifications to be made and for all relevant people to come together. All officers, Dimitri and I met in front of St. Peter's Church. Ensuring security in the dangerous area, where the rocks have rolled down, warned their colleagues working on top of the mountain and we went inside the church cave, led by the Public Prosecutor.

We approached the tunnel and, as I saw at night, we saw the corpse of Nikola, whose back rests against the wall of the tunnel, sitting as if he was resting. I took Dimitri out of the cave with difficulty, as he started to cry and shout. I tried to whisper him words to calm him down; it was meaningless, everything I was trying to do was meaningless, it was of no use – and Dimitri couldn't recover for a long time.

After a while, I heard that the prosecutor, who went out, called the security guards, and when he was talking to them, he ordered the court clerk next to him write something down. We quietly watched the officers who did the work to be done without any rush and we set off with the convoy.

We waited for the autopsy to end, sitting on the benches standing against the walls of the small and gloomy waiting area in front of the morgue hall of Antakya Training and Research Hospital. The face of the young prosecutor, who came out of the autopsy room at the end of the minutes that felt very long and overwhelmed our soul, was quite anxious and sulky. They knew each other, so he approached Dimitri with this intimacy, wished him condolences and invited us to the courthouse building.

Afterwards, he said that there was an important topic he needs to talk about and quickly left us. We looked at each other and stood up without wasting time. When we reached the new courthouse built outside the city, I helped Dimitri get out of the car by taking him from the arm, he was having trouble standing. I also supported him walking.

While we were waiting in front of the door of the Prosecutor's room, I thought I wanted to call Solmaz - call her immediately to Antakya and share all the heavy loads I had difficulty carrying alone. I took my phone out of my pocket, touched the keys, and listened to the metallic sound of the same uniform voice that said the phone I was calling was off or out of reach. I couldn't understand why and the moment we were going to try calling again, we were called in the Prosecutor's room.

The young Prosecutor greeted us standing, he showed he seats across his desk and sat in his own seat without waiting for us to sit. He was lookign at us with a sulky and extremely worried facial expression, which made me understand that he was thinking of how to start the conversation, what to say and how much information to give. He told the young clerk sitting at the computer next to the desk to leave us alone and the moment she left, the Prosecutor started speaking in a low volume. He was almost whispering.

"I actually wanted to speak to you about this yesterday. We wanted to be sure and research into it more; but after we found the same thing on the body of your other relative, it became inevitable that we talked as soon as possible… I have to warn you."

"Warn you!" We did not understand this, and we looked at each other with Dimitri, with expressions that revealed our difficulty to understand the situation. We turned back to the young Prosecutor and waited for him to continue speaking.

"As we were working on the body of the young girl we found at the bottom of the Iron Gate, we were thinking that the incident could be an accident and that it was just a case of falling from a high level. And the cause of death of Nikola Çağlayan today initially seemed like suicide. He was carrying an empty box of medicine. In the careful studies we made in both autopsies, with such thoughts, as well as in the studies of the forensic medicine specialist, unfortunately proved that the causes of their death weren't what we thought and predicted."

He opened his desk drawer and took out two small, transparent bags; they looked like their mouths were tied and sealed. He placed them on top of the papers in front of him. He continued speaking in a way that was careful and he looked like he was trying to not miss anything to tell us. He was trying to choose words, force himself and that's why he sometimes paused.

"We found these identical metal objects stuck in the hearts of both people. Neither incident was caused by an accident, suicide or a similar reason. Unfortunately, we are faced with two separate murders... Gizem Başaran and Nikola Çağlayan were both killed first, then one was thrown from a very high place and the other was left where we found him, with an empty medicine box in his hand, as well as with these thin metals in their hearts."

I was fidgeting to speak and ask a few questions about what he told us, but the young prosecutor raised his hand. He almost said, "Wait a little," to emphasize that he almost came to the most crucial point of his speech.

"The murderer, or murderers, seem to want to say: 'We could Show these deaths like suicide or falling from height but we don't... We leave you with information that can be easily understood in an attentive autopsy; so we announce those who must hear it, that we have committed two murders... Fear us! We challenge all of you!"

The young prosecutor was speaking very precisely and assertive. We waited for a while without waiting. We looked at the identical shiny metal bars, which were about the same fifteen centimeters in length and with ends finely thinned up to five millimeters thick at the tip, inside the transparent bags. White labels were attached to the bags; we paid our full attention to metal bars, regardless of the inscriptions on the labels.

"These two events are changing course now, so you have to be very careful. We may encounter more negative events at any mo-ment, you should immediately report everything you hear or doubt. Now I want to ask you a few important questions: Have you ever received a threat; Do you have any enemies, will-give cases, or people in hostility towards you? It is very important that you give us the answers correctly and completely, so think about it for a while, if you want.

Now that was so much, really too much. The burden to learn that our relatives were killed, when we could not even accept their deaths, was really heavy. Dimitri's voice, that almost sounded like it was coming from a distance, cut the silence in the room.

"I don't know if it makes sense for me to speak about this but I guess I have to," he said. Both the young prosecutor and I looked at his face with worry. "Last year, someone in his forties came to my Office at the museum. He was speaking in a crooked Turkish. It must have been Jul yor August. The man told me that he just wanted to meet me, in his first visit. Then the next day and the following days, he visited me unannounced and I started encountering him on the street of my house – as if it was a coincidence. They all started to disturb me, but I couldn't react. One day, the unannounced guest showed me a newspaper article from his pocket, which depicted the Picture of the skillfully crafted, pure golden Winged Seahorse that was stolen from the museum of another city and was replaced with a fake. Then I immediately understood what he was trying to tell me, what he wanted me to do as well as his continous visits.

First I tried to ask him to leave politely and tell him that he was asking the wrong person to do wrong business. When he started to tell me enthusiastically that even the famous *Mona Lisa* could be stolen a hundred years ago and that the man who kidnapped the *Trojan Treasure* to his country is still remembered by his country with praise; then I could understand his true aim. He was openly and clearly wanting me to replace the originals of the most valuable historical artifacs in Antakya Museum with cheap counterfeits and that we could earn huge sums of money, doing that.

When I found that my polite rejections were insufficient, I kicked him out in a language that he would understand – and I warned him that in case he shows up again, I will inform the police about him. He never came back, but I received threats a few times – I couldn't understand where or whom they came from. A hoarse voice was threatening me and telling me that people close to me were in trouble as well. I didn't take any of those threats seriously and I didn't feel the need to report them anywhere. Now I understand that I should have…"

Dimitri paused for a while, stood up and walked right across the young prosecutor. Bowing, as if he wanted to be approved, he asked, "Mr Prosecutor, could any of the things I said have an importance? Would they be of use to you?" The young Prosecutor didn't say anything – he looked extremely thoughtful and worried. He stood up, opened the door of his room and summoned the clerk girl back.

He told us that what Dimitri just told us are very important and that he has to testify in order to record these statements, make them official and add them in the file. He asked him, with a soft but very confused attitude, to tell us everything he just said, in great detail, without leaving out anything that he might be thinking that they aren't important – including the visit, the offer, and the threat.

As Dimitri was explaining everything fort he clerk to write, slowly and with thinking, I asked the Prosecutor for permission, in a low volume. I told him I had to call my relatives. I looked at the Prosecutor, who approved my request with one nod without speaking, then threw myself out of the room. I was overwhelmed and I started to worry about Solmaz more after what Dimitri just said. I thought of calling Solmaz's parents, but I thought I should be with Dimitri as he was testifying. I could call them later. Then I returned to the Prosecutor's room, knocked on the door and entered the room without speaking.

The young prosecutor took my written statement too. He politely questioned all I did, the plaes I went and the people I met from the first day I came to Antakya, until the last moment of my statement.

I compared the roads, streets, sidewalks we passed on our way back to Dimitri's house with ancient roads and streets; I thought of the two or three thousand years of difference between the ancient streets and the new. I looked at the new streets of today with wide, regular, under and overpasses that provide uninterrupted traffic flow, and then I looked at the ancient road known as "Kurtuluş

Street", which today tries to survive with its narrow, old and history-scented houses, pavements and workplaces. I knew it was the first illuminated street in the world.

I thought of the glorious old years of the city, I tried to revive the years when five hundred thousand people lived here, when it was called the "Queen of the East". I thought of the warrior structure of Antioch, which was destroyed with eighteen great earthquakes, fires, sieges and invasions and was always repaired, resisted against all negativities with determination. I remembered that even the name of the river passing right in the middle of it was "Asi*", which symbolized rebellion, revolt and war.

I turned my head for a moment and looked at Dimitri's face; I forced myself to overcome the despair created by his helpless, tired and desperate image in my soul. I couldn't. We parked the car in its usual place and walked to the door. He took out the keys of his house from his pocket, stretched out his hand to put it in the lock, but we saw it open with the touch of his hand before he could put it in; the door had to be locked, its wing was open. I remembered very well that we locked the door as we left the house, and it was now open with a reason we couldn't understand why.

*Asi [Turkish]: Rebel

We entered the house quickly, without thinking of anything. Everything in the house - the pots in the courtyard, tables and chairs, furnitures in the rooms, under the beds, inside the wardrobes, the oven and the refrigerator in the kitchen were all searched in detail, without any skipping. According to our first observations, nothing was stolen or missing from the house. It is as if those who did this work wanted to say, "We have entered your house, we have searched everywhere and we can re-enter at any time, so be good and do what we ask!"

As I called the young Prosecutor, Dimitri was calling an executive he knew at the Security Directorate. We didn't touch anything. We looked at each other with expressions that meant to say that it was time to tell those brutal murderers, whoever they were, that as two unhappy and angry relatives of two youngsters whose lives were extinguished, we would never be frightened of such mafia-like threats. Difficult and uncertain days were ahead of us.

CHAPTER TWO

33. WHERE ARE YOU SOLMAZ?

The events had moved to a completely different dimension... At the beginning, we were waiting for the two young people to escape with their sudden and great appreciation for each other, to hide and appear soon to say that they wanted to marry each other. Since we found out that these innocent young people became victims of brutal murders, we perceived in pain that we have completely lost them and they disappeared completely from our hands. We were trying to understand where our desperation, which deepened every passing day, was driving us.

Before we could digest and accept these desperate moments, we found out that our house was broken into and this attempt of burglary that also involved a threat and intimidation increased not only our desperation, but also carried us in the middle of a blind fight with the anxiety and fear we experienced.

The police officers arriving at our house smeared black dust all over the place to take fingerprints; and the young Prosecutor informed us that he is uneasy with the recent developments and that he will be protecting us – thinking that we would be glad for his decision. I could understand it from his attitude, which was the proud, arrogant and self-seeing attitude of those who do good and want to announce their deeds.

We turned down his offer to protect us, Dimitri and I; we tried to explain to him, in calmness and with the anger we were trying to suppress, that we could protect ourselves - that these people who brutally murdered our relatives are the same people who broke into our home and that we wanted to face them.

We asked the young prosecutor when we could get Gizem and Nikola and when we could bury them. He told us that this could take a few days, that we have to wait for the pathology and toxicology examinations to be complete, and that everyone has to abide by the rules and the law even if he dislikes them thoroughly as well. We wanted to do everything to bury them as soon as possible so that their souls rested in peace.

The moment the prosecutor and the other officers left the house, I called Solmaz once again. I dialed up her number with fear, wanting her to pick up. I waited a while, then I was frozen, I became quiet…

This wasn't supposed to happen, this couldn't and should have happened. I called Solmaz's mother with a thousand negative thoughts surrounding my mind. When I couldn't get an answer, I called her father's cell phone, but I couldn't hear anything else other than the call signals. I called their house… The phone rang and it rang and then it became quiet. I prayed inside so the thousand negativities in my mind, which I couldn't quite understand, are not true.

I turned and told Dimitri that I couldn't reach Solmaz. I told him that she should have answered to each of my calls for possible information on Gizem, and that she herself should have even called me to receive information from me. I told him that I don't think it's normal that I couldn't reach her by now. Dimitri always asked me what he was supposed to do, with his desperation, and now it was me who was asking him that. I was crazy with desperation, and scared.

I ran across the courtyard and opened the front door. I took the car key out and opened the trunk of the car. It wouldn't be a surprise to me even if I couldn't find the backpack I left there, so I looked at the trunk, but there it was, where I left it… I bent over quickly and felt whether it was still full. It was. I opened it, and yes, there it was. I touched it and felt the soft texture of the leather that was there, waiting for hundreds of years, together with the wax-like structure on it. I took a deep breath, closed it back and then I entered back home as if I carried a regular backpack. Looking at my hectic and meaningless behavior, Dimitri was trying to understand what I was trying to do.

I left the backpack on the table next to the small fountain, stood next to it and stared at it closely. I was still hesitant whether I should tell Dimitri about it or not. I sat across him, without speaking, I took two white notes out of my pant pockets and placed them in front of him. He looked at the folded papers, then he looked at my face. He took one, unfolded and read it, left it back on the table. Then he took the other one, unfolded, read it, and placed it next to the other. He looked at the notes as they were next to each other and when he understood that there was no difference between what was written on the two papers, he stared at me with questioning eyes.

I told him that I found one of the papers in Gizem's pocket an done in Nikola's. I told him that I found Gizem's dead body completely out of coincidence and that I found Nikola based on the clues I had from what was written on the note I found on Gizem's body as well as the pictures I brought back from the walls of the apartment in Ankara.

I then told Dimitri that this is everything I knew and that I knew it all, except one matter. He looked at me carefully, and I understood that he not only was curious about the matter but also why I wasn't telling him about it, with that one look. Sometimes a small glance, a simple hand gesture can tell what thousands of words, hundreds of pages can't explain – that was the kind of look Dimitri had on his face.

I told him that it could be a simple precaution that the two notes Nikola had written were the same, so that even if no one could find the paper on him, he might have thought that the one on Gizem's body could be found and that he could have aimed to lead whoever found the note to the places he wanted.

I wanted him to read what was written on the paper, once again. He started to read: "You will find it in the holes / Of the cracked walls / Of the destroyed temple –" Then I said, "Stop! Not this one, read the second part." He nodded and started reading the second part. "You will surely find it / In the great void / Of the cave in the middle / Right above the temple / Where it waited for two thousand years…" Then I raised my hand towards him and said, "Stop!" once again – "That's enough." I stood up, opened the backpack, took out the scrolls, held them like an object that could be easily broken, and slowly placed them on the table.

When I sat back in the chair, I saw Dimitri looking at and reading the two names written on the scrolls with growing eyes. I felt myself tremble as I listened to his voice, that hardly came out of his dry mouth: "O Theophilus"

I told my archaeologist friend that I never opened the scrolls I found with the clues I got from Nikola. We tried to untie the scrolls, which were bound with leather cut like strings, but we couldn't manage to do it. When we forced it once again to untie it, the leather strings tore from the knot.

We started to turn the pages of the scrolls one by one, with extremely slow movements; all Greek writings on the pages were visible and could be clearly read – there was no deterioration, wear and decay.

We turned a few more scrolls. When we found the scroll right in the middle and raised it to place it next to the others, we saw a piece of broken ceramics. It could be part of a ceramic cup or a bowl, but it didn't look anything like the pottery used today. My heart started pounding. Neither of us knew what to do out of excitement. We started to sweat, remained silent and couldn't speak for a while.

Dimitri took the ceramic piece in his hand. It was matte white. He examined it and gave it to me with incredible care, wanting me to examine it too. "It must be very old," he said, as he looked at the white piece with bedazzled eyes. I nodded, approvingly, and slowly placed it on the scroll that it was waiting for, who knows how many centuries. Without moving our eyes off this finding, without speaking, we thought what we were supposed to do. Even though I knew what he meant with the "old" when he said, "It must be very old," I couldn't really imagine and perceive what he meant.

"There isn't much to think about, really," said Dimitri. "We have to hand these in the museum and have to do it as soon as possible. I started to resolve the reason for the incidents, pain and destruction we've been experiencing." Sometimes his eyes were caught on a specific point, he thought, squinted, looked away and forced himself as if he could read what he couldn't think, somewhere he looked at.

"Both the uninvited guest I told the prosecutor about, as well as other people Nikola was interacting with, have to be investigated. I am a person who was born and raised here, and I have authorised knowledge on the city's history due to my profession, whereas I don't have the knowledge to understand the information written on Nikola's note."

His thoughts were all over the place. He was speaking, telling me something and as he was doing that, he seemed to be organising new thoughts. "Finding that man, who continuously visited me last year and disturbed me with his visits, could help with the answers to most of our questions. Now, let's first hand these scrolls and the piece of ceramics to my colleagues at the museum, let them make a record of it and get a copy of that record. Let's then try to find visuals of that uninvited guest of mine from the archive of security footage in the museum and if we can find it, let's hand them to the officials as well. Afterwards, let's try to find out whether the investigation on the phone records of Nikola was concluded or not. We are in a difficult situation and I don't think this brutality will end anytime soon. We alla re under serious threat. The house being broken into, everything being scattered around but nothing being taken means nothing but a threat."

I accepted to hand in the scrolls and the piece of ceramics to the Antakya Museum, however, I told him that I wanted to take photos of the writings on the scrolls, including the very last detail. Dimitri didn't react. I took out the camera from my backpack and took photos of all writings, words, signs, any inscription from different angles, without missing anything.

When I moved onto the piece of ceramics, I took photographs first where it was initially placed, perhaps where it was protected for hundreds of years. Afterwards, I took it out away from the scrolls, placed it on the table next to the fountain and took photos of it from all angles. After I was done taking the photos, I scrolled them back like I found them, placed them inside a plastic bag and then in the backpack. As we were heading to the museum in the car, the undoubtedly ancient and valuable scrolls and the piece of ceramics were on Dimitri's lap and not in the trunk.

34. CARBON-14 VE OPTICALLY STIMULATED LUMINESCENSE

We have completed all the procedures that needed to be done at the museum. We each took a copy of the official records issued by the officials, and went out. We sat on the wall next ot the Asi River. The water of Orontes was flowing fuzzy yellow. Even though I already told the museum officials that the procedures need to be done have to be done in Turkey, I repeated the same words to Dimitri, who was another official of the museum. I told him that those scrolls and the piece of ceramics to be sent abroad for any test or procedure may never return to this land again.

I told Dimitri a few more times about the importance of the piece of ceramics, that I could imagine whom it belonged to, as well as the importance of the scrolls that I could understand who wrote it from the first two words written on it. I also told him that when they are completely resolved, even though they may not be able to change any beliefs, they may have significant effects. What I was doing was to sell ice to an Eskimo, and I was going it – and act that should not have been taken normally.

Even the possibility that I might have found a piece of an important object, that was a subject of wars, novels, poems, fights, religious and political debates; which could not be found for thousands of years, was enough to excite me.

I took the phone in my hand with negative, dark and pessimistic thoughts that shadowed all my excitement, and called Solmaz once again. I called her parents and their home, but nobody was there, no one was answering. At that moment, I knew I could call anyone without hesitation, even if there were hundreds of people I could call – a relative or any other person.

As I continuously dialed up her number and couldn't reach her, Dimitri was looking at my worried face and couldn't say anything. I put the phone back in my pocket and told him, with the hundreds of negative thoughts in my absent mind, that I had to leave for Istanbul tonight.

Even though I resisted and insisted that it would be better for him to stay in Antakya, Dimitri didn't listen to me and bought two tickets for the plane at 22:00 from the ticket sales office – we were going to fly to Sabiha Gökçen Airport.

I waited for my friend to complete the procedures, sitting on the wall next to Asi River. I looked at the Parliament building of the old Hatay State and the sign on it, that said, "The Parliament Cafe." I looked at the sculpture of Atatürk right in the middle of the city square on the left of the Parliament building, at the old buildings of the post office, municipality and the bank around the square; at the magnificent mountains on the south of the city, and at the city walls that could still be seen in some places. I looked at them all and I felt sad.

We were happy when we recently arrived in the city. Our desperate lives were carried from the days when even the existence of Solmaz next to me calmed my soul against the depressed mood I was in due to my nightmares, to these days full of hellish disasters that we didn't know how to resolve. If only she called me, if only she could, I would never reproach the woman I loved. She wasn't calling and this situation, which was outside the normal, was making me very uneasy and unhappy. There must have been something negative happening to her or her loved ones, there could be no other explanation fort his.

I felt invisible, evil hands, strangling me from the throat and chest – I was having difficulty even breathing. I wished inside that my soul, full of fear and anxiety, would not strangle me. I had to keep thinking healthy and right.

As my back was turned against the old museum building, I looked at the Silpius Mountain spreading in front of me. I quickly turned around with the touch of a hand on my left shoulder, with fear. He was looking at me with a facial expression that was surprised against my sudden reflex. I apologised from Dimitri. He told me that he turned in his letter of excuse and that he could extend the period of his excuse by calling them if necessary.

We got in the car, we first fot home and then took our belongings and started to head towards Hatay Airport in the middle of the wide plain, which was obtained by drying the Amik Lake of the past years. It was as if a car was constantly chasing us and we were constantly being watched. I could always feel someone watching us, transferring duties to each other and collaborating, as we went home from the museum and from home to the airport.

We completed the flight procedures and took the plane without waiting. The cabin was not very full. The young officer lady gave us the seats, one next to the window and the one right next to it. When the plane took off, I tried to explain to my friend the happiness I felt from the empty seat next to us. Dimitri, who lost all his joy and humorous character, responded to me with a slight smile.

I understood that all passengers have arrived from the door of the plane, that seemed to be very heavy but could easily be shut with one movement of the arm. My aim was to provide a more comfortable trip for my heavyweight friend sitting at the seat next to the window. We were goint to fly for an hour and a half, so we could talk about many things. Just when I opened my mouth and prepared to say something, that feeling that we were being watched suddenly and without reason, collapsed on me. I looked at my left; a young woman and her mischievous son, who seemed to be around three years old, were talking and laughing to each other. I stood up and opened the door of the closet above us. As if I was checking our bags, I quickly scanned the rows of seats behind us; I was looking for a familiar, previously seen or a suspicious face. There was none, I couldn't see anyone who could create suspicion and sat down again under the scolding gaze of the toothy stewardess again.

Dimitri was looking outside, his head turned towards the cabin window and his forehead on the glass-like transparent window cover. I asked him what kind of procedures are to be made on the piece of ceramic that we handed in the museum between the scrolls. I waited for a while, but he didn't answer. I told myself, "It's time," and I asked the question that I wanted to ask him since the beginning but had difficuty asking – the question that made me suspicious and uncomfortable. I told him, without breath, about my suspicion and fear from thinking whether we have done the right thing by handing in the scrolls and the piece of ceramics to the officials at the museum.

If I didn't do this, I wouldn't be able to tell him about these any other time – my old friend was working at the same place with those officials, with the same position as them. I was also directing my concerns, doubts and insecurities – which seemed righteous to me – to him as well.

He turned to me with his heavy body, looked at my face and started speaking slowly. He told me that I was both right and wrong in my doubt, anxiety and distrust. The powerful sound of the engines of the plane, which started to accelerate on the airport runway, made it difficult for me to hear what he said.

He initially told me I was right, because in case it was proven that the scrolls were written by whom we thought wrote them and that it was used for the last supper with thirteen people, a museum anywhere around the world would offer checks with large amounts written on them – perhaps not a few billions, but definitely a few hundreds of millions. Afterwards, he told me that I was wrong. He told me that people tend to direct all their analysis towards the places they want, when facing events they can't resolve. At that exact moment, the plane was off the ground and was heading towards the sky at an angle of about fourty-five degrees – so now I could hear what he said more clearly. Soon after, the plane leaned towards the side and from the window Dimitri was resting his forehead a few minutes ago, I could see the sparkling lights of the Silpius Mountain.

He said again that I was wrong. He explained that the parchment roll we delivered to the museum was organic, and the white ceramic piece was inorganic and how many years their ages determined by going through different processes. This was mixed with the talk of the toothy stewardess, who was scolding us that we should not unfasten our seat belts, keep our tables closed, and turn off all our electronic devices. In fact, I remembered that she had told us all of this at the time of departure as well; I looked in front of me and quickly fastened my belt with the embarassment I felt over not fastening it before.

He told me I was wrong, once again. He told me that the findings we handed in the museum will be sent for a Carbon-14 test, that this method is called the "Radiocarbon dating" and with that, the density and the radioactivity of a Carbon-14 isotope that is found in certain amounts in organic findings involving carbon will be measured and the findings will be dated like that. At that moment, I could see that the upper front two teeth of the stewardess, who told us that our lifejackets were under our seats, were visibly large compared to her small face.

Without telling me I was wrong once again, Dimitri continued speaking: He told me that the cosmic rays spreading around the top layers of the atmosphere from space come in equal amounts from all directions. He said as the rate of composition of the Carbon-14 isotope and the density of it in living beings are carried to this day with the same amounts; the Carbon-14 starts to dissolve and reach a rate of balance in the atmosphere. At that moment, I smiled as I looked at the large front teeth of the stewardess disappearing as she showed us how to blow on the lifejackets.

He continued speaking, as if to underline how wrong I was, that this Carbon-14 entered the structure of carbondioxide, thus goes in plants through photosynthesis and then is placed inside the bodies of animals eating those plants. He said that when plants and animals are alive, the Carbon-14 in their bodily structure have a certain rate, but that plants and animals can no longer receive any more carbon from outside once they are dead and that the amount of Carbon-14 will have to decrease over time – decreasing by half in exactly 5730 years. Meanwhile, I started to understand how organic findings, which were thousands of years old, could be dated. At that moment, I saw the cheese-and-lettuce sandwich the toothy stewardess presented to me from the cart she pushed along the narrow hall.

Dimitri took the sandwich presented to him, together with the one that was presented to me and left them on the small table he opened from the back of the seat in front of him, without opening the transparent packs the sandwiches were in. He took a deep breath and turned his head towards the pitch-black plane window. He didn't feel the need to say that I was wrong once again.

He told me that found ceramics, cups, bowls, pots, bricks, even ladles, spoons made from pottery, tablets with writings on them, paintings on walls, stones used in bridges, potteries, amphorae to store wine, large cubes to store grains and many other cooked earth products can be dated through "thermoluminescence" and "optically stimulated luminescence." My head was spinning from what he told me, I thought he shouldn't have gone in such detail; I thought it but couldn't tell him anything. I wanted him to speak and thus get rid of the anxiety, feat and the unhappiness in him, even a little.

I turned around and looked at the toothy young stewardess; to see an ugly, black-bearded, sulky and evil face of a man around his fourties, taking the cheese-and-lettuce sandwich she was presenting to him, three seats in front of us.

35. GAZELLA GAZELLA

They were missing for exactly two thousand years. They were gone, even thought to be extinct. The people living in the old city thought that they had abandoned the mountains, plains, valleys, paths and sacred caves where they lived in; suddenly - and incomprehensibly.

There could be an explanation for a butterfly, insect, mosquito or even a bird not being seen for centuries; however, how could it be explained that a gazelle or sheep, a horse with its majestic mane, a wild goat appearing suddenly after never being seen for centuries!

They were gone for centuries, missing, their species was thought to be erased by now. It was as if they fulfilled their duties with the bodies they presented to the old masters, eating thyme, narcissus and minty herbs, suddenly disappearing as if they were drawn into the sky by a magical hand.

Even the waters of the Asi river they they drank, extending their thin and beautiful heads among the bushes and trees growing on the shores, as well as the paths in the mountains, caverns, rocks and stones were missing them.

"*Gazella gazella*," said Dimitri. "None of us could believe it when we first heard the news that one of the most beautiful animals in the world, which were never seen for centuries and were thought to be extinct, were seen again on the sacred mountains of Antakya. As a person who smiled at the scientific environment, where a new snail found in the rainforests with a low density of human population is presented as an important discovery, I was tearing up at the sight of these sweet and beautiful *Gazella gazella* coming to the Stauris Mountain from the neighboring valleys."

I could understand what he was trying to say and where he wanted to bring the subject; I couldn't make any comments with the shame I felt from the opinions I had just expressed, which made him doubtful as well.

He was telling me that the ancestors of the gazelles he was talking about have lived in the mountains of this city two thousand years ago as well, and were thought to be extinct. He was saying that their appearance centuries later could only be explained with a miracle. My friend was referring to the genetic relativity of these *Gazella gazella's* with the gazelle-skin I found in one of the monk caves in the high parts of the falling temple; trying to explain, in his own way, that the scrolls we handed in the museum are undoubtedly very old.

I realised that Dimitri, who was explaining to me all these, did not give any satisfactory answer to my question. As I gazed through the hallway of the plane, I saw the small face and the large teeth of the stewardess once again and rested my back in my seat. I listened to what the stewardess was saying in the phone in her hand: She was announcing that we must keep our seats uprights, close our table-trays and open the shades of our windows. We did all she said and started to wait. The moment the plane landed, I stood up, opened the luggage closet above my head, took the backpack from inside and waited for the toothy stewardess to open the door, as she stared at my face with a frowning, stiff expression. I turned around and saw the evil face of the man sitting three seats in front of us; when our eyes met, he turned his gaze towards the window.

We got off the plane and rented a car. Solmaz's parents' place was in Moda, Kadıköy. I told Dimitri that we must go there first. It was midnight and Istanbul looked like a calm, quiet and ordinary city, away from its usual intense traffic. As I was driving, I was checking whether we were being tracked. Even though I haven't seen anything, anyone besides that evil-looking man who glanced away when I realised he was staring at me; I had this uncomfortable feeling in my head that we were being watched, some people were following us.

We arrived in Rıhtım Street in Kadıköy around 45 minutes after leaving Sabiha Gökçen Airport, which looked calm and quiet as well. A few drunken people were loudly conversing, sitting with their backs on the walls next to the street. They were shouting at each other and sometimes drinking up bottles wrapped in newspapers. Three street dogs standing a few meters away from them were shaking their tails continuously, waiting for a few bites of food the drunk people would throw their way.

We arrived in front of the old, two-story house Solmaz's parents were living in, passing through narrow streets I have been through so many times. I parked right in front of the building, leaving the car in the middle of the road, and walked right towards the window of the building without shutting the car door. The building door was locked, so I rang the bell with the name of Solmaz's father on it, and waited.

I was imagining her voice, asking who it was, and I would answer to her with the great relief I'd feel, saying, "It's me, Solmaz!" There was no sound. I rang the bell once again, this time for a long time – I couldn't keep my finger off the bell. I found myself back in the arms of the depressing and uncomfortable, strangling negative thoughts surrounging my head. I waited a while in front of the door, looked above, the windows of the high floor were dark. I returned to the car with my rekindled hopelessness.

As we were about to leave the street, which was full of parked cars on one side, I looked at the rear-view mirror and saw a car that turned its lights on, starting to move. When we were on the main street, I pulled the car to the side and started to wait. The car behind us slowly passed next to us. The car's windows were covered in dark film, so we couldn't see how many people there were in the car or who they were. I waited a while longer and I told my friend, who was at least as uncomfortable as I was, that we were heading towards Kartal, where Solmaz and I lived.

The coastal road was full of fast taxis, youngsters racing with their top model cars and crazy people exhibiting acrobatic shows on their motorcycles. We continued our journey on the coast for 5-6 kilometers more after passing Maltepe. Soon, we were in Soğanlık district of Kartal. The neighborhood was Soğanlık village before and now it was called "New Soğanlık," divided into a few neighborhoods. The apartment we were sharing with Solmaz was on Yalnız Selvi Street in the Middle Neighborhood of his region. This was a complex of buildings where security guards were on duty 24/7 with a swimming pool, gym an deven a sauna and a steam room.

The humble apartment had one bedroom and a living room, the kitchen was at a corner of the living room. The bathroom was a comfortable one on the right upon entrance in the apartment, it had nothing missing. This small apartment was enough for us. We weren't those people who thought they lived inside apartments with may rooms but could only use two of them.

We lived happily and at peace. We could see the Prince's Islands, pale in the evenings but bright at midnight. The scene would create a feeling in us that we were looking out the window of a magnificent palace. I and the woman I loved - we would turn off the lights of the room, light small candles and put them on the table and on the window frame; we would sip red wine, holding hands. We would whisper our love to each other and promise to each other that we will never be separated until we die. All the nights we'd spend like this would continue in the bedroom we would go in, hugging each other with the head-spinning effect of the wine, turning into new styles on the satin bedsheets of our bed, and would continue crazily and with enthusiasm until we laid there, exhausted.

We were happy, and I could now understand it better.

After the incidents I recently experienced, I started to feel this occasional emotion more intensely. That state of happiness, which I couldn't perceive the moment I was experiencing it, would come before my eyes a while later and I could feel that happiness of the past more intensely then. Just like health… The state of goodness you never would think about and know its value when healthy, would remind itself with a small headache, a hurt wrist, an ordinary wound, a simple inflammation and other similarly small issues. It would make us understand the value of being healthy and explain it to everyone we would come across, and we would continue doing what we were used to, starting from the moment the wound began healing – no matter how wrong it is, we wouldn't do anything to protect our health.

It was not a strange feeling or behaviour, neither to me nor to the majority of society – not knowing the value of what we had, and grieving after what was lost, understanding its value only after losing it. Yes, we were happy and I could understand that better now.

I stopped the car right in front of the barrier at the entrance of the complex of buildings, with my mind full of such thoughts. I waved at the security guard, who looked at the license plate of the car and at me by leaning from the wide window of his cabin. I saw him pressing on the remote he had with a smile the moment he recognised me, and saw the barrier moving upwards. At that moment, I looked at the rear-view mirror and noticed the car that was parked on the other side of the road. It was waiting there with dimmed lights. It was the exact same car we saw in Moda, as well as near the stadium in Kadıköy. I now understood that this was too much and that these men were trying to follow us in an extremely fearless manner, as if to let us know, even, that they were following us.

Even though the barrier was completely lifted, I didn't move the car; I opened the door, got out and started walking fast towards the car that was waiting on the other side of the road. The car started moving suddenly and unexpectedly, with the uncomfortable sounds of a strong engine and tires; disappearing from sight completely.

When I was back at the entrance of the complex, the security guard was out of his cabin and Dimitri was waiting for me on the pavement. The security guard told us that the car had arrived there around ten-fifteen minutes before we did, but no one came out of it. He further added that he didn't record the license plate of the car because he didn't think it was important. I also couldn't record it, the car had moved so fast that I couldn't see anything else other than the number 1098 on the plate.

The security guard made me even more uncomfortable and tense. We went to Moda in the middle of the night… As we thought nobody knew that we were coming here today, a car followed us, arrived at the complex before we did, waited right across the entrance and the moment the person/people in the car saw me marching towards them in anger, moved quickly as if to escape. I thought that these people could be given the order, "Watch them by showing them, maket hem uncomfortable, make them afraid, but never face them!"

I was sure now, we were being followed. I told Dimitri about what I was thinking as we were heading towards the closed parking lot of the complex, leaving the security guard behind.

Yes, we were being followed. Now we had to act differently, take more careful steps and request necessary aid from the authorities.

We took our bags from the trunk and walked towards the entrance door of the building, which was inside the parking lot and had a password-lock. The password was 2103, it was a combination of my birthday and Solmaz's. We arrived on the 14th floor of the giant building, taking the elevator.

I took my keys out of my pocket. I was thinking back and forth – I wanted to move fast in order to reach the happy environment of my home, and I wanted to move slowly with the fear that I might face a terrible scene there. I opened the door. The moment I touched the switch at the entrance, two yellow lights illuminated the entrance hallway. I took two more steps. I looked at the living room, the bathroom, the bedroom, everywhere else – Solmaz wasn't there. I opened the curtains of the living room ad there they were, the Prince's Islands, blinking at me with their lights.

It was almost three in the morning. I prepared the sofa in the living room so that Dimitri could sleep on it; put clean bedsheets on it and turned on the air conditioner. As I turned to go to sleep, I heard my cell phone ringing. I look at the phone's screen and saw a number I didn't recognise, that started with the numbers 0216. This was the area code of where we were, the Anatolian side of Istanbul, and I didn't know the rest of the number. I answered the phone without hesitation and listened to the speech of a rude and ugly-voiced man, who was cursing and threatening me without giving me a break to speak.

He was cursing and forming unrecognisable sentences, shouting at me, but he didn't say what he wanted…

36. FIRUZ DEMIRCI'S INTEREST IN TYCHE

It was late, I wouldn't be able to call anyone. I started walking back to my room to sleep and my phone rang again. It was the same number. I pressed the button that gave the sound on speakers, moved next to Dimitri and this time, I pointed to the phone so he would understand and listen with me.

The caller was the same one who called me the last time, with the same voice and the same style of speaking. He was shouting, cursing and threatening meaninglessly again but he never actually said what he wanted. His style of speech and accent was quite different, he had a rough and incomprehensible style, he was always struggling at each word that people who learned Turkish later in life would struggle, and he wasn't able to pronounce the letter "r". We listened to him but we didn't respond in any way, and after a short while, he hung up.

When Dimitri said he thought he recognised this tone of voice, his style of speech and especially the different pronunciation of the letter "r", I looked at his face with wonder. He said this could be the person who came to the museum in Antakya and offered him money in return for his collaboration in a kind of theft. He told the young Prosecutor about all these as well. When I remembered the words of the caller, I understood the magnitude of the problems, the unresolvable issues we had in our hands and how desperate we were – and I trembled with fear.

As soon as we woke up the next morning, we called the Prosecutor in Antalya. We told him that we came to Istanbul and that we weren't just followed on the way, but that we were tracked all the way until home in Istanbul, together with the calls of threat. We told him that it would solve great mystery if he could receive the recordings of the security camera placed in the museum, which are protected in the archives, for the last week of July last year. We also told him that the man who threatened us on the phone last night could also be the person he would identify in the camera recordings. The prosecutor tried to learn the details, asking small questions here and there as we spoke. He told us that he will do everything we told him, that he will inform us on the state of affairs and that in case something new happens, we can call him 24/7.

Now we understood what happened a little better. We thought about the harassing visits faced by Dimitri a year ago, their offers for collaboration in the planned theft, and at the point we are at a year later, we thought we were able to resolve what the two murders are related to – bringing together many details and trying to complete the missing pieces of the puzzle of secrets.

I noticed that we never talked about the man who offered to do illegal stuff to Dimitri and constantly visited him, after I have testified at the Prosecutor's Office. When he said that the man who called me, whose voice I especially wanted Dimitri to hear, could be the same man, I thought that he had more information than what he told the Prosecutor and that I had the right to know them as well. I expressed this opinion of mine to him, openly and clearly.

Dimitri said what I thought was correct and that he couldn't have told the Prosecutor everything, that there are sensitive balances and that the protection of these balances have vital importance. Afterwards, I begrudgingly told him that I wasn't able to understand what he was trying to say and that he should speak in a more clear and understandable way.

He understood me – I know that he was also bothered by the mysterious way he spoke. At the time he started speaking and continued to speak, as he prepared himself with the words he spoke and his style of speaking, I should have understood that his aim was to create an environment in which he could voice what he was going to say more easily.

He should have understood me as well. I have found the dead body of the only sibling the women I love had, and I wasn't able to reach neither Solmaz, nor his parents for days. I was in a tough situation, I was desperate, depressed and I was in no mood to tolerate any mysterious, cryptic or metaphorical way of speech.

He understood me and immediately changed his mysterious way of speaking. I understood from the way he squinted and looked away in an exhausted, tired and melancholic manner, that he was trying to go back to a year ago and that he was trying to force his memory and thoughts – and from his determined tone of speaking, I was sure that he was going to tell me everything he knew.

"About a year ago, in the last week of July, I was sitting in my office at the museum and was reading the news on an importance bronze sculpture we found, with a weird but ordinary coincidence, on local and national newspapers – and I was cutting the articles with a scissors, feeling excitement and happiness. Whatever those articles are called! The sculpture we found wasn't so big. Even though it was a small sculpture that was around eight centimeters, it was very important. Even though we weren't certain, we thought it was a great possibility that the sculpture was older than two thousand years. We also distributed its pictures fort he press, calling it the "Tyche of Antioch." We found Tyche in a small niche somewhere on the wall, in a late excavation around the old stone wall that a farmer found while plowing his field.

"The statue, which we call the Tyche of Antioch, could be considered a serious expression of the advanced Hellenistic style and was a figüre of a woman. The woman named Tyche was sitting on a great rock (which is the Silpius Mountain), wearing a crown with a tower (these towers symbolised the Walls of Antioch) and she was stepping on the shoulders of a young man, swimming through the waves flowing through her feet, with spica in her hands – you probably understand that the spica represents the lush shores of the Amik Lake and the young man swimming through the waves is the Orontes River itself.

The pictures we've handed to the newspapers and our comments on the statue awakened great public interest. Soon after we informed the press that the statue was older than two thousand years and that a similar one is stored in the Vatican Museum, we got numerous phone calls and invitations for interviews. We were both happy and exhausted with the interest in detailed information on the topic.

Tyche is a Greek work that means 'fortune', as the personification of the power that determines the occurence of events outside of what humans are capable of.

The woman sitting on a sacred mountain, taming it, determining the limits of the mountain and its area of domination with the walls built around it, waiting with the crown on her head and the bundles of spica in her hand, controlling he Orontes River with her feet despite its crazy, harsh waves – represented the importance of knowing one's limits, taming the extremities and bringing together all necessary elements, which are destiny, luck and hard work.

Thanks to the information, comments and tales like these, the number of visitors in the museum was increasing every single day and we were receiving praising messages from all around.

As we enjoyed the success we achieved, that man I was telling you about came to me. He was extremely polite, well-cultured and gentle. I don't want to lose time by telling you the details of the first meeting again, for you already know it.

He reminded me of the incident in Uşak Museum, when the "Winged Sea Horse Brooch" was replaced with a fake – that a lot of people have earned serious money from such a simple act of exchanging two items, that they got rich, that their lives have changed and that I could easily access the same happiness. In the meantime, he placed a bronze sculpture he took out of his briefcase on the desk in front of us.

I was shocked and my eyes were popping out of my head, I was looking at him with fear and disbelief. The sculpture before me was the sculpture of Tyche itself. Seeing my worried face, the man told me not to worry, that what I see is merely a copy of it, and that the thing I had to do was extremely easy, simple and ordinary. He was speaking in the most innocent manner one could have.

He was telling me to replace the actual sculpture of Tyche with the one sitting on the desk, perfectly crafted to look exactly like the original; to hand him the original and that he would give me fifty thousand American dollars in return for my simple service. I stood up and told him that I will call the police if he doesn't leave my office immediately, that he is offering to bribe a government officer and that he is a thief. In fact, I should have already informed the officials about it, but I didn't want to mess with whatever was going on with that man.

The cheeky man stood up, smiling, and told me that his name is 'Firuz', that he was a blacksmith for many years, that he is a talented sculptor and that in case I decide to collaborate with him, he could sculpt copies of many sculptures out of metal, marble, bronze and clay and that we could earn so much money that it would even be enough for our grandchildren. When he said all that, I dismissed him from my office with even harsher insults and I reached for the phone on my desk.

At that moment, he made a hand gesture, telling me to drop the phone and that he will leave. He also said that he was not going to make me get away with these insults, that he has very powerful colleagues both in the country and abroad, that I was making the biggest mistake of my life by denying this opportunity and that my loved ones will also be affected by the negativities to come. At that exact moment, I stoof up fast, walked towards him, held him from his collar and dragged him out of my office.

Even as he said his name, 'Firuz', he couldn't pronounce the letter 'r'. When I heard the voice from the call you got, and when I heard that pronunciation of the letter 'r', I understood that it was definitely that Firuz man calling you."

I listened to what Dimitri had to say without interrupting him. As interesting and important as what he had to say, it was far from explaining the two murders. I told him that there must be even more important things he had to tell me, emphasizing the importance of him sharing them with me, and I pointed out the significance of us having to evaluate all data together with the slightest detail. I told him that we don't know where Solmaz and her parents are, that they could be in great trouble and could need our help, that they could be in a secret spot, waiting to be saved by us. He thought for a bit and started speaking once again, in a manner that made it clear that he understood the vitality of him sharing 'everything' with me.

"Alright, you're right," he said. "I will tell you about the events that don't seem too important to me as well." I told him that he better start before it's too late and that we don't have a single second to lose – he looked at me with a guilty expression.

"That man I sent away from my office at the museum, who told me his name was Firuz, never called me for an entire month. Right when I was thinking that He could never come back and I would never see him again, the envelope I received from a postman at my office was an indicator that the disasters were about to begin for me.

I shut the door of my office, sat at my desk and opened the envelope. When I looked at the photo I took out of the envelope, I was shocked. My hands started shaking and I started sweating. In the photo, Nikola and that man, Firuz, were sitting across each other, making cheers with the beer glasses in their hands and smiling to whoever was taking the photo. I couldn't believe it, I didn't want to believe it and I thought I and my brother were being dragged into a serious disaster.

When I noticed a folded white paper inside the envelope as well, I immediately unfolded it and started reading the twisted handwriting:

'I'd think again if I were you, Mr Dimitri! Think about it and don't forget that the offer we made to you is so good that it can't be turned down. In the meantime, I'm sending you a photo we got taken together with your brother Nikola on Bestekâr Street in Ankara, so you know that we are close friends now. If you want, you can frame this picture and put it on your desk. Best regards, Firuz Demirci.'

He was threatening me and making fun of me at the same time. I immediately called Nikola and asked him how he knew his guy named Firuz Demirci. He told me that he met him at a pub and that he hasn't seen anything wrong with him. I got angry and yelled at my brother. He told me to calm down and to remember that he is no longer a small child and that he is free to see whoever he wants, adding that he couldn't understand why I was so upset. So he asked me how I knew Firuz Demirci.

I told him that I couldn't tell him anything on the phone, but that as his older brother, I asked him tos tay away from this man. I forced myself to speak without getting upset, slowly and calmly, in a way Nikola wouldn't react against. He told me that he couldn't understand a word I said, but nevertheless he was going to listen to me and that he will never meet this man again. So I was relieved and thanked my brother.

My brother was smart. If he lived to graduate, he could be a great doctor. He was an idealist and he loved people. I still can't believe that his life has ended with such death, and I think I never will. It's as if I'm in a terrible nightmare, I want to wake up from this dream as soon as possible."

I had a hunch that he wasn't done with what he was going to say, and that the things he was about to tell me were even more important. He stood up from the armchair he was sitting in, walked towards the refrigerator and poured himself a big glass of cold water. He put the bottle back in the refrigerator and came back with the big glass of water, sat across me, back in the armchair.

I begged him to tell me faster. "I know now that the disappearance of Solmaz and her parents are related to Firuz Demirci, I now have no doubt about it. I called Solmaz once again, her phone is still off and we still don't know what happened to them."

He gulped down the water and left the glass on the glass surface od the coffee table in front of us. He turned his head towards the Prince's Islands, squinted like he just did, and started speaking again.

"The next day after I received the envelope, I heard the door knocking lightly as I was working in my office at the museum. I stood up, opened the door and saw Firuz Demirci, smiling at me with that disgusting face of his. I couldn't understand how he could come to my door, with what courage and dare, I was extremely upset.

I reached and grabbed him from his jacket and pulled him inside my office, shutting the door fast with a small kick. The man couldn't understand what was happening and he raised his arms as a reflex to protect his face from possible fists, so I showed him my fist, right in front of his nose, looking at his scared eyes. I told him about the discomfort I had from his mocking tone of his letter, and that I was in a state in which I couldn't control my anger. Afterwards, I mocked him and that I wasn't taking any of his steps or threats seriously.

He couldn't understand it. He wouldn't be able to understand it and he was never going to. A murderer, thief and conman could never be turned away from his direction, for he was prone to think, believe and say that there is no harm in trying any way to put the theft, deception and corruption in action.

I wasn't aware that these things I was doing would increase the man's anger and that he would resent me. In fact, I didn't care that he resented me. When I released his jacket, he looked at me as if nothing had happened and told me that he was doubling his offer. The cheeky man told me in case I handed him the original of the sculpture of Tyche, he would give me one hundred thousand dollars and that more could come over time as well.

I now knew, no matter what I said or did, he wouldn't be able to understand me. So I spoke to Firuz Demirci in the same mocking tone he spoke to me, without raiding my voice. I told him to get up, disappear without looking back, never approach Nikola, that I was so full of such threats, he should find other slaves to conduct such theft and corruption, and that in case I saw him again, there could be worse consequences he had to face, together with many other things.

My anger and my mocking tone was scaring even me but my warnings had no effect on the man. He grabbed the handle of the door of my office, looked at me with that dirty smile of his, and told me, hissing like a snake, that I was really going to regret it – that I was going against an organisation that had international connections and that the consequences of that will never be good for neither, me, my surroundings, nor my job. The entire time he spoke to me, he always mispronounced that letter 'r', and the momet I walked toward him, he opened the door and walked away from me."

At that exact moment, my phone rang and I saw the name of the young Prosecutor in Antakya on the screen of my phone. I answered the phone immediately and listened to what he had to say. He told me that he went to the museum and took the camera recordings out of the archive for the dates Dimitri told him, that he found the visuals on the man around his fourties, confiscated the entire recordings. He also added that the visuals of unidentified people are in the related units of the Security Directorate, that he ordered the officers there to complete the identification process urgently and that he himself was going to follow the developments first-hand. I thanked the Prosecutor and told him that the man's real or fake name was Firuz Demirci, and that my friend has just remembered his name. At the brief pause we had the moment I said it, I understood that he jotted the name down. He repeated the name back to me and I confirmed it.

After a moment's pause, I told the Prosecutor about who Solmaz was and that I wasn't able to reach neither her, nor her family members, and that I was very worried. I asked him what I should do and what his suggestions would be. He asked me questions on the identities of Solmaz and her family members, took their residence addresses, noted them down and told me he was going to take care of it. He further added that I should inform him about all developments without losing time, before he hung up.

As I was telling Dimitri about what the Prosecutor had said, I flinched with the sound of the phone I left on the coffee table. Because of the fear I was in, I was giving sudden and unnecessary reactions against almost all sounds; I didn't like the fact that I was constantly flinching when I heard sounds from the surrounding apartments like music or TV sounds. I looked at my phone's screen and couldn't recognise the number. When I answered the phone, I heard the ugly pronunciation of the evil voice I now knew very well: The man could not pronounce the letter 'r'.

37. THE RECTANGULAR YELLOW ENVELOPE

It was Firuz Demirci. Now he was forcing himself to speak more politely and sincerely. He was whispering to me as if he was telling me an ordinary, daily and simple matter – that I must bring the stubborn man next to me to reason and that otherwise, my loved ones would be in great trouble. He was also telling me that it would be of no use if I attemped to save the number he was calling from, for he was always going to call me from a different number. In the meantime, he was laughing in an annoying way, making weird sounds on the phone.

He was telling me that in case I informed the police or any other authority on the matter, my loved ones would be in a direction they could not go back from, and that direction was not a very long road, ending at a steep and high cliff. At that moment, the evil man laughed outloud.

Firuz Demirci waited for a bit without speaking, afterwards, he wanted me to write down a phone number he was going to tell me. I wrote it down. He told me to call the number he gave me, order four loaves of bread, and that after the breads arrived, he wanted me to call him – only for this time – from the number he called me. Then he hung up without speaking further.

I couldn't understand what he was trying to do. I immediately called the number he made me write down and I looked at the name that appeared on the screen before I took the phone to my ear. The phone was saved on my phone because I called that number many times in the past to order food – it was the number of a grocery store nearby. When the store employee answered the phone, I ordered four loaves of bread and gave him my address. The employee told me that my order will be at my door in five to ten minutes, and I replied to her by saying that I will pay in cash. I thanked the employee and started waiting in distress after I hung up. The request was odd. I didn't know what I was going to face, but I was afraid.

This order of four loaves of bread was odd and I couldn't understand the meaning of it at all, but I did it anyways in desperation, since I could do nothing else.

Ten minutes later, I flinched with the sound of the phone on the wall next to the front door of the apartment. My reaction was sudden and exaggerated, in a way that always happened recently, and I didn't like it. Each moment, I felt like I was about to face something terrible. As I was listening to the voice from the phone, I was looking at the screen of the phone, showing the lobby. It was the security calling me, and I flinched once again as I saw on the screen a ten-year-old, holding a grocery bag in his hand. I told the security that the order indeed belongs to me and that he could send the kid upstairs, as I opened the door and started waiting.

Soon after, the kid arrived on our floor and handed me a grocery bag full of bread, as well as a rectangular, yellow envelope. I looked at him with questioning eyes.

The innocent child told me that a man approached him as he was heading towards my building and asked him whether there are four loaves of bread in the bag. Afterwards, the man gave my name and my number to the child, told him that he was my friend and asked him to bring the envelope to me together with the bag. He also gave him ten liras for the service and immediately left. I asked the kid about the way the man spoke to him, the tone of his voice and how old he thought the man was. The cute kid told me, "He was as old as my older brother". I smiled and asked him how old his brother was. He said his brother was around twenty.

It wasn't him, it wasn't Firuz Demirci, who handed the mysterious envelope to the kid.

I gave the child another ten liras and closed the door to sit back at my seat across Dimitri. He was looking at the envelope in my hand, waiting for me to open it at once.

I carefully opened the rectangular, yellow envelope from where it was glued, placing the four photographs I took out carefully on the coffee table – one by one. I looked at the pictures with eyes full of fear, terror and an increasing anger. It was getting difficult to balance my emotional state after the recent incidents; as well as to control my actions due to my depressed state. I often was not able to recognise myself.

At that exact moment, my phone rang. I didn't answer right away, because I knew who was calling. I waited for a while. It rang and went silent. Immediately afterwards, it started ringing again. This time, I answered the phone and listened to the only sentence the evil man said: "What happened, you didn't call?!"

I didn't reply to him. I didn't speak and hung up on him.

38. DETAILS IN THE PHOTOGRAPHS

I was far from the moments that could be told, from the meanings of the moments. I was looking at the photographs in front of me, not able to understand anything. I was trying to understand it, forcing myself to understand, attempting to focus but I wasn't able to understand a single second of the present time I was in.

I was looking at the reflection of my own face from the glass surface of the coffee table in front of me, next to the begging eyes in the photographs. I was cursing my desperation.

I was a strong, fearless man who wouldn't bow down to anything. I couldn't believe this weak, poor state I was in, looking at the photographs in front of me with terror and trying to grasp the moment of capture in these photographs. Despite my best effort, I wasn't able to understand anything and I was trying to find something to break down and tear apart with my increasing rage. I spoke to myself, "Is it that easy to be a murderer, to just erase a living person?" I was starting to think actions that were up to no good.

In one of the photos on the coffee table, there was Solmaz's parents. Their hands and feet were tied, they were left at a dark corner of an old, dirty room and were looking at the person taking their photo with eyes full of terror. This photograph should have never happened, we should have taken every precaution to prevent this photograph from ever being taken.

The woman I loved, my Beautiful Solmaz, whose single strand of hair I couldn't bear seeing hurt, should not have been looking at me with that expression in that photo. She was standing with her white underwear, forced to stand in front of a dirty window. I was the sole responsible of what was happening.

I looked outside the dirty, dusty window she was standing in front of. I didn't want to see her face with an expression that was exhausted, ready to die. I shouldn't have seen it.

"Get up, get ready, we're leaving. We must leave the apartment. There is nothing left for us to do here any more," I told Dimitri and I started getting ready with hurry.

The phone rang once again. Forcing myself to act calm and reasonable, I answered the phone – for I knew the number now. Firuz Demirci started speaking to me in his usual careless, immoral and cheeky attitude. He asked me whether I liked the photographs he sent me, then he spoke words that enraged every fiber of my being... He told me that it's hard not to like the beautiful woman in the photograph and that there are other pictures of her in his hand, with a tone full of fake excitement.

He told me that it would be of no use for us to waste time in Istanbul, that we should immediately go back to Antakya and that I should convince the stubborn man next to me to do what he asked him to do – that otherwise, he would take new photographs of my loved ones, send them to me and that the ones I would receive next would not be as innocent as the ones I now have in hand, and that I wouldn't like them one bit. As I listened to him, I was holding myself hard not to yell and scream insults at him.

He told me that he is aware of the latest findings we handed to the museum, that he found them exciting and that he had certain plans to be implemented later about them. He was trying to tell us that he had connections with certain officers or ordinary employees working at the museum, that he could receive insider information.

He slowly told me that he wasn't expecting much for now, that he could very well make it with the Tyche sculpture that would be seen in newspapers and on TV screens for days, that it would only take him a few seconds for Dimitri to replace the fake bronze sculpture he would give him with the original, and by doing that, not only all our problems would be over, but we would also earn one hundred thousand American dollars.

He paused for a while and said that when he gets the sculpture of Tyche, he would place it in front of him and watch that beautiful figure for hours. He added that if he can't get the sculpture, he will have to watch the beautiful woman he has now and that this one is much more beautiful and lively than the sculpture. He told me that she awakened many feelings in him as well as other similar ugliness that he knew would enrage me.

I was determined not to get upset. With an attitude that made it very clear that I was forcing myself not to get angry, I told Firuz Demirci that we were going to do what he says and that he should wait for us without doing anything to our loved ones.

We left the apartment on Yalnız Selvi Street. As I looked around me on the way towards Sabiha Gökçen Airport, I thought I was bothered by the different architecture of the buildings standing on each side of the road, by the ugly buildings right next to others looking like chicken coop as well as by the modern, glass-windowed and aluminum-walled business centers. I was disturbed by this complex, unstylish, ugly scene made up of all these elements.

I told Dimitri that I didn't want to inform the young Prosecutor in Antakya about the latest developments just yet. He asked me why I thought so, but without waiting for my reply, he told me he agreed. There was no complicated way in the way I thought. A criminal organisation that could find intelligence from the museum could very well find other accomplices in any institution or organisation. We had to be careful and try to find ways to approach Firuz Demirci and his accomplices, without upsetting them.

When we arrived at the airport, it was almost 13:00. We handed the rental car and found out that the next flight to Antakya was at 16:00. We bought our tickets and took our place at one of the tables in a place that was a mixture of a coffee shop and a restaurant inside the airport, that was well-lit, spacious and airy.

The moment we sat down, I took out the yellow envelope I had placed in the front pocket of my backpack and started to examine the photos once by one. The first picture was of Solmaz's parents. The photo was obviously taken in a dim room with the light from the ceiling and possibly with a flash. The visuals were not clear and didn't involve a detail that could give me any clues, so I placed that picture at the very bottom of the others in the pile. The other three pictures were of Solmaz.

The first photo of Solmaz was taken during the day, in a well-lit environment. All of her clothes were off except her white bra and underwear, and she was photographed from right across her as she was sitting on the wide bed in the middle of the room. The round bars of the bedstead and the blanket on the bed looked quite ragged and old. On the wall behind the bed Solmaz was sitting on, there was a two-winged rectangular window with a muslin curtain. It was clear from the picture that the curtain was very thin.

The second picture was clearer. Solmaz was standing and the thin muslin curtain that was seen from afar in the first picture was now open and she was standing next to the window, trying to cover her breasts with one hand and her groin with the other. The silhouette of a high mountain was visible out of the window.

I focused completely on the mountain silhouette outside the window. A line descended from the top of the mountain to its skirts, that looked like a wall, making an 'S' with sharp edges. I felt like I saw what I was seeing some other time before, from another perspective. The silhouette I was looking at was no stranger to me. Before I moved onto the last picture, I examined the one in my hand extensively and looked for further details, colours I couldn't see, and new clues. I couldn't find anything else, other than the silhouette of the high mountain and the wall descending from the mountain, making an 'S' with sharp edges.

So I started examining the last picture and I realised that different from the other two, the muslin curtain was pulled to the side and the picture was taken to include that detail. Solmaz was standing next to the window, with her back turned against whoever took the picture, touching her hips. I knew that she wouldn't be able to pose like this under normal circumstances; I knew she was forced to pose this way in order to prevent something evil happening to her parents.

I looked at the edges of the strong walls, descending from the mountain towards its skirts, making a sharp 'S', right outside the window in the picture. I brought the picture even closer to my eyes and examined it. I handed the photograph to Dimitri, who was trying to understand what I was trying to do. I pointed at the mountain seen outside the window in the picture and asked him where this could be. He took the picture in his hand, looked at it caregully and he answered in a confident, certain way: "Silpius Mountain." "This is Silpius Mountain and the Walls of Antioch, descending down from the mountain."

My guess was right, I could recognise the place as well. The photographs they took to provoke, upset and scare me to make me do the things they wanted me to do, gave us important clues in the identification of where Solmaz and her parents were kept in.

I contantly postponed the insults I was about to say as I was enraged more, all the attacks I was planning to make against them, as well as my increasing feelings of revenge, rage and resentment. The slightest mistake I'd do with my current feelings and would possibly be meaningless, could have great damage against the woman I loved and her family members.

Firuz Demirci and his accomplices knew that even if he only sent me pictures of Solmaz's face, they could scare me. However, they didn't just do only that. The message of the photogaphs, taken with her underwear after Solmaz was forced to take her clothes off, was clear. They were trying to say, "In case you don't do what we ask, you will see that even those underpants will not be there in the second batch of photographs. We would go even further and send you pictures in different positions you would never wish to see."

I promised to myself that I would stay even calmer and more reasonable in all the calls he was going to make after that moment, that I wouldn't get upset. I now knew that they were in Antakya and that they were alive. They were prisoners of Firuz Demirci. I believed that a simple Exchange of the sculptures could save the woman I loved as well as her loved ones.

I told Dimitri about what I was thinking, that we could get a replica of the Tyche sculpture made and we could save our loved ones by giving it to Firuz. He didn't feel the need to speak, remained silent for a while, looked at me with worry and told me that the moment we hand him the fake Tyche sculpture, we would have the cruelest consequences of all, for the man we're dealing with was more knowledgeable and careful than a serious expert. I never brought up the subject again and forced myself to find solutions that are more coherent, reasonable and smart.

I heard the continuous announcements of the airport, constant speaking with the metallic sound, but I couldn't understand anything that was being said. I knew that there was a logic behind the irregular, random movement of all the people around me, going back and forth, right to left – but I couldn't understand any of the tules of this irregular logic.

Then I heard Dimitri, who told me that the last announcement made by the steady metallic voice was about our flight – so I put the pictures back in the envelope and the envelope back in my backpack with mechanic movements. We stood up and started walking in an unwilling, exhausted, sad, desperate way, not knowing what we were doing on the slippery and shiny granite floor.

The plane took off at exactly 16:00 and it was half empty. Before I put the backpack in the closet above our heads, I took out the plastic bag I brought with me to look at it when necessary, to find new details. From the plastic bag, I took out columns and articles cut out from newspapers. I read some of the articles. They were those I took from the apartment of Nikola in Ankara. I sat in the seat next to the window and looked outside – there was the same busy, irregular and fast complexity, whose logic I couldn't figure out. Dimitri was sitting next to the hall and was fast asleep in his seat, shortly after the plane took off.

All the articles were cut out of a local daily newspaper in Antakya, and they were all written by Mehmet Ali Öztaş. I've read his writings before and his style drew my attention. Besides his unique style that absorbed the reader and sparked curiosity, the stories and events he was telling were also quite interesting.

I couldn't just sit there without doing anything, whenever I paused to think, hundreds of negative and meaningless thoughts attacked and invaded my mind. I looked at the vast space covered by white clouds outside the plane window. Now I understood our situation better and I know that everything bad happened to us had to do with an international gang of historical artifact theft, led by Firuz Demirci. I could go directly to the young Prosecutor, tell him about the latest developments, show him the pictures in my hand as well as the place I identified from them, and perhaps I could help them save Solmaz and her parents with an operation.

I couldn't. Without thinking caregully and determine all consequences with the slightest detail, I wouldn't be able to take such steps. There was no joke in a criminal organisation that could likk two young people without mercy. I wouldn't be able to take the chance of all negativities Solmaz and her parents could face in the slightest misstep of the security forces. Even the thought of it made me shiver. I put the articles I read below the others. I looked at the headline of the one at the top and look at the smiling face of Mehmet Ali Öztaş on the black-and-white picture of him above he headline. I read the headline, written in Latin, once again:

"Homo sum; humani nihil a me alienum puto."

39. "HOMO SUM, HUMANI NIHIL A ME ALIENUM PUTO."*

I am human and nothing about human is foreign to me.

We begin our article today with a famous and well-known phrase from Terentius. This sentence explains that someone who knows himself should not be surprised by any other person's behavior, neither friendship, nor enmity, betrayal, brutality and tyranny, and when he encounters such behavior, he should not feel estranged.

As the inhabitants of this city, we know them very well. They set out with a large army and thousands of warriors to take Jerusalem, which is considered the most blessed of the cities for Christians, to capture the sacred relics in this city, the pieces of wooden crosses where the Prophet Jesus was crucified, and to protect the temple of the Prophet Solomon. There were big cross marks on their outfits. When they were called "Crusader Armies", they felt great pride and joy from it, which they could not hide.

I will not tell you about the cities they burned down, destroyed, the men they killed with their swords, the women they raped, the children they grilled and ate with skewers until they arrived in front of the Walls of Antioch.

On October 21, 1097, observers waiting with fear on top of the Castle of Antioch at the peaks of the Silpius Mountain, shouted with fear towards the farthest point of the plain, to the giant cloud of dust they saw near the Amik Lake – announcing the arrival of the army they were waiting for, to the notables and all other citizens of the city.

The commander and chief of Antioch was an old man named Yaghi-Siyan, who has been serving the Seljuk sultans for at least fourty years. He was very experienced, survived despite all betrayals he faced. He was a smart, cunning, skeptical man who liked to rule and he would mostly make the right decisions.

Yaghi-Siyan knew very well that Antioch could never be taken with an attack, and that the people of Antioch couldn't be left to starve by blocking the entries and exits to the city. The most trusted feature of the city was that it was like an impenetrable fortress. The twelve-thousand-meter-long walls had three hundred and sixty bastions. Although other sources wrote fourty-four thousand steps for the length of the walls, which makes thirty thousand meters, we accept that the walls were twelve thousand meters long in 1097, when the Crusaders surrounded Antioch.

The walls built of cut stone and brick climb all the way to Silpius, or Habib Al-Najjar Mountain in the East, and there is a fortress in the east of this mountain that is almost impossible to capture. The crazy river Orontes, named as "Al-Asi" [The Rebel] by the Arabs, was flowing at the West of the city. The river was indeed rebellious; instead of constantly dlowing towards the Mediterranean, sometimes it would get irritated and started flowing backwards, from the Mediterranean to Antioch. The bed of this Orontes River was watching the walls of the city and this created an in-surmountable, natural obstacle. The slope of the deep valley in the South of the city stood upright like a solid wall and did not give passage to anyone.

The people from all religions and sects were living happily in the city, surrounded by the walls. They had a large cultivated land. Everything could be planted in these fertile lands – olives, figs, many other fruit trees as well as vineyards spread over large areas. In other words, Antioch was a city that would not suffer or experience any problems, being satisfied with what it had for many years even if it was surrounded for years.

Although the city's chief Yaghi-Siyan relied heavily on the walls and food stocks of the city, he thought that a traitor, who would open one of the city's gates org ive up one of the bastions, could invalidate all security measures.

It was not difficult for this traitor to emerge. Jews, Christians and Mus-lims lived together in the city and some of them saw themselves as sec-ond-class people. Those who saw themselves as "second-class people" could take the pain out of this situation in cooperation with those who surround-ed the city. Yaghi-Siyan said that this could happen and that it would not surprise him at al lif it did – through this belief, he actually fulfilled the requirements of believing the words of Terentius, who said, "Humani nihil a me alienum puto" – "Nothing about human is alien to me.

We may find it difficult, now more than nine hundred and ten years after the siege, how Antioch, a city that could resist the surrounding of the Crusaders for two hundred days and countless attacks without any outside help, was taken down due to a dishonourable traitor. As difficult as we find it, this betrayal shouldn't be foreign to us in any way.

For the moment, we will not talk about the Ridwan, Tuqaq, Shams al-Dawla, Kerbogha, the delayed aid, the armies stuck on the way, those who have turned back, power struggles, jealousy, tricks, frauds and cunning schemes. What we really want to talk about is the betrayal. We would like to explain how a magnificent city, which could resist a two-hundred-day siege, fell overnight due to the betrayal of a single man:

In the night of June 2, 1098, when the cool, humid and crazy winds were blowing, all the lights of the city went out, the conversations of those sitting in front of their homes were exhausted and everyone fell asleep. Except for one person.

In the early hours of the morning, the curly bearded evil man listened to the rubbing sound of the rope hanging down from the top of a bastion on the walls in the South of the city and made hand gestures to the soldiers of the Crusader Army waiting below. The man's name was Firuz. He was a Muslim of Armenian origin and an armour manufacturer.

He has been very close to Yaghi-Siyan for a long time, but was recently accused of blacksmithing and forgery and sentenced to a very high fine. Because of this punishment, he carried extreme grudge against those who ruled the city and swore to take revenge. By contacting the Crusaders, he reported to them that he was responsible for a bastion facing the valley in the south of the city and that he could help them get in the city. The Crusaders offered Firuz, the armour manufacturer, many things – money, gold, land and others.

Collaborating with traitor Firuz, the Crusaders climbed the windows on the Two Sisters Bastion, which was under the responsibility of the armour manufacturer, with the help of ropes, and thus entered Antioch on June 3, 1098. Noise and chaos gradually increased, pipes crowded, people ran around and tried to hide. No good was going to happen to Yaghi-Siyan now, as he was trying to escape with a few soldiers he took with him through one of the gates – believing that the sounds of the pipes came from the city, even that the impenetrable fortress has fallen.

In fact, the number of Crusaders entering the city was only five hundred. The old Yaghi-Siyan, who fled like a coward after resisting for two hundred days, was extremely sad, desperate and devastated because of the fact that he had left his family, sons and Muslims behind. He started to cry and fell from the horse he was riding, due to the great pain he felt. He was severely injured due to the fall. Suffering, he died where he fell. Those with him left him where he died and continued to escape, whereas an Armenian woodcutter passing by there reconised him. Cutting off Yaghi-Siyan's head, he brought it to the Crusaders in Antioch.

The city was in flames and smoke was rising from every corner of it. Women, children and even babies were killed brutally by the Crusaders — no matter how they tried to run and escape. All the houses were burned down, women were raped, stray animals were fried in the flames of the burning houses. Antioch has fallen now, into the hands of the Crusader Army.

The city could resist two hundred days of siege and all attacks, deceptions and frauds — and it was fallen due to the resentment, vengeful feelings and betrayal of an armour manufacturer named Firuz. Antioch was conquered by the Crusaders and a new era has begun on June 3.

Firuz did not hesitate to betray the city, where he was born, raised, benefited from everything the city had to offer throughout his life — he had eaten the city's food for years, made children, and lived there with his relatives and friends.

Should we be surprised by these? Is such betrayal, anger, revenge, brutality and soldness so foreign to us?

What must the traitor Firuz have felt, when he sawthe cruel soldiers attacking and raping his neighbour - or when he smelled the burnt meat from the body of a baby, which was grilled like an animal on skewers, as he remembered the day the baby was born?

Should we be surprised by these?

Are the unbelievable actions, betrayals of the people we think we know very well, and how low they can be, so foreign to us?

No, we must never be surprised and feel any foreignness against such betrayals; we are human and no action, no attitude and no behaviour of humans must make us surprised and feel alien.

"Homo sum, humani nihil a me alienum puto."

40. TURQUOISE* IS A MIXTURE
OF BLUE AND GREEN

*Turquoise: Firuz

I fell asleep with the newspaper clippings in my hand as I was reading the story of the surrounding of Antioch after resisting for two hundred days, due to the betrayal of Firuz, and the story of Yaghi-Siyan, who escaped the city he ruled for many years one night without thinking about anything else.

Yaghi Siyan returned the city he ruled for years as a cut head shortly after he left it. The moment the Armenian woodsman raised the head of Yaghi Siyan after cutting it off his body, I jumped awake with a bump from the bottom of my seat. The plane had iht its rear wheels hard on the runway. I sat up, look outside the window and tried to understand where I was. I felt myself somewhere between the dream I had and the real time I was in.

We picked up the car we left at the airport's car park and proceeded towards the Antakya-İskenderun road through the Amik Plain. My phone rang right at that moment. Although there was a number on the screen that I did not know, I knew who was calling. I thought that the evil man, who was calling just ten minutes after we got off the plane, was watching us; in particular, he was trying to let us know that we were being watched and that he wasn't doing it secretly. He was trying to point out that the more he scared us, the more we would fulfill his wishes and unfortunately, he succeeded in all of his actions. Yes, I was going to do anything he would ask me of, I would force Dimitri as well and try to save the lives of three innocent people, who had no idea what was going on.

Dimitri was right in saying that Firuz Demirci wanted only the statue of Tyche for now. By taking the Tyche statue, he was going to get us involved in a crime as well and he knew the more we struggled to get out of that swamp, we would become tools in the dirty hands of the network of international smuggling with the coins, mosaics, statues, parchments and other thousand-year-old artwork we provided them with our own hands.

Dimitri was telling me, in a manner of a museum official, that what I desire can only be fulfilled through collaboration with the authorities. I told him that any step that would not endanger the life of Solmaz and her parents would be alright with me.

I mentioned briefly about the historical betrayal of armour-maker Firuz to Dimitri, from what I read in the column, I pointed out that the name resemblance is interesting between the gangster "Firuz Demirci." My archaeologist friend, who knew the history of the city very well, nodded with approval. He told me that this name and surname he was using can not be real, that no international smuggler or thief can use his real name and that I probably have thought that as well. He even said that the name of the bastion armour-maker Firuz used for the surrounding of Antioch by the Crusaders was the Bastion of Two Sisters.

I listened to him and tried to remember the brutally murdered corpse of Gizem. The woman I loved, Solmaz, was in his hands, that he could do any evil deed to her, and I tried to understand that hundreds of years after the great betrayal of the first Firuz at the Bastion of Two Sisters, another Firuz was committing a betrayal through two sisters – Solmaz and Gizem. This Firuz was either an incredibly smart and creative man, or he was a true idiot, who was a tool for some smart and creative people.

When we arrived at Dimitri's house it was almost dark outside. We went inside, looked at the courtyard and tried to distract ourselves from the heavy clouds of bitterness upon us. It was no trime to stop, pause, get bitter or sad. We have to search for logical ways and take correct steps that we are able to reach healthy results. A slight mistake we could accidentally make, an unreasonable decision we could take or a simple sentence we could utter out of anger could suddenyl bring an end to three lives.

I told Dimitri that I was going to go to that place, where I thought was photographed in the picture of Solmaz, from the same angle of which the mountain and the walls on the mountain skirts were visible the same way. I told him I was going to go there before the sun rises and that I would make research. Without answering, Dimitri stood up from his chair next to the fountain, went to the kitchen and came back with a rectangular metal box he was carrying. He left the box in front of me and wanted me to open it.

I opened the box and looked at the gun, spare charger and the cardboard package with a picture of a yellow bullet on it. I couldn't understand why he did that. He looked at my questioning eyes and calmly told me the importance of him being there with me. He wanted the yellow envelope from me, he said he was going to call the Prosecutor, show him the pictures and tell him about the merciless, even vulgar dimensions of what it came down to.

I placed the envelope I took out of my backpack, on the table. I photographed with the camera of my phone, the one which showed a window with an open curtain, outside of which the Silpius Mountain and the walls on the skirts of the mountain were clearly visible. I photographed the other pictures as well. Then I gave the envelope to Dimitri, as he was already waiting for the Prosecutor to answer with the phone on his ear.

Apparently he received a positive response from the Prosecutor after he told him that he had to see him as soon as possible. He stood up and started walking towards the front door with the envelope in his hand. I told him to be careful and not to make any other phone calls.

I locked the door behind him and came next to the fountain once again. I took the phone on the table and started to examine the photos I just took. I thought I could recognize new details, besides the ones I have notived as I was looking at the pictures themselves. The electronic device gave me the option to zoom in and show me details of the photos and I thought I had to use such features.

I looked at the angle the window was seeing the mountain, tried to calculate the location of the house on that angle, the distance of the house from the mountain seen from the window, the height the picture was taken from, the direction of the shadows created by the sunlight at the time the picture was taken, the roofs, walls of the buildings visible outside the window and many other details. As I was noting all these new details I noticed and tried to make a conclusion, I stopped thinking about the reasons why I missed a detail that was right in front of me and look straight at the windowsill.

I zoomed in on the wooden windowsill and noticed that it was painted clumsily in a bright paint that was a mixture of blue and green. The outside of the windowsill was the same colour. This detail of indispensable calue would make it a lot easier for me to find the house during my search in the region I thought I could locate.

I could no longer wait fort he next morning, I shouldn't have waited. My breath was fast and I was excited. I opened the box on the table and took out the gun. The charger was empty. I took the cardboard box with the bullets in it, charged the gun and placed it back. My hands were shaking. Hoping that I will never have to use it, I placed the gun between my pants and belt. I tied the thin cardigan I took out of my backpack on my waist and left home without waiting another second.

I locked the door, put the keys in my pocket and started walking upwards on the street that went towards Kurtuluş Street, the first street in the world to have been illuminated with lights. As I was walking towards the mountains, the old, narrow and stone-paved streets smelled of history and mold in the night.

41. IN THE SQUATTER SETTLEMENT

I, Yiğit Kaya, walking on the old, narrow, stone-paved streets that smelled of history, was in the mind of nobody.

I thought I could hear the silent, joyful screams of the stone on the floor of the streets as they were smiling at those walking on them, with their shiny whiteness that looked polished from being walked on for hundreds of years. Was I going to be able to prevent the negativities Solmaz could face?

The narrow streets of Antakya I was walking on were looking at me with their old faces smelling of mold, moisture and history. A wall covered with green grass, a rusty iron door, a free vine trying to experience its adolescence by stretching its arms over the walls, any branch of the vine full of green leaves, a woman sitting aimlessly in front of the walls full of moss from moisture, a wrinkled-faced man, a young and tender-faced boy and a baby with arms and legs swaddled, trying to explain its hunger by puckering and crying; it seemed to me as if they were all telling me, "Go, progress and reach" at the same time, together.

I walked non-stop. I walked and tried to reach the place where narrow streets expanded with slopes, hills, caves and dark streets full of trees, shrubs, grass and thorns. I was going to reach the neighborhood I had to reach by breathing the bad smells of the sewage waters flowing through the open waterways between the unpainted walls, even though they were plastered, passing through the stone roads.

I walked outside the area with ugly, uncoated, unpainted houses, which were placed everywhere in the hills, steep rocks, plains without a gap. I nautiously walked next to the sewage, flowing directly through the street.

I walked for a long time and climbed non-stop, I walked through the dark forest, through narrow paths and reached the city walls stretching at the highest parts of the Silpius Mountain, overlooking the city from above.

I touched the stones, I tried to feel the texture of the mortar between the walls, the bricks and the stones, kneaded with egg white and lime. I sat at the bottom of the destroyed wall. I was tired, losing my breath, sweating.

I thought that I should not be at the top of a mountain, in the darkness and at the bottom of a ruined wall in the middle of the night. My eyes teared up, I tried not to cry, but I could not succeed, the drops dripping from my eyes wet the gray and warm surface of the rocks that had been waiting there for centuries.

I stood up and started walking again, proceeding quickly, without thinking about anything and not letting myself get caught in negative emotions. The Parmenius River, flowing into the city that experienced earthquakes, fires, sieges and unhappiness for centuries by collecting all the water in the mountains, was flowing so little and weak that it would embarrass the huge Iron Gate built to restrain it.

The majestic Parmenius River, the owner of one of the world's first dams, the crazy river that once dragged the rocks, stones and trees in front of it, smelled as badly and uncomfortably as the sewage waters flowing through the narrow streets in this late night.

I walked without looking at the hollows in the mountains, with my darkening soul as I I saw the poor, stinking and blackened walls of the ugly houses on the right and left of the Parmenius, and the widespread, stinking and blackened walls of the caves in the holy mountains, that now became barns.

I walked through narrow, ugly, dusty and insanely windy roads, hills and ancient paths in the mountains of Antakya; I passed the slums, houses without plaster, thick, thin, windowless, doorless.

I walked, then stopped, paused and looked all over the old Jewish neighborhood. I raised my head towards the sky and looked at the sharp corners of the city walls extending from me at the peaks of the silhouette of the Silpius, illuminated by the moonlight. I looked at it and understood; I was now where I was looking for, I was in the right place, in the neighborhood I had to reach and find.

I looked at the little boy, who stood for a moment as he was jumping by my side and stared at my face with an ice cream cone in his hand, smiling. With his short trousers on his legs and a shirt that was a mixture of green and blue, he was looking at everything carelessly and took nothing seriously, except for the ice cream cone in his hand. I looked at his face once again, but he didn't care, he didn't take me seriously, ignored me.

"Oh!" I said to myself. "Oh, if only I could ignore everything as much as you do, if only I could feel the moment just like you feel the ice cream in your hand. I wish I could be as innocent, thankless and sincere as you are."

I ignored the white, yellow fluid flowing on his hand from the ice cream, I smiled again by looking at his face and said to myself, "Know the value of the moment you live in!" "You are a child and you are experiencing the poorest, truly poorest, the most innocent and sincere moments of your life."

The smart, adorable and sincere boy stared at my face, smiling continuously. I asked him, I questioned him... I asked him to show me the houses with blue-green painted windows, pointing at the color of his shirt.

He took me around the streets under the dimly lit yellow lights as if he performed a miracle. I was almost flying in the air. I was having a dream and I wished I never woke up from the dream. He showed me around and stopped right below the windows with the blue-green painted windows. I stopped and looked up.

The moon that had risen well was illuminating the house in the dark. It was illuminating the windows, glasses, walls and branches, leaves of the vine hanging from the walls; as if a bright white pol-ish was applied to them. Grape bunches hanging from the branches and the blue-green wooden moldings of the windows of the house also had their share of the brightness of the same moon.

He looked suspiciously into my hand that reached to his, he did not take the money I gave him, threw a final glance at the ice cream cone, stuck his teeth in it and jumped away from me.

Was the child eating the ice cream real, an illusion of a mystery guiding me or a deception of my strangely functioning brain?

42. AT THE SILPIUS MOUNTAIN

I was in the slum that saw the hills south of Silpius Mountain from the angle in the photo. The roads and the paths on the mountains did not tire me. I walked around the not many streets of the neighborhood with the mysterious boy next to me and found the house I was looking for at exactly where I thought it would be. The wooden moldings of all windows, balusters on the balcony, the television antenna were all painted with the blue-green oil painting with irregular brush strokes.

I stood in front of the two-story house. I pushed the front door and entered the courtyard of the house through the door that opened without difficulty. No light leaked from the downstairs windows, it was dark and it was as if the house was sleeping with the people inside it.

I took a few steps to the right of the courtyard and looked up the steps of the concrete staircase rising upwards. There was no protective iron or wooden railing, I climbed the steps before approaching the edges and found myself in front of the entrance door of the upper floor. The wooden door, painted with the same color oil painting, seemed to open wide with the smallest push.

I took the gun that was on my belt, I opened the safety, I drove a bullet on the barrel and I started knocking on the door iwith its grip. I waited for a little click from the inside, a door creak, a human voice. However, the ugly house's walls, windows, and the rooms behind the wooden door accompanied the silence of the night.

I knocked on the door a few more times; I leaned my ear against the turquoise surface and waited, holding my breath. First, I heard a deep, low and incomprehensible sound as if it was coming from a distance, and then footsteps of someone walking towards the door.

I walked away from the door and started to wait. Impatiently, I was standing breathless in front of the door that I expected to open as soon as possible, and I was pushing myself to wait without making a sound.

The footsteps halted right behind the door and a sleepy voice said, "Who are you?" I answered the question without waiting, "It's me!" I said. He probably thought the answer I gave was enough so he opened the door and asked the man he saw in front of him with a sleepy tone, his last question: "Who were you looking for?"

"I was looking for you," I said, "I've been wanting to reach you and get to know you for days." I said to the man who spoke without being able to pronounce the letter 'r'. I said, "I was looking for Firuz Demirci," and then I hit him with the grip of the gun he looked at with fear, right in the middle of his forehead. He staggered and took a few steps back.

I entered the house without waiting. When I hit him once again on the forehead, he fell on his knees, tried to look at my face but fell face down on the bare concrete floor of the house; his forehead started to bleed.

I closed the door, took off his shirt by ripping the buttons off and tied his arms with the same shirt. I quickly untied the laces of the boots standing next to the door and tied his feet together on the ankles. Holding his hair, I lifted him up and looked at his face. The blood flowing from his forehead was also smeared on his face, he was lying unconsciously. I did not tie his mouth. I said, "Shouting is free, Firuz Demirci, you can shout as much as you want." He didn't hear me, he couldn't hear me.

Four separate doors were opening to the hall after the front door. The doors of the kitchen right at the entrance and the bathroom opposite to it were open. Right across me, I could see one closed and one open door.

The light was on in the room with the open door, the dusty and bare lightbulb hanging from the ceiling radiated a pale yellow light. I entered the room immediately but there was no one. In the middle of the room there was a messy bed, a chair in the corner of the room and on top of the chair were clothes of Firuz Demirci, thrown on it.

I looked at the wall with the window and quickly reached the tulle curtain of the window I knew. I pulled the curtain with my empty left hand, looked out, and saw the giant silhouette of the Silpius Mountain, shining under the moonlight. I was next to the window, which Solmaz stood in front of in the picture. I was angry and in a state that I could do anything. Angrily, I knocked on the windowsill with the grip of the gun in my right hand, and cleaned the spilled turquoise coloured oil paint.

I searched the entire room. I looked for a trail, a familiar item, but there was nothing. There was no trace, no smell that I could combine with the presence of Solmaz; not even a strand of hair. I bent down and looked under the bed. There was also no trace in the dusty and dark place.

I went to the room next door and quickly opened the door. It was dark. I couldn't understand what were the dark spots that the light leaking from the corridor could not illuminate, so I touched the switch of the lamp. There was a bedspread at the opposite wall of the room, and the room smelled bad.

I approached the bedspread, waited for a short time and quickly pulled the blanket with my shaking hand. I looked frightfully at the bodies of two dead people, whose hands and ankles were tied, and their faces were starting to turn blue and swollen with their mouths, and a scream broke out of my throat that I could not believe. They were the bodies of Solmaz's mother and father.

I kneeled next to the dead and shaking, I started shouting, shouting and crying. I was having difficulty breathing, making sounds similar to the sound of an animal whose throat was cut. My face was wet with all fluids coming from my eyes, nose, and mouth. I was crazy and devastated, and I cried to my desperation as well - I did not know what to do.

It was like I was in a dream, I wanted to believe that I was having a nightmare. It all seemed like it couldn't be real life. I was screaming and crying ceaselessly, wishing that all these were nothing but nightmare and saying, "my God, I beg you, let this be a nightmare." It was real, the two dead bodies I touched, with their hands anf feet tied, were turning purple and they were real.

I couldn't do anything. I could not reach them on time and save their lives, I could not prevent them from suffering.

I stood up with my desperate mad temper, went up to the killer on the floor next to the front door, kicked him hard on his ribs. A bitter scream spilled from his mouth, he bellowed like an animal. He was conscious. I put the barrel of the gun in his mouth; he looked at my face and the black metal in his mouth with his eyes wide open from fear… I held my finger over the trigger.

I didn't, I couldn't, I shouldn't have pulled the trigger. I took the gun out of the mouth of Firuz Demirci, who started crying, and I demanded him to tell me right now, this second, where Solmaz is and whether she was alive. He was crying non-stop and could not speak.

I stood up and went to the kitchen right next to the hall, took a pot standing upside down on the counter, turned on the faucet and filled it with water. I went to the murderer who was still crying from fear, and I poured the water in the pot on him, hitting his face with it.

Momentarily, he was out of breath and then he forced himself to speak in meaningless, empty, absurd words. When I looked at his face, I could understand that he wanted to speak, form meaningful sentences and beg for his life. I pulled him from his hair and sat him up, leaning his back against the wall. He was looking at me with his hands tied behind him, knees bent, and he trembled with fear.

"So that's it, Firuz Demirci," I said. "I will make you just like that Tyche statue you wanted so much. Now talk, where is Solmaz?" He started trembling and mumbling even more. He was in an extreme shock and I couldn't care less.

Three of my relatives and the only person Dimitri had died in a very short time, and the woman I loved had suddenly disappeared. I didn't even know whether she was alive or not and the person who knows what happened was in front of me, trembling and mumbling. I was barely holding myself from not filling his brain with the bullets inside the gun.

"Is it that difficult to kill a man?" I asked myself. I looked at the man in front of me, who could kill four people, perhaps all by himself and without getting help from anyone else. I looked at the cowardly, treacherous and pleading expression on the brutal face of the man.

I was questioning him, asking them one after the other. "Did you not pity the two young people? How about the two old ones in the other room, lying dead, who harmed no one?" I was pushing the barrel of the gun towards his nose.

I could barely hold myself. "You are a shameless man, you are not even a man. The woman whose naked photos you sent me and threatened me with was a women with such a heart that couldn't even hurt an ant. What was that manner on the phone? Where is you manner now? Is your courage only that much? Even if you knew all the money in the world would flow to you, would all these people you killed be worth it?" I couldn't hold myself, I was speaking and asking questions relentlessly, getting angrier as I did so.

"I am asking you for the last time," I said and pushed the barrel right in the middle of his left ear. "I will not ask again. Where is Solmaz?"

He replied to me in a manner that was even more scared from my rather calm voice. "I don't know," he said. "I really don't. They took the woman away when you landed at the airport, and before they went away, they killed the parents. I didn't know that it would come to this." He couldn't pronounce the letter 'r', was speaking fast and trying to express himself with hurry. He mumbled for a while and started crying again.

I thought that he couldn't lie, knowing that he could have been killed at any moment and that I could really do it –his life only depended on a small movement I could do with my finger.

"I don't know who you are, how you can be so cruel and treacherous but soon you will speak like a little bird, I promise you that. Your name is Firuz Demirci, is that right?" I asked him, and watched him trembling. He couldn't speak and was shaking his head from side to side.

"Yes, it's not easy to kill a man, even killing a brutal murderer like you isn't an easy job to do, but there are other ways to make critters like you speak." He didn't understand what I was saying, he forced himself to understand it. He wanted to say something, words didn't come out of his mouth. He swallowed them and looked at my angry face.

I took the fake Firuz Demirci to the room where his clothes were thrown on the chair. I untied the shirt and the bootlaces on his wrists and ankles and pushed the barrel of the gun on the side of his forehead. I ordered him to get dressed and threatened him with the most determined tone that in one wrong movement, I would not hesitate to pull the trigger.

Trembling and not looking away from my face with his eyes wide open, he got dressed quickly. I held him from the back of his neck and took him to the room next door, told him to look at the faces of the two old people, who were strangled to death. He couldn't look at them, he shut his eyes and said, "I didn't want it to be like that."

So who wanted it to be like that? Although I didn't yet know the answer to it, I knew very well that a long time was not required to find out. I knew that this fake Firuz Demirci was going to start speaking like a little bird soon enough.

I made Firuz sit down on the bed, in a way he would face the two old dead bodies. I stood behind him and this time, I pushed the barrel on the back of his neck. I took my phone out and without waiting, I dialled Dimitri's number. He had called me six times. He answered the phone immediately and started listing his questions one after the other: He asked me where I was, why I haven't answered the phone even though he called many times, and what I was up to now. I listened to his entire questions without speaking and I answered them all in a tone that was sad, bitter and frustrated.

"I found the house Dimitri, I'm in it now. They strangled Solmaz's parents to death. Solmaz is missing, I don't know where she is or whether she is alive."

Dimitri interrupted me with a sharp scream, so I paused and waited for a moment. "Fake Firuz Demirci is with me now, watching his brutal painting of death with a barrel on the back of his neck." I knew he couldn't understand what I meant with his last sentence of mine.

I made Firuz Demirci give the exact address of the house. He spoke to the microphone of the phone and I described all the roads I passed, the streets around the house and the neighborhood in detail to Dimitri, as I asked him whether he was taking notes. I asked him to come as soon as possible with whoever he was with.

"We're on our way, we are with Mr Prosecutor now," Dimitri said, but I told him that we were going on a short trip with Firuz Demirci. As I was hanging up, Dimitri was insisting on telling me that I must wait for them without going anywhere, but I couldn't understand anything he was saying.

I stood the fake Firuz Demirci up on his feet, tied his wrists in front of him and made him walk until the front door of the house; we went down the stairs and walked towards the door through the hall.

We went out on the street and I showed him the giant silhouette of the Silpius Mountain. I demanded him to look at it, especially at the Walls of Antioch on the skirts of Silpius Mountain, with sharp edges that made an 'S'. I told him that I wanted to meet his treacherous ancestor Firuz with another treacherous murderer, Firuz Demirci, nine hundred years later, at these historical walls. I dragged him from the lonely, quiet and narrow streets towards the skirts of the mountain.

He didn't understand what I was saying, he couldn't – perhaps he didn't want to. However, I was determined to take this brutal, evil critter to the most magnificent place at the Walls of Antioch.

43. FROM BAB AL-HADID TO THE PARMENIUS RIVER

The night was dark. The wind was blowing wildly from the valley between the Silpius and the Stauris Mountains. Twenty minutes after we left the house, we passed by the last houses of the neighborhood and continued our walk on the old path twenty, twenty-five meters above the Parmenius River.

The stones of the road were well worn after having been walked on for centuries by merchants, clergy, Muslim and Christian armies, horses, camels and donkeys carrying soldiers, as well as sheep, cows and goats. I thoroughly memorized the trees, rocks, caves, weeds and shrubs surrounging thei pathway I went through. I was always going to remember this historical pathway with bitter memories and it extended to the city gate, also known as the "Aleppo Gate" of ancient Antioch.

I watched the fake Firuz Demirci walk in front of me, with his hands tied at the front, with fast steps and an attitude that knew where he was going. I was waiting for him to start talking as soon as possible. He should have told me where Solmaz is, should have told me whether she was alive.

Right in the middle of the passage between two big rocks, I stopped him, walked next to him and looked at his face. He looked at me with his face sobered up with the strong winds blowing, the paths we walked and the air of the mountains. He had evil eyes under his forehead with a big bump from my hit. "Who are you?" I asked him again. "Was it necessary to kill so many people, was it worth what you still couldn't achieve?"

He continued walking without answering the questions I asked, saying nothing. He took a few steps that stopped; started to speak with a crushed, desperate and regretful attitude.

"Bohemond is my name. I am a French of Turkish origin. My ancestors are from Antakya, they went to Lebanon about a century ago and from there to France. Many members of my family still speak Turkish and teach it to their children… We make a great effort not to forget this language among our family."

I did understand that he was not Turkish in our first conversation on the phone, I did not tell him that. I wanted him to continue his speech.

"I am a member of an international network. We have branches in France, Germany, Great Britain, Italy, America, Israel, Lebanon, Egypt and many other countries, and Turkey of course. I speak four languages.

Our best clients are private museums, colelctors, businessmen, rich people, holding owners, cult leaders, some clergymen and so-called believers who live in the bondage of bigoted beliefs. Any historical finding they set their eye on, a statue freshly discovered, a painting in a museum with poor security is always on our target.

When our clients set an eye on a finding that will fill the gap in their collections, they cannot sleep until the morning and do not make us sleep until we deliver this missing piece to them. We try anything to get the piece they set their eyes onto. Anything you can think of…

We play it safe. The day we agree on the amount, that is usually in millions, at least half of the amount is transferred immediately to our bank accounts. Our clients know that the piece they set their eyes onto will be handed to them under all conditions; because when an agreement is made and some of the money is transferred, there is no turning back for us."

The old Firuz, new Bohemond, was speaking willingly. Our tempo slowed down even further as I was listening to him on the pathway. I listened to him without interrupting and expected him to bring the subject to Solmaz as soon as possible.

"About a year ago, a highly important client we couldn't refuse offered us five million Euros for a statue here. The job seemed easy, we were going to bribe someone at the museum, change the statue with an identical one and hand the original to our client.

We set our eyes onto your friend, Dimitri Çağlayan. I assume you know these parts of the story so I'm skipping it. We couldn't succeed in bribing your friend. We looked into his past, his family and we found out that he had a brother. He was in medical school and he didn't know what he wanted to do with his life due to his young age. We approached him, became friends, gained his trust and we discovered the existence of even more important findings, thanks to him.

Nikola Çağlayan himself was quite interested in and informed on the history of Christianity, its mysterious past as well as the importance of Antioch in the development and spreading of this religion. In the long conversations we had with him, we could always learn new things and track every step of successful archaeologists. So we threw another hook at another museum worker and we easily could bribe him. I won't tell his name, you will find out soon enough anyway."

Bohemond was gasping. I stopped him and made him sit down on a rock. I sat down in front of him. A light rain had begun, he wiped the drops wetting his face with his tied hands. First he looked at his wrists, then at the gun in my hand that frightened him, and continued speaking.

"The other museum official, who was making research on the cracked, destroyed mountains and caves on the St Peter's Church, found the leather scroll completely coincidentially but he hid it somewhere only he knew and started to seriously bargain with us. We called the man to Ankara and saw the pictures the man took with his camera with great excitement and enthusiasm.

There were two possibilities: Either the museum official was trying to deceive us with fake scrolls he prepared himself, or he wanted to sell us the scrolls, which he claimed were at least two thousand years old (the third book of Luke from Antioch, that was known to have been written but could never been found) without registering it in the records. We had to take it seriously.

If the scrolls found were indeed the third book of Luke, who wrote the Bible, and if we could get our hands on it, we could sell it to any museum or collector in the world with a very high price.

However, the man wanted five million dolalrs from us and said that pre-payment was an indispensable requirement of this agreement.

We weren't fool enough to pay five million dollars for leather scrolls we have never seen or touched before, not knowing whether they were real or fake – but we also didn't want to scare off the man. We were very excited. We could clearly read, in one of the photos he showed us, the inscription, "O Theophilus". Luke from Antioch has written both the Bible and the Acts of the Apostles, addressing someone named Theophilus.

The rain was getting heavier. I was listening to him carefully and wondered where he was going to get to.

"We decided to get to him through Nikola Çağlayan. He knew the man from the museum his brother was working at and he could speak closely with him. We asked Nikola to not mention knowing us. We told him that this man has found some ancient documents that were very important for the history of Christianity and that he was trying to sell it. We said in case he succeeded, these documents could never return to this country, where they belong. So we took on the role of good men and told him never to tell anyone, including hs brother, about this matter until the documents are handed to the officials.

We succeeded – the young and innocent Nikola believed us. They met a couple of times, spoke but Nikola Çağlayan gave us no significant information. We suspected that he was receiving important information but we didn't push him in order not to scare him off or drive him away. The Tyche statue, which we were after, was in the museum anyway and we were in no hurry to complete that job, even though our client was pushing us to hand it to him. Our new target was to get those scrolls.

We called the man to Ankara about a week ago and he told us, despite our best efforts, that we will not be able to touch the scrolls in case he doesn't have the money he asked for. After he left us, we followed him. Our men, who were trying not to lose sight of the man where he went, photographed him with a young man he met at a shopping center.

The man he met was Nikola Çağlayan. That night they took off with the man's car and we followed them. The next morning, they arrived in Antakya and Nikola went to that house you were in as well. We waited for him until the afternoon, when he left the house that day, in street corners and under roods. He came out of the house in the afternoon with a girl we didn't recognize. We followed them everywhere they went on foot.

If you don't have a reason to worry, you usually don't notice you are being followed – so even a ten year old can follow you. We followed them and when they were next to the Charon relief on the Stauris Mountain, it was easy for us to catch them both in that lonely, quiet place, threaten them and make them speak.

The young man didn't speak. We forced him, threatened him, we told him that we would hurt the young woman, but we couldn't succeed. He took out a few pieces of folded paper from his pocket. As we were trying to understand what he was trying to do, he gave one of them to the girl next to him, the second to me and he read the third one outloud, without hurry, slowly and deliberately. Although I understood that what was written on the piece of paper in my hand was the same as what he was reading, I couldn't understand what he was trying to do. "If you could wait a little longer, it was going to happen the way I read it. You didn't wait, you couldn't wait so you lost," he said to me. I couldn't understand what he was trying to tell me.

He told us to follow him and started climbing upwards from Charon, which was carved in the mountain. We thought he obeyed us and that he was taking us to what we wanted, so we followed the two. We hiked for about an hour or two and we reached that ancient structure that is mixture of a bam and bridge, called the Iron Gate. He started lecturing the young girl next to him about history, telling her, "This structure is exactly one thousand and five hundred years old."

We wanted him to tell us what we wanted him to tell, the location of the scrolls, but he never mentioned that. We threatened him again and tried to scare him by saying that we would hurt the young girl next to him. He answered us with one sentence, saying, "I said what I had to say." He didn't say anything else besides that, we couldn't make him talk... And you know what happened to them.

You found the young girl under the giant walls of the Iron Gate and Nikola Çağlayan in the thousands-year-old tunnel inside St Peter's Church. We killed the girl first and Nikola got scared, screaming terribly. At that moment he was about to speak, so when he was trying to take us to the cave church, he was almost convinced to talk. He wanted to enter the church. As one of our men distracted the guard, we entered the cave. However, the moment we entered the church, he started to pray, beg and gave up speaking.

We did what we had to do, we did it... I have nothing more to fear, I stuck the steel bars into their heards. You will kill me anyway... I am not afraid any more, I say it, I killed them both, I destroyed them. I removed two obstacles in front of me earning millions of dollars. I also strangled the parents of your wife. You were asking whether I regret it... I don't, not at all. I was also going to kill your wife but we postponed it. For a short time only though; if you won't give us what we want, she will die as well. She will die. I will kill you sexy wife with my bare hands, I will kill her by tasting her..."

He was speaking ecstaticly. He spoke without a pause, breathless, he laughed and tried to continue his speech, which began to become meaningless, in a crazy way. I raised my hand and slapped him hard in the face. I couldn't understand from his wet face due to the heavy rain, whether he was crying or not. He seemed to come to himself after the slap. I put the barrel of the gun in his mouth and tried to prevent his speech, which upset my nerves quite a bit. He couldn't speak, so he went silent. He came back to himself and started to look at my face in fear.

The crazy Bohemond let it slip that Solmaz was alive. I didn't feel the need to ask the lunatic in front of me how they followed Solmaz in Istanbul, why and how they brought Solmaz together with her parents to Antakya. After what he told me, I knew how this international criminal organisation worked, what sort of cruel methods they could use to achireve their targets and earn that dirty money, that they would try to bribe anyone that would be useful to them and that they would not hesitate to commit countless murders.

I lifted Bohemond. I started pushing him through the narrow street and made him walk fast, holding him from the back of his neck. He did not give up, he continued to repeat that it was not late for anything, that we could work together, that we did not have to die with the dead, that life was ongoing, that if I forgave and released him, he would immediately tell the place they hid Solmaz, and even come with me and convince his other friends. Even as he was trying to continue his walk after me hitting him in the back of his head at the end of every sentence, he still tried to find new ways to persuade me and save his life. He tried, but failed.

The rain became heavier and started to prevent our walk on the narrow path. I stopped him, stood in front of him and told him that if he told me where Solmaz was, I would release him. He looked at me one moment, as if he believed me, and told me, almost begging, "Let's go back then, what are we doing at this time of the night on top of this mountain. Let's go home and there I will tell you where your wife is." I told him that we will not go back if he doesn't tell me now, that he will not go back, more correctly. I told murderer Bohemond that his end is here – he understood that he had no chance of survival.

My phone rang at that exact moment. It was Dimitri as I expected. He told me with excitement that they found the house, that the house was searched, the young Prosecutor was wish him and that the police has surrounded the entire neighborhood. "Don't you do anyhing and become wrong and guilty when you're right. Mr Prosecutor has found five different SIM cards in the drawer of the nightstand where Firuz Demirci's phone was. The numbers will be determined immediately and the phone records will be found out, to catch his criminal partners."

I told him to tell the young Prosecutor that Solmaz was still alive, probably kept somewhere in Antakya and that they must take action very carefully. I told them that I had only a small business left and that I would be with them the moment I am finished with it. Dimitri asked me what my small business was. I told him that I was on a quick walk towards the Iron Gate. He told me with worry, "Alright, don't be late and come here quickly so we can find Solmaz as soon as possible." "Okay," I told him." "By the way, that Firuz Demirci's real name is Bohemond apparently, he didn't tell me his name yet – I will inform you when I know."

We walked through the thin, curved path leading to the giant structure of the Iron Gate and going downhill. We reached the giant structure and proceeded on the stone pathway. We stood right in the middle and looked at the dark, bottomless cliff-like space below. Bohemond's feet were trembling.

"Do you regret?" I asked. "What does it change?" he answered me with a question. "Perhaps it can change something. Do you regret it? Was all you have done worth it? Did so many people have to die?" I insisted. "If I tell you I regret it, will you not kill me?" he asked his previous question in a different way. I told him that killing a person is not an easy task – even if the person to be killed is just a disgusting, ruthless, dirty money butler. I understoof that he was trying to save time. I could understand that he was trying to delay his end, even for a few minutes, by speaking to me longer.

"Although the Crusades seemed to have started with innocent and justified reasons such as taking back the sacred relics of Christianity from the hands of the Muslims and giving the city of Jerusalem to the administration of Christians, did you know that the actual reason was economic, as in every war?

Do you think they would continue on their way if the Crusaders, who went to Jerusalem, a city far away from here, to find the Holy Grail, the tree pieces of the cross where Jesus Christ was stretched, the nails with their hands nailed, knew that they were here in Antioch?

How do you think history would have happened if Bohemond, the commander of the Crusader army, who conquered Antioch on June 3 of 1098, had found the third book of Luke, the Holy Grail, that year?"

"Bohemond?" I cried. "Is it a lie that your name is Bohemond as well?" He looked at me with a smile and said, "No," "This is indeed not a lie, my name is Bohemond, and it is a complete coincidence that my name is the same with the commander of the Crusader army." I couldn't understand whether what he said was the truth, or whether there was a brutal irony in it, as there often was.

This speech became too long now, I had given Bohemond enough time. I pushed the man on the edge at the end of the Iron Gate's pathway. I told him that he was now at the end of the road, that he could be able to regain his freedom with the help of the power and the criminal organisation he was a part of, so that I couldn't let something like that happen, because such freedom he would have would hurt my conscience, knowing all the murders he had committed. He looked at me once again under the rain and said, "Alright, it will be as you wish." He looked down again and suddenly turned towards me, pulling my wet shirt towards himself with his tied hands. Suddenly, we started to fall rapidly towards the Parmenius River at the bottom of the Iron Gate. I looked into his eyes as we were falling. He was tightly holding onto the collar of my shirt and never let go even as we were falling… In those last seconds I fell, six words were on my mind only: "I could only come so far."

CHAPTER THREE

44. "O THEOPHILUS, YOU CAN ONLY LIVE FOR THE TIME THAT IS GIVEN TO OR SET FOR YOU."

Dear Mr Theophilus,

Living is not easy. It is not easy to live and write things that could be read even hundreds of years later, as one attempts to leave permanent work that could reach the future. It is not easy to pause for a moment while doing your daily chores, get away from everything, to understand by taking a short journey to your inner world, to express your belief with your heart and to make all unbelievers believe.

If you lived like a weed, aimless; it wouldn't matter the years you were born, raised and grown up, it also would have no value whether it was short or long.

In your ninety-nine years of life from the day you were born until you die, you could live like a weed, meaningless, worthless, and without any benefit to anyone, or you live for thirty-three years; you can be a good person who is full with meaning, has goals, even works to be remembered for thousands of years, and makes people believe in living in brotherhood.

Do you want a life that lasts ninety-nine years, meaningless, immoral, and each day the same as the previous and the next day; or do you want a much shorter life - thirty-three years, full, meaningful, moral and capable of influencing the world for thousands of years?

I would not change a single hour of my life, in which I relieve the pain of a patient, breathe comfortably and help him hug the arms of life, with the empty, hollow and meaningless millennia of a man who lives a life as ordinary as an insect.

Dear Mr Theophilus,

We are sent to this life with a specified time. What we can do is written on our forehead, our heart, and even the smallest point of our brain.

We live for the time given and set for us; neither a second less nor a minute more.

We can do work that we are authorized and determined; neither a missing job nor a single surplus.

You can live as long as you deserve, O Theophilus; moments when you fall off the edge of a cliff are just a dream.

If you fell, think why you fell. If you were made to fall, stop and think twice; look into the eyes of the one who made you fall and ask, where is the place you will reach in the deep cliffs that seem so short but you have actually fallen a period that is actually centuries long?

O Theophilus,

If you have a right, if you have a single second left from this world to live, know that you will live. As you fly like a bird in the gaps of the deep cliffs you fell and try to reach the hard rocks at the bottom, know and believe that the life you lead will not end.

O Theophilus,

Read the first two books I wrote to you and deliver them to a time that is thousands of years later.

This third book I have written, you will never be able to read it, and you will never be able to tell anyone. But I know, I know very well, I believe with all my heart that a man who can protect himself from the rocks rolling from the peaks of a ruined temple will find it, read it and announce it to all who deserve.

The man who will find and be able to read them should never take the sacred prize I have presented to him out of the city he found them in, as Cephas wanted so.

O Theophilus,

You can only live for the time given to and set for you; not a minute less, nor a second more.

45. LIVING… BUT HOW?

I heard birds singing continuously. It was as if I was sitting on one of the chairs next to the fountain in the middle of the courtyard and stretching my feet to another. I was half asleep, if only I could open my eyes, only if I could open them, I thought I could see the little birds singing to each other.

Even though I pushed with all my power, with my best effort and will, I couldn't open my eyelids. I was tired and exhausted. Let alone opening my eyes, I couldn't even move them a bit. I fell back into a deep sleep.

I was in a sleep that was moist like rain, even wet – walking towards the wet visuals of dreams waiting for me under a bright moonlight with small steps I took with my feet. The moment I saw you, I was going to stop and hug you in the surrender of out memories – and you, were you going to hug me?

I was not going to hug the things you tell me, I was not going to listen to you and not tell you anything – you couldn't understand me… You were going to stand before me as colourful and wet as the rain, even wetter than the shores of my soul, with an attitude that is as slippery as the visuals of nightmares waiting around the corners of desperate moments. You were going to hug me silently, unquestioning, with the irresponsilibity that left the past in the past. How about I – was I going to be able to hug you again?

I couldn't perceive how much time has passed. I woke up and this time I heard mechanical sounds – a ringing, a high-pitched sound, beeping and others I couldn't describe. None of them sounded like the birds chirping. I forced myself once again, I wanted to open my eyes and not sleep any more. I made an effort, forced myself and could only open my eyes halfway… *Where was I?* I could first see the blurry silhouette of the place around me and it wasn't next to the fountain – nor the sounds I heard were of singing birds… *What had happened to me?*

The last moment I remember was falling fast into a void with someone clinging rightly to my collar with his hands, and the moment he looked into my eyes with eyes wide open from fear.

I tried to open my eyes a little more. Thin and transparent pipes were coming out of both holes of my nose, my mouth and my arms, reaching somewhere. Red, yellow, white, and colorless liquids flowed through the plastic pipes. There were clips attached to the fingertips of my hands, glass bottles of different sizes, plastic bags held up higher than the bed where I was lying and turned upside down. I could hear all the sharp, intermittent, monotonous sounds emitted by a device, I saw everything but I could not perceive where I was and what all these things around me were for.

Suddenly I was startled by a face, whose mouth and nose were covered with a white mask, two brown eyes and a gentle voice coming from under the mask, which I saw not far from my face, above my head. "Hey! He opened his eyes… I can't believe he is conscious, he really is, he is looking into my eyes!" Who was this masked person?

Who was she, why was she hiding his mouth and nose with a mask, and what did her last words mean? What was she saying she couldn't believe, what could she not believe? I could hear and see everything but not understand what they were, couldn't put anything together.

"Sir, are you okay, can you hear me?" I didn't know what to say and how to respond to the masked face with brown eyes only, asking me that! I fell asleep again into the deep sleep. I was extremely tired and exhausted. I wanted to sleep, rest and feel better. *Where was I?*

I opened my eyes again. This time I was able to open it without difficulty and saw more masked faces looking at me from above. They were in an enthusiasm and joy that I could not understand and words were constantly pouring out from their mouths behind the masks… *Who were they, what did they want from me?* Suddenly I saw two dark blue eyes with red sclera and started looking at them constantly; I knew those eyes, I knew them from somewhere, I knew that shade of navy blue very well, but I couldn't remember who it belonged to... *Who were you?*

I felt the light touch on my hand, I looked at the hand that was gently touching me, then I looked once more at the masked face of the owner of that hand, the dark blue eyes above the mask. I forced myself to remember, and suddenly a current that shook my whole body, brain, self, memory passed through me; I sensed the blood flow attacking all my cells. My dry lips moved with difficulty. "Solmaz," I said and I didn't say anything else, I couldn't.

The masked face came closer to my face and two drops of tears dripped from the dark blue eyes. She blushed even more and said "It's me." "It's me Yiğit, did you recognize me? I knew it, I knew you were going to win this battle and not leave me alone here," she said. Now I could see her sobbing and happily hugging the brown-eyed white-dressed girl next to him. Once again all the images blurred up and despite all my efforts, my eyes suddenly closed. *Why couldn't I stay awake?*

I did not know how long had passed, but I could open my eyes much more easily, I could move my head more easily. There were four more beds in the large room besides mine,thin, transparent pipes went out of all of their nostrils, arms and hands, hoses came out of their mouths, reaching out to devices with blinking lights, plastic bags and glass bottles.

There was always someone around the bed I was lying in, and they were constantly talking to me, asking or answering questions I asked. The man who had a deep voice examined me with a listening device hanging around his neck and with the reflex hammer in his hand. I understood that he was my doctor despite the green mask on his face. He was telling me that I was better now and that they would soon progress with my treatment in the normal patient room. *Why was I in this state?*

Now I could feel all emotions like sadness, joy, sadness, happiness, enthusiasm, excitement, boredom and everything alike. I could distinguish the heat, I was uncomfortable with the cold, I was trying to move my numb arm and legs and I could move them, despite the difficulty. The hose in my mouth was gone and I was now able to swallow the liquids given to my mouth with the help of the masked people. Was I getting better now?

They tied me with belts. The officers who took the stretcher that I was placed on out of the intensive care unit were extremely careful and slow. After pressing the button of the large elevator that could only take the stretcher and the two attendants next to me, I felt the cabin rising upwards. It was the opposite, the exact opposite of the feeling I had when flying down the heights of the rock body of the Iron Gate.

They were waiting for me right in front of the elevator door. Solmaz and Dimitri were looking at my face with love, longing and happiness. The door of the patient room, wide enough for the stretcher to pass, was light blue. The officers set the height of the bed to the same level as the stretcher I was on and skillfully transferred me onto the bed with the help of Solmaz and Dimitri. My pain was less than it was a few days ago, when I first came back to myself and opened my eyes. However, I still couldn't move any part of my body as I wished.

They placed me on the bed, made the backrest of the bed upright by thirty degrees and explained Solmaz and Dimitri about everything they should pay attention to. They showed the button of the emergency call bell, which we could use in emergency situations, and left silently with their smiling faces and eyes. *To live, but how?*

It was as if I woke up from a damp or even wet sleep - wet like a rainy weather. I have now reached the wet visuals of dreams, awaiting me under the shiny moonlight, with the steps I took on my toes.

You should not have stood before me with a pale manner, as pale as the visuals of nightmares waiting around the corners of desperate moments, colourful and wet like rain, even wetter than the shores of my soul. Hug me with the irresponsibility that is silent, unquestioning, that destroyed memories and left them in the past.

I looked at Solmaz's face. We were finally alone. Solmaz was standing on one side of the bed and Dimitri was standing on the other side of it, they were looking at my face with longing and en-

thusiastic love. They were waiting for me to speak, to say something; whereas I expected them to speak, tell me and answer dozens
of questions I had. I moved my hand to tell them to sit down, looked
at them lovingly and in a way that made it obvious to both of them
that I wanted them to tell me what was going on – that I was ready
to listen. I wanted to understand, be understood and live – I wanted
to live a happy, healthy and fulfilled life… *To live, but how?*

46. I CLOSED MY EYES AND DIVED INTO OUR DANCE WITH GHOSTS

"We found you at the foot of the Iron Gate, together with the man called Bohemond. You were inside a wide waterhole in the river bed at the bottom of the giant structure. Bohemond was under you."

When I started to listen to Dimitri, who started speaking, I remembered Bohemond's eyes opened in fear, who, with his tied hands, clung to the collar of my shirt and pulled me down with him from the deadly height.

"The water in the pit you fell into and the man who was under you reduced the effect of the fall and saved your life, according to the opinion of the experts who examined the crime scene."

I interrupted Dimitri at this point of his speech and explained in a slow and tired manner how he suddenly clung to me with his hands I tied and suddenly dragged me to the river bed at the bottom where I initially wanted to send him to.

"This was one reason we wanted you not to do anything crazy and to come back right away in our last conversation on the phone. The man next to you was crazy; a cunning, ruthless murderer who could make very good use of even the smallest opportunity he could find. Now when I listen to what you say, I realize that I was not mistaken.

Soon after you and Bohemond left, we arrived at the house you described. The prosecutor on duty and specially trained security forces took the necessary precautions. When we entered the house, we were all terrified by the painful sight we saw. That was when I realized the severity of the anger you had. I knew very well what you could do with the feelings of revenge and resentment any normal person would feel, seeing that state of the two old people strangled to death."

Dimitri went silent as Solmaz started sobbing. He should not have described the last images of her parents next to Solmaz. He apologized and said he would be more careful from now on. Solmaz wiped her eyes and said "It doesn't matter, don't mind me, I can't hold back, even if you don't tell me anything, the same thing happens when I think about what we have experienced, I cry, I cry constantly," she said to Dimitri. He looked at me and, with the silent approval I gave with my head, continued to explain what happened.

"They collected everything in the house that could be useful to them, mobile phones, sim cards lying out in the open, papers, books, brochures, and so on. When you did not answer our calls, we set out for the Iron Gate, where you said you were. It was raining and when I think about it, how fortunate that it rained. When we climbed on the structure, we were going to find nothing and go back - but the officials we sent down to the river bed to examine the shadows we saw from above and couldn't identify told us what we never expected and never wanted to see, on the walkie talkie. Then we went down to the Parmenius River as well.

Bohemond was still in the waterhole, and you body was on top of Bohemond except for your head and arms. When we looked at your pulse, we realized that it was still, lightly, beating. Both your legs and one arm were damaged, you were laying there as if you were dead. With great care, we took you out of the waterhole, laid you on a flat stone, and quickly called the medical teams, paying attention to let you have open airway. It took them a while to come, naturally. Doctors and other paramedics who found our location next to the Iron Gate took the necessary precautions to carry you safely on portable stretchers, in a way that would not endanger your life, and took you to the ambulance they left near St. Peter's Church. We carried the body of Bohemond with the dead bag we took from the paramedics and handed it over to the officers who would take it to the morgue. "

My friend was tired of talking fast and continuously. He took a break and rested for a while. He looked at my face and asked if I was tired. I was in fact tired, but there were so many things I was curious about - that even if I knew that I would faint from fatigue, I would endure and continue to listen to him as long as I could. Making a slow and tired hand gesture, I asked him to continue.

"We followed the ambulance that took you to the hospital and came to the university hospital where you were taken in with the Prosecutor. The crowded group of doctors made all the necessary examinations, evaluations and told us that it was a miracle that you were alive and breathing despite the many wounds and injuries you had. They could operate you immediately, so they put you to sleep in the intensive care unit for a while. At the end of that period, you had three major surgeries. Your body was strong, you continued to resist despite all adverse conditions and managed to hold on to life.
"

He paused again, made a thumbs up gesture with his hand and shook it twice. The expression on his face said something like, "You were amazing, well done, I congratulate you." I looked at Solmaz… She wasn't in the same mood as a few minutes ago, she was sending a nice and sincere smile towards me.

"Exactly twenty-one days have passed since we brought you from the riverbed under the Iron Gate and brought you to the hospital; so as you can understand, it is the first time we are able to talk to you in twenty-one days. The doctors were sure that you would die in the first days that you were here, but then they got more pleased seeing you get better and gave better news to us every day."

As Dimitri as talking, I sometimes turned my head and looked at Solmaz. She was looking back at me with her beautiful eyes and face in cute and loving glances. My understanding friend saw that I was looking at Solmaz more frequently and that I was looking at her for longer periods of time, and suddenly whispered that I should not worry, that it was now time to talk about what happened to Solmaz. I smiled and with a low voice like his, I told Dimitri that I was indeed very curious how and when the woman I loved could be rescued.

"We couldn't get information from Bohemond anymore. Simultaneous raids were carried out to all addresses identified from the phone numbers Bohemond spoke to, with the examination the Prosecutor made on the mobile phones and a few sim cards found at the location. There were people we never expected, among those whose homes and workplaces were raided. There, in one of these raided houses, they found Solmaz. She was taken out of there and taken to Istanbul. When she was rescued I was so happy that I sat down and cried with joy."

Standing up from the seat she was sitting in, Solmaz came to me and kissed me softly on my forehead. Then she continued to tell me what happened, from where Dimitri left off.

"I was very scared Yigit, my parents were alive when they took me out of there. I was so scared that something would happend to them."

She was silent for a brief moment. She gasped and two tears dripped down her cheeks. When she finally started speaking again, I reached towards her and affectionately squeezed her hand, trying to tell her that I was as sorry as she was.

"Unfortunately, all my fears have come true… Now I don't have my parents, and nor do I have Gizem… What am I going to do?" I squeezed her hand so much that it almost hurt her. With my tired voice that I couldn't raise, I said, "I'm here, and I will be here for as long as I live and you live too." I looked at her face, trembling between crying and smiling. The woman who knew me best for many years understood, right at that moment, that I was impatient to hear the rest of the story.

The man you call Bohemond was a very bad person. When he said he wanted me to undress and that he would take pictures of me, I reacted very strongly. I understood that he wouldn't hesitate to harm my parents if I didn't do what he said, from his sinister, evil expression. I undressed and sotood as he wanted me to. He was aiming to anger and scare you by sending you those photos. I still get angry as I recall his laughter as he told me that he would include increasing immoralities in the pictures he was taking and that he would particularly enjoy them, if you didn't do what he said."

I briefly told Solmaz that Bohemond has sent me the pictures and that I found the house they were hiding from the little details in those pictures. She reached with her hand and lovingly caressed my hair. At that moment, Dimitri intervened: "Two of the houses raided by the Prosecutor belonged to the officers working at our museum. One of them was an ordinary officer carrying out secretariat work and the other one, which was the biggest surprise to all of us, was a high-rank officer. Even though he initially said that he didn't know anyone named Bohemond, when the Prosecutor laid out in front of him all phone records and text messages, he started telling us everything he knew about Bohemond and his gang. The gang's information sources at the museum were those two."

I could now better understand how they had heard about the scrolls we found and handed over to the museum for examination as well as the ceramic piece among them. I continued to listen to Dimitri.

"Oddly enough, this colleague of mine had found these scrolls long before we did, with great coincidence, and even though he was obliged to hand them over to the museum, he didn't do it. He confessed on the very first day he was caught that he contacted Bohemond and his historial artifact smuggler partners and had a serious bargain with them. By the way, there were some allegations about Nikola, and we will find out about them later together, in case the investigation is concluded properly."

I told him not to worry about Nikola, that I knew from what Bohemond told me that his brother was not involved in any crime. His face lightened up with joy; I knew that he would ask me to tell him right away and ovewhelm me with dozens of questions if he knew that it wouldn't tire me.

I squeezed Solmaz's hand lovingly as I was listening to Dimitri telling me how Solmaz, who was rescued the night I was brought to the university hospital and was taken into the intensive care unit, never left the front of the intensive care unit and the room that was assigned for her stay.

I told them I was very tired and that I wanted to sleep for a while, even if for a short time. I can't recall if I could finish my sentence but when my eyes closed and I surrendered myself in the soft arms of a deep sleep, I was far away from the real world. I could now only see through a pale and thin tulle curtain. We were moving together with the dreams dancing before me, twisting and turning. I surrendered myself even further into the soft arms of sleep and dove into our dance with the ghosts.

I was somewhere between sleep and wakefulness. I could hear Dimitri and Solmaz in the room, speaking softly, but I couldn't understand them. I could remember what they had just told me, and now I could attribute very different meanings to what I remembered now that I was inside the passage hall, the jumping board, the intermediate corridor, the stopover – that short interval resembling to be between life and death, which I could give many more names to.

Could life change so quickly and mercilessly in a very short time now, for no reason, after being able to hold onto the wings of a happy, peaceful, carefree and fearless life?

Two young people, both having good professions, who were both successful and could benefit the society and humanity in the next few years… Should they have been the ones to vanish, disappear and sent off to eternity for reasons that seem meaningless and insignificant to me?

Could life be so fast and cruel, changeable, meaningless and bad?

47. SOMEWHERE BETWEEN SLEEP AND WAKEFULNESS

I was somewhere between sleep and wakefulness. I was somewhere between hearing and not being able to hear, seeing and not being able to see, feeling and not being able to understand anything.

I owed the life I have been continuing to a pit, where the waters of the river flowing under the one-thousand-and-five-hundred-year-old Iron Gate accumulated, as well as to the body of a murderer that was left under me, after he wanted to end my life.

In that short moment of flying down from the highest point of the Iron Gate, I could not remember anything I thought, saw, or felt, except one: Bohemond's eyes opened with fear and his disgusting smile – the smile of an evil man who was approaching death in a desperate and pitiful way, and who couldn't digest this way of approaching death. His face, which reflected his fear, could smile in the meantime and this was very strange to me.

I knew that the similarity between the name he attributed to himself, Firuz Demirci, with the "treacherous armourer Firuz" and that Antioch, which resisted the Crusader siege for two hundred days, had to surrender with the betrayal of this armour repairman. I also knew the name of the commander, which took over the city by managing this Crusader siege – Bohemond. I was trying to resolve the irony of the similarities between the two names, but I couldn't reach a healty result despite all my efforts.

At that very moment, I remembered what the expression appeared on Bohemond's face told me, as we were falling down on the Parmenius River. It was saying, "Sometimes, what lies behind all the glorious victories of great commanders is a little betrayal of an ordinary traitor." His face was hurling with his ugly laugh, coming from his evil spirit, and I was plugging my ears shut not to hear this ugly sound that filled the void we were in. It was as if I was dreaming – I was somewhere between sleep and wakefulness.

I was trying to understand the efforts made to restore the magnificent city to its former glory after eighteen major earthquakes, but I could not perceive anything; I was somewhere between sleep and wakefulness.

Antioch was destroyed by great fires, floods, floods, epidemic diseases as well as big, deadly and destructive earthquakes and was repaired each time despite all the disasters and was brought back to its former glorious days. There must have been a reason why it was called "Theopolis" once – which meant the "City of God." I was trying to understand exactly that, forcing myself to understand it but despite my greatest efforts, I could not reach anywhere. I was somewhere between living and dying.

As I was trying to get rid of the nightmares, which I couldn't understand initially, and the effects they created, I had to face real images that were far worse, scarier, terrible, evil, crushing, humiliating and destructive than those nightmares. I wanted to resist this reality, I wanted to rebel, oppose them, to shout out all the cruelties of life to everyone in loud noises – but I always found myself in the arms of a desperate submission, with my hands tied. I was somewhere between reality and dreamworld.

I was forcing myself not to think about our life after these days, the difficult and unsolvable situation we were in, what we would do and how we should behave. Unfortunately I could not manage to find answers to that as well. I did not even know if I could be healthy, vigorous, active and free again like the old days, after the operations I went through like a dead person. I was somewhere between existence and non-existence.

I did not yet know anything about what Solmaz went through. I also did not know how she was treated and what had been done to her. I was overwhelmed by the negative thoughts attacking my brain, which I tried to get rid of every time they came. I couldn't find any way to get her out of the injury of these terrible and desperate days, in which she lost all her relatives.

I was struggling somewhere between sleep and wakefulness, death and life, surrender and resilience, existence and extinction – I was trying to decide which side I should choose, but I couldn't make any choice despite all my efforts and determination.

48. WHERE COULD LUKE FROM AN-TIOCH POSSIBLY WROTE THE BIBLE? WHAT ABOUT MATTHEW?

I thought that all criminals had been caught, the veil of secret over the events had been lifted, and I could never even imagine that I would be wrong, that I might be mistaken in these thoughts. However, there were other brutal events to go through, and they were waiting for us in places we never expected, all in ambush.

The city, which had not witnessed such a major conspiracy for years, was seriously shaken. With the murders committed in a very short time, four people losing their lives and these people belonging to two different religions, the involvement of a well-organized historical artifact smuggler gang in the affairs, the fact that only the pawns of this gang could yet be caught, and strong doubts that new murders could be committed, constantly increased the tension in the city.

In this tense and uneasy environment, word was out about the scrolls made of gazelle skin we found and the ceramic piece hidden in between the rocks. This created not only an increasing tension but a rising curiosity as well; with the rumors changing from one mouth to the next and turning into strange, mysterious stories that had nothing to do with the reality.

It was said that in addition to the known canonical Bible written by Luke from Antioch and the books, "Acts of the Apostles", a third book has been found - and what this "Dear Physician" from Antioch wrote in the third book, which is thought to have been written after the first two books, could lead to significant changes in religion, belief and knowledge. Therefore, the wave of curiosity, excitement and interest that emerged depending on these events was growing day by day.

In addition to the country's important journalists and television reporters interested in the issue, important journalists from abroad were also pouring into the city. The job of promoting Antakya with the importance and value it deserves, which Dimitri wanted with all good intentions, unfortunately, seemed to be realized by itself with bad and painful events.

All journalists from Turkey and abroad told their eagerly awaiting readers and audiences that the gazelle skins have not yet been examined, that no results have been obtained, but that it was highly possible that they were written by Luke, the physician from Antioch, since the first page of the scrolls read, "O Theophilus" and this form of address belonged to Luke. They were writing and speaking in a style that would increase one's curiosity, without break. In order to keep the subject alive, they were covering news, publishing columns and comments on the interesting history of Antakya with the new findings, murders committed and the smugglers.

I was reading all the newspapers brought to my room and the news articles, columns and comments on them carefully, looking at the pictures with interest and trying to pass the time in bed by getting angry all day long with the speculations and distortions made on the events.

I finished reading a column describing Marcus, the author of the Greek Bible written for the Roman Church in 60-70 AD, staying in Antioch for a while and I immediatelymoved on to reading another column. I was reading with high interest and learning that during the Jewish wars, which broke out with the death of Saint Jacob in Jerusalem in the sixties and the destruction of the city of Jerusalem in the seventies, the Church of Antioch underwent profound changes, and the Gospel of Matthew was written in Antioch to meet the theological and religious needs of the second generation Christians living there during this period, that this canonical Bible is the same as the Bible that is known today and that the Hellenistic teaching, this Bible written in Antioch (the center of the Greek language) in 80-90 AD, reflected the development stages of the Church of Antioch, as well as common Jewish and pagan influences. I read with interest and learned that all these could not be a coincidence, that it was a

Bible that was used in religious lessons and rituals in those years, that the style used pointed to the possibility that its author might be a Jew, that the text was directed towards the people of the city who spoke Greek but adhered to Jewish traditions, and that its content was prepared for educational purposes.

The news, articles, images, comments and latest developments about Antakya were kept alive every day, and the journalists who did not want to repeat the same words and sentences were continuing to tell the history of the city while constantly providing new information.

I was reading all that's written with great interest. It was told that 300,000 people lost their lives in the great earthquake of 526 in the city, which experienced eighteen destructive earthquakes that destroyed and burned the city and that walls of the city were completely destroyed in another earthquake that took place just two years later. Immediately after this great destruction, Justinianos had Antioch rebuilt, renovated the walls, built the giant structure known as the Iron Gate, and entrusted Antioch, which suffered many disasters, to the protection of God and thus named the city "Theopolis", "The City of God". I was reading with curiousity the words of columnists, who wrote that the name of Mount Stauris, which dominated the City of God, was also called "Cross Mountain" and this was because during one of the great earthquakes, a very large fire was seen on this mountain in the shape of a cross.

I was forcing myself to read carefully all national newspapers and especially local newspapers published in Turkish, as well as all the news published in newspapers in English, magazines published in French, and news by Italians who especially showed great interest in the matter. I was especially careful not to miss any of the articles written by journalist and columnist Mehmet Ali Öztaş, whom I knew from his previous articles. All his writings would tell about the rich history of the city. I was trying to write careful, accurate, non-contradictory articles, and I found his articles quite successful. He would research all details of the subject he was covering, then try to convey the results of his research without boring the readers. What I read lately were never a repetition of the articles I had read before.

One day he was telling about Antioch Theology School, another day he was giving information about Stylism and he would most certainly combine every subject he wrote with the magnificent history of Antakya. Besides what he was writing, his narrative style and different style also drew my attention.

From the very first day I read him, I thought that Mehmet Ali Öztaş could actually be a very successful history researcher and writer in the national level.

I looked at the long title of his column about Antioch Theology School, and started reading it with interest.

49. ALL OF US WERE REALISTS THROUGHOUT HISTORY – US, THE HEIRS OF ANTIOCH SCHOOL OF THEOLOGY

According to Origen, who was born in the early 180s after Christ, some parts of the Bible could not be explained in any way without the "Perspective of Rebirth".

A new interpretation tendency emerged in Antioch, with a reactive approach against the Origenism movement that had an intense influence in the city of Alexandria during the IIIrd and IVth centuries. The Antioch School of Theology strongly criticized the Alexandria School of Theology, highlighting the human nature of Jesus Christ and attaching great importance to this approach, interpretation and thought.

The Exegetical School of Antioch was able to reach its approaches different from Alexandria by relying on scientists and theologians who shared the same views in the fields of Anthropology, Exegesis and Christology.*

**Exegesis: Critical explanation or interpretation*

*While the School of Theology in Antioch was working on literary interpretations, historical facts, and language features, the School in Alexandria was making an extraordinary effort to see the figure of Jesus behind every holy word or sentence heard through allegory**.*

**As a literary device or artistic form, an allegory is a narrative or visual representation in which a character, place, or event can be interpreted to represent a hidden meaning with moral or political significance.

These two different approaches and styles of interpretation were based on Plato and his student Aristotle. One of the ancient Greek philosophers,

Plato, lived between 427-347 BC. While the speculative nature of the School of Alexandria highlighted Plato as the basis of their perspective, the Theology School of Antioch based their perspectives on Realism and Aristotle, who lived between 384-322 BC, who was the representative of Realism. There was mysticism on the one hand and rationalism on the other. Eustatius, Bishop of Antioch, the first proponent of this approach, accused Origen of turning the whole Bible into an allegory. After that, Diodorus, who was born in Antioch and was elected as the Bishop of Tarsus, played an important role in the efforts for the approval of the Iznik declaration by fighting for it in the consul in Constantinople.

On the one hand, knowledge, universal birth, ideas, the state and the immortality of the soul were mentioned with the speculative approaches of the Platonic Alexandria; on the other hand, the realistic approaches of the Aristotelian Antioch Exegetical School were expressed, mentioning the power and the ability to do things, philosophical knowledge, practical wisdom, direct comprehension and philosophical wisdom.

These two different approaches, one talking about speculation and indispensable allegory, the other defending realism and the mind that directly conceived, were constantly arguing.

Now, centuries after these discussions, there is an important fact that we want to remind all our friends who ask whether the third book, which is alleged to be in our city and thought to be written by "Dear Physician Luke" from Antioch, is real or fake: Like our fellow countrymen, we believe in power and abilities, philosophical knowledge and science, practical wisdom, philosophical wisdom and, most importantly, the mind that conceives directly - and like every person who has such an approach, the importance and value of these gazelle skins and ceramic bowls will only be able to debated with consistency after scientific studies are made, determining how old they really are.

We are excited and enthusiastic like the whole world and we look forward to it with curiosity, interest, longing, patience and respect like everyone else.

50. STRANGE VISITORS IN THE HOSPTAL ROOM

7nths. The surgeries performed gave very successful results and no complications developed. Physical therapy was applied to the areas that were weakened by inactivity and operated on, I was getting stronger day by day and I felt better. The physicians, nurses, and caregivers who came to my room and made their daily visits could not believe the level of health I achieved in a short time, and they told me that they had never met another patient who was able to heal so quickly and said that I added new miracles to the miracle of returning to life, which they say with their own eyes. I could not understand whether what they said was true, or if they had used a fake discourse to raise my spirits and help me recover faster.

By the way, my boss, who said that he has been following all developments closely from the first day onwards, came to visit Antakya. I liked him more with his sincere and friendly approach. My boss was a good businessman, he quickly started developing new projects related to the subject and shared them with us. He was talking with a smile, saying, "Include Antakya in tour programs, Yigit" We were looking at your face with interest when we said "Even a small part of your fans would fill this program". He continued his narrative with seriousness, and as soon as he said, "Especially female fans will show great interest in the Antakya tours", he laughed and I joined his laughter, ignoring the pouting face of Solmaz.

He told me and Solmaz that we were on paid leave since the beginning of these events, and that he will continue doing so until we recover and return to our jobs, asking us to check our salaries in our bank accounts. Our boss was a really nice and honest man. This behavior touched Solmaz and me, and we thanked him with moist eyes.

Although more than three months had passed since the events, the anticipation and the visit of the reporters to the city continued. There were journalists who wanted to talk to me from time to time, to interview me, but I could not accept any of them.

Although my health was getting better day by day, my doctors, to whom I had sent journalists' requests for interviews, were refusing and saying that I had not yet recovered, that I should have a little more patience and that they would definitely allow the interviews when the time came. They had the mature attitude of adults affectionately trying to relieve the impatient desires of a young child. I couldn't understand if what they said was real or they were just saying these; however, I bowed down to everything they said, as if I was obeying a law.

Whatever happened, the physicians who always said that I should not tire myself, could not resist the insistent requests and eventually informed me that I could have a half-hour interview with a group of maximum three or four journalists. I had to choose among the reporters who wanted to meet me. So I selected four journalists, two Turkish, one Italian and one German, from the list I was given. We were going to have the meeting in my room; and I had to accept the requests of my doctors, who said photos and videos were not allowed.

On the day of the meeting, besides the four journalists, there were two translators, Solmaz and Dimitri. I knew both of the Turkish journalists from their articles. I smiled and said that we had only half an hour, that I did not want to annoy my doctors by exceeding this period and that I wanted to listen to the questions from them first. The first time I heard the questions, I realized that even though the questions seemed different, they all wanted to get the same information. So I started to answer them all at the same time.

First, I told them where and how I found the scrolls and the ceramic piece between them. I told them that there were cracks due to the ground movements that have been happening in Mount Stauris recently, that dozens of rocks rolled from the high parts of the mountain to the skirts in a dangerous way, that the cracks that happened due to this movement do not appear in any other part of Stauris Mountain and this situation seemed very strange to me.

I explained that I thought that any object, scroll or similar object that was hidden somewhere and could not be found two thousand years ago might have become visible with the mountain's movement. If our predictions are confirmed by tests to be carried out and the findings turn out to be two thousand years old, I explained how important it would be to conduct serious research in the cracked, collapsed and rocky area of Stauris Mountain just above St. Peter's Church. I said that the authenticity of the findings can only be proven by scientific investigations, and that they should not believe anything said before these investigations are completed and asked them to not mislead people, readers and viewers who believe in them.

They recorded everything I said with the devices they left on the nightstand next to my bed, and they took notes in their notebooks. During a break from my speech, the Italian journalist told me that he wanted to ask me an important question, through his translator. The Italian journalist was shy, asking his question with difficulty, in an intermittent manner of speaking. When I listened to the translator who translated the question to me, I understood the reason for this attitude, which I could not understand much at first.

I listened to the translation with anger at first, then forced myself to be calmer – for he told me there's a rumor that from the things I've found, I had delivered the leather scrolls as they were but had replaced the bowl, which was originally metal, with an ordinary ceramic piece. He was asking me whether this was true or not. I listened to the translator, who went further and continued to explain that I had found other, very important things in the cracked walls on the mountain above the same cave, meanwhile I looked at the Italian journalist with furious eyes. First I asked him if he could speak English. With a red face and shy attitude, he nodded and told me, in perfectly fluent English, that I should not be angry, that these allegations are being debated all around and that it was his job to investigate into these allegations; it was therefore natural to ask the person at the center of these allegations when he found the opportunity to do so.

I listened to what he said until the end and I answered the Italian calmly, without anger and with a smile. I said that I lost four of my relatives, who did not have any fault, in this incident; that I was able to escape from death by miracles that came together at the last second, that no one would know about these even if I did not hand in anything I found, that I handed what I found to the authorities as they were, and that the rumor was extremely cruel and unfair. The Italian journalist was staring at me apologetically. The group left me unreluctantly after I said that I was tired now and that the half hour was up.

I looked at Solmaz, who never spoke during the entire meeting, and at Dimitri, whom I prevented when he was going to interfere with the Italian journalist who asked the last question. I knew they were also affected by the discomfort I was experiencing. The rumors that came out and reached me while waiting to be appreciated and thanked were at the level of neighborhood gossip. We could hear some things spoken in the university hospital where we had been staying for months, but no one had even hinted at it, let alone tell me about such rumors. The television channels we watched, the newspapers and the magazines we read had never included such incriminating questions or statements. Dimitri, who had outside contact and was involved with the findings as well as the circles where these matters were being discussed, did not tell me anything. I looked inquiringly and asked him if there were any other rumors. He simply stated that he had never heard anything other than a few trivial rumors, and he didn't care about them either.

He told me that the question of the Italian journalist was actually things that he himself was curious about, that he could not ask them directly, because he was too afraid to ask them or was afraid of our reactions, and that he took refuge in the lie that there were rumors in order to be able to ask the questions. I told Dimitri that this was a good method. You cannot tell anyone that they were a thief, smuggler, rapist, deceitful, dishonest, liar, and so on, directly, but instead say, "There is a rumor that you were sleeping with people for a fee. What do you say to these rumors?" and that this would make everything so much easier, that one could tell anyone anything, any insult, without any repercussions.

As my friend left the room, I greeted him approvingly, with gestures that made it clear that I was ready for anything, as he was telling me, calmly but anxiously, that the events we experienced and the things we found were very important and thus we could face even heavier accusations after this point, that we should all be ready for them.

The doctors came to my room in the evening and made their routine checks, seeing my sullen and anxious face. I told those good people, who told me that they warned me about it and that I should not have worn myself out, whom we became almost like a family, that my sadness was not caused by fatigue but by the rumors I heard from the journalists. I was using short, concise and clear words. They told me that they would no longer allow such meetings before I fully regained my health, got stronger and fully stood up. The moment I looked at Solmaz's face as if to ask for her help about this, Solmaz was smiling sweetly, to comfort me and tell me that she was thinking the same way as the doctors. Wen ever talked about this again when we were alone. I told her that I was feeling tired and that I wanted to sleep, closing my eyes immediately. I wanted to quickly cross the threshold between sleep and wakefulness and fall into the arms of a deep sleep without dreams, nightmares, or fear.

At some point after I dived into and was embraced by the arms of a deep sleep, I felt the squeezing, choking touch of a tourniquet wrapped around my left arm. I slowly opened my eyes and saw the tall, athletic young, beautiful woman standing on the left side of the bed. She was wearing a white coat, tight jeans under the apron, and a yellow t-shirt on that. I had never seen the woman before, and she was tring to poke the syringe in her right hand into the bulging veins inside my left elbow. I quickly pulled my arm away from her and asked her what she was trying to do.

I looked at the full lips of the athletic woman, her face trembling with excitement and her sweaty forehead, as she was saying that it was time for my medicine. I pressed the emergency call button next to my right hand and loudly shouted at Solmaz, who was curled up, sleeping on the sofa. The beautiful young woman approached me again and, without using any antiseptic, she tried to poke the pointed end of the injector into my vein. I quickly pulled my arm once again and told her that she should use an antiseptic before injection, trying to seem calm. I was trying to gain time and avoid a bad accident until the staff I called with the emergency call button came in.

The athletic woman leaped towards me with the injector in her hand, without saying anything, so I hit her hand hard and started shouting for help. The doctor on duty, nurse and the other overweight nurse entered the room right at that moment when the door opened; looking at me, at the woman in front of me, at Solmaz, who stood up trying to understand what was happening, and at the injector on the floor.

I pointed to the woman, who said it was my treatment time and was trying to inject the thing on the floor directly into my veins.

Without giving me the opportunity to ask them whether she was a new officer, the athletic woman walked at the doctor and the nurses and knocked them down on the floor as if she was doing something ordinary and usual. Walking quickly towards the door, she turned back and told me that this is only the beginning – that we were going to meet again as soon as possible, and that she was happy to get to know me, in a sarcastic, condescending manner that made it clear she had no concern about me.

As Solmaz was trying to catch her, the doctor and the nurses trying to get up, she pulled the door behind her and suddenly disappeared.

51. IS STRYCHNINE THE PUNISHMENT OF STRAYING?

The young woman disappeared like a ghost; suddenly, just like she appeared. In our assessment, considering her movements, attitude, composure and her mastery of martial arts that can overpower a few people at once, we could understand that we were dealing with a professional gang member, or perhaps a master killer.

The young prosecutor, police chiefs, the crime scene investigation team and private security guards of the university hospital filled the room shortly after the attack, and they were telling each other that they would try to find the woman they could not even see sliding next to them like a ghost, by examining the security camera records.

The officer took the syringe on the floor with his gloved hands, removed the needle before placing it in a transparent bag, and explained that the substance in the syringe he sniffed could be strychnine, but the final result could be obtained after laboratory examination.

I looked furiously at the young prosecutor, who apologized, saying that it was a serious mistake not to take me under close protection despite the four murders committed and the intense interest of all media organs and that he was the culprit of this mistake. I told him that apart from such temporary protection measures, it is necessary to work for a definitive solution of our problems and that the ruthless gang we are facing will not stand idle from now on and will constantly attack with new methods. I mentioned the rumor the Italian journalist told me during the day, the question he asked, and the discomfort we felt about it. I said that simple, ordinary protection measures would not work in this case, and that the young woman, who could not be caught, could easily stab the injector in my vein if she wanted to, that I thought she probably did not complete the mission intentionally because the injector contained a highly lethal poison.

I could understand that the prosecutor, who looked at my face with an expression that he did not fully understand and expected me to give him more details, was thoroughly confused by my sentences.

"They won't kill me yet," I said. "It is not their job to end my life without buying the ancient artifacts that they think are extremely valuable, sacred and can easily be sold in international markets for two or three-digit million dollars. What just happened was only a threat, for them to show me, "We can destroy you whenever we want"; they threatened, tried to intimidate me and succeeded in their own way. Actually, they think they succeeded. After that, they will attack us with new methods. You, dear prosecutor, should take precautions to protect Solmaz rather than me. Although they want it so much, they cannot do anything but frighten me before they receive the relics they think I have and which they claim rights on anyway; however, they will not have mercy on my relatives. Please try to protect Solmaz. "

The prosecutor listened carefully to all I told him and tried to tell me that he understood me very well, looking at my anxious face, and ordered two official security guards to wait twenty-four hours at the door of the room where I slept, despite all my objections.

I knew that the non-functional protection measures that could not protect the heads of state, army commanders, dollar billionaire businessmen living under the most intense security measures in the world, could not protect us. We were faced with a secret and powerful gang, a crime machine that took all the risks, did not hesitate to even commit murder, and will not hesitate after this moment. We were in danger, they could end our lives at any moment; however, I especially wished Solmaz would live longer. This is the only reason the truly loving person could ask for the way his loved one dies.

The prosecutor, who came back to our visit the next afternoon, told us that the result came from the laboratory and that the substance in the syringe was strychnine, and that the amount of the substance in the injector would be enough to kill ten people like me, in great pain and in a very short time. I saw Solmaz cover her face with her hands and try to cover her terrified eyes as she was silently listening to us, standing next to my bed.

I was very nervous, I started laughing. I said, laughing, that Strychnine was used by ruthless municipalities to reduce the number of stray animals, more precisely, for their destruction and murder; and that I knew the "massacre of stray dogs" was done with this poison, as these brutal municipal officials said, but I could not understand that sentence back then. In other words, stray dogs were "executed" when they committed the crime of "straying", that their species was tried to be destroyed, that if they did not commit the crime of straying, that is, if they could wander around in the streets by taking conscious steps for a purpose, those human-friendly dogs would not be executed. I tried to explain all this with my wrecked nervous system and my laughter.

My different and strange attitude caught the attention of both the prosecutor and Solmaz; they looked at me without saying anything or smiling. They were trying to explain to my depressed soul, who was able to stand upright and maintain its consistency through difficult, painful, unacceptable events, that they were tolerating this short-term strangeness and nonsense.

I told them it might mean one more thing if the poison that came out of the injector was strychnine. I explained that the cute dogs, who consumed the meat casually thrown around by pouring strychnine on it, died in pain after just twenty minutes, writhing, contraction and bleeding in all their internal organs. The attempt by the criminal gang to kill me with strychnine, gave the message to me that, "You are a dog and you will die like a dog!" I added that they tried to humiliate me in their own way.

With my rising anger, I told them that I understand the message they wanted to give me, and that the next time we meet the criminal gang members, I will never accept being likened to a dog as humiliation; on the contrary, I love those cute animals very much and even a single fur of a dog is worth more than this filthy, disgusting, scavenger, despicable crime gang supporters, who can commit ruthless murders, who are thieves, smugglers, dishonest traitors.

I was really angry and nervous and started to sweat; my heart was beating rapidly and I was aware that I was starting to talk nonsense. Solmaz came next to me and took my hand, stroked my hair, whispered in my ear that I should be calm. She leaned softly and gave me a gentle little kiss on my forehead; my eyes filled suddenly, I hardly held myself from crying and forced myself not to cry.

52. IN THE COURTYARD, NEXT TO THE FOUNTAIN

We became very close and almost like relatives with all the faculty members, specialists and assistant physicians, nurses, physiotherapists, laboratory technicians, and even the cleaners of the university hospital where I had been staying for months. As we sincerely thanked the staff who said that I was now fully recovered and that it was alright for me to leave the hospital, we quickly started getting ready and packing our belongings.

After leaving the hospital, we would spend our days at Dimitri's house and, depending on the situation, we would move to Istanbul after a while. Apparently, Dimitri saw that the car I left in the space in front of his house was broken and the people who broke into it searched the car, and he didn't say anything about it until the day we left the hospital, as well as what he did after he saw it. Although they knew they wouldn't find anything, the stupid assault on my car could serve their mission of intimidation, but I was not in the mood to take any intimidation, threat and assault seriously; I have just returned from death, I regained my health and now I was leaving the hospital where I had been lying for months.

I said to the hospital staff that I did not want to use the wheelchair brought to the room and that I could walk, so they greeted me with understanding.

We tried to explain to the young and respectful police officers that we did not want to get into the police car waiting for us in front of the exit door of the hospital, that it would be more appropriate for us to take a taxi, and they said that they received strict instructions from the prosecutor, that they would take us to our destination by themselves and keep watch alternately in front of the door of the place where we will stay. They told so sincerely and friendly that the prosecutor would cause problems in case of any other objection, so we did what they said and headed towards Dimitri's house.

Dimitri was continuously pointing to and explaining about the factories, gas stations, student dormitories, car sales galleries, furniture stores, giant hypermarkets, truck garages, sign shops, grocery stores, baklava shops, kebab shops, kokoreç shops, soup shops and restaurants, hummus producers, bakeries, butchers, private hospitals, hotels, apartments, houses and workplaces with gardens, car rental offices, police stations, police stations, gendarmerie commanders, public confectioners, künefe producers, fan-sellers, bagel ovens, car wash stations on both sides of the wide street we were driving from the University Hospital to Antakya. He was saying that not so long ago these places were completely empty, even fields, and that he was not happy with this rapid development and crowding.

I looked straight ahead through the windshield of the car where we turned left from the street we were on and reached Asi Avenue; what laid in front of me in all their glory, side by side, were two mountains that left their mark in my life: Stauris and Silpius, or Cross and Habib Al-Najjar ...

I looked and thought about the changes that they have brought to the ordinary, still lives of mine, Solmaz's, Dimitri's as well as the lives of many other people we do not know, maybe we will never know, in the last few months. Who knows what more great secrets they kept in their secret caves.

We passed over one of the bridges over the Asi River. I looked at the ruins of the city walls and aqueducts that stretched towards the bank of the river, only a small part of which could be preserved, and I tried to get rid of the thoughts of Yaghi-Siyan, Shams al-Dawla, Bohemond and armor manufacturer Firuz, as they were attacking my brain.

After a short while, we reached Dimitri's house in the middle of a narrow street on the left side of Kurtuluş Street. We thanked the police officers who brought us there and we got out of the car with our belongings. My car wasn't where I left it; My thoughtful friend said that it was a little damaged, that he sent it for maintenance and repair, that it will be brought back in a few days.

It was mid-November. Nearly four months have passed since our arrival in the city and the days of scorching heat were over. There were days when cold, misty, rainy and mad winds were blowing. First, Dimitri and then we entered the courtyard of the house, and sat on the chairs next to the small ornamental pool where we sat and had long conversations, had dinner and got drunk. It was the hour when the light of the day was about to end, and the night was approaching with all its sadness.

I thought of Gizem and Nikola; I remembered the sincere intimacy between the two of them when they first met, suddenly I felt that my eyes were full and I raised my head and tried to look at the sky.

I could not see the sky, I saw long wooden-metal sticks scattered from the center in the middle of a large garden umbrella that I had not seen before, and the thick dark blue canvas attached to them. At that moment, I listened to the sound of the rain falling on the cloth of the umbrella and looked at the ripples on the surface of the water in the ornamental pool.

I forced myself not to see the sadness on Dimitri's face, who opened the lights of the courtyard. I ignored the sorrow of Solmaz, who was sitting next to me unhappily and watching me with the same expression as mine. The night, the falling rain, the darkening sky and the cold wind that started to blow were preparing to flow into our depressed souls.

I had begun to tell Dimitri, who wanted us to eat in the kitchen in order to be protected from the cooling weather and the increasing rain, that I was overwhelmed by staying in a bed between four walls in a closed place for months, and he silenced me with a sign of his hand. He told me not to tire myself and started running towards the kitchen with Solmaz.

After a short while, they were with me again, with the trays they were carrying. I was not looking at the plates, glasses, food and drinks they placed on the table. I was listening to the sound of the pouring rain, and I was looking at the drops hitting the flowers, leaves and branches of the trees in the courtyard. The thick fabric of the umbrella could protect us from the rain coming from above, but could not prevent the drops coming from the side. We were all wet, and I still did not want to be crammed into a confined space, to get away from the smell of the earth created by the rain, and to enter the limits of spiritual condemnation, much like the captivity of someone who has completely lost his freedom, seeing nothing but four walls.

"Can we drink something, can you drink?" Dimitri asked me, as he tried to hide his sadness with a pretentious joy, and I told him I could drink, that I wanted to drink, that I even wanted to get drunk by drinking a lot.

Dimitri immediately ran to the kitchen and rushed back with a large bottle of raki, evident from its steamed exterior that it was taken out of the fridge a while ago. He sat down and filled our tall glasses, added water, and drank half of the raki in the thin glass, which he put to his mouth without saying anything. I did the same thing and looked at Solmaz as if I wanted to say, "You drink, too...".

I wanted to drink, relax, walk away even if temporarily from

my problems; I wanted to run, to hide, and to bury my head in the sand. Everything happened suddenly and I was suffering as I thought.

Could we prevent what happened? I did not know the answer to that either.

When I asked Dimitri when the examinations on the scrolls and the ceramic piece would end, he finished his drink in the thin glass before answering me completely and said that he could not give me a certain amount of time... I took my mobile phone and found the image of the cover page of the scrolls I took pictures of.

O Theophilus.

There was only one sentence on the first parchment, I looked and quickly moved to other pages on the screen that I swiped with the tip of my finger. I said that I wanted to translate this Greek text as soon as possible, that I was curious about what the parchments had told, and that no matter how many years it was determined in the examinations made, I did not care much about it anymore.

I finished the drink in my glass as well. Although we had finished the first glasses, we hadn't eaten anything. Solmaz warned us in an anxious tone; she wanted us to continue drinking slower and to eat something. The rain, which reduced its intensity, continued to fall with light, delicate, fine and small drops, as if to ensure that its existence would not be forgotten. A bright wetness covered the whole courtyard, the umbrella above us, the doors, the lamps, the flowers, the trees; and the air smelled of earth… The night was quiet, calm, melancholic and sad.

Dimitri was just starting to prepare our second glasses, when we heard a knock on the door. We didn't expect anyone, and we didn't need anyone but ourselves. We looked at each other's faces with concern. I touched Dimitri's arm as he was turning the lid of the bottle in his hand, and stood up. At that moment, there were three more knocks on the door.

Solmaz looked at my face with a frightened expression and said that we do not have to open it, that we should not open it; but I told her that it might be important, that there might be news, and I started walking towards the street door. I stretched my hand to the lock, turned the key, and opened the door.

I looked at the man standing outside the door, his hair, face, and clothes drenched in the pouring rain. I was not expecting this. I still did not think he could be in Antakya, nor did I expect that he could find the address of the house and arrive at this time of night.

53. A STRANGE GUEST: TANCREDE

Under the yellow lamp on the rod that illuminated the old, narrow street, the Italian journalist was standing after we met in my room at the hospital – the man who stretched mt nerves like a bow with his question. I told the police officer waiting behind him that it was alright.

"Good night," he said in English that made it clear that he was Italian. He was wet with rain and water was dripping from his face. "I'm Tancrede, we met at the hospital."

I never expected this man… Judging by the way his clothes were soaked, it was obvious that he walked a lot in the rain.

"I heard you recovered and left the hospital. You must be fine now, so I wanted to visit you. Sorry if I disturbed you at this time of the night. " The man was extremely polite, and even though I wanted to tell him, "Yes, you did disturb me and I do not accept the apology!" I couldn't. I stepped aside from the doorstep since I was blocking the entrance and pointed with my hand, meaning that he could come in the courtyard. I wanted him to understand me not speaking, my welcome without speaking, as well as my anger that still didn't go away; and I also wanted him to understand that the source of all this was the ridiculous question he asked me at the hospital, making unfair accusations against me.

He quickly entered the courtyard of the house. With his wet clothes, hair and face, he walked with tired, nervous and timid steps towards the side of the pool. Solmaz and Dimitri shook the hand of the man, whose name they did not know, without standing up. This was their own way of reacting to the Italian journalist. As I was taking a seat, Tancrede sat in the empty chair next to Dimitri. He was scraping the water from his hair and face with both hands and trying to breathe the mystical atmosphere of the courtyard with an expression of relief.

"Sorry again, I interrupted your meal and disturbed you. I realized that I unintentionally made you sad, even hurt you, with the question I asked in your room at the hospital, next to the other journalists. I shouldn't have done that, I came here to apologize and explain that you misunderstood me. If I had left the city without expressing myself more accurately, I would feel a great bitterness and discomfort, please believe me. I did not direct you anything I thought or believed could happen under the guise of asking a question; I actually conveyed a rumor circulating, and believe me, if I knew that I would make you sad or hurt you, I certainly wouldn't have asked that question. "

He was speaking very calmly, politely and sincerely. Solmaz and Dimitri, who carefully listened to his apology speech in English, which they spoke well, were looking at Tancrede with suspicious eyes. I was trying to understand and analyze the true purpose of the man.

After what happened, I was suspicious of everyone, everything and whatever is being said. I doubted whether he was really a journalist, the sincerity of his apology, or even whether his name was Tancrede. It was also doubtful to me that he came alone to the house where we were staying. I even thought that the aggressive members of the smuggling network, who were waiting outside, on a corner, under the eaves of the old houses, who could perhaps commit brutal murders, would raid the courtyard of the house with a cryptic sign of this man, guns in their hands. I was trying to understand his true purpose and all negative thoughts were flowing rapidly through my mind at that moment.

If he was indeed a journalist, I could take it natural for him to stubbornly and try every way to get new information by avoiding his colleagues, to adopt artificial attitudes, to try to be extremely polite and sincere, to use word games, to appear in unexpected hours and unexpected places. But what if he was not? If he was not really a journalist, but a man of a criminal organization who disguises himself under the mask of a journalist… That's when I thought that our job was really difficult, that we still could not get rid of the men and that we would experience other negativities and I was seriously afraid of possible attacks.

"You don't have to apologize," I said, kindly and calmly like him. "We know very well what we are doing, and we calculate very well where the steps we take will lead us. I was not angry with you asking that question. I reacted to the accusation we never deserved in that question, to the rumor that officially accused me of stealing. If you are a journalist, which you say you are…" Right at this point in my speech, I fell silent and looked carefully at the man's face; I realized that he was trying to take his gaze away from me with hesitation, and I continued my conversation with the same calm and polite demeanor without taking my gaze away from him.

"We are well aware of the importance of the package we found and delivered to the museum officials. Both of my friends are archaeologists. And I am a historian. We know well the history and the past of the country we live in and the events that took place in these lands. We estimate that what is written on the leather scroll to be at least two thousand years old, which will be concluded in the examinations. We are all aware that with such a conclusion, its content could change many things known up until now. We, too, care about what has been found, and we want to find out as soon as possible whether we are dealing with a truly historic find or an ordinary leather scroll produced by fraudsters who want to leak money from historical artifact collectors and rich people through ingenious methods and manipulations. "

I stretched out my hand and took a small sip of the glass Dimitri had prepared, looked at the man and waited for him to speak. Our host asked Tancrede, who I understood he disliked, with his hospitable, friendly and sincere personality unique to the city he was born in, whether he wanted to drink anything. Surprised by this unexpected and sincere attitude, the Italian was able to get away from the tension of the first moments while trying to explain that he could accompany us. He had a more relazed attitude and facial expression, so we were also a little relaxed from the previous tension.

He said that he could have that white-coloured drink we were having, even though he did not know what it was. I could easily understand that Dimitri found the man cheeky and unreliable. Tancrede was looking at the prepared glass with interest; the drink, which was clear and colorless at first, turned milky-white when combined with the added water, which obviously attracted his attention... We all took a sip from our raki glasses.

I didn't want to talk any more; as soon as I finished what I said, I thought I was talking a lot and I regretted it. The Italian took another quiet sip of the raki in his glass; He grimaced first, looked at our faces and immediately filled his mouth with a bigger sip. We could not tell whether he liked it or not, so he set his glass on the table and started to speak in the same calm, polite manner. The rain, which started to fall again at that moment, was increasing gradually.

"We believe everything you say, Mr. Yigit," he said, clearly pronouncing the letter 'g' in the middle of my name and this was pretty strange to me. "The findings are really important. The news dropped like a bomb not only in the Christian world, but for all people who have knowledge about these things. The fact that Luke from Antioch is the author of the third Canonical Gospels and the *Acts of the Apostles* increases the importance of the scrolls found in Antakya, you understand, right?

Luka was a physician from Antioch and you found the scrolls in Antakya. It is very meaningful to us that the first page of these scrolls begins with the address "O Theophilus!" because the Acts and the Gospel of Luke begin by addressing a person named Theophilus. Another important point is that the scrolls found were written in Greek, like the Bible and Acts of the Apostles, written by Luke, who knew Greek well. You may have wondered where we got this information or how we learned it, it is no longer a secret that it is not just us, the whole city knows it, and all the newspapers are full of this information.

So I have to say without further ado that we believe those gazelle skins are real and at least two thousand years old. We believe that "Dear Physician" St. Luke wrote them in Antioch, where he was born, and hid them in the hope that they will be found when the day comes. "

As soon as he finished his speech, Tancrede reached out his right hand and brought the glass from the table to his mouth. As he was doing that, I asked him, "Who are you?" He looked at me while he was trying to swallow the liquid in his mouth. I asked once again: "I'm really wondering, is it a group you call 'We' or what?" Throughout his speech, he kept saying "We", never using the word "I". Was he trying to describe a community, a sect, or a professional group he belonged to while using the third plural constantly; or was it an ordinary word?

"Please don't get me wrong, when I said 'We', I was trying to describe the journalists and colleagues who watched this incident from the first day," he said. Should I have believed the man or not? By pushing aside these and similar questions that came to my mind and had no answers, I continued to listen to him.

"Of course, these scrolls are very important. If the age determined after the Carbon-14 test reaches two thousand, which I think will happen, then what is explained on the scrolls and the information they contain will gain importance. However, the most important issue is that this is also of great importance for you: the age of the ceramic piece that is said to be found among the parchments."

While forcing myself to understand what he meant, we were observing with strange feelings that the umbrella on us could not protect us at all from the rain that started to pour much faster and that none of us was disturbed by it even though we got thoroughly wet. We continued to listen to Tancrede.

As he said, "The age of the ceramic piece is important, Mr. Yigit," I was angry at myself that I was being bothered by his pronunciation of the letter 'g' again and forced myself to focus on the main subject. "If the age of the scrolls is two thousand and the age of the ceramic piece is close to this, then there is no problem. You will then be declared a great hero and recognized all over the world, respected wherever you go, and welcomed as a guest of honour wherever you go. "

I hoped it would be like this and continued to listen with interest.

"If it turns out that the scrolls and the ceramic piece found between them are new, that is, if these finds are determined to be new in age by any of the methods of Radiocarbon, Archaeomagnetism, Thermoluminescense or Optically Stimulated Luminescence, then you are in trouble."

I could understand the importance of what he was saying. If the findings were determined to be new, we would either be accused of producing new and fake scrolls and items to draw attention towards us, or we would be accused of replacing two thousand-year-old finds with fake ones.

"And the last possibility, Mr Yigit…" I was finally able to listen to Tancrede despite his inability to pronounce the letter 'ğ', who continued to say, "If it is determined that the scrolls are old and the pottery that comes out of them is new, which is exactly what the rumors are about, this would mean the beginning of really difficult days for you.

When I remember your experiences, the relatives that you've lost, and the serious accident you returned from death, I can't help but ask "What could be worse than these?" There is another issue that confuses people: the announcement that a bowl that everyone thought was metal turning out to be ceramic… People can believe this only in the light of scientific data."

He reached down to the glass in front of him, to signal that he had completed his speech.

I said that the only action I took was to deliver the findings, which I found while searching for my disappeared relatives, to the authorities of the relevant institution, and I suddenly stood up; I looked at his face with an expression telling that he had to go now and extended my hand to Tancrede.

As my hand was in the air, he took the glass in front of him, finished the entire glass, stood up and gently shook my hand. I walked beside him as he moved towards the door. He asked me if he could come again. I did not reply, opened the door and waited for him to step out.

We were alone again, after the Italian left, and began to question the reasons for this interesting visit... It could have been anything: this man could have been a journalist, a smuggler, an organization manager, a thief, a murderer, and many other good, bad, positive, negative people imaginable. However, the only and most important feature or personality structure that was impossible for me was that Tancrede could be a reliable man. It could be seen clearly that he was trying to hide something with his constantly moving pupils and his hectic, insincere manner, not knowing where to put his hands and arms; Tancrede was not successful in this at all.

While trying to tell Dimitri that I no longer wanted to drink, that I was tired and I wanted to retreat to my room, the beautiful woman did not listen to our friend who said, "Go together with Solmaz, I'll tidy up here." She sent me upstairs and started to carry what was on the table into the kitchen with our host. It was still raining and the air smelled of earth.

54. THE RAIN POURED CONTINUOUS-LY, HEAVILY

I climbed quickly up the steps leading up to the room. I was wet enough and I didn't want to get more wet, get ill and have to lie in bed. I had just recovered and my immune system was pretty weak. A micro-organism that could not affect a normal person, a simple parasite, cold weather, or even an exaggerated activity could put me in bed.

I was cold. I hurried into the room, touched the heater button, and threw myself into the bathroom. I undressed, raised the handle of the faucet, and waited for the hot water to come. I put myself in the arms of the hot water. I felt warmed up, refreshed and free from fatigue. I got out of the bathroom in the bathrobe I was wearing, sat on the bed and transferred the photos from my mobile phone to my laptop.

I have illustrated each of the parchments separately. I took a notebook and pencil out of my bag and started to examine the images. The first image had two words and a single sentence, I knew this before. As I read, I wrote on the first page of my notebook; "O Theophilus..."

I looked at the second parchment and, without any hurry, I began to read what was written in Greek and translate it into our language and transfer it to my notebook with a pencil. In places I could not translate, words I could not remember, the internet, the world's largest library or information bank, which I connected wirelessly with the help of the computer at hand, supported me like a loyal butler, a reliable partner or a skilled secretary, like a ready-to-order assistant in all matters.

I had completed the first part when Solmaz entered the room. The sound of the pouring rain coming in the moment she opened the door of the room, the cold air mixed with the smell of moisture and earth, and the beautiful woman made a good trio. "I'm cold," she said. "Take a hot shower right away, I got it, and I'm better now," I replied.

I looked at the beautiful woman who was undressing in front of the mirror opposite the bed I was sitting in and rushed into the bathroom, leaving all the clothes she took off on the seat next to her, and suddenly all my focus was distracted ...

I forced myself, trying not to think of anything other than the work I was doing. I started the translation of the second part and, following the same method, with the same help, I continued to transfer every sentence I translated to the white pages of my notebook. The more I translated and understood what I was translating, the more I was interested in what was written on the scrolls. All the stimuli from the outside, the strong and frightening sounds of thunder, the stubborn blows of large raindrops beating the windows, and the white light of lightning that sometimes filled the room could not prevent me from working.

Yes, now the beautiful woman was coming out of the bathroom with the white towel on her, walking between the mirror and the place where I sat, drying her body, bending, twisting, leaving the white towel on the bed, leaning towards her suitcase, the small and delicate laundry she took out, and similar little things… Only such small and provocative things could prevent my work.

I transferred everything that stood in front of me and was unnecessary for the moment on the nightstand, I stood up, threw the white robe on the floor and I met the beautiful woman at my best. She looked at me in amazement. I reached and grabbed the little piece of clothing in her hand and threw it on my robe. I hugged, embraced the woman I loved, filled the scent that I had longed for, for months. I felt her hug and her arms tightly around my neck, and we fell over to the wide bed.

Outside, the pouring rain opened the gates to a wet, hot and slippery world, and thunder covered our frantic screams. It was raining heavily, gasping for breath... It stopped after a while... It became silent... The world became still.

We hadn't touched each other for months, we couldn't get close to and hug each other. From the day we met ten years ago to this day, we have never left each other except for obligations. I sometimes used to think we had become a habit for each other and I would tell her that with hesitation. "You're right," she used to tell me. "You're a good habit for me." We used to smile and hug each other with enthusiasm at such moments. "I do not have bad habits such as drugs, smoking, excessive alcohol, you are my only addiction, Yiğit Kaya, and I regret to inform you that I have not thought of getting rid of this addiction for many years and coming," she would say, smiling, and we would hug again, trying to live and understand that moment - just that moment.

In the conversations we had throughout the nights, I would remember certain days in the past and longingly tell her how happy we were in those moments. "We are also happy today," she used to tell me. "If you can perceive the day you live, even the very moment you can breathe, understand the value of being alive, breathing comfortably, if you know that life is a chance and privilege given to you, and you can make all these the principles of your life, like the days of the past and the days that you longed to remember, then both your today and your future turn into feasts full of happiness, health and peace. "

I got up from the bed where we hugged each other, and put a long, appetizing kiss on her lips. I put the bathrobe back on me, transferred my laptop on the nightstand, the notebook I wrote the translations on, the pens and whatever I used, all to the small table in front of the window. I lit the table lamp and smiled and told Solmaz to get dressed. She looked at me with an expression that said, "I am in no mood, I want to sleep as soon as possible" and buried her beautiful head in the soft pillows. I put the blanket on her and sat on the chair by the table.

I was able to zoom in or zoom out the images of the parchments I transferred to my laptop, and could even zoom on one letter, making it clearly visible. What I read sounded quite interesting as I studied and read and translated what was written in Greek into my own language.

I worked non-stop for hours and completed the translation of two more scrolls. My eyes were closing spontaneously, I was very tired. I brought the swinging head of the lamp close to the table; now it was very dim but bright enough to distinguish everything in the room. I threw the bathrobe I was wearing on the floor and pulled the light quilt I had covered on Solmaz, who was in a deep sleep. I watched her beautiful curves for a moment and quietly curled next to her.

Solmaz used to say that a man who entered the bed with a woman lying naked in bed wearing clothes would be deemed to have insulted himself first and then the woman in bed with him. She even laughed and said that it was an expression of the man's incompetence. I remembered what she said, and yet turned my back to her, I was extremely tired and wanted to sleep as soon as possible.

I woke up quite early, shivering. I immediately got out of bed, got dressed and opened the curtain completely. I looked at the first light of the new day, trying to rush to other areas and fill the places emptied by darkness. I sat down, turned on the computer and flipped one more section from the images on the screen.

At the top of each parchment was a heading written in larger letters and under these headings, the author of the scrolls was telling about the different days.

He was telling about the Stauris Mountain, which I now knew very well, the cave on the mountain, the Silpius Mountain, the Orontes and Parmenius rivers, and the important personalities who came to these places and told their beliefs to the people living in this city. He was also talking about himself; He repeated his name, his work, his birthplace many times in the writings. As I was continuing to translate and write them in my notebook, I felt that I was never bored with these poetic repetitions.

When I completed the translation, I wanted to see what I wrote as a complete, whole text. The more I progressed, the more I was interested in the text. This situation enabled me to work more intensely and ambitiously and to overcome the difficulties of translation, which was actually a boring job.

At that moment when I was sitting by the window, I decided to write what I could from the very first days we came to this city - the good, the bad, the beautiful, the bitter, the sweet, the mystical, the understandable, the incomprehensible, the accidental, the calculating, the believable, the incredible that I could have experienced, until the very last day. Everything I could remember, understand and perceive; I was going to write as I remembered, understood, and perceived them.

I left the room and looked down into the courtyard, which took on a new look in the pouring rain. I looked at the rings created by the drops hitting the water of the fountain; The branches and leaves of the soaked trees, the steps leading up to our room, and the thick fabric of the big umbrella looked very different. The air was hazy, damp and boring.

I looked at the chairs by the pool and thought about the unexpected guest who came at night, and the conversations we had with him. I tried to derive new meanings from what the Italian journalist Tancrede told us; what he said was seriously important.

Tancrede said that the results of the laboratory examinations were very important to us. He was right when he said this, and we were eagerly awaiting the reports much like those who were following the events.

I entered the room again and, saw the owner of the dark blue eyes staring intently at me, sitting up on the bed. I approached her and gave a kiss on the beautiful woman's lips with my cold lips.

I quickly explained to her my decision and what I wanted to do; I said that I wanted to write about all our experiences, and even all the things we have experienced since the first day we met. I explained that I was going to add the things written on the parchments, which I did not finish translating, in this book as well. The dark blue-eyed blonde told me that even if she could not help me with the translation, she could help me in bed when I got tired of working and took a break, and that she could help me rest, hugging my neck with a mischievous smile. I could not resist her and instantly laid down next to her.

55. THE PUBLISHING HOUSE IN ISTANBUL

I called Istanbul. I especially called our boss from the switchboard of our workplace. The switchboard clerk, then the assistant of the boss, and finally the boss, spoke to me in a cheerful and enthusiastic manner. They asked about our situation, they said they missed us. I responded to all of them with the same enthusiasm. The boss said, with his usual mischievous attitude, that my fans abroad (!) watched the events from the press, wondered about me and insisted that when I regained my health, they wanted to participate in tours in Antakya under my guidance. At the end of his sentence, he did not fail to say that almost all of my fans were women. While he was saying these, I visualized his smiling face in my mind.

My boss told me that the doctors, who said that I should rest for a month, gave a medical council report, whereas that the report was not important and that whenever I felt ready and well, I could return to work and my health was more important than anything else. I thought I really loved him, as he was saying all these with his usual sincere and friendly attitude.

I told Solmaz about all the things my boss had just said, she pouted and looked at me with anger especially when I told her about my fans (!).

It was still raining, and the weather was hazy and extremely dull. We went down to the courtyard with Solmaz, Dimitri was in the kitchen, he brewed tea and prepared the table. We sat down and had breakfast in silence. Dimitri told us that the rain would not stop and that the heavy rain would continue for at least three more days, suggesting that we stay at home and rest well.

Those three days were a good opportunity for me. If I worked hard, I could complete most of the translation and start my own story that I was thinking of writing.

The rain never stopped for ten days, not three. We had breakfast with Dimitri every morning, and as soon as he left, I locked myself in the room and worked for hours, non-stop. I would translate the scrolls from the images on my laptop for a few hours and then sit down and write our own story for hours without a break, often forgetting to even eat.

The rumbling sound of the sky mixing with the sound of the rain, the fragrant tea that Solmaz would always bring, and writing, doing nothing else but writing… I was slowly starting to love this life. I could not respond to even Solmaz, who praised my typing speed with the computer I placed on the desk by the window, and I was continuing to write without wasting time.

We were sitting at the rich tables that our host, who came home from the museum in the evenings with full bags in his hand, prepared at the table in the kitchen due to the cold weather and heavy rain, we were eating well, drinking well and having hours of deep conversation.

I was giving them brief and summarized information about what I learned from the translation and saying that I could not answer Dimitri's insistent questions about the details before completing the translation of the entire text.

However, from the repetitions of the writer and the events he described in a poetic narrative, I understood that he was a person who was born in Antioch, lived here and worked as a doctor in this city and learned Greek, and I did not see any harm in saying that the repetition was "Luke is my name".

When I carefully put together the information I obtained from the Bible and the connections between these new information, I said that "Dear physician" Luke probably knew Virgin Mary and the Apostles in Jerusalem and Antioch, most likely met with Jesus Christ in Jerusalem, became his disciple, and that when he returned from Jerusalem to Antioch he had become one of the important leaders of the community here. I was also telling that if I brought all the details together with the completed translation, we could achieve healthier and more accurate results. Almost every evening, I was curiously asking Dimitri if the laboratory examinations on the scrolls and the ceramic piece were completed.

Whenever we sat down every night, we drank and chatted, when we came to our room from the kitchen, I was sitting at the desk without wasting time and was immersed in my work system that I had made a habit. First, I continued translating and then write a narration of our own story for hours, until I was quite tired and my eyes were starting to close spontaneously. I have benefited from this hard work and made significant progress in both studies.

On one of the rainy mornings, I went to the room right after breakfast and before I started to work, I called Kemal Kır, who was the editor-in-chief of a publishing house in Istanbul. He was one of my old friends, and as soon as he heard my voice, he cried out with joy, told me that he was watching news about me from the press, wondering where I was, about my health, about Solmaz and the course of other events, in his usual fast and enthusiastic way of speaking.

I briefly explained what we went through, said that I left the hospital and wanted to rest in Antakya for a while. He gave me an enthusiastic response, and at the exact moment he paused, I whispered to him about the translation I had made, my own story I had been writing, especially the events we had experienced in the last few months, and that this should remain between us for the moment. In the silence that occurred for a moment, I could only hear the sound of his breath. I was silent and waited for a while.

I told him that I would combine all of these, meaning the translation of the scrolls and our own story, what we have experienced in the last few months, the events, the murders, the suffering we have experienced, our return from death and the rich history of Antakya and its important place in the history of religions, and that I wanted to publish it.

Kemal Kır said with excitement that he himself must be the publisher of this book. In particular, he told me with increasing enthusiasm that I should be quick, write faster, and if necessary, he could send an official from the publishing house to help me.

I told my friend that in case he published what I have written and what I have translated just as I have edited them, in case he maintained the order I created between the sections in the same way and did not interfere with my style, words, sentence structure, that his publishing house could be my Publisher. He promised me that he would not interfere and make no changes except small things (!) like punctuation.

I told Solmaz about the phone conversation I had with Kemal Kır. She thought about it for a while and said that it would be better to publish the translation and what I wrote after determining the age of the scrolls. I told her that she might be right, but we still had time to decide. The only thing I had to do, for now, was to write, write, and to write…

Suddenly and out of nowhere, Nikola was in my mind. I remembered the pictures, posters, writings, newspaper clippings, books and brochures I had taken from the drawers, that I had taken off the walls of his apartment in Ankara and filled in a bag. I picked up the backpack and took out the plastic bag, emptied all of its contents on the table. I stood and looked at them all, and suddenly I was heartbroken. At that moment, an upside-down, white and shiny paper caught my attention. I would turn it over to see what picture it was, when I noticed the words and phrases of the faded lines and the handwriting I now know of Nikola's. With my widening eyes and rapidly beating heart, I read the faded lines with excitement

56. SCREAMS YOU COULDN'T HEAR, TEARS YOU COULDN'T SEE

I picked up one of the pictures I collected from Nikola's house. I recognized the writing behind the picture now. It was Nikola's writing. First I flipped the front of the poster in my hand. On the poster, the Antakya Walls stretched all the way and the old walls reached the castle on the top of the mountain. I started to examine the picture that I had seen before, which previously did not interest me much.

With collapsed columns, rocks, stones and bricks, the wall that rose, descended and curved in accordance with the slope of the mountain, it looked like it was incapable of even protecting itself. It first stretched to the skirts of a further hill and then to the ruin of a building on the hill that was understood to be a castle.

I turned the picture over and looked at the words of the faded text behind it. I knew Nikola's writing style now. He wrote them in two separate sections of six lines each. Each part contained thirty-one words and all that was written was sixty-two words. The text was a pleasant, ingenious and poetic narrative of the picture on the front. I paid attention to each word, the structure of the lines, as well as each punctuation mark. I examined the two separate parts individually before and after I read them together; I tried to compare what I understood and what I could perceive when I read them separately.

I read the faded text a few more times. It was a purely poetic narrative, but it was not poetry. I counted the words one more time, studied the lines again. I turned the picture and looked again at the walls on the peaks of Silpius Mountain, the forest passing through the walls, the cramped view of the trees, the collapsed and complete ruin-looking old castle that tried to remain intact, brick and stone pillars rising like a few rotten teeth into the sky. Trying to find a new password, a different sign, a meaningful image, I looked at the picture, forcing myself but unfortunately could not find anything that could be of use to me. I tried to visualize the twelve-line narrative written on the back, but I could not succeed and I did not force myself any more; I turned the picture and started reading it aloud this time.

You will cross a mad forest; cross it you must.
You must pass by great trees gushing out of steep rocks,
By the ruined city walls stretching for kilometers,
By the souls stuck on the stones that have fallen to the ground,
By the cries you can't hear, tears you can't see,
And by the flood of blood.

Proceed to the castle rising on the mountain peaks; proceed you must.
You will find what you seek for, and what you have lost,
Inside, between in the Heart and Spirit of the Castle Walls
Inside, between the baths, houses, rooms, windows
able to withstand the calamities of hundreds of years
Under, between the thick stone walls...
Find it you must.

I thought of the significance, value and mystery of our findings, which were possible through his written and directing narratives, the things that we had delivered to the museum, and which are now being examined with advanced techniques in the most advanced laboratories. He was sending us to a different, more mysterious path that I could not fully understand, telling us that we should overcome the difficulties on this road, talking about the sad moments we will encounter on the road, giving clues about where and what we could find on the road, and almost forcing us to take the journey. The poetic text, consisting of two parts, six strings and thirty-one words, ended with the words, "You must find them."

I looked at the huge drops of rain hitting the window; they hit the glass first, seemed to stick to the glass for a moment, and then flowed slowly downward. The same thing happened to all of them, and no drop could stay where it struck and seemed to hang for a very short moment, forced to flow downwards on the glass, towards the window sill, the balcony and the garden. No drop had any privilege over another.

I brought my head closer to the window, my forehead to the window, and looked down at the courtyard, the trees, the flowers, the fountain, the table and the chairs, which I could only see in blur. Although it has only been a few months since the lively, enthusiastic, warm and sincere conversations we had as friends accompanied by good food and drinks, I could not believe my memory, which thought that they were far behind in the old days, as if they happened centuries ago. I caught on the sick wings of my memory and wished it would fly me and take me to our happy, joyful hours. At that moment my eyes were full, the image behind the glass blurred by the falling raindrops became even more blurred and disappeared completely; I was not crying, I could not cry, but tears were flowing from my eyes.

I sat on the chair and filled everything, except the picture of the Antakya Walls with faded lines behind it, in a bag and put it back where it was in the backpack. I looked at the picture, placing it right in front of me. I wanted to look at it from time to time. I completed the translation of one more chapter by looking at the images on the computer screen, zooming in and out, searching the Internet for Greek words I could not remember; I re-read this whole last chapter in my notebook and felt impressed.

I opened the file on my laptop where I was telling our story and resumed writing where I left off. I wrote for hours without a break, without eating, drinking tea, coffee, or even water. My fingers never separated from the keyboard keys; I was writing constantly, quickly, as if someone was chasing and running after me.

I thought for a moment what Solmaz had said. Should this, the chapters I have written and translated, have been published after the age of the findings are determined, or before? I couldn't come to any conclusions, unfortunately, and I delayed thinking about it for a while. I had to continue writing without wasting time, quickly and without missing any memories, and complete the translation, as well as our own story, as soon as possible.

I was aware that life, the time we were alive for, was not very long and that every person could reach the end of the time given to him, at any moment, unexpectedly; I had been through painful events and bad experiences that taught me to complete all the work I had to do as soon as possible. I was pitying the days which passed wastefully, purposelessly, empty and doing nothing, and I was writing non-stop without wasting a single minute.

If I knew that I could live without eating and drinking, I would not even eat or drink water, and I would not devote a single second to the brother of death, which is called sleep, if I did not feel the blows on my energy, exhausted with the passing hours and hard work.

As I wrote and read all of what I wrote in a holistic manner, I was able to evaluate what happened more accurately, healthily and consciously. The events we experienced, the people we encountered, the different environment we were in, the different cultural structure of Antakya, the human communities representing many religions, beliefs, sects and groups, the endless tendency of tolerance, the importance given to the details of life, food and beverage traditions and culture; All of them carried me to a more accurate and conscious evaluation of what happened.

As Nikola wrote, we were crossing crazy forests and were constantly hungry for the summit, like great trees gushing through the steep rocks, we were aiming for the sky, the highest, the steepest hills we could reach.

All the streets, houses, walls, windows of the Jewish Quarter of two thousand years ago, including the house we stayed in, were strained under the overwhelming weight of spirits stuck in their places, and they were constantly shaken by crazy screams that I could not hear, but could feel with my soul.

In fact, there was no point, or need to try to push it too hard, to search for complex meanings, to find difficult and incomprehensible ways out. You were born, you grew up and you died; and it was up to you to make your life difficult or to make it easier.

The conclusion in all attempts to find out what the hidden meaning of life, if any, was actually one. The difference between the meanings explained manifests itself in the method of explaining this single and absolute result, the way the method is explained, and the perception level of the people. Yes, the meaning of life was absolute and unique.

When I sat down and asked myself, "What would I wish for a person I loved the most?" I realized that I have actually figured out the meaning of life.

What could I wish for a loved one in life, who could be anyone I couldn't give up on, for whom I could sacrifice my life, who could be anyone... My mother, my father, my wife, my child, my sibling, my friend, my confidant, my master, my teacher... What could I wish for them?

The answer to this question gave the clues of understanding the meaning of life and the secrets of living in a consistent manner, perceiving them and as well as the methods of resolution.

Yes, the result that can be achieved was that simple and clear. The sincere wishes that I would have for someone I love very much were the simple and clear expression of the meaning of life itself.

I thought of the person I loved the most in life. I looked at the image I envisioned in my mind with love and I listed the most important concepts I could ask for, for that indispensable person, for that person I adored, and I sincerely wished. I wished for her.

"I wish her a happy, successful, healthy, dignified and long life," I said to myself.

This was the result: This was the meaning of life and the resolved form of its supposed mysteries that could seemingly not be resolved; to be able to lead a happy, successful, healthy, dignified and long life and to find ways to do this... No, life had no other meaning; it didn't have any secrets. It was like that two thousand years ago, and it would be like this two thousand years from now.

In particular, the last few months I've been through, the incidents I encountered and could not resolve, the desperation, the relatives we lost, and the uncertainties that continued in spite of these discouraged me, pushed me to definite judgments and forced me to come up with the clearest and simplest solution.

I walked away from the window, left the door open and climbed onto the balcony in front of the room, glanced once more at the courtyard under the same heavy rain. I realized that the image I saw more clearly now did not lead to different thoughts from the blurry image of the previous one, and did not affect my mind and soul differently. Like in life, the destination was always the same, whether you lived in blur or clarity - always the same.

The two small sparrows, wet and clinging to the edge of the window, were huddled well together, trying to warm up, and they weren't afraid of me. They shrugged as if trembling, flapped their wings and tried to cleanse the water trapped in their feathers. I looked at their tiny heads and eyes; There were traces of mere anxiety, fear and timidity on their faces, even though I could not see any expression like joy, sadness, laughing or pouting. Trying not to frighten them, I walked away from them in small steps and entered the room again.

I sat in the chair and looked at the photograph of the city walls again. When I remembered that the Roman city walls were nineteen kilometers and the walls of Istanbul were sixteen kilometers, I thought that the twelve kilometers of the Antakya city walls were a considerable length. In Turkey, the walls of Antioch were the longest walls that survived after the Istanbul Walls, so I thought of the importance, the value in the history of Antakya, as well as what happened a thousand years ago, when it was still the most important obstance against the occupation of the city.

They were the walls that were built during ancient and important ages, destroyed by earthquakes, repaired again, destroyed again by bigger earthquakes, and finally rebuilt by Justinian a thousand and five hundred years ago. While it was trying to resist earthquakes, fires, sieges, and wars, I could see the screams, tears and blood flowing like a flood of spirits caught on the stones falling on the ground, and I remembered Nikola's writings.

You must pass by great trees gushing out of steep rocks,
By the ruined city walls stretching for kilometers,
By the souls stuck on the stones that have fallen to the ground,
By the cries you can't hear, tears you can't see,
And by the flood of blood.

57. YOU WILL CROSS A MAD FOREST, CROSS IT YOU MUST

The rain, which lessened in intensity, finally allowed us to use the courtyard of the house as in the summer months. The whole city, the mountains, the stones, the plains, and the land were saturated with water.

Dimitri, who came home with full bags in his hand when he got out of work in the evening, told us that he had not seen such a long and heavy rain in years, that even the Orontes River overflowed, the lower floors of the houses and apartments near the river flooded, and people barely escaped from drowning.

Solmaz and I hardly ever went out of the house due to the rain and stormy weather that had been falling for days. We sat in our warm room and talked for hours, trying to bind up our wounds, heal our souls, and get ourselves together by resting well. I had devoted almost all of the remaining time from our conversations to translating the scrolls and writing about what we had experienced in the last months.

We sat with Dimitri, who came from work in the evenings, in the large kitchen, tasted the local and delicious dishes he prepared, and had pleasant conversations on every subject that came to mind with the ecstatic enthusiasm of the fig rakı produced in the villages of Antakya.

At the end of the hours we spent in the kitchen because of the heavy rains, I went to our room, ignoring all the voluptuous calls of Solmaz, who was ready to go to bed and sleep immediately, and slumped down on the table and worked for hours without stopping, until dawn. The barking of dogs and the sounds of crickets, which I remember from the summer months, that interrupted the silence of the neighborhood's nights, were replaced by the sounds of the constantly pouring rain and the startling noises of the sky.

I was tired of working and I wanted to rest my mind and soul by doing a different job, and as I have been doing recently, I took the newspaper clippings in the bag I brought from Nikola's house again, looking at all the columns of Mehmet Ali Öztaş. I read the article breathlessly until the end…

Victimhood of the Translator

Could it be a statue of a prophet carved with two horns on his head, despite the images of devils that are usually depicted with horns?

It's possible…

If the translated texts fall victim to the translator, even if the translator who translated these texts is a true saint, there can really be a horned prophet statue.

Saint Jerome (Eusebius Hieronymus Sophronius) was born in the region of Pannonia near the present-day Italy-Croatia border around 340 AD. In his early youth, he was more interested in pagan texts and poems.

Between the years 374-379 AD, he lived a completely reclusive life in Orientis Apicem Pulcrum (Queen of the East), that is, in our city, in the southwest of today's Antakya. This is the very region where the Sect of Stylism would later develop, and Young Simon would live on a pillar for forty years.

In 379 AD, he was given the title of priest by St. Paulinas in Antakya. He returned to Rome in 382 and began working as assistant-secretary to Pope Damasus. The most important request of Pope Damasus from Jerome, whom he referred to as "my wise friend", was to review the Latin versions of the Old and New Testaments.

Everywhere, in every city, there were so many Latin translations of the Bible, and there were great differences in meaning between them. Jerome first edited the four Gospels and later the Latin translations of the Psalms. Upon the death of Pope Damasus, he went first to Antioch and then to Alexandria and Bethlehem. Settling in a monastery in Bethlehem, the city where Jesus was born, Jerome learned Hebrew from a Jew.

In the monastery where he settled, he translated the Old Testament from Hebrew and the New Testament from Greek to Latin. These translations were accepted as the official version of the Bible by the Council of Trent eleven hundred years later and were called the "Vulgate Bible".

Jerome succumbed to a protracted illness in Bethlehem on September 30, 420.

Even Though He Was a Saint

Regarding translation errors, Jerome says, "Of course I'm not so stupid as to think that any word of God needs to be corrected or written without divine inspiration; but the changes in the different Latin translation texts of the Bible show that they are wrong," he says, adding that he and all translators can make mistakes.

One of the most important translation errors of St. Jerome is the horns on the head of Moses... In the original Hebrew text of the Bible (Exodus-34.29), the Prophet Moses descended from Mount Sinai: "Moses went down from Mount Sinai with two tablets of covenant in his hand. His face was shining because he was talking to the LORD, but he was unaware of it. When Aaron and the Israelites saw Moses' shining face, they were afraid to approach him."

Here, the Hebrew word "chorn, chornus", which is actually used, means "sparkling, halo of light", but unfortunately also means "horn", and Saint Jerome used this second meaning in his translation. According to him, Moses descending from Mount Sinai with two tablets in his hand does not shine but has two horns on his head, not halos of light!

We can now answer the question at the beginning of our article together: Why not carve a horned prophet statue if the translator did that? Even if the translator himself is a true Saint!

Can the horn, which is sometimes depicted as a single and sometimes in pairs, and is usually attributed to demonic faces, can be carved on the head of a statue of a prophet?

Famous Italian sculptor Michelangelo depicted Moses with horns, based on Jerome's translation, in the Moses Statue he made in 1515. The horned Moses Statue, two meters and thirty-five centimeters tall, can be seen in St Pietro in Vincoli in Rome.

Michelangelo, who completed the Statue of the Horned Moses, stood across the statue when he finished it and, "Speak!" he exclaimed; he waited for a while, then threw away the hammer in his hand and said, "Come on, let's go" with feelings full of excitement, faith and curiosity.

Here, in order not to be unfair to Michelangelo, it would be appropriate to mention a different view: The famous sculptor is aware of everything and the double horns that Moses placed on his head is a reference to Pan in Greek mythology with a goat's body and double horns; in other words, the statue is actually a statue of Pan-Moses. Pan, the son of Hermes and Penelopia, is famous for appearing out of nowhere in the fields, mountains and plains, frightening everyone; He is a master of creating panic, and the word "panic" is rooted in the same Pan.

In our next article, we will discuss the story of St. Simon, who lived for forty years on a marble column on the same hill, from the Mount of Miracles in the southwest of present-day Antakya, where St. Jerome led an reclusive life for five years - the story of the ascetic life St. Simon led while trying to approach and reach God by looking at the shores of the Mediterranean's Samandağ district, towards the Asi (Orontes) River from a pillar. We will also discuss the Sacred Vessel extended to him from the stairs on the side of the marble column, the Sect of Stylism and today, the images of the propellers of the wind turbines that are constantly rotating in the same region, and the disturbing noises of the hums created by these propellers, which in no way allow seclusion.

Could it be perceived as a disrespect to Saint Jerome, who is considered to be the ancestor of the translators and whose name is mentioned as "Hieronymus of Antioch" in some texts, to complete the article with a word from the Italians? We do not know, and we leave the comment to you, our readers, by writing the expression as it is.

*"Traduttore traditore".**

* * *

In the evening of the day when the rain stopped, next to the small pool where we sat for the first time in days, I asked Dimitri about the laboratory investigations of the findings. He told me that the studies are ongoing and that soon we will learn the result - the approximate age to be determined.

I told him new information from the translations I made to the master archaeologist; I tol him about the style, method and expression characteristics of the author of the scrolls, I talked about the words he used, the sentence structure, the way he spoke about himself, his profession and belief. I also said that I expected the gazelle skins to be old, very old, and if it was to be determined that they were two thousand years old, this result would not surprise me.

Dimitri said he agreed; however, he said that he could not say anything definite about the ceramic piece, that he could not make any predictions, that it would not be more than a good wish or even fortune-telling to make an estimation. He was speaking in a thoughtful style and eyes unique to the masters of his work, fixed on a point. He stated that the young prosecutor called him several times, got information about the studies, asked about us and said he wanted to see us. He added that the prosecutor had secretly whispered to him that they had found the trace of the woman who attacked me and raided our room in the hospital with a syringe filled with strychnine, in Istanbul, and that they had been following the whole gang. I was startled suddenly and felt myself shiver. Learning that the attacker was in Istanbul made me uneasy.

The translator is a traitor.

That night, I told Dimitri for the first time... I talked about the twelve-line narrative of Nikola in the poetic style that he wrote on the back of the picture with the walls. I told him about the style of his brother's writing and what I read as far as I can remember; I spoke of the ruined walls stretching for miles, of the spirits stuck in the fallen stones of the walls, of the mysterious places that can be reached by passing by the inaudible screams, invisible tears and endless streams of blood of these spirits.

I suddenly thought that Dimitri, who was looking at me with eyes full of tears as if he saw his brother before him, might have heard what I said before, and I realized that I was not wrong about this.

Dimitri's eyes started to fill with tears when he said that Nikola had sent him this two-part poem by e-mail about a year ago, that he had read it many times, liked it and was impressed. He recited the last three lines to us with his voice starting to tremble:

Able to withstand the calamities of hundreds of years

Under and between the thick stone walls

You will find what you seek, you must find yourself and what you have lost; you must find them

Solmaz and I both had tears in our eyes; we stretched out our hands at the same time and touched our friend's arms that were frozen on the table.

I told Dimitri that I wanted to see the walls and the castle, the remains of which can be seen when looking at Mount Silpius, which I had seen pictures of before, the subject of which was mentioned in some lectures at the university, and which can be seen from almost every neighborhood, avenue, street, windows and balconies of Antakya. I also told him that I could not help wanting this after reading what Nikola wrote.

My friend, whose eyes were red with the effect of the sincere and emotional moment we had just experienced, looked at me for a moment with an attitude that still maintained his sadness and said that we could go if it didn't rain the next day. He told us that he would go to the museum in the morning, that he could return home after taking leave in the afternoon, and that we could visit the walls, the castle and the forests of the old Silpius, now Habib Al-Najjar Mountain for three or four hours.

I closed my eyes for a moment and read the first line of what Nikola wrote:

You will cross a mad forest; cross it you must.

I was going to listen to him and go to the mad forests, carrying what he wrote in my hand.

I would pass by the mighty trees sprouting from the steep rocks and the stones falling from the destroyed walls that stretched for miles. I wanted to hear the cries of the souls stuck in these stones and see their tears. I wanted to reach the castle rising on the top of the mountain and find what I had lost, what I was looking for, even to find myself.

58. ANTAKYA CASTLE AND ITS WALLS

I wrote nonstop until dawn in the morning. The rain, which started again with thunder at around four o'clock in the morning, almost exhausted my hopes, but after about two hours it stopped completely. I got up from the table and went out to the balcony in front of the room. I filled my lungs with the incredibly clean, cool and fresh-smelling air, breathed in deeply, filled the sunrise and listened to the crazy sounds of chattering birds from the courtyard.

I threw myself into the arms of the sleep that I knew would be enough even if I slept for five hours until eleven in the afternoon. I plunged into mad, crazy, impassable forests. Nikola, me and Gizem, whom I always remember with that smiling face, the three of us walked together in the crazy forests, and leaned with our backs on the trunks of the pine trees. Nikola was playing with Gizem's long hair, laughing endlessly, joking with Gizem, reaching out and boasting about his quick reflexes as he grabbed a hairpin from her hair like a little kid and placed it in his pocket.

He says to Gizem, who looks at his face with a fake anger, "Stay upright and smile even in the most difficult moments, let them wonder why you are smiling", then turns around, shows the walls that stretch out from the forest to the hills and the cut-stone bodies poured from the walls with his hand. He was telling me the importance of walking past these walls that have resisted the calamities of hundreds of years.

I finally fell into a heavy sleep that I couldn't remember anything else from.

I opened my eyes with a pleasant smell coming to my nose and the caress of a soft hand on my face; I opened it and met two beautiful dark blue eyes. Solmaz was smiling at me, showing her white teeth. I stretched out my arms, hugged her and pulled the beautiful woman towards myself. I kissed every part of her face, her neck, her ears and her hair. "Get up!" he told me. "Get up and take a shower. It's eleven o'clock and the rain stopped. Let's not keep Dimitri waiting." Desperately, I obeyed and followed the strict orders of the cruel and beautiful woman!

Dimitri and I, who came home at noon, got into the car after a quick snack with a mixture of breakfast and lunch and started driving on the first illuminated road in the history of the world, Colonnaded Street, today's Kurtuluş Street, to reach the road that leads to Altınözü district, which were going to lead us to the city walls.

The road to Altınözü district stretched uphill on the opposite side of the Stauris and Silpius mountains facing the city, and crossed the road, climbing on the mountain, a few kilometers later, where the sign saying "Antakya Castle" appeared on the right side of the direction we were going. The moment he saw the sign, Dimitri told me to slow down and take the path that lead up the mountain. I slowed down and carefully entered the rough road. We reached the summit of the Silpius Mountain, which was visible from the city, by curving left and right along the dismantled asphalt, large and small pits and patched road in some places and continuously going up. We parked the car in a place near the concrete building, the exterior of which was tried to be given the appearance of a wooden house. I looked with dismay at the crowd of dozens of televisions, telephones, radio transmitters, antennas, cables, wires, and base stations.

We got out of the car and started walking on the dirt road leading to the hill where Antakya Castle is located. The first parts of the walls we saw seemed to reveal several periods at once. Grass had sprung up between the brick-sized stones, which were obviously very old, in the middle of the wall, and the mortar had begun to fall. Just outside this inner wall, large stones, like rectangular cheese blocks cut with a sharp knife, were lined up to create very regular walls. The inner wall from earlier periods in the sections where these smooth cut stones were poured in places; it was creating sadness in me with its irregular, indented, wrinkled, worn, overgrown and old appearance.

The young and dynamic stance of the coniferous pine trees, which were obvious to have been planted a few years ago, was in stark contrast to the tired appearance of the weathered and collapsed walls. We continued our walk, passing by the ruins of some bastions, which were said to be only three hundred and sixty of them when all the walls were still standing. These bastions and the rusty appearance of the old electric poles erected right next to them, the drooping wires running from these poles to the other old and rusty poles, seemed to be competing with each other to look older.

These walls, which were built, developed, and destroyed every time by severe earthquakes starting from the Hellenistic period, seemed to be looking at everyone who passed by them with the proud, smug and mysterious eyes of being able to resist for centuries and to be restored in new periods.

The dirt road we were walking on came to an abrupt end, as if it had been cut with a knife, when we reached the edge of a forest. Giant pine trees, thickets reaching our height, vines wrapping around the trunks of trees, thorns hurting our legs, almost seemed to say, "The road you came from is over, you must prepare for narrow roads, paths, steep slopes; if you are ready, we can embrace you." Without hesitation, we entered the forest and came across the thick, solid and strong trunks of pine trees, which stretched upright towards the sky, bent towards the walls, and stretched out towards our faces.

You will cross a mad forest; cross it you must.

The mighty trees spouting from the steep rocks…

Yes, just as Nikola wrote, in his first two lines; we passed through a "Mad forest" without ever seeing the sky.

I was left with a new feeling of distress at the sight of plastic bags thrown on the floor, tin beverage cans, used napkins, old and torn newspaper papers, crumpled cigarette packs, plastic water and glass wine, rakı, beer bottles, broken glass, eggplant, onion and tomato peels, stones were brought together and used as barbecue, charcoal residues that had been extinguished without being exhausted, ash hills and the image of wasteland created by all of these. I thought that those who built these walls a thousand, and two thousand years ago and the inhabitants of the city living in the areas surrounded by these walls could not have been so filthy, scruffy, disrespectful and hostile to the environment.

We walked along the path through the mad forest, trying not to step on the food leftovers, dried vegetable peels, broken glass and ash heaps. After a short while a wide light filled the forest; it was as if our eyes had passed through a tunnel and caught the light at the exit. After a few steps, we saw the walls stretching before us like a painting by a master painter, and the ruined bastions of the Antakya Castle, which these walls reach.

We walked from a steep hill, the highest point of Mount Silpius, to the castle, which overlooked the whole city and guarded it like a watchman. We proceeded by the walls, which remained intact, some partially destroyed, sometimes by having to step on them. The wind was blowing wildly. The grasses, bushes, vines, greened by the rain that had been pouring for days, shimmered like a lush ocean with every shade of green. It was as if the notes of a song sung centuries ago were flowing by our ears. We could hear their words.

> *Proceed to the castle towering over the mountain peaks;*
> *proceed you must*
> *Inside, between in the Heart and Spirit of the Castle Walls…*

It was as if the words of Nikola's poem were flowing through our brains. We were looking at the ruined walls of the bastions, some of which remained intact; We were trying to understand the easily crumbling composition of the wall, the outermost stones of which were poured out, the stones of all shapes and colors, large and small, pointed, round, cube, cylindrical, and the mortar that has been trying to hold them together for centuries. The green leaves of a plant that grew between two stones and stretched parallel to the ground, the yellow, white, purple flowers stretching between these leaves and the sun's rays hitting them were shining before our eyes like skillfully shot brushstrokes of a beautiful painting.

We reached the castle, where we expected to find heaps of stones as we saw from afar that had completely collapsed and, thanks to its surviving walls, merely delineated its borders; We reached it and we couldn't believe our eyes. The areas under the vaulted stone roofs, pits, carved rocks, large and small windows in the walls, the ventilation holes in the ceilings still seemed to groan at the cries of people bathed there a thousand years ago, and with the cries of delight from people exploring each other's bodies.

We entered one of the buildings that we understood to be used as a house, bath, kitchen or warehouse, listened to the songs of the blowing winds, waited for a short while and moved on to another building right next to it. We could even feel the heat and vapour of the hot water that was filled into the pits on the ground a thousand years ago.

We took shelter in another of the vaulted roofed building, where we escaped from the heat that we were uncomfortable with despite the insane winds. In the space under the stone ceiling, which we understood from the black soot in the corner that it was a kitchen, we were closing our eyes and trying to hear the sounds of knives from the cooks and their apprentices, to take in the raw smells emanating from the vegetables they chopped, and we were trying to feel the bubbling of the food boiling in large iron, copper, earthenware cauldrons.

The soot of the fires were alive, fresh and new on the smooth Stones of the walls, as if the fire had been lit the night before to boil the sheep. I approached a small gap in the wall and looked; there stretched ancient Antakya, the Orontes River and the Amik Plain.

The inhabitants of Antakya Castle, the gentlemen, the wealthy, the rulers and all the residents of the castle, who spend hours of pleasure in the baths filled with the steam rising from the hot water, could see the cooks and apprentices cooking the meals through the large and small windows they reach by taking a break for a while and taking a few steps. I asked myself, whether this incredibly impressive and beautiful landscape could make every viewer feel privileged.

Inside, between in the Heart and Spirit of the Castle Walls
Inside, between the baths, houses, rooms, windows

I came out of the vaulted stone kitchen, reciting the four lines of Nikola's poem; I advanced to the farthest end of the castle; I walked along the pristine roof of one of the most magnificent of the stone structures and looked at the city from the highest point of Silpius... I looked and thought of hundreds of years ago, today and tomorrow that rushed into my mind.

I looked down and across from the frightening height of Mount Stauris to the cracks, collapses, and shards of the farthest reaches; I tried to see the pagans, the Jews, the first Christians gathered in the cave at the very tip of the mountain, on the thin, long ancient path stretching hundreds of meters below me, and the "Rock" Peter, Cephas, who was the first leader of the community in this cave.

I set my eyes on farther places and forced myself to determine the location of the airport where planes, landing and taking off, awaited in the middle of the Amik Plain.

I forced myself to think and see the dust clouds rising from the places where the soldiers and horses of Bohemond, who came towards Antioch, commanding the Crusader army of thirty thousand people, right at the place where this airport was built.

I tried to see the city gate from the height where I was sitting, through which the Turkmen Bey of Antioch, Yaghi-Siyan, who resisted for two hundred days and did not surrender the city to the Crusader Army under the command of Bohemond, was afraid of the Crusaders who went beyond the walls and their number was only five hundred.

I forced myself to understand the reasons for the betrayal of Firuz, the armour manufacturer, who had forced Yaghi-Siyan to escape in fear, selling the city by hanging a rope from the Two Sisters Bastion to the five hundred Crusader soldiers.

I turned and looked again at the other parts of the Antakya Castle, where I was sitting on the roof of one of its buildings; I thought that Yaghi-Siyan's valiant son Shams al-Dawla and his companions might have spent days full of fear, far from pleasure and sinful delights, in the rooms and baths of this castle, where they took shelter and resisted for days and fought with the Crusaders.

I turned my head a little to the right and looked hundreds of meters above the Stauris and Silpius mountains, standing side by side like two loving neighbours; I tried to see Peter, Barnabas, Marcus, Matthew, John, Luke and Paul, who came to Antioch by walking the narrow and winding old path stretching between the two mountains.

I tried to think of the merchants trying to reach the city from Jerusalem, Damascus, and Aleppo, and the camels, horses, donkeys, and herds of sheep and goats they brought to sell.

I looked at the bed of the Parmenius River, which ran just below this narrow and winding path, rushing between two mountains - at that moment I shuddered; my legs contracted and I felt my whole brain go numb as I tried to forget the pain that stabbed me like a knife in my stomach.

Further in the direction I was looking, there was Bab al-Hadid, the Iron Gate, hidden behind a hill of mount Silpius and where the river curved to the right, was where my life would almost end. I started to feel dizzy and have cramps in my stomach. I tried to understand why I was on the edge of a precipice, much higher than where Bohemond had grabbed my collar and dragged me into the void with him.

I clung tightly to the stones on the roof of the building I was sitting on, took deep breaths and tried to fill my lungs and perceive myself, my soul. I tried to close my eyes, which kept startling with images all around, and not to vomit; I forced myself to calm the contractions in my stomach. I tried to lean back slowly, to lie on my back on the stones of the roof with my whole body, without letting go of the stones that I was holding tightly with my hands. I made it with difficulty, and I saw bright yellow rays seeping from the sun hidden behind a cloud in the sky.

The words of Nikola's poetry, accompanying the symphonies that the winds blowing on the highest mountain tried to compose, were on those white clouds that hid the sun. I have seen and read:

Inside, between in the Heart and Spirit of the Castle Walls

Inside, between the baths, houses, rooms, windows

able to withstand the calamities of hundreds of years

Under, between the thick stone walls…

You will find what you seek, you must find yourself and what you have lost; you must find them.

59. INSIDE, BETWEEN, IN THE HEART AND SPIRIT OF THE CASTLE WALLS

I was brought to my senses by the sound of a strong thunder, as if it exploded in my ear. I was on the vaulted roof of the old stone building, I was lying on my back. I heard and understood all that Solmaz was saying, complaining continuously, and what Dimitri said as well, who agreed with everything she said - but I was taking on an attitude as if I did not understand them.

Ignoring the continuous scolding was the safest way to get rid of all these things aimed at me – that I haven't fully recovered yet, what was I doing on this mountain top in this cold weather, why did I come here when I could have a good rest...

I slowly sat up, I didn't get up for a while, I took a deep breath. I looked at Solmaz, who said that my blood pressure might have dropped, with an approving expression; I thought that if I confirmed everything she said, her scoldings might decrease. Again the sky roared and I felt small, thin, light raindrops on my face. I got up quickly and we started to turn back the way we came.

I looked at the harmonious combination of the collapsed walls, the strong bastions of the walls, the columns that surrounded the castle and remained upright, the grasses sprouting from them, bushes and flowers of all colors along the way we walked; I looked and remembered that I had to do this climb with the refreshing, startling effect of the light rain. I was trying to unravel the secrets of Nikola's last writings, which were directing the reader to find something, but unfortunately I could not reach the tangible and visible data that would tell me that I had reached the right conclusion and that I was not wrong.

I was looking at the dry grass, tiny flowers with bright yellow and bright leaves coming out of the bushes, standing upright, the irregularity of the trunks of the trees in the pine forest that is visible ahead, the descending, rising, ever-changing curves of the path we walked, and the rain-filled clouds that gradually darkened the sky, trying to make sense of them all.

However, when I first read it, I found what Nikola wrote was extremely clear and understandable. While I could have walked to the place he was trying to tell me from wherever he had led me, by every road and by every tree, and could have perceived all his writing more accurately, I quickly came back because of an ordinary low blood pressure, a brief moment of fainting, and the opening ceremony of the insane rains that forced us to return. And who knows how many times I had recited Nikola's poem in my heart.

There was a shortcoming that I missed, I couldn't understand and couldn't explain what it was. There was a secret, something hidden between the words, something that was smiling and winking at me incessantly; I couldn't find it. I was pushing myself, running the sixty-two words he had written before my eyes with every cell of my brain, but despite all my efforts, I could not reach any results.

As he said and wrote, I went through a really mad forest, walked along the walls stretching for kilometers, reached the castle rising on the mountain peaks, wandered all over the houses, rooms, baths and kitchens that people once lived in the castle, I tried to feel their speeches, anxieties and fears from centuries ago and forced myself to hear the sieges that lasted for days and the cries of the people who were brutally murdered in the occupied city.

On the last line of the poem I read accompanied by the notes of the song that the wind, the sun's rays and the raindrops that started to fall are trying to sing, he said "You will find it" and declared nothing with a definite verdict - and I had not found what I was looking for, neither myself nor what I had lost.

I raised my head to the sky in the mad forest, which the narrow path lead to, and I looked hopefully at the branches and thin leaves of the crazy trees; unfortunately, they couldn't tell me anything either.

In the poetic narrative he wrote, there should have been other data, supplementary information to support what he wanted to tell. I looked at the dense vegetation of the forest and thought again what to do. I thought about how and where I could find new data, new clues to support what was described in the poem. Nikola was no longer alive; there was nothing I could research about him except his apartment in Ankara, his friend circle, the house in Antakya that he used with his brother, his room in this house and a bag full of books, photographs, posters, newspaper clippings and papers he wrote with his own hand that I brought from Ankara.

The number of people from whom I could get healthy information by talking was only two. Of those two people, I was already speaking to his older brother Dimitri and we were discussing everything down to the smallest detail. The second person, on the other hand, was one of the museum staff, who was still a mystery and was arrested in the first hearing after the recent events. All of Bohemond's ties to his gang had been identified, his phone calls and negotiations had been tapped, yet he had never spoken or given any new information during all interrogations.

When we came near the car we parked next to the high antennas, transmitters, poles and wires, I did not respond to Solmaz, who asked for the key, and did what she wanted. They opened the door and carefully seated me in the back seat.

The rain continued to rain slowly, lightly and with thin drops as it had been in the first moments, without increasing in intensity. Solmaz, who was turned on wipers of the car she drove carefully and meticulously downhill from the top of Silpius Mountain, looked at me with concern from the rear view mirror. I told her I was feeling better. I asked Dimitri about his arrested colleague; I tried to find out if there was any information, development or new situation other than what we knew about how he got into Bohemond's gang.

Without taking his eyes off the rough road in front of him, Dimitri began to speak. The name of his colleague, who started working at the museum about three years ago, was Rıdvan. He was overly ambitious, talkative, argumentative, unreliable. He studied at the university's archeology department for three years, and he had to leave before completing it, whereas he could not resolve the confusions created in his soul by being a semi-university graduate, and he was unstable. He explained that when his personality came together with this depressed structure, such a dangerous and cruel man emerged. He told me that he was too cruel to shy away from stepping on or destroying his own relatives, even his siblings, let alone his colleagues, in order to earn money, success and advancement.

Rıdvan had close relatives in Aleppo and he visited his relatives frequently in this city, he earned additional income by selling the goods he brought on these trips, he tried to earn a lot of money and get rich as soon as possible. Dimitri said he might have gotten together with Bohemond's gang because of such ambitions. He paused for a moment, stopped as if he was thinking about something, and when he started to speak again, he calmly said, with a thoughtful voice, that he could not guess how he was able to establish a close relationship with Nikola, he did not know what their degree of closeness was, what secrets they shared, and what role the historical artifact smuggling network played in this closeness and confidentiality.

I reminded him that what was written on the papers I found in the pockets of Nikola and Gizem took me to those scrolls that we thought were very important. I said that I thought the poem I found behind the picture of Antakya Walls described the location of another mystery item that I thought was very important – although I couldn't know what it was.

I also told him that the real reason for this mountain climb and our visit to the walls, the fortress and the old stone structures inside the fortress was the poetry of Nikola. However, I explained that there was a deficiency that I could not fully understand, a password I could not decipher, or a symbol I could not see.

We completed the mountain road and started to head home from the wide asphalt road through the streets of old houses on both sides of Antakya. People escaping the rain, which increased in intensity, were trying to reach their homes with running steps. I looked and saw that they all had their hands full. They were walking fast with the bags they were carrying, or they were taking shelter under the eaves where the raindrops could not reach. I looked at the people walking on the road with the respect I have for the innocence and benevolent appearance of anyone walking with bags filled with groceries while returning home with little or much money, working in an easy or difficult job all day long.

You wake up at the earliest hour of the morning, go to your workplace, work all day long, and if you have earned money, you return home with food, drink and similar loads that you bought with little or much money. You eat, you nap by the stove or in front of the TV, spend time with your children, make love to your wife at night, sleep, wake up again in the morning and go on with your life repeating almost exactly the same daily actions of what you went through the day before. I knew there were people who lived in this repetitive fashion for ten years, twenty years, maybe even longer. They said they were happy… Were they really happy? I was openly asking those with whom I could talk closely, trying to learn the secrets of this… What was the secret of this?

Before speaking, they would look at me with smiling faces and say, "Don't think, don't think too much; if you think too much, you will question too much, if you question too much, you will dive into details; then you will find yourself in a vicious cycle and be unhappy…" I couldn't understand… Was it that easy?

To live, but how? What they meant was, "Wake up in the morning, go to work, earn a some money that can help you live, no matter how small, don't lean on anyone, don't have too high expectations, file your ambitions and live happily". Could I, could I live like this? I didn't know yet. I was constantly thinking and forcing myself to give healthy answers. *To live… But how?*

I asked Dimitri if I could meet Rıdvan, who is in prison. He turned back with his broad torso and said he would discuss this with the prosecutor. He paused for a moment and looked at me with a questioning expression, trying to understand why I wanted this. I explained that I wanted to complete the missing link, that I wanted to find clues, if any, which could complete what Nikola wrote. I said that I wanted to understand the secrets of ruthlessness, murderousness and cruelty, which started with the ambitions of an ordinary man working in the museum, with the desire to get rich - an ordinary smuggler who was going back and forth between Aleppo and Antakya. My friend, who rubbed his neck, which hurt from looking back, looked at me with a face that expressed that he did not fully understand what I was saying, nodded his head in approval and turned his gaze back to the windshield of the car.

I knew that I could find what I was looking for, myself and what I had lost, in a place, person or any conversation I had never expected, in some seemingly unnecessary sentences of the conversation. *Diabolus est in singulis.**

The devil is in the details.

60. IT WAS BAD, IT WAS REALLY BAD, IT WAS INCREDIBLY BAD

Dimitri and I sat inside the thick concrete walls of Antakya Prison, behind thick glass partitions. I wanted to calm my friend, who was behaving in an excited, impatient, and angry manner, I was trying to make him just listen to me, but unfortunately I couldn't do this. It is difficult to calm down a man who has lost the only person he had in his life, his brother, his indispensable, best friend; especially in front of the people who caused him to experience such pain...

Nothing could be more important than a person's life, even if it was about the most important findings of the world - the subject of wars, fights, debates, novels and stories belonging to the people who came from two thousand years ago, establishing and spreading the most widespread religion. Even if the findings were important, you couldn't tell that to an older brother who has lost the only person he had in his life.

A sip of wine at a dinner with friends in the innocent hours of the evening is like a few drops of water, it cannot extinguish the fires of the lips and heart that burn like fire. The life of a lost person cannot be brought back!

I looked at Dimitri's face. I looked into his angry, devastated, disillusioned and hopeless eyes; I tried to read the words he was going to say, or the words I hoped he would say, to Rıdvan.

"Don't say it," I told him with my mind, "You shouldn't say it, you just have to listen, understand and perceive. You shouldn't perform any attack that comes to your mind and that you think is right."

I felt weak, hurt, defeated, and tired. I did not know Rıdvan who would come to the meeting room. I had never seen his face, his height, his eyes; I didn't know what the man who influenced all of our lives, our present and future looked like.

I looked at the metal handcuffs on the wrists of the tall, slender man walking towards us behind the thick glass in the interview room, and the dark gray clothes of the prison guard who was trying to unlock the handcuff with the key in his hand. I turned and asked Dimitri, who was sitting to my left, "Is this him?" I asked. "Is this Rıdvan?" His face was sad and sulky, angry, his eyes were red. He was angry at this man for his role in the death of his brother, but he was also saddened by the miserable state of his colleague.

Rıdvan sat across from us. He looked at us with an air of self-confidence that we had never expected. I looked at him with the same determination; I tried to show him his cruelty and immorality. I tried to get him to express the negativities he brought us all to, I forced myself to tell him about the captivity he reached with his evil personality and that his life has turned upside down now. He did not understand, could not understand; it was bad, it was really bad, it was unbelievably bad.

One drop. Just a drop... If I were just a drop of rain... *What am I saying?*

If I were one of the raindrops reaching the ground, if only I could be one and hold on to the edge of the turmoil that Rıdvan was trying to stand upright in front of me, if I could be a single word of the sentences that Nikola wrote, even a grain of dust vibrating at the end of a single letter in the word and understand... *Understanding... But how?*

Rıdvan looked far from all miseries. He was telling me, "Read, re-read, read again," from the telephone receiver he was holding. He was saying, "You will find it in the mad forests that Nikola told me, you must find it...", he was giving me orders even though he was bad, ugly and captive, telling me the places I should go. *To go... But where?*

"You will find it if you go," he said, and described the crazy forests himself as well. "Don't question, don't ask, find it in what we wrote to you, if you force yourself, you will definitely find it." *Finding it… But where?*

He suddenly started talking about the new life we will find in the forest, in the trees in the forest, at the base of the trees. Even talking about the new life it was bad, it was really bad, it was unbelievably bad. *Evil… But why?*

"Ask," I said to Dimitri. "Ask your colleague anything you want to know."

"I won't ask," he said. "I won't ask anything to a poor man who has adopted the rules of cruelty."

"Why?" I asked. He looked at me first and then at Rıdvan's evil face that seemed to have sunk hundreds of meters into the ground, then turned and looked at me once again. "Is it worth it?" he asked. "All the precious metals of the world; are diamonds, rubies, emeralds, even all the money in the giant bank vaults - worth ending a person's life?" I looked at his face, he was thoroughly enraged… "Is it even worth spending a second to explain this to such ruthless wretches?"

Rıdvan was talking about the rebellious branches of the crazy pine trees of the mad forest that stretched to the right and left. He was talking about the importance of achieving goals, and that he would not shy away from destroying other people's siblings, even his own younger siblings, in order to achieve these goals, with the same malicious and ruthless attitude.

The moment he stood up, he looked at me through the thick glass with meaningless, empty and ugly eyes. "You have to understand," he said. "Why don't you understand?" he asked. "Look at the trunks of trees in the forest," he said, "find the secrets engraved in their bark," he said, "are these not what you must find and seek?" he asked again, and I looked at Rıdvan in disbelief.

Could it be that he was giving the codes for a new and mysterious journey that would extend from Antakya to Aleppo, from the Iron Gate to the Parmenius River, from the sacred paths of Stauris Mountain to the summits of Silpius Mountain? *Secrets… But what are they?*

"Go!" Rıdvan was saying that he was the real author of every written sentence, word and letter, he was saying that if I went there, I would find it. *Finding... But what?*

* * *

Able to withstand the calamities of hundreds of years

Under and between the thick stone walls

You will find what you seek, you will find yourself and what you have lost; *you must find them.*

I heard the lines of the poem whispered in my ear and I woke up with a jump. It was dark in the room, I tried to sit up. *Where am I?*

I wiped my sweat-drenched face and hair with my hands, sat on the bed and turned on the lamp by my bedside. I tried to not think of Rıdvan in the nightmare I had, I turned and listened to the quiet, calm and regular breathing of Solmaz in the arms of a deep sleep, looked at her beautiful face, gently stroked her hair.

61.

61. "MOUNTAIN OF HOLY MIRACLES" ON THE SHORE OF THE ASI RIVER AND STYLISM

I got out of bed after a rough night of bad dreams. I got ready and went downstairs with Solmaz. It was seven o'clock in the morning. We entered the kitchen and started preparing breakfast. We brewed the tea. Half an hour later Dimitri came, rested and refreshed.

I reminded him that I asked him to speak to the prosecutor and ask permission to meet with Rıdvan. He said that he did not forget, that he would go to the courthouse after visiting the museum and that he would try to get the Prosecutor's permission by speaking to him in person.

We ate breakfast differently than usual, reluctant and lacking in appetite, as if fulfilling a mandatory duty. After Dimitri left, we sat in the kitchen; we looked at the half-empty plates, reluctantly ate the leftover tomatoes and peppers, gathered the crusty cheese crumbs on the edge of the plate, threw out the breadcrumbs, and listened to the attacking sparrows chirping that broke the silence of the courtyard as they beat their beaks aggressively. *Living in the moment... But how?*

The day was just like how days were lately, the weather was still cloudy and the rain seemed to start again. I told Solmaz that I would go up to the room and that I would work during the day. I placed a kiss on the cheek of the beautiful woman, who, with the attitude of a loving mother advising her child, told me not to tire myself and remember that I fainted the day before. I stood up and went out to the courtyard. In an instant, breadcrumb-friendly birds flew away.

The sky, full of dark clouds, was boring and depressing – it had an attitude that it could empty the water it had collected at any moment.

I went up the room and opened all the curtains, sat on the chair, turned on the computer that was on the table. The weather was cold but I was not feeling cold. I opened the images of the scrolls that I had transferred to the computer and translated another chapter from where I left off. I also worked on the part where I wrote about our own story; I wrote, non-stop, without giving a break. As soon as I felt that I was getting tired, I looked at my watch. Time was flying, it didn't stop and it didn't hesitate. I got up, lay down on the bed, closed my eyes and tried to sleep.

Short or long, every moment of sleep is to get away from the truth; you dive in sleep and break away from real life; you cannot understand which one is happier or more devastated... You cannot understand what happened, where you've been.

I reached out and grabbed the cell phone on the nightstand. I called the editor in Istanbul; in his usual enthusiastic and fast-talking style, Kemal Kır asked me how my health was and how my work was going. He explained to me that he had completed all preparations, included my book in the publication program, and even instructed the printing house to make a stock of paper.

Like pessimism and sadness, enthusiasm is contagious. I answered him with the enthusiasm he had infected me with, I told him what I had done; I said that I was getting close the end of the translation of the scrolls, that the telling of our story was progressing, but that I had a small problem. I said that I wanted to tell what happened in the last few days and write until the last day I left the city.

I also explained to him how I was thinking of arranging the chapters of my upcoming book. I explained that the first part of the book would be the part that I translated from the parchments, the second part would consist of our own story, in the third part I would switch to the parchments again, in the next part I would return to today's narrative and this order would continue until a certain part of the book.

"You thought well," he said. "Do it as you tell me now and send it to me as soon as possible. My friends, to whom I told about this book project, are also looking forward to it." At the end, he said goodbye to me in his distinct style and hung up.

When I started to talk to Kemal Kır, I was not completely determined about the order of the chapters, I was just thinking that I could rank them as I explained. However, when the line-up came to my mind and I got approval from the editor, I made my final decision; I was going to rank the sections as I explained.

With the comfort of my final decision and the enthusiasm of Kemal Kır, I got up from my bed and quickly started working again. Even when I told Solmaz, who came to the room and invited me to lunch, I couldn't take my eyes off the computer screen and continued my work with great desire, ambition and enthusiasm. I worked for hours. Forcing myself not to hear the heavy rain, lightnings and thunder outside, I wrote with passion. At the moments when my brain, arms and fingertips went numb from exhaustion and my eyes started to close on their own, I would go to the bathroom and wash my face with ice-cold water.

Dimitri called around three in the afternoon. He explained that he could hardly meet with the prosecutor, told him that we wanted to talk to Rıdvan face-to-face in the prison, but that the prosecutor could not allow this due to the ongoing investigation, and gave many other similar reasons why he can't allow it. There was nothing to say, I thanked my friend and left the phone on the nightstand. I left the room and went downstairs, distressed by the news that destroyed all my desire to work. The rain had stopped but the sun had not shown its face, the sky had darkened as if evening fell.

Solmaz, who was sitting next to the small fountain, got up as soon as he saw me coming, hugged me tightly and kissed me. He pointed to the steaming steam from the glass tea cup in front of him, which she said she had just brewed. "Sit down," I said uneasily. "I'll pour my tea."

First, I told her about the meeting I had with the publishing house in Istanbul, the enthusiastic and impatient attitude of the editor, and the order of the chapters I had decided on. Afterwards, I told her about the phone conversation I had with Dimitri, that the prosecutor did not accept our request for meeting Rıdvan in prison, and that I felt sad. Solmaz said that she already did not expect such a permission to be granted while the investigation was still in progress. I looked at her and briefly tried to explain that I did not agree. Just then, I got up and poured another cup of tea and turned off the stove. I was just about to say that I was cold, that I wanted to drink these last cups of tea in the room when she got up and started walking towards the stairs.

As soon as I entered the room, I took the bag out of the backpack and spread the contents again on the table. I ignored all the complaints of Solmaz, lying on the bed, that she wanted me to get some sleep and rest. I reached for the bundle of newspaper clippings on the table; I quickly looked at the titles of articles by Mehmet Ali Öztaş, the columnist of a local newspaper in Antakya, which I had not read before…

Luke of Antioch

Mark's Days in Antioch

Matthew Wrote his Gospel in Antioch

All Sixteen Chapters of Didache Written in Antioch

Saint Ignatius of Antioch

Golden Mouth of Antioch: John Chrysostom

The word "Catholic" used for the first time in Antioch

The Principality of Antioch

Stylism and the Mountain of Holy Miracles

All of them intrigued me… I took the article about stylism in my hand, leaned back on the chair and started reading with interest.

Stylism and the Mountain of Sacred Miracles

Did you know that Constantine gave Christians freedom of belief in 313 AD, a new society was born in a short time, a new Christian lifestyle different from the previous one emerged and its principles were determined, that comfortable, free, peaceful and happy days were experienced after years of great suffering, and that over time, the "Asceticism" movement emerged as a historical reaction to this comfort?

Have you heard that the purpose of the hermits was to stay far away from those who live for the day, from the whole society, from the Greek wisdom, and to continue their lives by establishing closer and sincere ties to God, only to God?

The movement of stylism first started in Syriac monasteries. A stylite, who lived on a pillar, stood between the earth and the sky, uniting solitude and asceticism. In fact, during the Paganism period, people lived on a pillar in certain months of the year, and the first practitioner of this in Christianity was Simon the Elder. Did you read anywhere that Simon the Elder's most devoted follower was Simon the Young?

Do you know that Simon the Young was born in Antioch in 521, lost his father in the great earthquake in 526, in which 300,000 people died, and when he was only seven years old, he retreated to a hill near the Orontes, that is, today's Asi River, where wild animals were roaming, and started his Stylite Life, that he lived for forty years on a marble pillar placed in the middle of the monastery, which was built under the direction of Simon the Younger in 551 and can still be seen today?

Would you believe that this hill is a place of pilgrimage and that it is called the "Mountain of Miracles" because of the many miracles performed by Simon the Young, and that this monastery, which is eighteen kilometers away from Antakya, can strangely affect people of all religions and beliefs, even if you didn't go to the monastery?

Can you understand the incredible magic of climbing on a high marble pillar, looking at the Mediterranean Sea, the Orontes River and the surrounding green pastures as far as the eye can see, trying to reach the inaccessible in infinity, trying to get all the life energy from the inaccessible in eternity, throwing real and temporary life into the plain arms of eternal life and having the power to live on that pillar for forty years?

Have you ever heard that on one of the four medallions made of fragrant resin-sawdust mixture found in the excavations carried out years later on the Mountain of Holy Miracles, there was a saint sitting on a pillar and a monk climbing the stairs on the left towards this Saint was extending a "Holy Grail" he was carrying to the Saint?

And today, dear readers, if you go to this Mountain of Holy Miracles, you would see completely destroyed churches, heaps of garbage dumped next to the remains of the marble pillar on which Simon the Young lived for forty years, a guard tent where not even a dog would stay, and the non-stop rotating blades of the turbines that generate electricity from the wind, that break the silence between the earth and sky, completely destroying the possibility of reaching the unreachable... Well, can you approve of this situation?

* * *

With this article, I realized once again that the columnist, who took me one thousand five hundred years ago, has a unique style that affects the reader in a strange way without the reader realizing it.

The columnist referred to this mountain as the "Mountain of Holy Miracles" and was talking about the medallions made of resin and sawdust found in the Monastery of St. Simon at the highest point of the mountain. One of these medallions mentioned seeing a saint sitting on a pillar and a "Holy Grail" was extended to him by the monk, who reached this saint by climbing the stairs on the side. This was where I stopped and read the lines again. I turned my head to the window and tried to count the drops hitting the glass; I couldn't count them.

I wished that the ceramic piece among the parchments I found was the other part of the holy grail, which was engraved on a resin-sawdust medallion found in St. Simon's Monastery and given to the stylite Simon, who lived on a marble pillar for forty years, by a monk.

I left the newspaper clipping in my hand on top of the others and turned all the pictures on the table upside down. I started to examine them one by one; I was hoping to find a new clue - a little note, a sign, a symbol, or a new poem, a password. There was another missing link in the chain. An incessant voice inside me said, "Search for it! You will surely find it."

I found it and realized that I was not wrong.

62. D. O. U. O. S. V. A. V. V. M.

Not of the paths walked on for centuries,

Find and bow down to new paths hidden by the bushes, grasses, vines and thorns, all the plants that cover the floor of the Forest.

First smell the soil of the mad forest,

Then find those carved into the trunk of the tree.

There, right under that tree, you will find what you are looking for, nowhere else.

I read what was written without being able to keep my hands from shaking. My heart was beating fast. I started sweating with a heat wave that covered my whole body from the tips of my hair to my toes. Once again, I read excitedly what was written on the glossy paper that I was holding in my hand, turned the front face and came across an image of a lush forest. What I saw was a photograph taken from inside an old pine forest that attacked all directions with every shade of green.

Despite the straight and upright images of dozens of thick pine trunks reaching towards the sky, some rebellious trees that had grown sloping to the ground, were leaning against other tree trunks like a ladder. Crazy vines sprouting from the ground swirled around every tree and shimmered with heartfelt images of close friendship. There was every shade of green in the image. The shiny leaves of a grass-green vine stretching through the dark, pointed black-green pine leaves, whispered to the ears that could hear the song of a lush brotherhood from the inside and out with the blueish green of another plant on the ground. I brought my gaze closer to what I thought was a stain in the lower left corner of the picture; there were numbers 3, 20, and 104 written in pencil – they were legible, albeit difficult.

I turned the back of the picture again and read the narrative again; I counted the lines and all the words of the last narrative. This time Nikola had an eight-line narrative, written in the same poetic style, and it contained forty-two words. I wrote the two chapters and twelve lines of narrative that I had found earlier on a piece of paper, and just below it I wrote all eight lines to appear as a third part. I reread the lines with schizophrenic doubts, counting all the words once again. The narrative, consisting of three parts and twenty lines, contained a total of one hundred and four words – just like the numbers written in pencil on the front side, where the picture was.

At the bottom of the paper, I wrote these three numbers first, with hyphens between them: 3-20-104; then I arranged the six numbers next to each other as if they were one number: 320104. I forced myself to find a clue, some hidden meaning, a password or a sign; I couldn't find anything. I summed up the three numbers: 127. The number I found didn't make any sense to me either. I multiplied the three numbers: 3x20x104=6240. This result could not get me anywhere either. I divided this number by two: 3120. I divided it by three: 2080… This also had nothing to say to me.

I frantically tried to add, multiply, divide, subtract, and find a meaning, a secret narrative, a hidden sign, out of these three numbers. I perceived that all the results that I struggled with and tried to reach, and that all the results I tried to reach, that I was trying to reach, made no sense, that they could not lead me anywhere, and I fell into increasingly dark moments of despair. I assumed that I no longer have a well-thinking brain due to the traumas I had gone through, and in order to calm the throbbing pain of my brain towards my skull, I went out of the room, filled my lungs with cold and moist air, and inhaled deeply.

3, 20 and 104… These numbers were flowing before my eyes non-stop. I looked down at the deserted and dim courtyard, wet from the pouring rain; It was twilight - the hour of day and night meeting and mixing with each other. We had lived the whole day like an endless evening and had reached the night with the absence of the sun that never showed its face.

As I continued to fill my lungs with the cold and humid air, I saw Dimitri walking in from the main door with bags in his hand. He looked at me with his usual kind and smiling face. I suddenly became aware of the sadness within him, despite his loving and smiling face - I perceived it despite the distance between us; only I could understand it. We had been injured by the same blows, experienced the pain of similar wounds, and now we were trying to heal our wounds with the same methods.

As I closed the open door of the room, I told Solmaz, who was lying on the bed, that Dimitri had come and I would go downstairs; she made a hand gesture, meaning "OK". I found Dimitri in the kitchen, trying to empty the bags he had brought.

The peace, comfort and happiness felt by anyone who worked all day long, bought what was missing at home, some food and drinks for the home, at that exact moment of arrival at one's own castle, shelter, could not be exchanged for anything. Working all day long, dealing with all kinds of problems, grappling with unsympathetic and ruthless managers and customers; constantly trying to explain things to people, instructing them, taking orders from managers, and the last meters of the daily marathon race were completed - the finish line was finally reached. That finish line was the door to the house where the marathon runner enters at the end of the day with bags in hand. Showers are taken, feet are stretched out on a coffee table, drinks are poured into glasses, and all is well at that moment; it is the perfect time to plunge into the peaceful arms of calm, quiet hours away from everything and everyone.

Our marathon runner, who arrived his house with bags in his hands, was smiling at me with a sincere but painful face, clearly due to not being able to get over the loss of the only person he had in life, his brother. While emptying the bags, we talked about the day, told each other what we did, and questioned what we couldn't do. Together with Solmaz, who joined us, we prepared the dinner with usual movements. It was cold, and the rain continued unceasingly; we said, "Let's have the feast of the night in the kitchen".

Dimitri told us about his visit to the prosecutor. He explained that the prosecutor did not accept the meeting we wanted to have with Rıdvan in prison, that it was not appropriate "in terms of the safety of the investigation", that our request was not accepted and that he could not insist so as not to cause new suspicions.

I told him that I could not understand what "safety of investigation" would hinder our meeting with a man who had lost four of his relatives with another one, who became a partner in this atrocity, a man who was involved as an accomplice in these events that had no "safety" anyway.

Dimitri smiled again and said that he thought the same as me, but that the rationale of those who carry out such works, investigations and hold a responsible position for evaluating, analysing, judging and reaching a conclusion was completely different from ours. When he said that we could create unjustified suspicions or even be blamed if he insisted or said that our request to meet is of indispensable importance, I understood that I had to close this issue to never open it again.

We continued our dinner preparations by talking about daily, ordinary and non-tiring subjects. The cold air that poured into the kitchen through the door we left open mixed with the smells of food and created a pleasant combination with the smell of earth created by the pouring rain. Dimitri explained that he had not seen such heavy and incessant rain in the last ten or fifteen years, that many houses near the Orontes River were flooded and that the inhabitants of these houses were saved from drowning only by construction equipment.

He asked what we were doing, whether we were bored or not. I told him what I had done, that I was about to complete the translation of the scrolls, that I was continuing to write our own story quickly and that I was getting close to the end, that I had spoken to the publishing house in Istanbul, how the chapter order of the book would be, and that I took this job very seriously, that I even wrote about his vast culinary culture, his taste in food and about his eating addiction.

"So write this down too!" he said, holding one of the lamb chops he had fried in butter by the end, bringing it to his mouth and scraping all the meat off the thin bone, almost like a powerful vacuum. I smiled at him and told him that I would definitely write this.

I said that I had found another poetic narrative written by Nikola. He moved back from the lamb chop plate he was holding, wiped his mouth and then his fingers with a napkin, leaned back and looked at me with a mixture of sadness and curiosity in his face.

I explained that there were eight lines and forty-two words in the narrative I ended up with, that when I wrote them under the first narrative, they formed a whole and I reached to a text consisting of three chapters, twenty lines and one hundred and four words in total. I read the first four lines to him exactly as I remember them.

Not of the paths walked on for centuries,

Find and bow down to new paths hidden by the bushes, grasses, vines and thorns, all the plants that cover the floor of the Forest.

As before, I saw his eyes filling with tears. He got sad, slowly got up, opened the refrigerator door, poured each of us a glass from a large bottle of raki he had bought, added water on top, and without saying a word, finished the glass in one gulp. I looked at Solmaz and I did the same.

"Exactly as he wrote it," said Dimitri. "He used to live as he spoke. He would say, 'Don't choose the way everyone else goes, you shouldn't. If there are two roads in front of you and you don't know which one to go, take the less trampled road and walk without fear. If you don't feel like choosing any of the two roads, you yourself create a new path and take that road, walk and move forward, without any fear…' In the last lines you found, he wrote about the philosophy that he believed in and made a principle out of, in his short life."

Dimitri looked at our two empty glasses and quickly filled them halfway; without leaving the bottle in his hand, "Don't do what we do, Solmaz!" he said.

Explaining that it is important that the two texts that Nikola wrote on the back of two separate pictures complement each other when put together, that his brother could do this and that he surprised him with such games in his childhood as well, Dimitri said that he could not understand what the numbers 3, 20 and 104 that

I found meant for now. He also said that he was going to work on them, as he was reaching towards his glass again.

He explained in his own slow, calm and wise manner that the methods in which symbols, signs, passwords, letters, numbers are used and the information desired to be kept hidden with these methods have existed throughout human history and that people hid information, concepts or items that they cared about, found valuable, and did not want others to learn or find – thus encoding the places they hid these information, concepts or things with these symbols, signs or numbers.

Dimitri complained that an important city like Antakya, where all believers of faith lived together in the past and even today, a city that has been the capital, albeit symbolically, of the Eastern Roman Empire, is full of such signs, passwords and letters but that we couldn't show, tell people about them enough. He paused for a second and continued speaking in the same calm manner.

"Now let's talk about what we all missed. From Leonardo Da Vinci to King Arthur, from the Knights Templar to the Crusaders, for almost a millennium, perhaps since even more ancient times, people have been fascinated by an item that is now legendary, whether it's a cup, a bowl, a goblet, or a symbol described with a symbol like that. It could also be a secret information or a concept, and people were after it for many years. Well, now I ask you; if it exaists, which city has the highest probability of containing this sacred object?

Now stop and think again. There is a city in which the most important people of the newly spreading religion came, lived in this city for many years, these people were the closest people to the Prophet, the first church of the world was founded in this city and today, there are over two billion believers of this religion. Imagine that even the name of the most widespread religion was given in this city for the first time! You guessed right, I'm talking about Christianity and Antioch... Now tell me, where do you think the holy grail, cup or chalice we assume to be, is - or what city is it most likely in?

Look, the investigations on the scrolls and the ceramic fragment we found are ongoing. What will be the fate of this city if, at the end of the investigations, it is determined that they are indeed about two thousand years old?

Come on, let me answer this question as well, but first I want to tell you a little story, I believe you will find it interesting; but after finishing my story, I want you to combine what you understood with what I have just told and interpret them, okay?"

He reached for the half-full glass, took it and finished it in one gulp. He began speaking again in a calmer and low tone.

"Near Staffordshire, England, there is Shugborough Estate. The owners of this mansion are from the Anson family. This family had a fountain built in the garden of the mansion in the 1700s, and they made a relief-finish of the mirror reflection of the painting *Et in Arcadia Ego*, the Arcadian Shepherds, by the French painter Nicolas Poussin, the grand master of the Knights Templar. So far it's all normal, ordinary and there is nothing special; however, they also engraved some letters under this relief:

D.O.U.O.S.V.A.V.V.M.

Starting from 1748, when these letters were recognized by some people, rumors spread rapidly that this was a code, that this code gave the location of an important and very valuable item, and that this very important and valuable item would be found once the code is deciphered. This valuable item was the Holy Grail, chalice, or cup that Jesus Christ used at the last supper where he met with his apostles. Everyone tried to decipher this code from Charles Dickens and Charles Darwin to Bletchley Park, who cracked the code used by the Germans in World War II. They made great efforts, but with no results.

Result: The result benefits Staffordshire, England, and the Shugborough Estate in that city. Every year, thousands of tourists come to see this city and this house, the Shepherd's Monument Fountain in the garden of this house and the ten letters engraved on the marble plate under the relief in the fountain, spend money, visit the city and wander... Who do you think has won? Were these letters really describing the location of the Holy Grail or are they just giving mundane information? For example, did it describe the initials of the members of the Anson family, their special days, their love, the food they ate or the characteristics of the wine they drank? Let's leave all this aside and look at the result. Who do you think was the most profitable out of this business, and who took the biggest share of the profits?

Solmaz and I looked at each other and, under the influence of alcohol, which dissipated all the pressures of the depressive days we had been living for days, we cried out at the same time and as if in agreement: "Dimitri Çağlayan is flooding like water!"

We all reached for the glasses and performed the action required by a table with alcoholic drinks.

63. I'M ASKING YOU: ARE YOU ME? HE REPLIES TO ME: "AM I YOU?"

An archaeologist was speaking. He was one of the officials of the Antakya Museum, one of the largest mosaic museums in the World, and everything he said should have been taken seriously. In our previous conversations, we learned that several times more of the historical artifacts exhibited in the current museum building were kept in warehouses, and it made us upset. The new museum building under construction is located directly across the Stauris Mountain, and this neighborhood was a special source of peace and happiness for me.

In fact, what he wanted to tell contained very plain and clear truths. He was underlining the benefits it would provide to the city when successful studies and promotions were made in an exaggerated situation, where even ten letters carved on the fountain in the garden of a mansion in a small city of a country were shown to be very important.

He was expressing his reaction that Antakya could not receive as many visitors as the fountain; even though Antakya, which is much older and more historically important than the city where that fountain is located, hosts historical artifacts of incredible value and is mentioned repeatedly in the Bible, the holy book of the world's most widespread religion. He was right, he was completely right with his reaction.

Dimitri looked at me excitedly when I said that Luke also mentioned the Holy Grail in some parts of the scrolls I had found in which I had completed the translation. This was the first time I was giving this information to anyone and I knew it would excite anyone who heard it. I went a little further and said that Luke, the author of the scrolls, said that Peter brought this holy grail to Antioch, used it in the rituals held in the cave church, gave it to him to protect and keep it, and wished that the first apostle would stay in this city forever, and I said Luke wrote that too. I even explained that I think that the reason why the third book Luke wrote apart from the two books, the *Gospel of Luke* (which is the third of the canonical Gospels) and the *Acts of the Apostles*, have not been found until today, may be that it was hidden with the holy relic inside.

Dimitri told me that what I said is logical and consistent with historical facts, that this information is mentioned in the well-known words of the Prophet of Islam and that even the tablets on which the first Torah was written, and the Ark of the Covenant containing some of the belongings of the Prophet Moses and Haroon, will be found in a cave in Antakya.

He was tapping the tips of his fingers on the table impatiently while he was explaining that the importance of what I said would be revealed by determining the ages of the scrolls and the ceramic bowl between them, and that the big city promotion that he wanted and wished could be realized very easily in this way.

Once again, I wanted him to help solve the possible secrets of the numbers 3, 20 and 104. He stopped and looked first at the wall in front of him, then at my face, he pursed his lips to tell me nothing came to his mind and told me he would investigate into it.

The clock was ticking. Despite the alcohol and the heavy meals, I did not feel any tiredness and I wanted to go up to the room as soon as possible to work until the morning. When I said this, both of them told me not to tire myself too much, that the days are still not over, that it would be okay if I finished my book in a day or two - but I had already stood up and walked out the kitchen door.

I ran up the stairs, entered the room, turned on the desk lamp and my computer. Only the last two parts of the scrolls remained… I started to work quickly; I was forgetting everything while I was working, I couldn't see anyone, I couldn't hear any sound, I was just concentrating on my translation or what I wrote. In those moments, I was experiencing such concentration. I had worked for days and now I was close to the end of the translation. I studied for another two hours and wrote the last sentences.

Solmaz entered the room just as I was about to start one of the chapters in which I wrote our own story. She said they had tidied up the kitchen and that Dimitri had gone to bed. I listened with a smile and turned back to the computer screen, concentrating on what I wrote with all my attention, not even looking at the beautiful woman undressing and getting ready for bed next to me.

I couldn't remember how long I had worked, but I stopped when I felt my fingers and hands go numb from sitting and typing non-stop, and my back was starting to ache. I went to the bathroom, washed my face, hands, arms, rubbed my neck with cold water and looked in the mirror in front of me. My hair was messy, my face was pale, the skin under my eyes were sunken - I didn't look good at all.

I dried myself with a towel, combed my hair and once again looked in the mirror in front of me. I looked at my face, my growing beard, my pale skin, as if I tried to recognize the face of a person I had never met. I could tell that I was losing weight, that I had lost a lot of weight compared to my old days, from the way my clothes were now loose on me; however, the thin, defined face in the mirror, which I had not looked at for a long time, with its unmistakable image, clearly depicted my misery.

That happens sometimes. You don't look at the mirror for days, you can't see or perceive the image even if you look, and when you look, see and perceive it one day, you will experience strange feelings and surprises with the appearance of the new face of the differentiated person you find in front of you. "Is this I?" you ask the image in the mirror, "Are you, me?" As you ask, the mirror image answers you at the same time and with the same lip movements: "Am I you?"

Sometimes you find yourself in places you don't know, don't see, don't know, without realizing it. Life has embraced you, loaded you and left you where it wanted. You lift your head and look around, forcing yourself to understand where you are and to perceive the situation you are in.

You whisper to the sky, you ask what you are doing in the new place where life left you, you question why, screaming, and most of the time you don't get any answer. After a short while you start looking for ways to adapt to where you are and to continue your life in this new place - helpless, alone and tired.

The sky and the trees around you, which you first whisper, then shout and scream at, begin to speak and answer to you after you adapt to them.

The answers to all the questions you ask are the new questions they ask. At that moment, you realize that while answering the questions asked of you, you have actually given all the answers to your own questions with correct, consistent and understandable words.

The mirror around you spoke up and, like the reflection of an image in a mirror, whispered its own answer to your question, which you could not understand at first. When you asked, "Are you me?" it has already whispered, "I am answering, am I you?"

I couldn't stand any longer in front of the mirror. I ran out of the bathroom as if I ran away from my hollowed-out eyes, my long beard, my thin and pale face, closed the door, and sat down at the table again, with the fussy and anxious attitude of someone who wanted to get something done quickly and knew that he had little time.

I was about to touch the keys of the computer when my eyes fell on the words of the last poetic narrative standing on the left corner of the desk.

First smell the soil of the mad forest

Then find those carved into the trunk of the tree...

I read the two lines I saw at the top of the glossy paper folded with the picture of the forest inside, a few more times. "Is it possible?" I asked myself. What I was thinking, what came to my mind while reading these lines - could it really be?

I stretched out my trembling left hand and touched the paper like a breakable object, gently picked it up, unfolded it, turned the picture, placed it on the desk, and began to carefully examine the trunks of the trees.

I noticed that on the trunks of some trees seen in the forest picture taken from afar, there were rectangular areas of gray-black color that were different from the bark of the trees. Gathering my full attention, I brought the picture closer to my face, then zoomed out and looked at it over and over.

I realized that I could not reach a conclusion from the very small and vague images, and I left the picture on the table again. First I turned off the table lamp and turned on the ceiling lamp, not caring that Solmaz might wake up. I took my smartphone, which had the features of a good camera, and took pictures of the forest image, the trees in the picture, the trunks of the trees, the rectangular gray-black areas, from different distances.

I quickly folded the picture and placed it carefully on the left corner of the desk again. I was excited and my hands were sweaty. I transferred all the pictures I took to my laptop, performed the necessary operations, and saved them with a program that would allow me to look at them in sequence, zoom in and zoom out when necessary.

I felt like someone who had found the decryption key of a very important cipher or was preparing to read a newly arrived letter informing the location of a relative who had been missing for years – anxious and fearful.

I first looked at all the pictures as I had photographed them, examined them, and switched to the slide show, speeding up and slowing down the images, and identifying which pictures I needed to examine more closely. I zoomed in on the tree trunks, the rectangular gray-black areas on the trunks that seemed very small from afar in the pictures I selected.

On the trunks of five trees, where I thought to be about one and a half meters above the ground, there were gray rectangular areas that looked like metal plates nailed to the trunk of the tree. And over all of them, regular and vague dark areas could be discerned; I thought the dark areas looked like letters or numbers.

Nikola's poetic narrative, consisting of three chapters, twenty lines, and one hundred and four words, came back to my mind. 3-20-104… While the numbers were flowing in front of my eyes, behind the picture of the forest I left on the left corner of the desk, the two lines that were now faded, were smiling at me like a friend who knew a lot about me.

There, right under that tree, you will find what you are looking for, nowhere else...

64. NOT OF THE PATHS WALKED ON FOR CENTURIES

I went to bed in the early morning, listening to the sound of the pouring rain and got frightened each time by the strong thunder. Solmaz was sleeping with her unique style, face down and with her right knee pulled to her belly. With her head on the pillow, breathing lightly and quietly, I stroked her hair slowly, bent over and kissed her cheek.

I turned off my bedside lamp, leaned my back against the pillow, and fixed my eyes on a point I assumed was right in front of me and couldn't see. I thought of places where the code I found, or thought I found, in the poetic narrative consisting of three chapters, twenty lines and one hundred and four words could lead me, help me find, or return from - empty-handed, without finding anything.

Someone who only looked at the picture of the forest would find nothing but the green fraternity of bushes, grasses, branches, and trees - not unlike the sight of any other forest, and would not be able to tell where and which forest this was. However, the front side of the first narrative with two chapters and twelve lines had the Walls of Antioch, and the integrity, continuity and the code pointed out by the two narratives were aimed at solving the same mystery. The forest was unmistakably adjacent to the walls on the summits of Mount Silpius.

When I evaluated the three parts together as a whole, the numbers 3-20-104 might have appeared as a code, but when I evaluated them separately, the two parts consisted of twelve lines and sixty-two words, 2-12-62 and the final narrative in a single chapter could be trying to guide me with the code 1-8-42.

I thought endlessly of all the possibilities, numbers, and combinations that could occur. Were all my doubts, hopes and expectations a delusion - or had Nikola really tried to convey the location of a very important item with his own encrypted messages? Would I really be able to find and reach an important well-hidden item, a writing, ain nformation; or were all of these thoughts an inconsistent product of the unhealthy functioning of my brain, which was affected by the traumas and accidents I had?

Right or wrong, healthy or sick, whatever the shape and origin of my thoughts were; I would definitely go where I needed to go and try to get correct, consistent and real answers to all my thoughts. The value I hoped to find was likely to exist and it was too important to give up on.

I closed my eyes and looked away from the invisible spot I assumed was on the wall across me. I forced myself to sleep, I wanted to sleep and rest well. I wanted to enter the new day in a healthy, vigorous, active and fast manner. I placed my hand on the warm back of Solmaz lying on my left side and felt that I was warming up; she murmured and whispered a few words to me that I could not understand.

Together with the birds of prey flying in the sky, we landed on the sturdy branches of the pine trees. We closed our eyes together and fell into deep sleep. They supported me with their wings, I held them with my arms. One of them pressed its pointed beak to my nose and we sniffed each other. It was as if I was one of them, they never felt alien to me, we were like connected members of the same family.

We hugged each other tightly in the cold of the night; I sniffed the strong and shiny feathers of their beautiful wings, they pecked on my arms, face and hair. They whispered in my ears that they missed me, and I cried wildly that I loved them.

They asked me to be quiet or to speak in a whisper, I said softly that I was not afraid of anything, with more frantic cries. I told the birds of prey that I missed the forests - our forests - and they said that they longed to perch with me on the branches of the pines.

We became a swarm with the young birds, who imitated the mother bird's matriarchy, the father bird's harshness as well as my disobedient, rebellious behavior - looked up at the sky and told the brightest star above to wait for us. We whispered that we would come near it; the star heard us, winked, told us it understood us, and we all closed our eyes. We made that star understand us, too. We slept, all together; arm in arm, wing in wing...

I woke up around ten in the morning. I was alone in bed and in the room. I listened for a sound in the bathroom, it was quiet there too. I quickly got out of bed, opened the curtain, and tightly closed my eyes, which were starting to ache with the bright sunlight pouring into the room. I opened the door of the room and breathed in the fresh air and filled my lungs, hungry for the air. For the first time after days, my new hopes were blooming in a sunny, bright and peaceful morning.

I looked down with curiosity and saw Solmaz sitting by the small fountain under the bright rays of the sun. She was holding a book in her hand, she was extremely concentrated and was reading without taking her eyes off the pages. I called out to hier from above, exclaiming with enthusiasm that I loved her; she fliched at first, and then scolded me like a naughty child, signaling me to be quiet. She brought her long, slender finger to her beautiful lips. I got silent, bent my head, and turned my back to her in the manner of a scolded child, entering back in the room.

I rushed into the bathroom, took a shower, dried myself, dressed up and went downstairs. I approached Solmaz's ear, who was still sitting by the fountain, and whispered, in a barely audible voice this time, that I loved her. She looked at me as if she didn't understand me. I bent down and whispered it once again... She must have definitely understood what I said, but she wanted me to repeat it over and over again, the cunning and cruel woman! I did not succumb to her cruelty and did not whisper again.

When I sat on the chair across her and said that I had completed the translation, she extended her hand and congratulated me. She also did not hesitate to joke about it, saying that she admired my speed. I told her about the possible codes in Nikola's poetic narrative, the rectangular plates nailed to the trunks of the trees in the forest painting, and told her that I would climb Mount Silpius once more, and that we could go together if she wanted to.

Solmaz looked at me with a smile. She was telling that she wanted to spend this beautiful, sunny day by the fountain in the lovely garden of the house, reading a book and drinking tea under the warm glow of the sun. Meanwhile, I had already stood up and started walking towards the street door. I opened the locked door and told her to lock it behind me.

I knew the way all too well now. Young girls and old women went outside after the rains that have been pouring non-stop for days, placed their pillows, duvets, beds, and the laundry they washed on tables, chairs, and stools they took out to the sun-dried streets, argued and joked with each other. The scene was nice, cute and sincere, filling one's heart with enthusiasm.

When I went out to the street, I saw the same images being displayed by the shopkeepers lined up on both sides of the road, and I looked at them with a happy expression. The sun had revived the whole city in an instant, and all the people were clinging to new hopes in the bright, warm and strong arms of the new day.

While passing through Kurtuluş Street, I looked at the Habib Al-Najjar Mosque on the left side of the road. I thought once again and tried to understand the respect, tolerance and vast culture that the name of the first Christian from Antioch was given to the first mosque built in Anatolia, that it was not changed afterwards, and that it has been preserved for hundreds of years.

Around noon, the roads were so deserted that they were almost empty. I rushed through the streets. I took a right turn from the wide asphalt road leading to Altınözü district and tried to reach the hills of Silpius by climbing the narrow, curved, and patchy mountain road full of potholes.

I looked sadly at the bent, wrinkled, hollowed out images of very old olive trees scattered randomly on the right and left of the road, in the fields, on the hills. Olive trees, which have been living for centuries even though their insides were now empty and some parts rotten, were giving new branches on their other sides and adorning these branches with lush leaves and olives, the fruit of heaven.

I looked proudly at the old olive trees and smiled. I knew that they could think, sense, and hear me. I said to myself, "Everything is expected from these olive trees – all that is good, true, beautiful and positive…"

I called out to all my relatives, whom I loved, valued, cared about, trusted and believed in, one by one, and shouted to the sky, saying, "I hope you live like an olive tree and be as free, productive, resistant, invincible and honorable."

I parked the car in the parking lot next to the concrete structure, which was a mixture of a casino, coffee house, hookah place, on the top of the high hill in the middle of the Silpius Mountain. On the hill next to the parking lot, telephone base stations, television and radio antennas, transformer huts, wires, poles and many similar devices that I could not name were saluting the spiritual capital of the Roman Empire from the most beautiful, airy and most commanding hill of Silpius.

Before entering the dirt road that started right next to the magnificent locations of the antennas, I opened the trunk and took out the bag full of everything I had bought on the way. I locked the car and started walking towards the mad forest with the sad demeanor of a calm, slow, stagnant and lonely man going on a picnic.

I was shouting all the numbers, signs, symbols, and ciphers that came to my mind against the thick bark trunks of the trees rising on the edge of the forest I had reached. I was shouting and reciting Nikola's poem, with all my might.

I wished that the forest, all the trees in the forest, could hear me, and the forest, with its trees and all its branches, kept repeating back to me every line I had recited, in a stronger tone.

Not of the paths walked on for centuries,

Find and bow down to new paths hidden by the bushes, grasses, vines and thorns, all the plants that cover the floor of the Forest.

First smell the soil of the mad forest,

Then find those carved into the trunk of the tree.

There, right under that tree, you will find what you are looking for, nowhere else.

65. FIND NEW PATHS HIDDEN BY SHRUBS AND BOW DOWN

I entered the forest by walking on the dirt road. The sun's rays, penetrating through the gaps left by the branches and leaves of the trees, illuminated the green base of the road. I stopped and turned my head up. At first, the branches, leaves and vines I saw high seemed to be responding to my curious gaze.

A few meters after entering the forest, the road ended and several narrow paths started, dispersed in different directions. I started to take a step in a perpendicular direction to the path we walked on the day we reached the castle, without setting foot on any of them. *Not of the paths walked on for centuries…*

Protecting my legs and hands from the sharp and hard thorns, and being careful that my footsteps were safe, I made my way to the lower reaches of the forest. Through the bushes, grasses, vines and thorns…

It was as if I was walking down from the highest point of Mount Silpius towards the city, and large and small birds, insects and reptiles, frightened by the sounds of the plants I stepped on, were escaping left and right, upwards, towards the branches of the trees. *All the plants that cover the floor of the Forest…*

I continued my lonely journey, being careful with every step I took in the forest where I walked through the unpaved areas, not to touch the new branches and sprouts that sprang up from the bottom of every tree I passed by. *Find and bow down to new paths hidden by the bushes, grasses, vines and thorns, all the plants that cover the floor of the Forest…*

In some places, I wandered around trees standing in impenetrable proximity, jumped over rocks, greedily plucked vines that were tangling at my feet, bent down and filled my lungs with the earth-grass-bush scent still rising from the wet grasses and bushes. I breathed in deeply and at that very moment, I looked and noticed the metal rectangular gray plate nailed to the trunk of a thick, tall, bent pine tree. *First smell the soil of the mad forest, then find those carved into the trunk of the tree...*

As if I saw a relative I haven't seen in a long time, I approached excitedly to the thick-bark trunk of the pine tree, on which the metal plate was nailed.

I reached out my hand and stroked the tree, reaching out and smelling its trunk. I looked at the rectangular gray metal plate; I touched the black and upright numbers.

I tried to perceive and read what was written, like a blind person trying to read, touching the ridges.

The numbers I saw and felt with my fingertips and their sequence, the dots between them – they were looking at me as if they were describing moments of sadness, full of quarrels, blood and turmoil: 3.06.098.

I now understood, that all my thoughts and my possible doubts could be true. I took the bag that I was carrying with my right hand in my left hand and started to walk down in excitement, by the lined-up trees.

The numbers on the metal plates nailed to the trunks of the trees must have had some logic. I solved it in the second plate I saw after the first plate I distinguished: 3.07.120

The number three was fixed, the number after this fixed point must have indicated the order in which the trees were located, and the last number must have indicated the position of the tree in the order. At that moment, I really wanted to know beforehand this marking system, which is in accordance with the rules and methods of forest officials.

I continued to walk down fast, on the same line. The 07, which came after the number 3 on the last metal plate I saw, was telling me that there were thirteen more to go. I continued my exciting and strange journey, sometimes leaning on trees, holding on to their branches, and drawing strength from the sprawling vines, but pressing the trunk of each tree to see if there was a nailed plate.

Despite the rain, and the misty and dark weather of the previous days, it was a clear, bright, warm and sunny winter day today and I was very happy about it. When I thought that if it had been like the previous rainy and extremely thunderous day, I would not have been able to complete even a small part of the distance I walked today, I wished that the sun shining above me would shine for at least one or two more hours.

I moved forward and saw the metal plate with the number 19 after 3. I was excited and even forgot the hard days I spent ill in bed when I felt I was getting closer to the end, to the goal I wanted to reach with all my heart.

The sequence of numbers 3.20.126 that I saw on a tree with metal plate nailed on the trunk of a tree next row increased my excitement even more. I walked to the right, facing the city from the tree where I saw this last plate, and the sequence of 3.20.120 numbers I saw in the same row, a few trees later, told me I was going in the right direction.

I walked faster. Without stopping or hesitation, almost without breath, I walked with sweat all over my body, forehead, face, hands, and read the numbers on the slightly curved, rectangular gray metal plate nailed to the thick bark of the tallest tree in the forest, almost curved towards the sky.

I read, paused and looked at it once again, but I could not perceive anything. I recognized the shape of the numbers, but could not understand what they meant, despite my best efforts.

I recited the last two lines of Nikola; I thought and at that moment I was able to recognize the numbers that I knew well and have almost been legendary for days… I approached the tree, extended my hand to the metal plate, touched it: 3.20.104

There, right under that tree, you will find what you are looking for, nowhere else.

As I silently recited the last two lines of Nikola, I saw white smoke rising from the middle of the Silpius Mountain and flames rising with red curls: the forest at the foot of the Silpius Mountain was unfortunately on fire.

66. ORIENTIS APICEM PULCRUM *

I had no time to waste. I quickly examined the tree, its trunk, and the metal plate nailed to the trunk. I took the wooden-handled incision from the bag I brought with me and began to dig under the tree; I hit the ground non-stop, cleared all the surrounding grass, plants, vines, dry leaves, made the soil at the base visible, and kept digging the exposed area.

As I dug the ground, dried and rotten leaves, bark, roots, and worms came out, and a sharp smell of earth and rot diffused into the air. I had no difficulty in digging the soil, which had softened with the effect of the rain that had been pouring non-stop for days, and I was working around the trunk of the tree. The giant pine stood as if it were the oldest tree in the forest with its majestic, thick and powerful appearance.

On the one hand, my desire and impatience to reach what I was looking for as soon as possible, and on the other hand, the forest fire that started in the lower and middle parts of the mountain forced me to work at an ever-increasing pace and to dig the ground ambitiously. At that moment I saw the helicopter hovering over the burning part of the forest and pouring water from the large vessel attached to a long rope; emptying the water it was carrying and quickly flying away from the burning area.

Queen of the East

I continued to work. With every blow I landed with the adze, I looked where the soil compound that came out of the hole I had dug had emptied, and continued to search for the tangible, visible, yet obscure item that I didn't know what it actually looked like, and even doubted whether I could find. I had reached a depth of forty centimeters around the trunk of the great pine and still had not come across anything. Even though I was tired, I couldn't stop and kept digging rapidly. The smell of smoke, soot and humidity rising from the lower parts of the mountain was taking away my right to stop, rest and take a break. The iron part of the adze in my hand was completely covered with mud, and I kept digging non-stop when, at the last blow, I was startled with the sound of metal hitting another metal, I stopped for a moment and, throwing the adze in my hand to one side, I leaned forward, bent down and I began to remove the moist soil with my fingers - softly and productively.

First, I saw the mud-soaked end of a thick plastic bag, and then I dug my fingers deep, felt the hard, smooth texture inside the bag, and pressed my fingers to the bottom to properly grasp it. I stopped and took a deep breath; I wished in my heart that what I was looking for, what I needed to find, was the thing, object, writing that was in my hands. Without haste, I grasped it like I was holding a breakable object and pulled my hands up. I took it out easily and placed it on the green plants next to the clump of earth that I dug, sat down next to it, gasped, just stared...

After a while, I stretched out my hands, caressed the plastic bag. The tired look of rusted metal from the part torn by the first blows of the adze was staring like the sleepy eyes of a newly awakened creature. I extended my fingers to the torn part of the bag, widened it a little more and felt the rusty, rough texture of the metal touching my fingers. I took it out of the plastic bag and looked at the cube-shaped iron box that barely fit between my two palms, about fifteen centimeters on each side and rusty on all sides, some of the rivets on the sides almost melted into the iron.

That was it, that was really what I was looking for. The numbers Nikola vaguely wrote in a way that nothing could be understood from them, which could only be found through the poetic narrative he wrote with three parts, twenty lines and one hundred and four words, were the same numbers on the metal plate that forest officials had nailed onto the trunk of the tree, under which the rusty iron box was buried in the ground.

I placed the rusty iron box and the adze in the bag I brought with me. I filled all the soil I dug into the hole I dug, pressed the soil with my mud-covered hands and feet, sprinkled dry leaves, twigs, herbs on it, and turned my gaze to the random location of the fire that I had forgotten. A thin white cloud of smoke was rising into the sky. The number of helicopters hovering over the burning place, discharging water had increased to two, and one of them was passing right over where I was. The ground, soaked by the rain that had fallen for days, did not allow the fire to spread too quickly.

I started climbing in the direction I came from. I couldn't hear any sound coming from the ground I stepped on, the dry branches I broke while walking, the tree trunks I was rubbing past, and the birds playing in the air - I couldn't think of anything other than the bag I was carrying and the precious relic inside. I turned back when I reached the top of the Silpius Mountain, out of breath, and looked at the Asi River, which continued to flow silently and brightly in the middle of the thousands of buildings scattered in all directions in one of the most important cities of the Eastern Roman Empire, that old city, Antakya - shouting the name of the city:

"Orientis Apicem Pulcrum / Queen of the East!"

I reached the car I had parked next to the place where there were antennas, the TV transmitters, the cell towers, the wires, the rusty poles, and the worn-out transformers. I was about to open the door of the car when a little puppy came to my feet, wagging its tail rapidly, sniffed the hem of my pants and looked at me with its almost smiling, innocent face and moist nose. I bent down and stroked its head, its floppy ears; the puppy closed its sad eyes and lived that moment, only that moment.

I started the car's engine. The bag was still in my left hand, I didn't let it go, I couldn't let it go. I felt as if I left it anywhere, I would never find it again and all my efforts and risks would go waste. I placed it neatly on the seat on my right and began to make my way back into the city through the narrow, twisting, rough, forest road full of pitholes. I waved with a smile to the tiny dog who greeted me off, running by the car with small, staccato barks.

The mud that dried on my hands spilled from the steering wheel I was holding onto the seat I was sitting on, on my pants, on the floor mat of the car, and I didn't care at all.

People sitting in the cars passing by me, throwing their chairs in front of the workplaces on the roadside, watching their surroundings sluggishly, drivers standing under the traffic lights waiting for the green light to come on, porters trying to walk while bent over the heavy load they were carrying, students returning from school with their bags in their hands and on their backs... Every woman, man and child I saw - adult, old or young - everyone seemed to be staring at me without taking their eyes off of me. And I was sending heartfelt smiles to everyone who looked at me; I was smiling and greeting everyone who looked at me like a victorious commander who had now achieved his goal, won the war, found and captured all he was looking for.

While trying to reach the house from Kurtuluş Street, this time I looked at the old, faded and yellowed cut stone walls of the Habib Al-Najjar Mosque, which was on my right. With all my enthusiasm and heart, I whispered "Dear Carpenter" as I felt the maturity, brotherhood and friendship of a Muslim temple, which had the privilege and distinction of being the first mosque of Anatolia that was named after the first Christian from Antioch.

I looked over at the seat on my right, extended my hand and touched it... I stroked the bag. I didn't know what was inside the rusty iron box, which I couldn't believe I had found or touched, where it would take us, what roads it would lead us to, the mountains, plains, valleys and rivers we would lead our lives from this day forward, and I did not want to find out yet.

67. NEITHER A MISSING WORD, NOR AN ADDITIONAL PHRASE

I parked the car in a place I found in the narrow street. My neighbors, who were now used to the fact that the place I parked my car almost belonged to me, looked at me curiously through the dusty glass of their windows, which smelled of history, obsolescence, and mold. I grabbed the bag in the right front seat, got out of the car, and waved to them. They walked away, smiling...

I knocked on the peeled wooden door of Dimitri's house. I stood in front of the weathered door with the self-confident demeanor of a successful man who carried the magic key in his pocket that would enable him to eradicate the troubles, difficulties and pain he has been experiencing for months.

I stopped and knocked on the door once more. The echoes of my knocks on the door came back to my face with the silent and calm reflection of the doors, which would not open. I waited and listened to the familiar rhythm of the footsteps to the door, hitting the stone floor. Behind the opened door, the dark blue eyes I wanted to see most in life were waiting. "Okay," I whispered. "Everything is alright, I found it, Solmaz, I found what I was looking for." She looked at me with a still and sullen face without a smile, saying nothing. She wiggled her eyes as if she was trying to say, "Look behind me, look at what's waiting behind me", turned her head slightly to the left, secretly showing me the man sitting by the small pond.

I looked and saw Tancrede smiling beyond Solmaz's shoulders. Without waiting, I entered the courtyard of the house quickly and greedily, I wanted to ask what he was doing, for what reason he came and what he wanted. I didn't ask, I couldn't ask. The rusty metal box in the bag I carried in my left hand, and my dried muddy, dusty and dirty hands, could have said a lot to someone with a high probability of being an enemy. I stopped and greeted this strange journalist with a fake smile that seemed strange even to myself.

He replied to me by telling me that he had not yet left Turkey, that he had traveled to Ankara and Istanbul and that he found this country very interesting, and that he was trying to seem close to me and Solmaz with a fake sincereness. He explained that Antakya was the city that he, his relatives and even his ancestors found the most livable, with the mischievousness of a pure child trying to seem sweet.

My mind and all my thoughts, all my attention, were on the bag that I had laid on the floor as if it was an unimportant object. I was not looking at the bag at all, I was forcing myself not to look at it.

While I was telling him that I was happy to see him again, Tancrede was looking questioningly at my shabby, thin face, to my beard, and to my clothes covered in dust and mud.

I told him I was mountain climbing. I also said that I love mountains, valleys between mountains, and rivers flowing madly. Without caring whether he believed me or not, I spoke about the endless happiness climbing gives my soul, as well as being covered in mud, Rolling in dirt and in crazy rivers

He was aware of my pretentiousness and insincerity in my speech, and he was listening to me in his own fake and stagnant manner, and I was aware of that as well. He looked first at the mud on my face, hands, and clothes, which had now turned into dust that could only be shaken off, and then hesitantly he looked at the stones on the floor of the courtyard and the bag I had left on those stones. He tried to explain to me in a hissing voice that a problem-free and endlessly happy life awaits me and Solmaz, and that he could not understand or resolve the reasons for our rejection of this happy life, without taking his eyes off my eyes. He fixed his eyes on the stones on the ground once more, looked at the waters of the small pool, and finally, turning his gaze to Solmaz, he continued his speech: "I care a lot about myself, it seems to me that nothing will happen without me. Last week I was driving around Istanbul in a cab and I asked the cab driver what the words written on the entrance gate of a cemetery we passed meant, he translated it to me in perfect, beautiful English that he had learned at university: 'Every living being will taste death.'

"I didn't care if he translated it right or wrong, with missing or more words, I was able to fully understand his translation; You should also understand what that sentence means, that the end called death is inevitable."

I could fully understand his English, which he spoke with an Italian accent. At this time of the day, I was trying to understand where his speech and the things he said inside an ordinary house in a narrow street of an old and historical quarter of Antakya would lead to - I was waiting with curiosity.

"One day, when I cared too much about myself, what I did, what I spoke, what I promised, what I wanted to do, and the steps I took, and when I thought that without me, the newspaper I was working for would never be able to be published, that the quality, number of prints and sales of the newspaper would decrease, and the articles would not be read, I came across an ordinary book. I just looked at the book; It was full of pictures, figures, charts and comments. As I was reading it with that attitude of being so self-fulfilled, not caring about anything else other than myself, I suddenly paused and all my attention to what I was reading - it was important, what was told in the book.

I have read that there were one hundred and seventy billion galaxies determined and calculated in the infinite void called the universe. I learned that one of these one hundred and seventy billion galaxies was the Milky Way Galaxy, and I was reading in astonishment and amazement that this galaxy contained an average of three hundred billion stars, when I stopped and read all of it once again and asked myself: What could the importance of one of the seven billion people living on a planet in one of a hundred and seventy billion galaxies, one, that is, me?

If it were you, ma'am and you, gentleman, could you care about yourself after this information you have learned? Could you continue to care about yourself as one of the seven billion people living in one corner of an ordinary three hundred billion stars in one hundred and seventy billion galaxies?

We believe in eternal life and we are running after certain values and symbols that we believe in with all our heart, which will ensure our permanence in this dizzying endless expanse. We are looking for them and we will take every step to find them. We will surely find them!"

Tancrede was thoroughly excited. We never interrupted his enthusiastic and impressive speech, patiently listening to him until the end. Even at this hour, long past midnight, when I write these, I remember vividly the moment he stood up, extended his hand to ask for our excuse and shook our hands, the minute he walked softly to the door, and his words: "You know what we are looking for, give it to us and get rid of it, live happy, healthy and peaceful days, all your life".

NOTE TO THE PUBLISHER

Dear Mr. Kemal,

I'm writing non-stop, without rest, and quickly. In fact, right after the parts where I explained that Firuz Demirci's real name was Bohemond, I should have written who the Italian journalist we met at the hospital was, who later visited Dimitri's house uninvited.

I should have written that according to known and accepted historical information, the name of the commander of the army that besieged Antioch in the Crusade in 1098 was Bohemond, as I wrote in the previous chapters, and that the name of Bohemond's nephew, to whom Bohemond handed over the administration of the city after capturing Antioch, was also Tancrede. I should have never listened to the last words of the so-called journalist who was speaking to me as he was walking out the door and should have slammed my fist right in the middle of his face. I'll explain later how I restrained myself and why I did it. I probably don't have to tell you that Tancrede was the head of the Principality of Antioch a thousand years ago and minted coins in his name, you probably already know it.

I know, the sections are all mixed up… It doesn't matter if it's mixed though; you are the master of writing, but as you promised me, you must not change anything, you must publish them all the way I compiled them and will send you. As you promised, as we agreed, I should be able to read all that I wrote as they are; there should be nothing different: neither a missing word, nor an additional phrase.

68. I FORGOT THAT SOLMAZ WAS A GOOD ARCHAEOLOGIST AS SHE EXAMINED THE RUSTY METAL BOX

As Tancrede was walking out the door, I stared after him. The man had made it clear which side he was on in an extremely intelligent and polite manner. He had told me who he was working for, and offered me serious amounts of money. The offer he made included a veiled accusation: "We know, you gave the fake to the museum and the original is still in your hands... Give them to us, and we'll pour money upon you!"

Tancrede did not speak openly; however, I knew which group he was from and what he was trying to do under the guise of a journalist. I couldn't openly blame him; because he didn't want anything directly from me. He was deftly telling through veiled narratives that death was inevitable, that everyone would definitely reach this end, that no one had any privileges, that we were as insignificant as a small spot in the infinite universe and that we should not care too much about ourselves - hiding what they really wanted to say.

I got up from my chair and washed my hands with the water from the fountain, splashed cold water on my face, and washed away dust, soil and the dried mud. I picked up the bag on the floor and walked up the stairs to the room with Solmaz, whom I told I had an important surprise for. I stopped right at the top of the stairs and, with an exaggerated politeness, gave way to her. From the mischievous expression on my face, she understood what I was going to do and started to climb the stairs with a careless attitude. I just looked, did not extend my hand and did not touch the sensual image floating in front of me. She turned her back and looked at me with an expression that showed her happiness for me being able to joke again.

We entered the room and, without speaking, I carefully placed the bag on the desk in front of the window. I took the rusty metal box out of the bag and told her all in one breath what I had done. She looked at the box with the patient attitude she had acquired from her education, and examined every part of it. When I said that we could examine it better if we washed it and removed the mud and soil on it, "Are you crazy!" she responded to me. "Is it possible to do something like this, didn't they teach you anything in the archeology school you studied for two years!" She scolded me quite a bit. I kept quiet and joined in inspecting the box. I forgot that Solmaz was a good archaeologist...

Solmaz was just looking at the box. She was examining every part of it from the right, from the left, from above, and she certainly did not touch it. She asked me for pen and paper, I reached and gave her whatever was on the desk. She started taking little notes. I needed to be thoroughly washed cleansed; I said I wanted to take a shower and went to the bathroom and left her alone with the metal box.

I took a long, warm and relaxing shower, shaved, got rid of my beard and my shabby appearance. I put on my robe and looked in the mirror. I looked at myself with a smile, feeling good and happy for the first time in days; I looked at my face in the mirror with the confident expression of a man who had achieved the success he longed for. "Are you me?" I asked, and as before, the image of the answer was reflected to me from the mirror. He answered me in the same way: "Am I you?"

I got angry and turned my back, grumbling. Just then, I felt a voice behind me said, "Okay, we get it, don't get angry. I am You." I could have sworn I heard those words. I stopped and turned around quickly, looked in the mirror again. The face in the mirror was also looking worriedly at my worried face. I thought that these moments were a new illusion of my brain, which was damaged by the accidents I had. I quickly left the mirror without waiting.

When I returned to the room, I found Solmaz still sitting in a chair in front of the metal box, taking notes. She said my phone rang while I was in the bathroom. I sat on the bed, grabbed the phone from the nightstand, and stared at its screen. The caller was the boss. I called him right away.

He questioned me with his usual sincere and enthusiastic demeanor... He asked about my health and Solmaz, in one breath he asked when we were going to come to Istanbul, and he listed all at once that he missed us very much, that he wished we could get together as soon as possible, and that all our colleagues sent the same wishes. I told the boss that we were fine, that it had been raining non-stop for days in Antakya, even a few people lost their lives in floods and dents, that we would like to return to Istanbul in a few days if nothing extraordinary happened and everything went well.

Leaving my phone back on the nightstand, I approached the archaeologist at the desk and looked down at the notes she had taken. I tried to read what she wrote. I looked at the picture of the metal box she had drawn on paper and was trying to emulate. Solmaz had written "13 cm" next to the edges of the cube, and the six rivets on each side were marked with small circles that she had thickened, and put sequential numbers on each of them.

I asked her what she was thinking. She tried to explain to me that there were many possibilities, and that all possibilities could be determined by laboratory examination, as being done with the scrolls, but one thing she was absolutely certain of - that the item, object, or whatever its name was that was so tightly guarded inside a metal box must have been very valuable.

She also mentioned the possibility that the contents of the rusty metal box may be the same age as the box, or much older than the box. I paused, fell silent with a thought that suddenly came to my mind. She looked at me, in an expression that asked me what happened. I told her that I was thinking, just thinking.

I did not tell her that the gazelle skins were at least two thousand years old, but the ceramic piece inside might be new or even a few years old. I also did not tell her that I thought Luke might have taken a precaution to prevent the relic, which he wished to stay in this city forever in the text he wrote, from being taken away from this city. I couldn't tell her that there might be a trick for those who find the scrolls and the relic inside so that they can leak more money to themselves; they might have hidden the things inside the scrolls, for instance this rusty metal box, someplace else in order to sell it later - first getting rich with real scrolls and a fake ceramic piece, then later with the real ones.

I was thinking and wishing that all the riddles that were becoming more and more intractable would be solved as soon as possible. The only way to solve the riddle and answer all questions was to complete laboratory investigations and determine the exact age of the findings. I looked at the clock on the wall. It was almost six o'clock, and it was time for Dimitri to come home.

I asked Solmaz, who was still examining the box beside the desk, if it would be right to tell Dimitri about the metal box. She looked at me hard, sharp, as if there were no other possibilities, and as if she was looking at an insect. "Are you crazy?" she said. "How can you think of hiding such an important finding from our friend with whom we shared everything from the very first day - the good, the bad and all information!" "Alright," I said. "We'll tell him, don't get angry right away. Let's go down to the kitchen and prepare dinner." She thought that she might have offended me, so she looked at me with a smile; reached out, took my hand and squeezed it lovingly.

I put the metal box on the desk back into the bag and took it with me with the attitude of a small child who couldn't keep his toy away from him with the thought that it could be lost at any moment, and went down to the courtyard. The weather had turned dark. Despite the rain and icy cold weather for days, a warm and dry night awaited us. I suggested Solmaz to prepare the dinner table in the courtyard, and she approved me with a smile, with the longing for the open air and the hunger for fresh air of people who have been locked in a room for days - overwhelmed, bored and fed up with this isolation.

We started to carry all the materials from the kitchen to the table in the courtyard. Plates, spoons, forks, glasses and all other necessary items were neatly placed on the table.

Just then, the doorbell rang. Dimitri must have arrived. I walked to the door, turned the key, opened the door, and faced the worried expression of the young prosecutor standing one step behind Dimitri, who was standing before me.

69. JUNE 3, 1098, 912 KNIFE CUTS, 912 MARBLES AND LUIGI

I honestly did not expect the prosecutor to come visit us at this time of the day. Dimitri hadn't told me either. I stepped away of the door, wishing nothing bad happened. They entered inside, greeting us. Seeing the table we had prepared for dinner in the courtyard, the Prosecutor apologized shyly for disturbing us at this inappropriate hour.

The young man, who had a tough, authoritative and determined look in his courthouse room, was now gone, and was replaced with a shy and naive young man who didn't even know where to put his hands. I smiled, thinking of about the sense of power and dominance that offices give to people.

We all sat on the chairs next to the table. "I wanted to visit you for a while now," said the prosecutor. While talking, he was constantly moving his hands, moving them pointlessly, but he could not find a place to rest them. "Fortune allowed me to do it today. Actually, I know that you are angry with me for not allowing you to meet with Rıdvan, the museum officer in prison, but please try to understand me. The rules tie our hands, we couldn't do a single unlawful act in an incident of four murders, even though they were your relatives."

I told him that we were not angry and that he was right. I couldn't tell him that we would ask for help from Rıdvan in solving the secret they had encrypted with Nikola! Nor could I say that I would ask Rıdvan about how and to what extent he had part in the death of our relatives, and other similar matters.

Finding a spot on the table to rest his left hand, the prosecutor continued his speech: "We continue the investigation. We have obtained most of the important information, operations were carried out in different provinces, and they are still being carried out, we carry out everything in great secrecy, but as you know, we are dealing with a criminal gang with an international organization. Not only are they smugglers of historical artifacts, they are powerful enough to carry out any filth you can think of, in a highly organized and ruthless manner."

He said nothing but what we already knew, he was quite well at keeping secrets and he was adept at going around any information that should have been kept a secret. He asked me about my health, what I have been doing, whether I was resting well - even, strangely and questionably, what I did today!

I explained that we had to stay at home because of the crazy rain and that I went out for the first time today, climbed mountains, took a walk to breathe the fresh mountain air and regain my strength. He looked at me with a smile, took a deep breath, and finally found a place to rest his other hand. He was suddenly relieved.

"Today, a fire broke out on Habib Al-Najjar Mountain. Forest fires are not uncommon this season, we think it was arson. The firefighting helicopters took some pictures from the air. When we enlarged and examined the pictures we received, we encountered an interesting view. We might have bothered you if you hadn't just told me, the first time I asked, that you were climbing the mountain." He stood up, reached into the inside pocket of his jacket, and left on the table a photograph of a man walking among the trees in the mountain.

"Keep it, you can keep it as a memory, we have a lot of them," he said with a smile. I got up, too, and shook his hand with the relief that he didn't know why I went up the mountain. At that very moment, he asked the crucial question: "I'm just asking out of curiosity, what was in that bag you were carrying in the picture?"

I said with a mischievous smile that I could swear I wasn't the arsonist who set the fire.

"No arsonist would say he was in the arson area as long as he can hide it. Although you were unaware of these pictures, you said that you were on the mountain; I no longer suspect you!" then, a mischievous smile identical to mine settled on his face, relaxed and starting to join in on the jokes. "Still, I wonder what you were carrying in that bag?"

I said with a smile that I listened to the doctors who specifically said that I needed to drink plenty of fluids during the recovery period, and that I went to the mountains with a few bottles of water I took with me and took a walk. I didn't know that the helicopters hovering over the fire area would photograph the whole mountain.

Despite all our insistence, he did not stay for dinner. I could finally understand that he had not made this sudden and untimely visit purely for the sake of asking for help. After we said goodbye to the prosecutor, I looked at Dimitri. He realized that I was going to question why he hadn't announced that the man was coming, and said that they had met at the door, without listening to the rest of my speech. Then he turned and smiled at Solmaz, "Since you prepared the table in the courtyard, you are tired, you have worked hard, then you deserved the award; I will reward you with a strong barbecue party," he said, and then, with one of his heartfelt laughters, which we missed, he picked up the bags he had left on the floor next to the table and quickly headed towards the kitchen. I walked after him.

In fact, all the ordinary conversations while preparing food, the daily events that are told while placing plates, forks and similar items on the dinner table, the memories told while transferring the prepared dishes to the plates in front of everyone, and the sincere laughter while drinking from the full glasses, all of these try to take us away to calm beaches, banks of rushing rivers and the peaks of high free mountains, which serve only one purpose: peace.

I have not used the word tranquility, which I have used many times in my writings, I could not use it, and I will not use it from now on. There are such words that no new word can replace, its full meaning; "Peace" is a word that is at the top of the list of words that you cannot change, cannot replace with a new word, and would not be accepted even if you replaced it, even if you wrote full pages, explained for hours, and even if all your mental confusions about the past prevented you from using that word.

Even while I was speaking, telling and trying to perceive these last lines I wrote, I was filled with peace, not tranquility…

We all gathered next to the barbecue that Dimitri prepared. We wanted to get rid of the chilling and trembling discomfort of the night that was starting to get cold. The ash-covered embers in the barbecue and the crimson color in some parts of it gave peace to our wounded hearts. The sizzling and rising smoke of the fat dripping from the meat on the shiny metal grill, which we placed without touching the embers, and the burning smell of the peels of tomatoes and peppers, went beyond the borders of the courtyard and spread to the whole neighborhood.

"I forgot something!" cried Dimitri, as he thrust the blackened iron tongs and the grill into my hand. "I forgot the most important thing!" While he was screaming more than laughing, he ran to the kitchen. Solmaz and I looked at each other curiously. He appeared before us again, like a cartoon character appearing in pictures on a time-lapse storyboard. In his hand was a small bottle of steamed rakı that he had taken out of the refrigerator and had forgotten on the kitchen table.

We told him that it was such a shame, but he couldn't tell whether what we said was shame was because he forgot the little bottle of rakı, or the small size of the bottle. At that moment, he quickly did the best thing to do: he filled our glasses.

As we carried the barbecue to the table, each of us held a glass of pure white liquid. Barbecued meats, tomatoes and the like were staring at us from inside our plates. Speaking with the effect and enthusiasm of the first glass, what Dimitri told was really important. He was telling us that the officials explained to him that the laboratory examination on the scrolls and ceramic cup was about to be completed, and that the official report would reach their hands in two or three days, and that they could not say anything about any preliminary information, guesses or the like – adding that it would be inappropriate for him to tell us exactly what kind of praises (!) he wanted to tell those officials at this peaceful table. Every time I looked at his face and every line of his face, I could understand everything he wanted to say and what he couldn't say.

We did not once again talk about the importance of determining the age of the scrolls and the ceramic piece; When the results came, that would be the only topic we would talk about anyway.

I asked him what the names Firuz, Bohemond, and Tancrede meant. He stopped and thought for a very short time. He said that the name of the commander of the Crusader army, which took the city on the day that Antioch was surrendered, defeated and looted on June 3, 1098, was Bohemond. He explained that the city surrendered to five hundred soldiers, who crossed the walls with the ropes hung by the treacherous Firuz, and the level of damage they inflicted on the city despite the protection of seven thousand Antioch soldiers. He was saying that Antioch was turned into a principality after this date and that Bohemond's nephew, named Tancrede, was appointed to this principality, when he stopped for a moment, stood up and anxiously asked, "Wasn't the name of the journalist who visited us also Tancrede?" He sat down again, looked at me, and when he learned that Tancrede visited us today again, he reached for the full glass in front of him.

"The date of June 3 is important," I said. "We should care about this date, it holds incomprehensible secrets in the history of the city and the events that followed."

Dimitri looked at me with an expression that said he couldn't understand what I was trying to say… He already knew that I was also writing a book in which I told our own story while I was translating the scrolls, and I briefly reminded him of this. I also told him how the order of the chapters I wrote and translated from Greek would be, and that I sent this order to my publisher in Istanbul. Then I told him about an important event that I stumbled upon, as I was researching during these studies. I asked him if there was a murder committed on June 3 of any year, that is, when the Crusader Army captured Antioch. I also asked him whether the number of blows to the body pierced with a repeatedly stabbed knife was the same as the number stated in the autopsy report.

"Luigi," said Dimitri. "I had a classmate named Luigi when I was in primary school; We had a sincere friendship and his birthday was June 3rd. When you said June 3rd, I remembered him. He was loving, he loved us all and everything. We used to play marbles together. He always waited for his father, who was working abroad, and wrote longing poems after his father. He would say, 'My father will come again when I collect exactly a thousand marbles, a thousand marbles' and look down with full eyes. He would greedily scatter what he had and always win our marbles lined up in the folds of the ground. Luigi's father really did come one day, then they packed up all of their stuff, loaded them into a truck, and got into a small, old, dusty car that followed the truck. "Where are you going, Luigi?" I asked him. We hugged each other and started to cry when he said, 'We are going to Milan, to our relatives abroad, we will live there from now on.' He looked at me sadly when I asked him, 'Could you manage to collect a thousand marbles?' and I remember him saying, 'It's nine hundred and twelve, but I could have collected more, I should have lived here more,' as if it were right in front of me."

I wanted to throw away the traces of what Luigi said to Dimitri and any scars June 3 left on my friend's soul, but unfortunately I could not perceive, with my brain that suffered traumas, the reasons why a man was killed with nine hundred and twelve stab wounds on this date, very close to this historical city.

We ate all the grilled meat we had prepared, and later in the night I briefly explained to Dimitri why I went to the mountain, as the prosecutor asked. As he stared at me in surprise, I stood up and brought the bag I had left in the kitchen, carefully placed it on the table, and took out the rusty metal box and placed it right in front of him.

70. LIVING IS SIMPLE AND STRAIGH-TFORWARD

Dimitri stared silently at the rusty metal box. While he was telling me how, where and when I found it, he was listening to me and continuing to examine the box without taking his eyes off of it. I could see that he was very excited.

After examining the box for a while, he waited for his excitement to subside for a while, and then, with his uniquely responsible museum official attitude, he explained that we had to deliver this box to the museum like we did with the scrolls, and that we had to do it as soon as possible for security reasons.

I wasn't thinking like he did and I told him that right away. I explained that the ages of our first findings have not been determined, that the studies have been going on for months and that the results have not yet come, that it would be better for us to hand over the metal box after the results come in, giving reasons that I think are justified, and I also explained my suspicions and their reasons.

He paused and thought for a moment. As he was telling me that the reports of the scrolls and the ceramic piece were a few days away and that it would be alright if we waited for this short period of time, but that we had to protect the metal box very well during this time, I was trying to show him with every line of my face the satisfaction I felt for his accepting my words without difficulty.

I put the box back in the bag. We carried everything on the table to the kitchen and I said I had to work and went out with the bag to the room.

I thought of my indecisive and inconsistent days when my desire to work changed every day. I was lazy, unproductive and reluctant, and I did not want to move even the tip of my finger, But when necessary, I could suddenly become a man who was extremely ambitious, willing, efficient and able to work for hours without interruption. I had to set myself a purpose and a goal so that I could throw myself into the arms of productive and hours-long work. I was telling an imaginary person in front of me about the goal I had set, searching for ways to reach the goal I had set, determining the arrival time, and leaping forward like an arrow that had been released from its bow. I never got up from the chair I was sitting in and continued my work non-stop, for hours, for days, except for mandatory breaks and a few hours of sleep; a purpose and goal were really important.

This was the goal I set for myself, my goal was to write down all our experiences. Until the day we returned to Istanbul, I was going to complete my studies and what I planned to write, edit the chapters and send it to the editor by e-mail. The editor-in-chief, who was impatiently waiting for the completed version of my book, could then make the necessary examinations, at least until we returned to Istanbul, complete minor (!) corrections such as periods and commas, as he put it, and could proceed with the cover work. I didn't want to waste any more time and I wanted to reach the finish line of this work marathon in two days.

Before I started working, I took out the rusty metal box again, and looked at it. If I knew I wouldn't damage the thing I thought was inside, I would have removed the rusted rivets one by one without waiting for a second. However, I had to wait and deliver it to expert hands.

I thought of Tancrede for a moment. If I gave him this metal box, which I now knew he was after, I thought that I would never work for the rest of my life with a few million dollars that would be deposited in my account with a good bargain and travel the world together with Solmaz, I smiled mischievously and quickly dismissed these thoughts from my mind.

"This is man," I whispered, "he thinks about everything, he thinks nonstop, even when he thinks he's not thinking about anything, he thinks he's not thinking about anything at that moment." I quickly placed the metal box in the bag, hid it in the corner of the bottom shelf of the wardrobe, under the clothes, and began to work greedily, pushing all the ridiculous thoughts out of my head.

I couldn't even understand what Solmaz was saying, who tried to talk to me after she entered the room, got ready for bed and laid down, as I was tapping my fingers on the keyboard without stopping, quickly and passionately.

"To be able to work," I said to myself, "what a great chance and happiness it is to be able to produce something, to innovate, and to have a healthy body with a strong, ambitious, and willing brain that can do them."

I remembered that I couldn't do anything, I couldn't produce and I was only trying to heal with my useless body during my days at the hospital, when I was in bed without being aware of myself - I thought of those desperate days. While I was waiting impatiently for the day I would regain my health, I now knew that one of the most important ways to get rid of diseases and to get rid of all the negative effects of diseases was to "want" something.

I could now feel with my whole being that I could apply this to any concept, purpose or ideal, and that I could achieve anything I sincerely wanted, reach any goal, and achieve any success.

Setting goals, completing the preparations for the journey and the long walk on the road, and leaping forward, repeating what you want along the way, believing, not getting tired, not giving up, not resting, and when the day comes, when the waiting period is over, when the journey comes to an end, to hold on to the goal you have reached and to follow it. to hug it tightly with your arms, never letting go – could this be one of the reasons for life, living, existence?

I thought that preserving the achieved success and keeping the gains were as indispensable as reaching and achieving a determined goal.

I thought that the most important shortcoming that businessmen, artists, politicians, bureaucrats, managers, athletes, scientists, academics, singers, models, traders, investors, entrepreneurs, bidders, smugglers, thieves, peddlers, doctors, engineers, lawyers, teachers, civil servants, workers, trade unionists, barbers, cooks, liquor manufacturers, tavern owners and hundreds of other manufacturers of jobs, ideas and services overlooked or ignored was that they did not take measures to protect the successes achieved.

The goal reached by running, fighting, suffering, tired and sleepless nights in sweat, for days, months, and sometimes even years – a captured castle, captured hill, the great success achieved, a small operation that was unfortunately interrupted because of a simple prevaution forgotten to be taken, all slipped from the hands of successful people, disappeared, and was completely erased from the pages of the history of miracles with a few attacks by scavenger vultures, opportunists and moneylenders.

If they ask me today, if they question me in a friendly, friendly and humane manner after all the events that have happened to me, and if they try to find out which one is important in the light of my experiences; I could say without thinking that maintaining the success achieved and keeping the gains are much more important than succeeding and winning.

Was it nice to never reach someone that one desired, missed and loved very much and regretted all his life, or was it better to be able to endure losing one day the loved one that he has reached with the great love he felt? Which one was right?

Undoubtedly, what was right and beautiful was to protect values. In spite of all that happened, if they asked me and said, "Do you prefer to suffer with the regret of never reaching a value that you desire and long for, not being able to reach it throughout your life, or to suffer by losing it one day after you have achieved it?" My answer would be clear and simple; even if I knew that I would lose it one day, I would say without hesitation that I would prefer to reach it.

If I couldn't reach it, I would experience the pain of writhing regrets throughout my life, whereas if I reached it, even though I knew I would one day lose it, I would only experience the regret and pain of what was lost, after the day I lost them.

I suddenly recalled my inexperienced, naive days when I sarcastically evaluated the words of sages who said that life was a game. After the events I experienced and the things that happened to me,

I was now perceiving life as a game; a simple, pure, easy and understandable little game. I could now understand that what was important was not to quit the game, but to try to succeed, to stand up again in the parts where you failed and lost, to dive into the playing field once again and continue the game with brand new hopes.

That's it; living is simple and straightforward.

A person who is born, develops, grows, learns, comprehends, aims for peaceful, happy and healthy days and spends his days with his loved ones, could not and should not have any other purpose other than to increase the number of such days. Now I truly believed that these were the meanings of life, and I wished that I could spend my coming days in line with this understanding.

I turned and looked at the keyboard of the computer. I quickly and passionately touched the keys; I continued my game, my own game, I wrote the words of the mountains, the hills, the valleys, the rivers, the paths, the grass, the bushes, the vines and the trees, the songs sung by the chatty birds perched on the branches of the trees, - I wrote for hours and told our story endlessly until the first light of the morning.

71. I PUT MY HAND ON HER CHEEKS AND MY FINGERS GOT WET

I woke up shortly after going to bed, it was approaching nine o'clock. I looked to my left and listened to Solmaz's deep, quiet and frequent breathing, she was asleep. I put my feet on the floor and grabbed my phone on the nightstand. There were two missed calls, one from Dimitri and another from someone else who was not on my contact list.

I immediately called Dimitri from where I was sitting. He answered it quickly and said, "Have you thought about it?" "What," I asked, "what was I going to think?", "I'm asking about the metal box, Yigit, will we give it to its owner?" I understood that when he said owner, he meant the museum officials, that he was trying to ask implicitly. "No," I said to him, "it will definitely reach its owner one day, but we talked and agreed that we could wait a day or two more, I agree and I will do whatever is necessary in a day or two."

I hung up and dialed the other number I didn't recognize. This call was also answered quickly, the person I didn't know answered it in English that sounded like Italian, saying, "Have you thought about it?" Even though I knew who he was from his voice and manner of speaking, I asked his name, and he said, "I am Tancrede."

Unable to understand whether his name was really Tancrede, or whether he was using it to intimidate me by referring to the name of the deceased Bohemond, I asked him too, what I was supposed to think about.

He told me once again that I shouldn't care about life, that I shouldn't take myself too seriously. He told me that I am a small point in the whole universe, too small to be ignored, and whispered in a calm and confident manner that if I wanted to, I could live my life after today very comfortably, happily, peacefully and with plenty of money.

I thanked him, I understood what he was trying to say, but I didn't think he could understand me, not even a little bit. I put on the same attitude - imitating his fake, polite and insincere demeanor - and hung up the phone.

I was just leaving the phone on the nightstand when I heard Solmaz's sleepy voice behind me. I turned and looked at her face, smiling, unable to understand what she was saying and looking into her eyes with questioning eyes. "Have you thought about it?" she asked, and I looked at her with a wider smile, bent down, kissed her lips, and gave her a big, hearty laugh.

"Is it so funny I ask?" she said to me angrily, and I was still laughing, and I told her with laughter that I couldn't help; that the three people I started talking to as soon as I woke up today asked the same question to me, as if they had agreed to do so.

As I asked the first two, I asked Solmaz as well, about what I was supposed to think, even at that moment I was forcing myself not to laugh. "Have you thought about when we will return to Istanbul?" she asked. "Tomorrow," I told her, "we'll be back tomorrow.

I explained to her that I would review all my writings today, make the final edits, complete the order of the chapters by consulting herself, and put an end to the work. I was about to send it to the publisher as an e-mail attachment when she wrapped her thin and delicate arms around my neck, pulled me over her, and suddenly began to smother all around my face with wet kisses.

"Stop!" I said, "I shouldn't get tired, please don't tire me out, I have to spend all my energy on working, otherwise I can't complete it and it will take another day to go back." As soon as I said that, she pouted with her beautiful face and slipped out from under me in anger, with the attitude of a teenage girl.

"You'll see," she told me, "I'll take bad revenge on you." Listening to these last words, I knew it well from my past experiences that she was going to make me "beg for it."

I got up, went into the bathroom, washed my hands and face, opened the window curtains, turned on the computer again, worked non-stop, and rushed towards the last section I was approaching.

In all my works that I started and continued for days, I was always like this, my heart beat faster no matter where the road would lead - good, bad, beautiful or ugly; I would get really excited when I felt that I was getting close to the end. I would start sweating for no reason, my hands would tremble and I could hear every beat of my heart loudly.

I was now reaching the end; I was constantly making mistakes in the last lines I tried to write, I couldn't rewrite what I deleted after I deleted a section that I shouldn't have deleted, I had to rewrite the whole thing from the beginning to put together the section that lost its integrity.

When I woke up the next day, I was determined to make the final checks and send it to the editor. At that very moment, I felt the smell of green apple-flavored cigarettes that Kemal Kır, sitting in his study room full of books at the publishing house, smoked by adding them on top of each other, the smell spreading all over his room, on the books, on the shelves, on the floor carpets and on the window curtains. The next day, after I had finished the study and sent the email, I thought I could buy as many green apple-flavored cigarettes as I could find and take them to him; I could already hear his screams of joy.

I looked at Solmaz, who was lying on the bed and immersed in the book in her hand, her face still sullen. To dispel the tension between us, I asked her in a low-pitched voice, if she wanted food, drink, or anything else from the kitchen. She answered me with two, just two words, never taking her eyes off the book in front of her: "Don't want!"

It was clear that she was still angry. I twisted my tail between my legs, almost as beloved little puppies do when they are frightened or startled, and continued my work.

We were about to reach the moments when the day bid farewell to the usual daylight and was going to experience their indispensable unity with the darkness of the night. I didn't look at my phone, which was starting to ring on the nightstand, and pretended to be immersed in work. Without letting go of the book in her hand, the navy-eyed blonde rolled to her right and picked up the phone, "Dimitri, calling," she said in two words.

She still maintained her harsh, angry and uncompromising demeanor. I turned a blind eye, she listened to Dimitri and turned to me, "He says don't eat anything, that we can consume what he is about to send home in maybe three days, what should I say?" she asked me, I pretended not to hear, and this time she shouted at me with anger. I looked startled and said, "Whatever he says, however he wants, I'm alright with it."

She looked at me with the same angry and aggressive manner and spoke to Dimitri with a softness that was completely opposite to the way she was looking at me. She listened for a while and then put the phone back on the nightstand. She sat on the bed and, with her suddenly changed demeanor, in a loving and calm tone, began to tell me what she had been hearing on the phone. She told me that the laboratory investigations were completed and that the reports reached Antakya with an official letter, and then she told me that the waiters of the *Antakya Cuisine Restaurant* would be home within an hour.

I paused and could not speak for a moment. I looked at Solmaz with the expression of a person who had a stroke in his hands, arms and all the muscles of his face, who did not expect this situation yet, could not accept it and was stunned. What could be the result, what could it be, what should it be? At that moment, I could not think clearly, I could not know, understand or perceive anything.

I got up and opened the door of the room. The full moon, the radiant absolute ruler of the dark night, was looking at me from the most suitable place it could be, and I looked at it, then looked at the courtyard, turned my head, listened to the pleasant sound coming from my right, that I could not recognize. It wasn't a guitar, it wasn't a violin at all, it couldn't be a revel, oud, mandolin, it was far from piano or oboe; it was like no other. I listened.

I listened and felt myself on the peaks of high mountains. I stood across the deep valleys, high cliffs, rivers and lakes that I reached by running through plains, swam in cool waters, encountered impenetrable walls, crossed bastions of a castle and entered the castle under the vaulted stone roofs filled with hot waters, I threw myself into the steam where I tried to understand life, death and love.

The person who was playing the saz stopped for a moment and shouted his love in a voice that was first low and then gradually rising. I listened to the words rising from the courtyard of this musty house in the old Jewish quarter towards the sky, towards the bright face of the full moon.

I turned and looked at the room, I entered the room quickly and I grabbed the thin wrist of the beautiful woman, who continued to look at me with an angry face, I took her to the balcony slowly, I wanted her to take a deep breath and listen to the Turkish-Arabic tunes of the music rising from the courtyard of the house next door. I made her listen to the bittersweet words of love, first told in a slow and then in an increasingly loud voice.

As I waited for the next words of the person I thought to be a young man from the voice I heard, I looked at the face of the woman I loved, shook her hand in my palm and looked at her with a determined expression that showed her that I wished, at that very moment, that she would understand the words of the song being sung, that she would look at me and see what's inside of me, grasp my heart, and burn me again. Listening to the tunes rising to the sky, I could now see the beautiful woman hugging me and softening, pushing aside her angry, reproachful, uncompromising and harsh demeanor.

I and the beautiful woman next to me were reaching the height of being impressed with simple, ordinary and not very meaningful sentences, while the impressive tunes of the instrument playing and the words compatible with our emotional intensity at that moment were rising towards the full moon, the absolute ruler of the night in the sky.

How could those words and tunes have such a profound effect on the woman I love, on me and all others who listened to the boy playing? I looked at her with the wetness dripping from her warm cheeks.

I thought that all mystical, impressive, emotional and loving people who had a say in the past and history of the city or not, might have said what the young man told with the folk song he sang.

I thought of words and phrases that active, determined and important men and women might say two thousand years ago and later, for instance; even I could have said, despite all the training and determination I've had so far, "How confused my mind is," I could force myself to reach a dark blue-eyed woman, a concept, an ideal, or the unattainable - yes, the unattainable.

I took her in my arms, kissed her questioning face, cheeks and eyes, I said, "Let's go back to the room now if you want". I was trying to understand where the easy-to-understand, clear words and tunes, the music that spread to the night, took those who listened - by looking at her eyes and her beautiful face. I put my hand on her cheeks and my fingers got wet.

72. CARPE DIEM, QUAM MINIMUM CREDULA POSTERO *

Live the day, trust in tomorrow as little as possible. (Horace: 65-8 BC)

We were living a night accompanied by the full moon and stars in the sky. We got ready and went down to the courtyard. I told Solmaz that we had to complete all the preparations for the next day's return and that we could set off at an early hour, after tomorrow at the latest. She thought for a moment and whispered to me in a sad tone that this city was to her as important as the city she was born in, and that she felt like she was from here since the day she buried his mother, father and brother in the city cemetery.

Solmaz was telling me with tears in her eyes that in the first days of my stay in the hospital, they managed to bury her relatives, who were handed over to them after the autopsy, in the Antakya Cemetery with the help of Dimitri so that their souls could find peace as soon as possible, and that Nikola was buried in the Antakya Christian Cemetery on the same day. I grabbed her hand and squeezed it lovingly.

I suddenly realized that we had never talked about it, and that she hadn't said anything until tonight. From time to time, I realized that I could not remember some days, events and special moments in the past due to the traumas I went through, and I felt great sadness for this fault. I couldn't understand whether we had never talked about these issues because of my abnormal recollection and forgetfulness caused by the concussions I experienced, or because of the usual protective instincts of normal brains that make us forget painful events and memories. I told her not to worry, without letting go of her hand that I was still clasping, and that we would come to this city at every opportunity and visit her relatives, who were in their eternal sleep.

I was able to let go of Solmaz's hand when we heard the light blows on the street door at around nine o'clock at night. I got up and opened the door; The young lad standing in front of me, smiling and apparently a waiter from his clothes, was speaking in a dialect mixed between Turkish and Arabic. He explained in an extremely naive and sympathetic manner that he came from the *Antakya Cuisine Restaurant*, that he brought greetings from his boss, Semir Yağmur, and that he thought we were going to serve food to a large group because of the large amount of things they brought.

Semir Yağmur, the owner of the restaurant that Dimitri took us to on the night of the first day we came to the city, was a very friendly man in his fifties, with a belly, a gray beard. He spoke non-stop in Arabic with Dimitri, and with me and Solmaz using a mixture of Turkish-Arabic and a language he produced with his own unique methods. I remembered the man, and the young waiter, whom I had told to send our greetings as well, nodded and smiled at me. He hesitantly told me that if we let him, they would carry the packages they brought from the car waiting in front of the door to the house. I stepped back from the front of the door and watched the transportation process, which was assisted by the driver who joined the waiter, by sitting on the chair next to the pool.

Watching the white bags brought to the kitchen, all full, being brought to the kitchen, I saw Solmaz looking in surprise at the multitude of plastic bags, and I was smiling sincerely. Now, as I saw those who moved into the kitchen, I could understand the meaning behind Dimitri's words: "We can only consume what I am about to send home in maybe three days".

The young waiter and driver completed their work and did not take the money I wanted to give them just as they were leaving; I forced the money into their pockets and thanked them. I turned on the pale yellow lamp of the courtyard, a pleasant and peaceful light filled everywhere. I walked towards the kitchen and met Solmaz's angry and simultaneously affectionate face, who was complaining that she was dizzy from the multitude of transparent and thin plastic boxes with lids that came out of every bag she untied. We could see the contents of the rectangular, thin and transparent boxes, but it wasn't enough for the boss Semir Yağmur; he had written or ordered his people to write on the small white papers that he had placed on the boxes, in a scraggly, squiggly handwriting, what the contents were.

"Oh, Dimitri!" Solmaz was saying, constantly and angrily, "who is going to eat all these?" In addition to the fact that he grew up in the city with a culinary culture from centuries ago, our friend, who has internalized this culture, had such a way of saying goodbye to his friends who were soon going to leave the city and his house. The right and proper farewell could have only been made with a rich table.

I looked at the richness of the sea of colors and varieties that Solmaz took out of the bags and lined up on the kitchen table in regular rows, and I began to read in a loud and cheerful tone what was written on the papers pasted on the transparent boxes. "Pepper yoghurt, taratur (it was written like this), çiğ küfte (I was reading it the way it was written), rich sahter salad (meaning thyme salad), roasted eggplants, oluve salad (spelling mistakes belonged to Semir Yağmur), sac oruğu, sürk salad (I learned that it meant çökelek salad), hummus, solid cacuk (it really said so), abugannuş (a type of roasted eggplant paste), strained yoghurt, yoghurt with carrots, peppers with walnuts, egglants with yogurt (this should have been 'yoghurt')), princess (I think it was named because of its pink color, from ordinary red lettuce), roasted hot pepper (I would be surprised if it was not hot), arugula with yoghurt (here spelled correctly), arugula salad and a few other varieties that I couldn't understand because of the papers I couldn't read despite all my efforts. I was tired, exhausted and told Solmaz that I couldn't read the others, it was as if we were swimming in an "Ocean of Appetizers".

I thought about the great importance that the Antakyans, who were rightfully proud of the rich, innumerable and all incredibly delicious appetizers (mezes) and dishes in their cuisine, gave to food preparation, setting and serving, hosting guests, and the importance of making these the culture of the city they lived in. I looked at what Dimitri sent, and I understood that his method of saying goodbye could not be so different from the centuries-old culture of the city where he grew up. A pleasant, warm, sincere and friendly night awaited us.

"Carpe noctem*," I said to Solmaz. She smiled at me and met my attack with the sentence of Horace, whom she had researched and worked on before; "Carpe diem, quam minimum credula postero." **

We took small, white ceramic plates from the shelves, transferred all the appetizers from the boxes, decorated them and carried them to the table in the courtyard one by one. Even half of the plates we prepared were enough to fill the table; we carried the one in the kitchen to the courtyard.

The hour when Dimitri announced his arrival was drawing near. We were both waiting with excitement and wanted to hear what he had to say as soon as possible. The ministry letter announcing the laboratory results could have changed many known facts. We would spend the next day in the city and leave the next day. Besides our preparations for our return, we should have discussed what to do with the rusty metal box.

We had spent almost five months in the city where we arrived at the beginning of July. If I didn't count the days when I was unconscious in the hospital, I felt as if I had just arrived in the city a few days ago.

The next day, we would send the work I completed to the publishing house, go to the museum for the metal box, wander around the bazaar for shopping and finally leave the city. I thought of all of those and for a moment I panicked at the multitude of things we were going to do.

  *   Live the night.

  **   Live the day, trust in tomorrow as little as possible.

Continuing to carry the appetizer plates in the kitchen and arrange them on the tables, Solmaz looked at the color variety of the appetizers in the plates and the harmony between them, and, "It looks like a painting, like a poem, as Horace said; 'A painting is a poem without words' is that right?" she asked me. I quickly evaded the risk of panic attacks and smiled back at her, "Poetry is a painting made with words."

73. FOOD APHRODITE LOVED

At about eleven o'clock at night, I opened the knock on the street door and saw Dimitri's face standing in front of me, smiling tired but not nervous, and I smiled back at him. Despite the large number of plates we had placed on the tables when we entered the courtyard, he said, "Well, it seems I did not exaggerate, that's enough for now", I couldn't understand whether he was saying it with conviction or to tease me. We sat across from each other; we were waiting for him to talk with curiosity and report the results of the investigations that we have been waiting for a long time.

"The scrolls are two thousand years old with a fifty-hundred-year margin of error, and are made from gazelle skins, as we originally thought."

The museum official, who paused at this point in his speech, was trying to gauge our reaction. This was really important news. I was excited and stared at him without saying anything. What was written on the scrolls flowed from my brain in an instant; Luke had achieved his goal. As he wrote, the scrolls he had prepared were found centuries later, his writings were read, and even translated into the present language of the city he loved so much.

I dismissed all the thoughts that invaded my brain and, having difficulty speaking because of a dry mouth, tongue and palate, I immediately asked about the ceramic piece.

"They could not determine a definite date, at most forty-fifty years; however, we can say that it is not very old."

This was the sad news of the day Dimitri reported. During the days I was in the hospital, I was faced with an annoying situation that overlapped with the question asked by Tancrede towards the end of the interview, who visited me in my room. According to the rumor circulating in the city and among the journalists, I, who delivered the scrolls to the museum officials as I found them, kept the relic hidden among the gazelle skins, and instead handed over any ordinary ceramic piece to the authorities. It was no longer a difficult task to guess who might have spread this ridiculous rumor. It was strange but not meaningless coincidences that especially Tancrede, whose side I could now understand, asked this question, constantly reminding me that I am not even an important point in the infinite universe, implying that I could get a lot of money if I wanted to, and most importantly, the fact that the commander of the army that occupied the city during the First Crusade, Bohemond's nephew also had the same name as the so-called journalist.

I told Dimitri everything I thought about and that I was deeply worried that the announcement of the laboratory results he had informed us would put me in a difficult situation, that the rumors that had already been spread by word of mouth would be heard more intensely and that I would face a variety of dangers.

"Is it possible?" I asked. "Could it be that the laboratory results would not be announced for a while?" I asked him if it was in accordance with their official procedure to announce the results after we handed over the rusty metal box to the museum authorities and we left the city. If this was not the case, I explained that even announcing that the investigations of the ceramic piece were ongoing during the announcement of the age of the scrolls would save us a significant amount of time, and that we could be protected from dangerous attacks during this time.

He thought for a moment and suggested that I go to the museum the next morning and inform the authorities that I would deliver the metal box to the authorities, provided that the announcements of the results would be made as I requested. His proposal was logical and rational, I accepted it. I was sure that the rusty metal box was indeed a relic among the scrolls. I forced myself to remember the pictures of the scrolls on the computer and the spots on the photograph in the middle sections, I remembered and had a sudden chill; They were rust stains, ordinary rust stains.

Suddenly I got up and went up to the room and said that I had to finish my work. He pointed to the ocean of appetizers on the tables and tried to explain that we were going to have a drink. Without listening, I headed for the steps of the stairs, entered the room, turned on the desk lamp and the computer. The screen soon lit up. I opened the folder where I had placed the photos of the scrolls, scanned them quickly and looked at the large and small areas that looked like stains and became evident with the orange, brownish, blackish colors that had permeated one of the midsections.

I opened the file that I had saved in chapters, translating from Ancient Greek, and realized for the first time that there were seventeen chapters. All chapter titles belonged to the ancient Jewish Luke of Antioch.

I placed the first part of the translation at the very beginning of the book:

"We Listened To Him In The Cave We Gathered."

I decided to place the translation in intermittent and successive parts one after another, I complied with my decision and placed the first lines of our own story in the second part, so the the third part naturally became, "Charon Without a Face."

I continued the work and placed each part that started with an odd number according to the order on the parchments: "We Used To Escape From The Tunnel In The Cave, To Hide" was the fifth part, for example; and the seventh was, "We Wrote Whatever He Said".

"Did He Bless Orontes, or Did Orontes Bless Him?" became the ninth part, and I placed the "Cave Church on Stauris Mountain" in the eleventh part.

I had chills as I typed the names of sections. When the thirteenth part became "We Were Fishing in the Orontes River", I looked around and once again felt the meaninglessness of the mystical moments. The fifteenth part became "We Were Listening to Cephas In The Cave" and I kept silent; I kept quiet as long as I could.

After placing the sentence "Students Named Christians in Antakya for the First Time" in the seventeenth part, the nineteenth part was "We Understood Our Temporariness, That Cephas Told Us".

While "Luke Is My Name" was shouting in the twenty-first part, we were starting to read the "Acts of the Apostles" in the twenty-third part...

"Beloved Carpenter", in which we were describing Habibi Al-Najjar, was trying to smile down from the twenty-fifth part, down from the cave in the mountain... Luke was standing there, starting to speak: "I am a Jewish Physician from Antioch", in the twenty-seventh part, and he was forcing himself to shout, "O Theophilus!" in the twenty-ninth and the thirty-first part.

I placed the thirty-first part in the same order and was about to file the last part as the thirty-third when I stopped; I thought that the special meaning of the number thirty-three and what was written and told in this chapter, coming after the chapter called "From Bab Al-Hadid to the Parmenius River" in our story, would suit the flow of the narrative, and without hesitation or pause, I filed it in the forty-fourth part of Chapter 3.

"O Theophilus, You Can Only Live For the Time That Is Given To or Set for You."

The title in this section and the sentences written under it were the last section written on gazelle skins. I have reserved the rest of this chapter for our own story. I recorded all of what I translated and what I said in successive chapters and in a single file. There were only a few pages left for me to write: the section where I was going to write about the meeting we were going to have at the museum the next day and the rusty metal box we were going to deliver.

While I was about to turn off the computer and get up, Solmaz entered the room. She was rubbing her belly and complaining... She explained that she had a significant contribution in the consuption of Dimitri's "Ocean of Appetizers" but they they couldn't succeed at finishing them, despite all their efforts.

Smiling and putting all the kind, sincere, flattering expressions on my face, I told her that these were all Aphrodite's favorite foods. She looked at me without understanding. I was determined to tell her, so I tried to explain in a more joking manner: I tried to explain to her in a more understandable style and words that the foods, even the drinks, that Aphrodite loved and consumed non-stop, were called "aphrodisiacs" and that the classifications were made under this title. "Get ready then!" she told me...

74. NOW WE ARE LEAVING THE CITY

I took a shower and got dressed. I asked Solmaz if she wanted to come with us. She muttered a few incomprehensible words... I took the backpack and placed the rusty metal box inside. I went down to the courtyard, carefully carrying the box and counting the steps I had descended. I looked all around the courtyard; I looked at the room doors that opened onto the courtyard. It was the hour of the symphonic concert given by the birds perched on the branches of the trees every morning, and I knew that if I did not listen to this symphonic concert on the day I left the city, I would feel a great loss. I stopped before I got too close to the trees and listened to the chirping of the little musicians rising to the sky.

We were in the last days of November. I tried to remember the happy and carefree days we lived in the city, which we came to in the hottest days of summer, which lasted only a few days. A pleasant wind licked my face. Now, nearly five months later, we were leaving our relatives in the cemetery of the city where we lived through difficult, painful and desperate days and establishing an indispensable bond with the *Queen of the East*. An unbreakable bond...

Without letting go of my backpack, I headed for the kitchen door. The door was open. I poked my head in and saw Dimitri inside trying to brew tea. "We're hungry," he told me. "We lost our appetite because of you in the evening, we couldn't eat much." If I didn't know what Solmaz had told me, I could have believed what he said.

We were finishing the first glasses and filling the second ones when Solmaz entered the kitchen. She sat quietly in one of the empty chairs and said that she would be able to eat anything, that she just wanted tea. She looked quite happy.

We jumped into the car waiting for us in the space in front of the house, left the narrow stone-floored streets of the Jewish quarter of two thousand years ago and headed towards the museum next to the old parliament building next to the Orontes River.

Now I wanted to complete all that needed to be done and return to my work as soon as possible. Tomorrow at the latest, today if possible... I didn't want to go back and test my boss' patience any longer.

When we reached the museum, I gave the key to the security guard who came to the car and I took the backpack with me. I was carrying the bag, heavy with the metal box, as if it were a part of my body. We entered the museum and walked, following Dimitri. The place we came to was a large meeting room with a high ceiling and there was no one there.

Dimitri said that we could sit on whatever chairs we wanted around the rectangular table placed in the middle of the hall, and left us saying that he would be back in a very short time. Solmaz and I sat on two chairs near the door, and I slowly left the backpack next to the chair.

All the walls of the meeting hall were decorated with framed photographs of mosaics, statues, tombs and old coins exhibited in the museum. In the picture opposite me was the beautiful Tyche, sitting on the summit of Mount Silpius and trying to restrain the rebellious Orontes with her feet; she was shaking the wheat she held in her hands with the crown in the shape of a wall on her head, and it was as if she was smiling at us.

Before the door of the meeting room, a tall, burly and rather overweight man with bald hair, who looked about fifty years old, and after him Dimitri entered.

They sat right across us. On either side of the long and wide table, we looked very far from each other and very formal. We watched together, without speaking, the walk of the young girl in a short skirt, who came to the meeting room at that moment with the files in her hand, and all the exaggerated movements she made until she sat on the chair next to Dimitri.

The balding man, who confidently explained that he was the head manager of the museum, went straight to the subject. He thanked us and gave us great compliments. His speech was fast and difficult to understand; it was as if his tongue couldn't keep up with the speed of his brain. I realized that Dimitri had already informed him when he said it would be alright to accept my terms.

First, I explained that I had only one condition and that I put forward this condition for our safety. I told them that revealing the age of the scrolls would cause no harm, but on the condition that they explain that the investigations on the ceramic piece were not completed yet due to the rumors, I would give them another very valuable find and that after the examinations on it were completed, the number of visitors to the museum would increase several times. The experienced manager was aware of everything.

The head manager said once again that they unquestionably accepted every condition I said, and he shouted that he was ready to give all kinds of assurances. I could see very clearly that his forehead and his red cheeks, which were gushing with health, were starting to sweat.

The young girl in the short skirt could not hand me over the file, sos he stood up and brought the file with her to me. I took the file from her, read the documents inside and signed it with the pen on the table.

The young girl in the short skirt waiting next to me took the file to the other side of the table with the same exaggerated movements and placed it in front of Dimitri. She looked at our friend, who signed the file without reading it and passing it to the head manager, with an attitude expressing that she did not approve of someone else doing a job that was supposed to be done by her.

The experienced manager examined all the documents prepared, took out his pen from his shirt pocket and signed every page. When he looked at his assistant, the young girl, I knew she would take the file with her exaggerated behavior and come to me with her unique gait. I wasn't wrong. She came to me with her hips swaying left and right due to the high-heeled shoes she was wearing, and placed the file in front of me.

I took the backpack I had left by the chair and placed it on the table. I gave the bag I took out of it to the young girl. She looked at me questioningly, as soon as I said she could give it to her manager, she turned and, with the same exaggerated gait, reached the man - whose hands were shaking with excitement.

I placed the file in front of me in the backpack on the table and stood up. We were able to complete the first and most important job of the day without any problems.

Dimitri explained to the head manager that we would be leaving the city today or tomorrow and that he must take care of us, thus asked for permission. The museum director, who looked at Dimitri with the most smiling face, told our friend that he was free with his ecstatic dreams of the successes waiting for him.

Although there was a parking ban in front of the exit door, just as we were getting into our car, which was waiting for us under the supervision of the private security guard, I looked carefully at the men wearing sunglasses, which were visible through the windshield of the metallic black minivan, which was standing ten meters behind.

I slowly got in the car and waited for Dimitri to sit in the front seat next to me, groaning and puffing, having difficult because of his growing belly. While I was moving the car, I watched the progress of the minivan, which was moving in harmony with our speed, on the rear view mirror.

We were going to say goodbye to the young prosecutor by stopping by the courthouse. Passing through the new and wide streets described by Dimitri, we arrived at the building that was built almost on a hill. We walked in and breathed in the sad, gloomy, depressing air present in every courthouse.

I wanted to finish our visit as soon as possible and leave that place. Old and young, men and women, well-dressed townspeople, peasants dressed in their field-work clothes, lawyers in their dark robes, walked back and forth as if they were on a set schedule, climbing the stairs, getting on the elevators, sitting in chairs placed by the walls.

Their sullen, sad, thoughtful facial expressions seemed to be the common denominator of the people in the building. I thought that not a single person without a problem would come to this building.

I thought that the bailiffs, who were looking at the lists attached to the panels on the wall in front of the doors of the courtrooms, shouting the names of the lawyers, plaintiffs or defendants with the loudest voices they can make in order to announce the names to almost the entire building, could make good peddlers, market merchants or session managers in auction rooms.

I knew that all the people waiting were looking at all the people passing by, but seeing no one. We walked along the corridors of the high-ceilinged building, ignoring these attitudes.

The young prosecutor accepted us during the break of a trial he attended. When he saw that we were waiting in front of his room, he smiled enthusiastically and entered the room himself before the door he opened. We followed him and sat in the seats across the table. When he asked us what we wanted to drink, we just thanked him. He looked at us with an involuntary expression that he was glad we didn't waste his time.

I said that we had come to announce that we would be leaving the city the next morning the latest, and to say goodbye by thanking him for his help. He paused and thought for a moment, I noticed the lines on his face loosening. He was relieved.

I couldn't tell if this relief of the young prosecutor was due to our tactful act of saying goodbye, or if the man, who was the cause of a lot of trouble, was finally leaving his area of responsibility!

He leaned forward from his seat as if to tell us a secret. His elbows and arms were on the table. He whispered to us that they had detained and questioned the Italian journalist a few days ago, but had to release him because they could not determine a suspicious situation.

He told us that he used the name Tancrede in the articles he wrote in the newspaper and in the news he made, but that they determined that his real name was Basilio. I remembered that one of the people sitting in the black van I saw as I was leaving the museum looked like Tancrede. The black van had followed us close to the courthouse, then suddenly disappeared. I considered whether to tell this detail to the prosecutor, but I said nothing. I did not want Solmaz to be disturbed.

He stood up saying that we should be careful and that we could always call him until these issues were resolved, and he apologized and informed us that the hearing he was supposed to attend was about to begin.

We sensed the command, "Go now, I have work!" and quickly stood up. We went out of the building that smelled of sadness, longing and issues.

As I opened the door of the car we had left on the sidewalks next to the walls surrounding the courthouse, I saw the black minivan parked with its back towards us, again about thirty or forty meters away. Its windows were covered with black film, and its license plate was too far away to be read.

For a moment it occurred to me to walk to the suspicious car and ask what they were trying to do. I didn't, I couldn't, I didn't want to drag Solmaz into an unnecessary and senseless panic and anxiety.

We drove through the windy, dusty streets of the city and parked the car in an empty parking lot next to the old Hatay State's parliament building near the museum.

We met here with Dimitri on the first day we came to Antakya. While getting out of the car and walking to the parliament building, Dimitri told us that there was a stone Roman bridge over the Orontes River, in place of the current concrete bridge, until the end of the nineteen-sixties and that it was brutally demolished.

We climbed the stone steps of the staircase leading to the glass-enclosed terrace of the old parliament building. We sat at a table overlooking the city square, the Atatürk statue, the stone buildings of the post office (PTT), municipality, Ziraat Bank and the museum.

The terrace where the parliamentarians, ministers and the heads of state, who discussed the problems of the former Hatay State, participated in heated debates and insulted each other, found relief when they were bored after the quarrelsome meetings, has now been transformed into a pleasant space where a café chain offered cake, ice cream, tea and coffee. We adapted to the atmosphere and asked for a baked rice pudding from the respectful waiter waiting next to our table.

I raised my head and watched the ancient Silpius, now known as Habib Al-Najjar Mountain, visible from this angle. I looked at my watch, it was getting close to noon, we had nothing to do but a little shopping.

I turned to Solmaz and told her that if she wanted, we could set out today. She looked at me happily and told me to decide in her most submissive manner. Just then, I heard Dimitri's stern and determined voice.

We listened to his reproachful statements - as if we were in a hurry, what would happen if we stayed one more night, would our company in Istanbul go bankrupt, did I not know the disadvantages of driving at night - so we decided to set off early the next morning.

We paid the bill and started walking down the street by the Orontes River towards the car. Sitting on a stool next to the glass-top booth by the sidewalk, an old man with rotten teeth asked us suddenly, "I have cheap cigarettes, do you want it?"

With a smile, I looked at the man with a gray beard, his face full of wrinkles, a man struggling for life. "I would like to," I said. He opened the drawer of his booth and showed me the packages he had arranged vertically. I took one of the green colored packets and read the writings on it. This was what I was looking for. Three packs of green apple-flavored cigarettes remained in the old man's hand. I bought all three. While paying his money, he said to me, "Come tomorrow, I'll bring more for you". Before I put it in the backpack, I wrote the editor's name on a transparent bag I got from the old man and carefully placed the packages inside.

On the way home, we took the longer way and passed St. Peter's Church. We looked at the solid iron shelters extending obliquely to the ground from the cracked and flaking parts of the mountain, the Charon relief visible from afar, and the intact walls on the steep rocks stretching from the top of the Silpius Mountain next to the Stauris Mountain, to the deep valley.

We put the things we bought from a few shops on the way, into the trunk of the car. Now I wanted to return home as soon as possible; I had only one job left to finish and I was determined to get it done this afternoon.

I felt very uneasy about the presence of the black minivan that followed us along the way we went, keeping the distance between us, but I did not show it to Solmaz or Dimitri. They seemed to want to Show us that they were watching us, but unfortunately I could not understand what they were aiming at.

75. JUST LIKE THE PAST I COULDN'T ERASE FROM MY LIFE, OR NEW PEOPLE I HAVE PLACED IN MY HEART

As soon as I got home, without wasting any time, I left the room and turned on the computer. I pushed the curtain right in front of me to the side, and I rubbed the light of the sun, which was shining despite the cold, into the folds of my wounded soul, trying to warm my heart.

Everything was ready now, I was going to do the final checks and send it to the publishing house as an email attachment. The last check I would make was irreversible and very important; I had just checked the translation of the scrolls and knew that there was no longer any room for correction. I started to read the chapters in which I told our own story; I was reading quickly and making the final corrections as needed right away. I've looked through all the chapters.

I quickly read about Dimitri Çağlayan – a monument of appetite, the places I lived two thousand years ago, *Historia magistra vitae*, learned behaviour, the world's first church, Lake Amik turned into a plain, barbecue parties, Charon in Dante's *Hell* - who looked at the city from Stauris Mountain - *Cur-quomodo-quando*, Nikola's apartment on Ankara's Bestekar Street, life changing in an instant, anyone who wanted to find something having to search for it, Carbon-14 and OSL tests, *Gazella gazella*'s, Tyche, Firuz Demirci, the indispensable details in the photographs, *Homo sum, humani nihil a me alienum punto*, turquoise from the mixture of blue-green colors, the slum, Bohemond, Bab Al-Hadid and the Parmenius River, my days in intensive care, my dance with ghosts, the mysterious places between sleep and wakefulness, the Antioch Theological School and our inheritance, the strange visitors to the hospital room, the innocent and adorable dogs killed by poisoning with strychnine for committing the crime of straying, the strange guest Tancrede, the pouring rains, the inaudible cries, the invisible tears, the crazy forests to be passed, the Walls and castle of Antioch, the inside, the heart, the soul of the castle walls, the Mountain of Holy Miracles and Stylism, the Shepherd's Monument and the coded letters in the marble sarcophagus, the mirrors that could ask and answer questions, the importance of finding new ways out of the paths that have been stepped on for centuries and bowing respectfully before these roads, the *Orientis Apicem Pulcrum*, the rusty metal box, The date of June 3, 1098, the 912 knife wounds, Luigi, the fact that life was actually simple and straightforward, cheeks that wet my fingers, *Carpe diem, quam minimum credula postero*, the oceans of appetizers, chapter titles of the scrolls, and the last scroll that could not arrive at chapter 33 - I quickly read all of the chapters, made corrections, additions, and removed everything unnecessary from what I wrote.

It was like life, literally like life. Like moments I corrected on, added to, or subtracted from my own life.

Just like the past I could or couldn't remove, could or couldn't erase from my life, or new people I have placed in my heart.

There was neither a missing word in my writings, nor single phrase too much; just as we talked and agreed upon.

FROM THE EDITOR: A FEW IMPORTANT NOTES

I am really sad.

I am really sad, sorry, devastated and wounded…

We buried Yiğit Kaya and Solmaz Başaran next to their relatives lying in the cemetery in Antakya. On the same day as I was returning to Istanbul, I looked out of the plane window and cried non-stop.

I had briefly examined the seventy-five chapter file attached to the e-mail he sent, and forwarded it to my friends who had already been getting prepared for days. I couldn't believe the news I got the next day, and in order to get over the shock I had, I locked myself in my room and started to cry.

On the day of the incident, dear Yiğit and Solmaz set out in the morning hours, lost their steering control as they approached the Iskenderun district, smashed the roadside barriers and lost their lives by falling into the deep cliff next to the road.

According to the information received later from eyewitnesses, a black-colored minivan with dark film-covered windows, watching the car that Yiğit Kaya was driving very closely, first jammed our friends' car by making extremely dangerous maneuvers and then caused it to crash into the cliff from the side.

The file of seventy-five chapters written, edited and corrected by Yiğit Kaya was almost ready for printing. I immediately ordered my friends to print it without waiting.

I flew to Hatay Airport on the first plane I could find and was able to catch the funeral. We met Dimitri Çağlayan at the cemetery; he was extremely sad and devastated. When he learned my name, he asked me to come talk to him after the ceremony.

It was officially announced that the scrolls found by Yiğit Kaya were about two thousand years old, but it was reported that the studies on other finds were still ongoing. In this sense, the narratives Yiğit sent me, based on first-hand testimonies, were of great importance and therefore had to be published as soon as possible. Although I had given instructions to my friends at the publishing house, I called once again and warned them to go to the printing process as soon as possible. I asked them to add the lines you are currently reading to the end of the book, under the heading, "From the Editor: A Few Important Notes".

Dimitri Çağlayan, who came to me as I was walking away from the graves, where Yiğit and Solmaz laid side by side, handed me a small bag that he took out of his coat pocket. We were getting wet and cold under the pouring rain. As soon as I saw my name written on the bag, I opened it quickly and when I saw the green apple flavored cigarette packs that came out, I couldn't hold myself any longer and started to sob and shake like a little child.

After a while, I returned to the graves where I had left, ignoring the intensifying rain, and spoke to him for the last time:

"Rest in peace, dear Yiğit. We will publish what you sent, as you wished. There will be neither a missing word, nor an additional phrase; just as we talked and agreed upon."

9 781913 680800